THE SULTÁN
and
THE CRUCIFIX

The Sultán and The Crucifix
by
Paul Anthony

The right of Paul Anthony to be identified as the author of this work has been asserted by him in accordance with the Copyright, Designs and Patents Act of 1988

~

This is a work of fiction.
The names, characters, businesses, places, events, and incidents contained in this novel are either the products of the author's imagination or used in a fictitious manner.
Any resemblance to actual persons, living or dead, or actual events is purely coincidental.

~

First Published 2019
Copyright © Paul Anthony
All Rights Reserved.
Cover Image © Margaret Scougal

Published by
Paul Anthony Associates UK
http://paul-anthony.org/

By the same author

~

The 'Boyd' Crime Thriller Series…
The Fragile Peace
Bushfire
The Legacy of the Ninth
Bell, Book and Candle
Threat Level One
White Eagle
The Sultán and the Crucifix

*

The 'Davies King' Crime Thriller Series…
The Conchenta Conundrum.
Moonlight Shadows
Behead the Serpent
Breakwater

*

In the Thriller and Suspense Series…
Nebulous, Septimus

*

In Autobiography…
Strike! Strike! Strike!

*

In Poetry and Anthologies…
Sunset
Scribbles with Chocolate
Uncuffed
Coptales
Chiari Warriors

*

In Children's book (with Meg Johnston) …
Monsters, Gnomes and Fairies (In My Garden)

*

To Margaret - Thank you, for never doubting me.
To Paul, Barrie and Vikki - You only get one chance at life. Live it well, live it in peace, and live it with love for one another.
To my special friends - Thank you, you are special.

~

With thanks to Margaret Scougal, Pauline Livingston and Pat Henderson for editing, consulting and advising on my various works over many years....   Paul Anthony

~

1

Daybreak.
The Banks of the River Euphrates
Deir ez-Zor Governorate, Syria

An acrid gut-wrenching odour escaped a rusting exhaust pipe and invaded the atmosphere when the first set of wheels crossed the city boundary and trundled along the sun-scorched highway into the concrete jungle.

To the uninitiated, the weary-looking single file of second-hand vehicles travelling along the sand-blown route resembled a circus coming to town. Weaving in and out of abandoned broken down wagons ditched on the road, the convoy made its way south towards the border with Iraq and the shell-shocked divided city of Deir ez-Zor.

The city had become the centre of the country's petroleum extraction industry following the discovery of oil in the Syrian desert in the 1930s. The oil industry took off in the early 70s and revealed Syria to be the only significant oil-producing country in the Eastern Mediterranean. Things changed when the Syrian civil war broke out and ferocious military clashes erupted between the Syrian Armed Forces and the Free Syrian Army together with other opposition organizations such as the Islamic State of Iraq and the Levant and Jabhat Al-Nusra.

The Deir ez-Zor district remained one of the few Syrian Government's strongholds in eastern Syria. In 2015, Islamic State militants launched an offensive. They captured Palmyra and cut off the remaining supply line to Deir ez-Zor.

Effectively blockaded by ISIS, the city became the site of a three-year-long siege with the Syrian Army. The siege ended following a long and bloody battle, but it had left the city divided and with no clear governance.

It was the last stronghold of Islamic State and the reason the bedraggled convoy had journeyed to this particular location.

A dozen children playing on the pavement knew this was no circus coming to town. They could see the motorcade was made up of a motley collection of trucks and lorries driven by an assortment of transnational drivers.

Raising rifles aloft, the battle-hardened Jihadis signalled their escape from the war-ravaged desert behind them and headed towards the oil and natural gas fields that dominated the region.

A mixed bag of vehicles and armaments stolen or acquired in clashes with the Turkish, Iraqi and Syrian army slowly threaded its way south. A German Leopard battle tank and an American M1 Abrams assault tank, both bought years ago from a Lebanese arms dealer in Morocco, led the way and were followed by armoured personnel carriers, jeeps, military trucks, transit vans, and commercial pickup trucks carrying machine gun emplacements.

Traces of black engine oil trickled from the Leopard's exhaust as it belched thick murky smoke into the sky. It was on its last legs and the driver knew it as he slammed the gear stick through the six-speed gearbox trying to find a responsive cog.

There was a worrying rattle from the twin-turbo diesel engine before the innards finally exploded and the vehicle came to rest in the middle of the road with steam escaping into the air from the engine compartment. Stuck, with no way of moving forward, the convoy huddled up behind the Leopard and eventually came to a standstill.

Opening the driver's hatch of the Abrams, a bearded Egyptian Jihadi emerged and shouted towards the Leopard in front of him.

'Get out! I will bulldoze you from the road. Get out now!'

As the crew of the Leopard jumped from the vehicle, the Abrams dropped into low gear and moved forward gradually nudging the Leopard from the highway.

Nearby, watching proceedings, a group of children ambled lazily along the edge of the road. There was a brief smile from one of them, but it didn't infect the group. They'd seen it all before. Such an occurrence wasn't new to them anymore.

One of the children suddenly pointed upwards to the sky and then pointed towards a clump of trees some fifty yards away.

Slowly pushing the Leopard from its place of death, the Abrams angled at forty-five degrees and decided upon the final graveyard of the lead tank.

Then the first Brimstone air to ground missile slammed into the turret of the Leopard and exploded. A heartbeat later, the second missile hit the Abrams on its gun barrel and blew it to smithereens

The noise was deafening. Pieces of lethal burning metal flew through the air in the aftermath of the two explosions.

Children ran to the trees for cover when three aircraft swooped low and unleashed an array of deadly missiles into the convoy.

There was no time to read the logos on the aeroplane wings. No time to watch the carnage that followed. There was just time for the children to escape the deadly air assault.

'Run!' they screamed.

More air to ground missiles were unleashed as the convoy occupants suddenly realised they were under attack.

Two Maverick missiles whistled through the air and slammed into a ten-ton military truck.

There was a huge fireball followed by a rake of gunfire from the third aeroplane that chose to pepper the convoy with its cannons picking out vehicular targets below.

Here and there, machine gun fire missed. Bullets scoured the tarmac below and then randomly found its target.

A windscreen in a jeep shattered and the two occupants in the front seats were killed instantly when cannon fire tore their bodies to pieces. Another military wagon erupted when lethal projectiles found the fuel tank and the Jihadis ran for cover.

Escape for the ISIS warriors measured a stride or two but no more. Moments later, the pilot above got his range and terminated more lives with a display of thunderous firepower that shredded the living into a mass of dead and mangled tissue.

More air to ground missiles followed when the aeroplanes returned for a second bite at the cherry.

Screaming voices added to the bloody carnage as the convoy met the visitors from hell at daybreak in Deir ez-Zor.

Dawn did not shimmer that day, neither did it burst forth in glorious unconquered splendour. Rather, it froze, a reluctant witness to the manmade storm of death and destruction taking place.

Galvanised into retaliation, the determined Jihadis were intent on revenge and scrambled to their vehicles. Clambering onto the rear platforms of half a dozen pickup trucks, the fighters manned heavy machine gun emplacements whilst others loaded shoulder-fired rocket launchers and pointed them at the enemy diving from the skies. There was a rapid exchange of gunfire between the combatants in the sky and the warriors on the ground.

Shooting wildly at the aircraft, the Jihadis were outgunned when the three enemy aircraft pummelled the convoy once more with a range of lethal fire.

Missile after missile pounded into the convoy, destroying, decimating, slaughtering, maiming, and killing.

More explosions lit up the day and revealed the long line of vehicles now ablaze on the main road into the city.

Silence!

Two and a half thousand miles away in the electronic weapons area of an American military base near Vicenza, Northern Italy, a drone operator engaged in modern warfare tactics.

A message was received, understood, and acted upon.

Two hands engaged a keyboard. A man's eyesight focused on the computer screen before him. The image of a faraway desert bounced back as he rattled the keyboard, increased the speed of the projectile, and glanced briefly to a map signifying his target zone.

Nodding, he snatched a mouthful of black coffee as the unmanned aerial vehicle – an MQ1 Predator, which had been launched by him from an airbase in Saudi Arabia – responded to his control mechanism and changed course.

With a length of thirty feet and a wingspan of fifty feet, the Predator weighed in at one tonne and flew at an altitude of four miles above the surface of the earth. When brought to maximum efficiency at about two miles above the earth's surface, the vehicle was capable of reading a car number plate and define facial characteristics from a cruising altitude of two miles.

Gently tapping the minus key, the operator watched the figures on the altitude monitor gradually drop towards the ten thousand mark.

The Predator descended like an eagle looking for prey.

Eventually, an eerie calm swept casually through the atmosphere. It was surreal as the hush seemed to infiltrate every inch of highway from the lead tank to a battered jeep at the rear. Gone was the noise of battle. Mangled tanks, broken wagons, twisted jeeps and battered pickup trucks littered the route. Next to the obliterated vehicles lay dozens of dead and dying soldiers. Only the low murmur of pain in the final throes of death could be heard.

The nauseous smell of spent fuel mixed with squandered ammunition hung in the air before invading the nostrils.

A child cautiously peeped out from the clump of trees in which he had hidden, peered into the sky, and then gave the all clear to his friends.

Moments later, the children were running away trying to find another place to play, to live and breathe again before the next brutal anomaly swept into their young lives. It's all they had known; fear. Most of them had grown to their present years without ever experiencing a lasting peace or a sustainable love. They were the product of a violent war that had no respect for age or gender and whose fallout was on a global scale.

Eventually, the victims gradually crept from their hiding places, crawled from beneath their vehicles, and stood up. Battle-hardened faces, pitted with the dirt and grime of war, occasionally scarred or bruised, studied the heavens above and the bombed-out buildings that sporadically bordered the highway on which they had travelled.

'Can you see them?'
'No,' peering into the sky.
'Where are they?'
'They've gone!'

'Are you sure? Maybe they are inbound low for another attack?'

Squinting his eyes, coughing, 'I can't see anything.'

Silence from the skies.

'It's over!'

'Who was it?'

'I don't know. Syrian? Coalition? American? Does it bloody matter?'

'Of course, it bloody matters. Who were they?'

'No idea but they're gone.'

'Who do you think they were?'

'I don't know! It all happened so quickly.'

A pair of dust-covered desert boots hit the tarmac, wrinkled in their contortion, and then took a cautious step forward.

'Yeah, they're gone. That's for sure. How many did we lose?'

'Too many!'

'Where's our leader?' from the boots.

'He was in the front passenger seat of the fourth vehicle. The ten-ton truck.'

The boots broke into a canter, reached the vehicle, and stood solid as their master announced, 'He didn't make it.'

Lying on its side, burning, the ten-ton truck had taken a direct hit which had killed all the occupants.

'None of them did. Allah has taken Abu Al-Ghamdi. Our leader is dead.'

A clutter of boots shuffled quickly in the dust of the highway as half a dozen Jihadis rushed to the scene.

'Allah be praised!'

'Abu Al-Ghamdi is in paradise.'

'Abu Al-Ghamdi!'

'Allahu Akbar! Allahu Akbar!' chanted the survivors.

They did not feel pity or compassion following the death of their leader. It was not inbred in them. It was the way they lived a life of constant warfare. It was their way, their culture, their very being that immediately sought revenge and not sorrow!

The man who was Abu Al-Ghamdi was no more. He had served his purpose. His name would be immortalised in the days and weeks ahead. He would be a legend soon, a hero, a name that would be revered and remembered by those of the faith. It was what those dedicated to securing and expanding the Caliphate did. They raised the status of such leaders to a level where they were remembered virtually as a deity of note – almost godlike beings that were honoured and revered once they had become part of fourteen hundred years of religious history.

Right now, it was time to vow revenge.

'Death to the Americans! Death to the Kefirs!'

'Kill the unbelievers. Death to those who defy Allah!'

The chanting continued until a new voice emerged and asked, "How many dead?' enquired Aishah.

A muttered reply offered no fact.

'I said how many dead?' repeated Aishah.

There was a confused look on the faces of those who had survived the attack.

'Wait!' commanded Aishah as he walked the length of the convoy before turning and revealing, 'Is everyone okay?'

'No!' replied Ahmed. 'We need medics. There are injured to care for.'

Both men dominated the convoy. Always dressed from head to toe in black, their drab attire clearly revealed them to be prominent leaders of the group. They were security men and had been the bodyguards of Abu-Al-Ghamdi. Now Aishah took charge and stepped onto the footplate of an army wagon.

Gaining height, looking over the group, his back clothing resonated with the culture of the ISIS warriors. He was the replacement, a natural leader, a man who had stepped forward and taken command at the first potential sign of weakness in the leadership.

In the traditions of Islamic warfare, Aishah had made the seamless promotion from feared bodyguard and security man to the leader of the pack.

'Aishah!' someone mumbled. And then another with quiet subdued respect, 'Aishah, our leader.'

'Allah will take the dead and dying, Ahmed,' suggested Aishah. 'Martyrs they will be. Inshallah! Or maybe their bodies will just wither away here until someone comes to get them. I don't know. What I do know is that this place might be in Syrian hands or our hands. Where are we, my warriors? We need to keep moving. Do you see others coming to help us? Can you hear their jeeps, ambulances and pickups?'

'No, is the jeep at the rear done?'

'Nothing is moving,' replied Aishah. 'The jeep is destroyed. The occupants are dead.'

'Then we have no medics,' declared Ahmed.

'How long have we?' enquired Aishah?

'Until the Syrian army comes?' proposed Ahmed. 'Ten minutes at the most. I'm guessing this stretch is under their control.'

'Who is with me?' shouted Aishah. 'Who fights with Aishah for the Caliphate?'

A murmur of approval grew to a crescendo of support.

A female body crawled from beneath a wagon, faltered, and then settled motionless on the tarmac.

'She is done,' announced Ahmed. 'They are all done.'

Elsewhere, a small group of Jihadi warriors emerged from their hiding places. Some carried rifles, grenades, and rocket launchers. Others carried sidearms and machine guns. They all carried the look of defeated fighters wearing the filth and stains of war on their stubbled rugged faces. Gradually, they gathered on the highway next to a pair of burning tanks emitting plumes of black smoke into the sky.

'We have no convoy,' remarked Ahmed. 'We are who we are. Just a handful left to fight for the Caliphate.'

'The Caliphate will never die,' declared Aishah. 'It rests, I tell you. It merely rests this day.'

A white man, unshaven and bedraggled in appearance, stepped forward shouldering a wireless system and offered, 'Funny in a way. Abu Al-Ghamdi always told me that a drone would get him. He was wrong.'

'But still dead,' replied Ahmed.

The wireless operator continued, 'We need to scatter before the aeroplanes come back or the Syrian army arrives in force. According to the radio, our comrades are holding out in the city centre. They're still fighting the enemy. It's street to street and door to door. That gives us time to escape.'

A voice from the group suggested, "Let's go and help them?'

'What with? The tanks are out of action and we've lost over a hundred fighters.'

Aishah nodded and said, 'Then it is time to follow the advice of the legendary Abu Al-Ghamdi and return to our homes.'

'Should we not look after the dead?' enquired another.

'We don't have time,' revealed Aishah. 'How many are we Ahmed?'

'Twelve! There are only twelve of us left standing,' replied Ahmed.

'One day a new Caliph will emerge,' declared Aishah. 'Until then each of us must return home and continue the fight. You know we are not alone. They have beaten us in the desert wastes but hear me, they will not defeat us in the cities, towns and villages of our homelands. There are over forty thousand soldiers heading home. Some will be captured and imprisoned, others will find their way to refugee camps and seek repatriation to their home countries. They know the war is lost but they know our dream of a global Caliphate will endure for generations to come. When the time is right our leaders – people like Abu-Al-Ghamdi – and those who follow him, will call upon our soldiers to rise again and fight the infidels on their home soil. The world will know when that day comes. Already our soldiers return to places like Morocco, Algeria, the United Kingdom, Russia, Australia, Indonesia, Malaysia, Italy, Denmark, Austria, Spain, Tunisia, Turkey, America, Canada, Scandinavia and…'

'Enough!' interrupted one of the fighters. 'You know me as Diego the Spaniard. Yes! I understand what you say. I well remember what our great leader Abu Al-Ghamdi told us. When we get home, we must lead the Jihadis in our country. They must be told to sleep and to keep the faith until the next Caliphate is planned and they will be called upon. We need leaders from our number to take control of the soldiers and use them wisely when the time is right.'

'Regional controllers?' suggested Aishah.

'Exactly!' agreed Diego. 'We shall all become Sultáns of our country. How say you all?'

'What?' raised a voice. 'You mean you want us all to take responsibility for the fighters returning home?'

'Yes,' nodded Aishah. 'Listen to Diego the Spaniard. He speaks my mind.'

'I am from Cordoba in southern Spain,' explained Diego. 'From this moment on I declare myself the Sultán of Cordoba. I shall identify my soldiers in Spain and carry on our work at home. One day, my friends, the Caliphate shall rise again and I, Diego, the Sultán of Cordoba and all of Spain, will be ready with an army of followers.'

A low humming sound gradually invaded their space.

Ahmed looked up and shouted, 'Drone! Surveillance drone!'

Emerging from the clouds, the grey coloured Predator cruised across the airspace at a speed of one hundred and twenty miles an hour. Equipped with four Hellfire air to surface missiles and various unknown technical equipment, the drone was no stranger to the Jihadi target below.

In Vicenza, a finger tapped the ENTER button.

In the desert, there was a slightly discernible twitch on the drone's nose cone before it changed course and flew directly above the decimated convoy on the highway.

The surprise appearance of the Predator drone was met by a salvo of gunfire towards the enemy in the sky. The survivors of the attack on the convoy knew that someone somewhere was watching them. It was common practice to send a drone over following an attack and they knew it. The drone would capture photographs of the aftermath and send them back to a control centre where they would be evaluated.

Ahmed seized a rifle and began firing at the drone shouting, 'Even here! Ground troops on the way. Hit and run!'

Numerous bullets pinged on the side of the metal drone but did nothing to dissuade it from its path.

The Predator lost altitude as its photographic technology came into play.

Far away, in Vicenza, the face of a drone operator flinched slightly, and unnecessarily, when tracer bullets raced from a gun barrel on the ground and seemed to attack the very image he was watching. But then he was at war too even though he was protected by distance. He was the unknown hand, the silent killer from above, the one dreaded and feared by each and every one of the Jihadis.

Aishah shouldered a rocket-propelled grenade launcher, took careful aim, and pulled the trigger.

There was the smooth sound of a small missile slicing through the sky like a knife going through butter.

In Italy, a finger dashed – too late – to a command key.

Aishah's timely intervention paid off when contact I and the drone exploded into a thousand pieces showering the highway on which they stood.

'Did it get us?' asked Aishah. 'Photographs?'

'Hard to say,' replied Ahmed with a scowl. 'Was it automatically recording or was it guided by someone? Does it matter? It's time to go. Come on!'

'Si, es el momento,' agreed Diego. 'Soy un Sultán. Yo soy el Sultán de España.'

'Speak English, Diego,' suggested a tall bearded man wearing a blood-soaked black and grey bandana and dark sunglasses. 'What the hell are you talking about?'

'Ahh! Eddie the Englishman!' ventured Diego. 'You have found your tongue, but you have not found your balls yet?'

'I'll shoot yours off and ram them so far down your bloody throat they'll be sticking out of your arse again, you stupid Spaniard,' replied the Englishman. 'Speak English, Chavo or drag your balls on the ground. Your choice!'

Laughing, Diego shouted, 'It is time to listen to my orders, Eddie. I am the Sultán of Spain.'

'I'm not called Eddie. I've never been called Eddie, you fool and you're nothing but a loud-mouthed Chavo,' snapped the Englishman.

Shouldering his weapons, Diego glared at his fellow combatant and replied, 'And I'm not called Chavo. You insult me. All these years fighting together and now you abuse me at the moment we are to part.'

'You're leaving?' queried the Englishman.

'I intend to return to the Great Mosque of Cordoba where I will speak to my fellow believers and persuade them that one day the Caliphate will rise from the ashes.'

'Good for you!'

'And you, what will you do, Englishman?' enquired Diego.

'I'm going north through Iraq, into Turkey, and then to Italy. From there I'll cross the continent and hitch a ride in the back of a wagon bound for home.'

'That might not be as easy as you think,' suggested Diego.

'I have the money, the means, and the contacts. It will take time but I'll make it,' replied the Englishman.

'Englishman!' remarked Aishah. 'What is your name? I mean your real name.'

'You guys have been calling me Eddie the Englishman since I arrived four years ago. Englishman will do. Where did you get Eddie from?'

'You had a king by that name once.'

The Englishman shook his head in annoyance.

'What do you need?' quizzed Aishah.

'I know where I can get guns and explosives when I need them,' replied the Englishman.

'What else do you want?'

'Nothing, I already have the faith. Allah will guide me to my destiny.'

Aishah scribbled an address on a piece of notepaper, handed it to the Englishman, and said, 'You can't travel with us. People will see you are European, hear your mother tongue, and report you to the police and the army. They'll know you are either Al Qaeda or ISIS. You'll never make the border unless you take the desert route. Here, head north to Al Hasakah and then cross the border into Turkey. Look out for drones. They are everywhere. You are more likely to be killed by a drone than one of the soldiers. The drones never miss. Make for the city of Mardin and go to the address on this slip of paper. I'll tell them to expect Eddie the Englishman and they will help you. They are of our people, of our faith. Allah will guide you to them. Do you understand?'

The Englishman memorised the address and chewed the piece of paper before swallowing it.

'Head for the Great Mosque,' instructed Aishah. 'The minaret towers above the city and is all-seeing. You will find the house on the side streets directly below the mosque and lying in its shadow.'

'Thank you, Aishah,' replied the Englishman.

Diego shook his head and ventured, 'What will you say in your mosque when they ask where you have been and what you have been doing for the last four years?'

The Englishman glared at Diego and then Aishah and Ahmed. Adjusting his bandana, he then reset the sunglasses on his nose and casually replied, 'All you need to know is that I'm from England and I don't need a mosque to do what I am going to do.'

'Listen to this on the radio,' interrupted one of the men. 'It's the Americans. They're preaching to the world that we've been defeated. They say the war is over and we're trapped in the desert waiting to be rounded up.'

'Trapped?' remarked Ahmed. 'Only if we stay here. Grab your kit. Take what you want from the convoy and move out. You know how to find Aishah and I. Go! Good luck!'

As the sound of approaching Syrian army vehicles grew louder, the twelve remaining Jihadis gathered their belongings, stepped from the highway, and sought the cover of the trees, bushes and vegetation bordering the route. Others broke into a jog and headed into the narrow lanes of the nearby concrete jungle.

'Trapped? The war is over?' remarked the Englishman softly. 'And here was I thinking it was just about to start.'

There was a sudden breeze that whipped around the black and grey bandana as a pair of desert boots moved quickly through the city towards a far-away destiny.

In an American military establishment near Vicenza, Northern Italy, a drone operator banged his fists on the desk when he realised the signal was lost. The computer screen wobbled and then displayed an image of black and white snowy static that played on his tired eyes.

Launched earlier that day from King Khalid Military City Airport, Saudi Arabia – but controlled completely from the American base in Italy – the operator knew the Predator was down.

*

2

The desert.
Syria
Later

Aishah had been right.

The Syrian army was all over the area looking for the stragglers and those who had survived the attack.

The Englishman set off on foot with a rucksack on his back and a rifle slung across his shoulder. The further he headed into the city the more he realised he was headed in the wrong direction. He was getting closer to the enemy, not evading them. There seemed to be army patrols everywhere, rushing to the scene of the burning convoy, chasing down escaping ISIS warriors, and following the pointed fingers of a bunch of kids who had been playing in the area.

He cut away from the city, turned his back on the broken building blocks that surrounded him, and sought his freedom. To his rear lay the flattened glass-strewn streets, countless tonnes of needless debris, and the torched shops and bombed out businesses of Deir ez-Zor. Behind him lay the government offices, windowless in most places, but in others re-designed by row upon row of zig-zag bullet holes made by those who sought to bombard their enemy with every ounce of ordnance in their possession.

Ahead of him lay his future, his destiny.

The Englishman ran as fast as he could through the streets, into the thinly wooded area that beckoned him forward, through the shallow sparse grasslands at the edge of the city, across the loose rock and dirt that bordered a billion grains of sand, and finally into the desert plains of northern Syria.

Collapsing on the loose soil, he felt a few of the harder rocks scrape his knees. He grabbed his legs, pulled them tight to his chest, and rolled into a ball. Blood seeped from a kneecap. He swore, derided himself for not planning his escape properly, and felt the pain shoot up his leg. Why had he not listened to those who had once told him what he would need to do if he ever found himself behind enemy lines?

Survival! He must survive so that he might fight another day.

Removing his bandana, he used it as a bandage and wound it around the worst of his knees so that the bleeding would stop. He dreaded the risk of infection. Small, he must remain small so that he did not present himself as a target. Tiny even. He twisted onto his back and closed his eyes, stretched out his legs, took in a deep breath, and lay there thinking.

Did those kids see me run this way and tell the army patrol? Whose kids are they? Where are they from? Do they live nearby? Did the lens on the drone catch me on the highway? Did the drone operator indicate where we were, which way we might choose to escape, where I am now? Where am I now? In the desert, away from the tarmac highway, the burning vehicles, hiding, escaping? Or playing dead by the side of a ditch until I get my bearings?

Scanning the immediate area, he realised he was on one of the many beaten tracks that crisscrossed the desert plains. These routes were mainly used by villagers who ignored the primary roads, took short cuts across the desert, and shepherded their donkeys and goats to and from the markets.

Often the donkeys would be laden with fruits and vegetables. Other times weapons and ammunition would be hidden beneath the foodstuffs. Most of the time, goat herders channelled their animals in specific directions where new grass might be found upon which the goats could feed.

Then he saw the wreck.

Ruined, the flat-backed pickup lay on its side, the result of a devastating earlier attack that had crippled the ISIS vehicle and rendered it useless, out of the game. Rusting now, its tyres had been removed and the machine gun that had once mounted the flat back area was gone, pilfered by the Syrian Army or who knows who. He didn't care.

Crouching low, he made his way steadily towards the vehicle, threw himself down by its side, and lay parallel to the length of the rusting heap.

Shade, he thought. I have shade from the sun and a place to rest and take stock of things. Moving to the rear of the vehicle he found a loose tarpaulin flapping in the breeze. The tarpaulin was trapped by the weight of the pickup.

He slid into the gap between the tarpaulin and the vehicle and closed his eyes.

When dawn smeared the sky the following day, he woke, checked his knees and tried to stretch out his limbs. He was stiff, burdened by the weight of anxiety in his mind, cold, afraid of being discovered in an old rusting wreck in the middle of nowhere.

He freed himself from the burnt-out vehicle. It had served its purpose. Hoisting his rucksack and slinging the rifle across his shoulder, he set off deeper into the desert.

Gradually, the soil gave way to the sand and the sand eventually grew deeper. The depth of the sand clawed at the Englishman's boots, tried to drag him into its depth, slowed him a point where the desert personalised its battle with him, caked his face with sand, burnt his lips, scorched the skin on his face, and sought to destroy him.

The Englishman carried on.

An hour passed before he saw the speck high in the sky and acknowledged that it might be a drone. He casually dropped into a shallow area and felt the pain in his back when he touched down in its belly. It was an irrigation ditch. I'm bruised, he thought, but not yet broken.

He lay, listening, panting, trying to control his breathing. Anxiety was the enemy, and fear. He fought them with time as the drone passed overhead to continue its search elsewhere.

Five minutes passed before he raised his head above the lip of the ditch, took off his sunglasses, and searched the area. It was flat, not a hillock or bush in sight. No cover. Just the highway and the far distant beginnings of the concrete jungle that was Deir ez-Zor. The gateway to freedom and escape had turned into the gateway of hell, a cold-blooded murderous inferno of carnage from the skies.

Destroyed! He knew they had been decimated.

Crawling into a ball once more he reached down to his boots and felt the heel.

How long had he worn those boots? When did he last take them off? Three, four days ago? Maybe a week or more, he could not remember. All he could think of was the escape along the highway into Deir ez-Zor.

He broke the heel and removed the compass and folded map which he laid out on the desert soil. He removed the creases with his hand.

The dirt on his fingers smudged the map but he found Deir ez-Zor, then Al Hasakah, then Madrin. Lifting himself slightly, he peered over the lip of the irrigation ditch, tried to find a landmark, a faraway junction, or a building that might give him a clue as to where he was on the map.

There were none.

The compass worked. Four years or more it had been secreted in the heel of his boot for just such an occasion. He gazed at the high brick buildings of the faraway city. They were like skyscrapers stretching their way skyward. Yet he knew they were no more than four or five levels high. The Englishman studied the area ahead and then decided on a route to take. He would follow the compass setting to the northeast and then take more bearings later in the day.

He folded the map, took a sighting with the compass, and set off hunched down and low. He did not run. Rather, he took short steps and picked his way through the desert sands. Here and there it was patchy and spontaneous in its fabrication. Deep sands were replaced by jagged pieces of rock that reached out of the earth as if to try and snare him.

Blisters! He felt the first of the blisters burning inside his boot.

Night fell once more. He dropped into a shallow irrigation ditch, removed a trowel from his rucksack, and began digging himself deeper into the land. There would be no bump in the landscape. No giveaway slight hillock that might betray his presence to a goat herder or tribesman who walked these lands.

He slept the night.

In the morning, he woke, stirred, and then suddenly reached for the knife in his thigh pocket when he heard a noise.

It was a lizard and for a moment the Englishman wondered who had been the more frightened. The lizard or himself.

Proud, almost arrogant, the lizard clambered up the side of the ditch and made the flat of the land. That was when the blade struck.

There was a twist of the handle when the Englishman's blade broke the lizard's back.

Breakfast! No water, nothing to drink, just the thin innards of a lazy lizard that had probably slept next to him for most of the night.

He was on the move again but now he was determined, hungry, and desperate to succeed. He moved only at night, heard the aeroplanes screeching through the sky on their 'hunt and kill' missions, and saw the far-off drones circling looking for a target that might satisfy the spook sitting next to the drone operator in wherever they were.

The Englishman didn't know, didn't care. He just wanted out of the desert.

Four nights went by and then the welcome glimpse of light that heralded dawn. And the thin yellow-green of the land that signified the end of the desert and the beginning of agricultural land.

Today, he thought. Today, I will skirt the town of Al Hasakah and make for Madrin.

Crawling along on his belly, he found the lake. It was on his map. He knew where he was at last.

For half an hour he watched the lake, looking for people, for animals, for an army patrol that might stop for water. There was none.

The Englishman slid into the water and drank slowly, almost casually, not wanting to end up with a bloated belly and a stomach breeding unwanted germs and a deadly disease. He washed, used the knife to clear away some stubble from his chin, and then took another compass bearing.

Almost there.

Night fell, he set off again. His desert boots were now worn to a mere thread and he sported blisters on his toes and both feet. His skin was stretched and tanned with the slightest of the sun and his weight was surely down a stone or more. He did not know. Yet his heart was on fire when he saw, in the distance, the minaret of the Great Mosque of Madrin.

He would rest. Tomorrow he would break cover, dump his rifle in the lake with his rucksack and excess gear, and enter the city. Head for the mosque, they had said. Find the address in the streets lying in the shadows of the minaret and they will help you, it had been said.

And then his journey would begin.

He found the house, was ushered in, greeted, and studied for what he was. His bandana was a bloody rag, his sunglasses cracked and broken, and his face tanned in places but cut and bruised in others following nights of hiding in ditches and days of crouching and crawling through the stony, soiled desert. Broken fingernails and lacerated fingers testified to his desert ordeal. His boots hung loosely, torn, with little tread left and a heel broken allowing the naked heel to burn into the hot leather.

Emaciated, gaunt, hungry, close to collapse, the Englishman was hidden in the cellar for the rest of the day before a woman came and tendered to him. A trusted doctor, he thought. She cleaned his wounds, bandaged his knees, tended to his blisters, and treated the sunburn that threatened his facial skin.

Later, they fed and watered him, read to him from the Quran, clothed him, and, when he was much improved, took him from Madrin to Ankara by car. His Arabic was slightly better than their command of the English language, but it did not matter. The Englishman was known to Aishah, recommended by Aishah and others in his company. Aishah was special now. He was the new leader of those who wanted a Caliphate. He was the local hero, a legend and an icon in the lands in which they lived. The Englishman was special too. He was respected and, more importantly, his escape through enemy lines, through the desert, was proven. Not only did he have the faith, love the Book, and enjoy Aishah's endorsement, he was a hero of a special kind. The Englishman was a warrior of worth.

In Ankara, he met others who clothed him again, gave him money, and put him on a bus to Istanbul.

Each time he would be met by those who valued him, wanted him, needed him to fight for their cause: to support the Caliphate. And every day he listened to those who told him of the contacts in the organisation of which he was now such an important asset. He was told where to find them, of how to contact them, of where weapons and ammunition might be retrieved or accessed, of who was onside and who was not. Of who to trust and who to distrust.

The Englishman was educated in the covert ways of an organisation that now valued his presence amongst their number.

In Istanbul, they took his photograph, prevented him from leaving the house, fed him, clothed him in good shoes, a couple of suits, shirts, ties and the fineries of an English tourist visiting the jewel of the Bosphorus.

Then they gave him a new passport in a name he had to learn, and papers and documents that portrayed his new standing in life.

The Englishman made his plan.

His plan of Armageddon.

*

3

Eight weeks later
Berkshire

Skirting the entrance to the village church of Saint John the Evangelist, Detective Chief Inspector William Miller Boyd ignored a black wooden notice board displaying the times of various church services that week. He left the gravel path and found the tarmac car park now full of saloon cars vying for a space to discharge their passengers.

Tall, broad-shouldered, with a square chin and deep blue eyes, Boyd sported a dark suit complimented by a white shirt, black tie and black slip-on shoes. He wore a gold wedding ring although his wife was not going to be with him at the forthcoming funeral service.

There was a nod from an attendant, a flurry of hand signals, and the mourners began double-parking as the smell of fresh cut grass competed with exhaust fumes and the occasional whiff of cigarette smoke coming from the waiting throng.

'You made it then?' remarked Antonia Harston-Browne. Dressed smartly in a crisp black trouser suit, the attractive redhead added, 'The traffic is horrendous.'

'It would be so wrong not to come to this one,' replied Anthea. Her auburn hair flowed to her shoulder but no further and her dark two-piece suit hinted at her good looks as she joined her colleagues and revealed, 'Apart from that, Boyd wouldn't have it any other way.'

Kissing the ladies on both cheeks, Boyd said, 'I'm glad you could make it.'

'And I'm sad to be here,' replied Antonia as she hugged Anthea. 'Where's Meg?'

'Staying with an aunt in Cornwall for a week with the children,' replied Boyd. 'I take it Phillip is unable to attend?'

'Unfortunately, he's been called to a high-level meeting with Maude Black, the Home Secretary.'

'You'd think the Director General of the Security Service would have given himself time off,' chuckled Boyd.

'Not this time,' replied Antonia. 'He asked me to officially represent the Service because of the nature of our working relationship. That said, I'd have been here anyway.'

Boyd smiled and enquired, 'Am I allowed to ask what Sir Phillip has been called to discuss?'

'No! You certainly are not,' snapped the lady from MI5. 'Changes! That's all I know. Changes! And I didn't tell you.'

'Need to know and all that,' quipped Boyd. 'Actually, you haven't told me anything.'

'The cortege is here!' interrupted Anthea.

Dressed handsomely in an extremely smart morning suit, the funeral director walked ahead of the hearse. Smoothly, he conducted his black ebony walking stick in a time-honoured tradition which dated back to medieval times when the Head of the College of Arms would walk in front of the cortege as a mark of respect to the deceased.

Expertly, the conductor manipulated his walking stick and led the convoy of black saloon cars as they gradually meandered their way towards the entrance to the church.

The mourners filed into the ancient building, took their seats, and waited for the bearer party to enter. It was as if they had all been summoned to respond to a higher calling in order to pay their respects to one now departed. Inside the church, on the wall behind the altar, a crucifix of Jesus on the Cross looked down on the gathering congregation. It did little to foster any warmth in the cold building.

Simultaneously, in the south of England, a tall well-built woman entered a block of flats on the outskirts of Rochester in Kent.

Ignoring the lift and obviously fit, she took the stairs and niftily made the first five floors before pausing for breath. As she did so, the woman, who wore a dark blue denim jacket with complimentary jeans, glanced casually down the stairwell to see if anyone was following her.

Retracing her steps, she casually shook her long blonde hair and then descended to the third floor where she ventured down the corridor to flat thirty-nine. The blonde used a key to unlock the door. Entering, she closed the door behind her and took stock of the flat. The place was deserted and didn't even boast a solitary piece of furniture. Glancing at the floor, she noticed a collection of letters that had been delivered. Stepping over these, she checked out the second room, figured it was a bedroom, and then poked her head inside a small kitchen.

Empty! The flat was vacant and there was no evidence of recent habitation.

The woman stepped cautiously to the window and studied the ground below. There was a play area for children, a piece of littered waste ground, and a car park. Watching the ground space for a while, she looked towards the highway adjacent to the apartment block, saw nothing suspicious, and let out a deep breath.

Kneeling by the door, she rifled through the post, rejected the dozen or so items of junk mail, and selected a medium sized padded envelope addressed to the occupier. Ripping the envelope to pieces, she read a handwritten note bearing an address and pocketed the contents – a collection of keys on a keyring. She then took a lighter from her pocket and burnt the note.

On leaving the flat, the blonde locked the door and made her way to the ground floor where she walked over the wasteland towards a housing estate.

Here, she located a row of garages, selected a key from the ring, and unlocked the up and over garage door. Once inside, she got into a white van and examined the contents of a holdall which had been left on the front passenger seat. The woman then drove the van outside, locked the garage, and drove off towards the A2 and the route into London.

The side of the van bore the logo of a courier's business.

Moments later, the vehicle crossed the River Medway and travelled towards Cobham where the driver turned from the main road into a system of narrow lanes surrounded by countryside.

The van pulled into a parking space adjacent to a wooded area. The driver sat for a while, studied the vehicle's exterior mirrors, and waited. Once sure that she hadn't been followed, the blonde took the holdall and climbed over a five-barred wooden gate into a wood.

Walking through the undergrowth, the woman found her marker and removed a shovel from the holdall. Digging a few inches into the soil, she unearthed a manhole cover and used the shovel's blade to edge the cover away from the hole. Reaching inside, she removed a bundle wrapped in cloth, covered the hole with the manhole cover, and then stuffed the shovel and package into the holdall.

Back at the van, the female undid the package and used years of guerrilla training to assemble the contents as quickly as she could. In amongst the tools of her trade, the woman noticed a pocket road atlas. Leafing through the paperback, she found a turned-down corner and opened the book at that page. Her fingers dropped onto the letter X written on the map. Following the route from X, she saw the letter Y at the end of the route and understood the cryptic message.

The blonde fired the engine and continued her journey.

There was a throaty roar from the mechanism when the sturdily-built courier eventually swung into the dual carriageway and put her foot down. Third and fourth gears followed in rapid succession as the driver threaded her way through the traffic, found the offside lane, and gunned the vehicle towards the capital.

Meanwhile, a short drive from Sandhurst, the Reverend Joseph Baxter climbed the steps to his pulpit. He acknowledged the crucifix with a slight bow and then turned to address the congregation.

'We are here today to celebrate the life of Sandra Peel known to many affectionately as 'Sandy'. Struck down by a sudden heart attack at the age of fifty-five, Sandy is survived by her sister, Lucy, and her estranged husband who is unable to be with us on this sad day.'

'Where's he at?' whispered from a pew at the rear of the church.

'They were in the middle of a divorce as far as I know. He was last heard of in Greece with another woman.'

'Oh…'

'Shush!' from an undisclosed mourner who turned and scowled at those who should have known better.

'As many of you know, Sandy was the deputy head of the Special Crime Unit in Scotland Yard. I now call upon the unit's commander – Edwin Maxwell – who would like to say a few words to you all.'

'Thank you,' replied Commander Maxwell as he climbed three short steps to the pulpit.

He removed his notes from an inside jacket pocket and prepared to read them. Then, looking up at the considerable audience, he stuffed the notes back inside his jacket and leaned forward onto the pulpit deciding to speak without them.

'Many of you here will not have heard of the Special Crime Unit so I will tell you what it is and why Sandra was a unique and precious member of the unit. The unit is a hand-picked team of detectives drawn from Counter Terrorism Command, together with some top detectives from all over the British Isles and some hand-picked individuals from MI5 and MI6. They are the best of the best which is why Sandy fitted the mould precisely. The unit's remit is 'to police and defend the freedom of the nation and its people.' I can tell you that Sandy filled the role admirably and will be sadly missed. Having served over thirty years in various departments including Traffic, Community Support, Crime Prevention, CID, and the National Crime Squad, Sandy found her true office far away from the rural solitude of Berkshire and ended up in central London. But she wasn't just a police officer, she loved photography and painting as well as reading and ...'

Elsewhere, traffic was building up.

The courier was through Dartford, Bexley Heath, Peckham, Vauxhall, and Pimlico. Slowing for the busy junction ahead, the van joined the queue and slid down the gears as Westminster Bridge came into view.

Stationary, the driver checked her mirrors and then studied the salon cars to the left and right.

The lights changed and the courier moved off over Westminster Bridge towards her destiny. Once over the bridge, she snatched a glimpse of vehicles on Parliament Street. In the distance, to the rear of the vehicles, she made out the Cenotaph on Whitehall and much of the Borough of Westminster.

Upgrading her gears, the courier adopted the offside of the road preparing to circle the area before finally ending her journey.

At the funeral service, at least half an hour had passed.

More orations, memories and tears, hymns and songs echoing from the late nineteenth century walls, and then the mourners slowly made their way out of Saint John's church into the fresh air outside.

'I'm going to miss Sandy,' remarked Boyd.

'She hadn't been long with us,' remarked Detective Inspector Anthea Adams, Boyd's second in command. 'I recall when she joined us she wasn't quite what we expected. But she proved a bonus and an asset.'

'Sandy had so much to offer and was just too damn young to be taken like that,' suggested Boyd.

'True,' replied Anthea, 'One day she was at work and in good health and the next, she was gone. It's dreadful.'

'Dreadful indeed!' agreed Antonia.

'It is indeed dreadful,' pronounced Commander Edwin Maxwell as he approached the trio whilst pocketing his mobile phone.

'Fine words, sir,' replied Boyd. 'You made a fitting tribute to our colleague.'

'Thank you,' smiled Edwin, the vastly experienced and popular detective who commanded the unit. 'But when I said dreadful, I was referring to my recent telephone call with the Commissioner.'

'It would have been nice if he'd put an appearance in but then I expect he was far too busy to attend,' proposed Boyd.

'No!' said Edwin abruptly. 'This will keep until we get back to the office. There's no need to discuss it now.'

The group began to stroll towards the car park.

'What will keep?' pursued Boyd. 'No disrespect, sir, but you've already let the cat out of the bag. What's happening?'

'I can't tell you.'

'The unit is a family, Commander,' proposed Boyd. 'Of course, you can tell us. Everything always stops inside the family. You know that.'

'I'm being moved sideways,' grimaced Edwin.

'What?' cried Boyd. 'What the hell for? There's been a mistake surely?'

The group made their way into a car park as the Commander explained, 'Family, you say, mmm! Sometimes families fall out. Well, there's no mistake, William. It was the Commissioner himself on the phone. Congratulations, by the way. You are now in charge of the unit.'

'Me? In charge of the unit?' voiced Boyd.

'I don't know whether to commiserate with the Commander or congratulate the Chief Inspector on his promotion,' ventured Anthea.

'Precisely!' added Antonia. 'But what an odd way to be promoted.'

'Promoted?' gulped Boyd. 'You mean I'm a Superintendent now? I didn't even have an interview for the job.'

'No,' chuckled Edwin. 'I'm afraid not, William. The axe has fallen on our unit. They need to save money again and we're in the firing line. I've got 'Organised Gangs' because Jim Bragg has retired. You've got the Special Crime Unit at the same rank as you are now.'

'Oh!' replied Boyd. 'I think we need to talk.'

'I'll know more when we get back to the Yard,' volunteered Edwin. 'Apparently, the powers that be have decided that ISIS has been defeated and we don't need the same amount of resources that we have now. There are changes afoot and it doesn't look good.'

'They've been listening to the Americans again,' suggested Anthea. 'ISIS will take more than a generation to defeat. It's inbred into the extremist system, isn't it?'

'Changes?' queried Antonia as she glanced at Boyd. 'I wonder if Phillip…?'

'That decision the Commissioner made seems to be wrong,' proposed Anthea interrupting. 'It's far too early. If you've defeated an organisation like ISIS then we need to see where they will regroup, who leads what remains of the establishment, and what state their finances, weaponry and manpower are in.'

'The Home Secretary has instructed the Chief Constables and the Commissioner apparently,' revealed the Commander. 'It looks like we are in a spiral of downward decline.'

'They don't have to accept,' remarked Antonia.

'But they will,' proposed Boyd. 'They'll accept the government line because it's what the present regime does best.'

'Wrong! It's completely wrong to close us down! They'll regret it,' voiced Anthea.

'You're not being closed down,' explained the Commander. 'You're being reconstructed in line with current requirements. I think that's the current word speak.'

'Still wrong,' repeated Anthea.

As they reached Boyd's squad car, Commander Maxwell held Boyd back and said, 'One moment, William. I'd like to introduce you to someone.'

'Who?' enquired Boyd as he noticed a smartly dressed gentleman approaching them.

'The new Chief Constable of Cumbria,' revealed the Commander. 'He's also expected to be the next one to sit in the Regional Chair of Counter Terrorism Command.'

'Oh yes,' replied Boyd. 'I heard there was a new man coming in. Where's he from?'

'Thames Valley!' said Commander Maxwell. 'On transfer to Cumbria in order to propagate the national agenda, I suspect. Don't repeat this but he's a spin doctor and that's what they want these days.'

'National agenda? Spin doctor! Word speak! That telephone call really did get to you, Commander,' suggested Boyd. 'It's not like you to get bitter and twisted. You sound as if you are not at all happy with things at the moment.'

'No-one ever delivers bad news personally any longer,' sighed Commander Maxwell. 'It arrives by either email, text or a very brief telephone call. There's rarely a face to face explanation but always an expectation that everything is hunky-dory.'

'I seem to have heard that one before somewhere,' replied Boyd glancing at Antonia Harston-Browne.

Cornelius Webb stood six feet three inches tall, was of broad build, sported a meticulously combed moustache, and enjoyed a head of thick swept-back dark hair.

The new Chief had a confident look about him as he extended a hand to Commander Maxwell and opened with, 'Edwin! How nice to see you! Wonderful speech from the pulpit. Well done. Sad times mind you, but you captured the spirit of the day admirably.'

'I didn't realise you knew Sandy,' offered the Commander.

'I didn't actually,' replied the Chief thoughtfully. 'But I thought it my place to attend in view of my next posting at Counter Terrorism Command.'

'So, you got the regional job?' asked Edwin.

'Oh yes,' replied the Chief. 'Temporarily! Sir Edward is on a fact-finding mission to America for six months. Between you and I, he's expected to prepare and submit a lengthy report when he gets back. Then he'll take early retirement. He has a heart murmur of some kind apparently. I'll take the chair every two weeks or whenever important decisions have to be made in the north-west concerning the terrorist portfolio.'

'Portfolio?' queried the Commander rather confused.

'My speciality,' replied the Chief. 'I'm very happy with the regional post but I've made it clear to the Home Secretary that I've only accepted this temporary position on the understanding that I'll get the top job at the Yard when the present incumbent sees their time out.'

'Oh, I see,' nodded the Commander forcing a slight smile

'Oh yes,' beamed the Chief. 'This is merely a stepping stone to the top job.'

'I didn't know,' replied the Commander.

'Well, you do now,' frowned the Chief. 'But in the immediate future, I'll be looking after things in the Lake District. Chairing one of the most important policing positions in the country whilst keeping the sheep in good order in Cumbria seems to be a nice balance, don't you think?'

'I suppose,' muttered the Commander.

'I'm told they get busy during the summer with holidaymakers but other than that I understand it's an ideal spot for someone destined for higher places. You just need to keep your head down and get the time in. Nothing much ever happens up north. But who knows,' continued the Chief. 'I might even have to pick up some sheep dottle if things get rough.'

'Sheep dottle?' queried Commander Maxwell.

'Sheep shit, Edwin,' smirked the Chief who laughed before continuing, 'Little to do on one hand and a lot to do on the other. Just the ticket, Edwin. Just the ticket!'

'Well, congratulations,' replied Commander Maxwell. 'I'm sure you'll enjoy the Lake District and the sixteen million tourists that visit Cumbria every year.'

'Sixteen million?' remarked the Chief, surprised.

'Yes, London has a population of over ten million people, not counting tourists,' explained Commander Maxwell. 'You'll find Cumbria is much busier than you might imagine, Cornelius. But then, it's just a small force in the backwoods, isn't it?'.

Boyd noted the twist of sarcasm in the Commander's voice.

'You've been there I take it?' queried the Chief.

'Obviously,' replied the Commander. 'And I am well aware of its policing functions. Didn't you know we have Cumbrian officers in the unit?'

Turning to the Commander's colleagues, the Chief rapidly changed the subject when he forged an enquiring smile and said, 'I'm Cornelius Webb. Who have we here?'

'Stepping stones plus a shepherd and his flock, sir,' replied the straight-faced Boyd. 'We pick up sheep shit for a living whilst being stepped on from those above.'

In Whitehall, the armed police officers on duty at the secure gate monitored the dozens of pedestrians thronging around the entrance to Downing Street.

Number Ten was the focus of attention for the sightseers. This was the headquarters of the Government of the United Kingdom and the official residence and office of the First Lord of the Treasury, a post which, for much of the 18th and 19th centuries and since 1905, had been held by the Prime Minister.

Photographs were allowed and resulted in a clamour to get the best view of the street, often with the gates or a police officer in the frame, as the public snapped away to their heart's content. Every few minutes someone seemed to take a selfie with the police, security gates, or the Downing Street nameplate in the background.

With two officers on the exterior of the gate, in Whitehall, there were at least another six on the interior of the gate securing the ground in the immediate vicinity of the prestigious address.

Unseen by the public eye, more officers patrolled the rear of the row of terraced houses that made up Downing Street. It surely wasn't parliament, but it was certainly the throne of government leadership. To the officers on a security patrol, it was Base Delta – Number Ten Downing Street.

The traffic flew down Whitehall in a never-ending madcap rush to get from A to B in the quickest possible time. There was no stopping. Double yellow lines, supported by obtrusive CCTV, clearly prohibited parking in the area and were a boost to security.

The courier's van slid to the near side of the road and idled.

A policeman on the footpath saw the vehicle stop and took a step towards the kerb.

The van's offside window lowered.

The policeman radioed the van's registration number into the central control room, 'Ten Four Six at Base Delta checking a white van registered number…'

The barrel of a gun poked out of the van's window.

'Down!' screeched the policeman as a hail of bullets zipped over his head and clattered into the iron gates behind.

Raising his firearm to chest height, the policeman radioed, 'Ten Four Six Base Delta is under attack. Shots fired!'

More shooting from the van. Bullets raked the air, took down half a dozen pedestrians, ricocheted from the iron railings securing the entrance to the street and zipped into the enclosure.

Police dived for cover as an array of gunfire raked the area and took down another civilian.

Screaming voices filled the air as a score of pedestrians ran from the immediate area. Bumping and charging into each other, a child fell to the ground and a woman found herself pushed against a wall as panic ensued. An elderly man wearing a trilby tripped over the child, hit his head on the pavement, and saw the blood spill from his head before passing out.

'Shots fired!' screamed the policeman into his radio. 'Am engaging! Base Delta is under attack!'

Immediately the two officers on the footpath dropped to one knee and took aim at the open van window.

More bullets spat from the deadly firearm as police returned fire.

'Take the tyres out!' yelled one of the armed officers.

Seconds later, there was an almighty screech from the van's tyres when the driver slammed the accelerator to the floor and drove off towards Westminster Bridge at high speed.

One of the officers moderated his position and ran down Whitehall in pursuit of the van. Taking careful aim, he hit the rear of the van with multiple shots. None of the bullets hit the tyres.

Peppered with bullet holes, there was a slight twinge from the van as it swerved from left to right, pulled hard across the centre of the road against the traffic lights, and then careered into a left-hand turn as the van sought to negotiate the traffic on Westminster Bridge.

'Ten Four Six ambulances required at Based Delta. Urgent! Multiple casualties. Shots fired! Attack vehicle has made off towards Westminster Bridge. It's crossing the river now.'

'Control – All received. How many occupants?'

'Not known at this time. At least one in the driver's seat.'

'Roger, Ten-Four Six! Ambulances dispatched. All trigger units, make Base Delta. Stand by for cordon activation.'

Fingertips glided across a keyboard as the various plans, practices and procedures flashed in front of the operator's eyes.

In the minutes that followed, Whitehall – at its junction with Downing Street – resembled a battle zone when ambulances, paramedics, and more police officers arrived at the scene to assist those already there. Over a dozen casualties were recorded in the opening minutes of the computerised police Command and Control log.

As the courier van made over Westminster Bridge, a police motorcyclist picked up the radio transmissions, saw the fast-moving van driving over the bridge into South London, and gave chase.

'Solo Two Nine-Nine in pursuit of the white van. Occupant believed responsible for a shooting attack at Base Delta.'

'Roger!' from Command and Control. 'Location and direction of travel?'

'Standby,' replied the motorcyclist as he gunned his high-powered lightweight BMW onto the bridge, overtook traffic at speed, and then radioed, 'South from Westminster Bridge on the A3036 towards Lambeth Bridge!'

'All units exercise caution. The occupant is armed and dangerous. Commentary please, Solo Two Nine-Nine. You have the air.'

'Target vehicle is through the roundabout at Lambeth Bridge.... Stand by..... And so am I... Left, left, left into Black Prince Road. Speed six zero and the van has two hundred yards on me at least. Through a traffic controlled pedestrian crossing on red... Stand by.... And so am I... Am making ground... No deviation. Solo Two Nine-Nine is gaining.'

As the chase continued, a blare of sirens and flashing blue lights descended on South London as the van escaped the scene of carnage.

With awesome speed, the police motorcyclist quickly closed with the van and radioed, 'Assistance required. Requesting a hard stop and firearm support.'

'All units converging!' from Command and Control.

An open top double decker sightseeing bus suddenly appeared turning from a junction into the main road.

There was a squeal of tyres when the blonde driver slammed on the brakes and mounted the nearside pavement in order to avoid the bus. Pedestrians screamed, threw themselves out of the way of the fugitive van, and watched helplessly as the van bounced back onto the highway and roared away from the scene.

Solo Two Nine-Nine saw the bus violating his space, hit the brakes, and then mounted the pavement intent on keeping up with the escaping van.

A woman with a pushchair emerged from a shop into the motorcyclist's path. The infant glanced sideways, allowed a dummy to fall from her mouth, and watched as Solo Two Nine-Nine, with nowhere to go, deliberately slid the motorbike into the building line in order to avoid colliding with either the bus or the child in the pushchair. More screaming, followed by a long scrape of metal and a score of flying sparks as the motorbike's fairing made contact with brick, the ultan windscreen shattered, and the wireless aerial sprouting from the radio mounted behind the rider's seat reverberated loudly on contact with building line. The motorcyclist's umbilical cord detached itself from the radio pod as the rider crash-landed on the tarmac and rolled over narrowly missing the wheels of the bus.

Snatching a lower gear, the van driver crunched through the gears as it disappeared from view.

Back in a secure office in Downing Street, a detective rewound the CCTV tape to the beginning of the attack and declared, 'ISIS! It has all the hallmarks of an extremist attack! Call out the circus!'

'Are you sure?' queried a colleague close by.

'Nope! But it's a big one. Hit those buttons.'

Outside Saint John the Evangelist's church in Berkshire, a finger and thumb curled the end of a moustache and the voice of Cornelius Webb boomed, 'Sheep shit collectors, is it? Sarcastic ones, I can tell! Indeed, sarcastic sheep shit collectors with no respect for rank Well, let me make things perfectly clear to you. I am the new Chief Constable of Cumbria, the Chairman and leader of North West Counter Terrorism Command, and the man who hires and fires those in the Command. I take exception to your disjointed comment. Misplaced humour and sarcasm should not be used to try and humiliate another and that's precisely what you have done. I'll have you know that...'

'Forgive me,' responded Boyd. 'I apologise if you did not find my remark useful. However, sir, the chair does not lead an organisation.

The chair facilitates discussion, ensures attendance at important meetings, and makes sure the secretary has the minutes up to date.'

'Guvnor!' whispered Anthea tugging the arm of his jacket.

'In any event, sir,' continued Boyd. 'You may hire and fire in the Command, but we work in the Special Crime Unit in London.'

'And you are on secondment,' bellowed Cornelius. 'A matter you seem to have forgotten.'

Rocked with the reminder for a moment, Boyd had no answer and could not deflect incisive glares from both Anthea and Antonia.

'My brief is to maintain the high standards that are expected of us whilst rescuing the budget,' explained the Chief.

'You mean reducing the budget?' queried Boyd.

'As applicable,' snarled the Chief.

'Gentlemen!' proposed Commander Maxwell. 'Must we? These are hallowed grounds I really think these matters might be better discussed elsewhere.'

A soft humming noise emitted from the area of Commander Edwin Maxwell's belt. This was immediately followed by more wireless signal activations as various personal bleepers were activated.

Edwin moved away, glanced at the Chief, and said, 'Excuse me.'

'One minute,' added Boyd as Antonia and Anthea reacted to their bleepers and scanned the screens.

'What's going on?' enquired the Chief.

'Base Delta,' murmured the Commander.

'It's a call out!' revealed Boyd. 'We're twenty-four seven on call and your sheep shit collectors are off to clear up some more dottle. It's what we do whether you like it or not. Sorry, but we'll catch you later. Perhaps next time, we'll have a better understanding between us.'

The team stepped away, got into Boyd's squad car, and heard Boyd murmur, 'I did it again. Why can't I keep my mouth shut?'

'It's your weakest attribute,' remarked Commander Maxwell. 'And Cornelius Webb is not a man who will easily forget what he considers to be an affront to his dignity.'

'It was a throwaway flippant remark, that's all,' replied Boyd.

'One too many,' added Anthea. 'Three or four actually. Mind you, he didn't have a good word for the Cumbrians. More contempt than affection.'

'Which is why I gave him both barrels,' revealed Boyd.

The engine fired and Boyd drove respectfully away from the funeral.

Reaching the main road, Boyd hit a button on the control panel and a pair of blue lights began to flash from the headlight unit. He gunned the car as fast as he could.

'An attack in Downing Street,' relayed Boyd taking charge. 'Operation Base Delta Attack Response. Make the calls, Anthea. Turn Bannerman out to deal and take charge of the scene. I want the following immediate actions. Secure number ten! Locate and secure the Prime Minister. Locate and secure the Monarch and the immediate line of ascension. I know they have their own protection teams, but we will assume the primacy of command until the situation is stabilised. Bolster the protection teams with Team Echo. That's our remit.'

'I'm on it,' replied Anthea. 'Ascertaining the cordon management system and locations.'

'Commander?' enquired Boyd looking for guidance. 'Are you going to tell me that 'phone call you took was a warning regarding an unscheduled exercise?'

'No,' responded Edwin. 'I wish it was. No, it's the real thing.'

'There's a lot to do then,' snapped Boyd.

'Perhaps we presume too much but then you never know. Make the nearest police station, William. We need site presence, site management, and a grip on the situation. It's a big one, whatever it is. I want our own satellite station set up here until we're on top of it.'

'Agreed!' replied Boyd. 'Antonia! Your mob?'

Engaging her mobile phone, the lady from the Security Service replied, 'I'm already on it, Boyd. I'll secure a lockdown on the mobile networks. Just concentrate on driving.'

Standing alone in the church car park, Cornelius Webb nodded to mourners passing by. He checked his watch, fumbled for his pager and mobile phone, and briefly felt the crucifix hanging from a necklace beneath his shirt.

As the sound of Boyd's siren drifted to his ears, Cornelius murmured, 'Base Delta? Whatever it is, why haven't I been informed?'

Outside a tube station in south London, the Downing Street assassin pulled into the side of the road. Leaving her firearm on the passenger seat, the woman abandoned the van. The nation's most-wanted killer legged it quickly down some steps into the tube station where she threw the van keys into a litter bin and caught the first train leaving the station.

Reaching the first stop, the woman joined the throng heading onto the platform, walked casually through the tiled corridors, and boarded a northbound train. Four stations later, and now north of the River Thames, the killer strolled out of the underground station, took in the fresh air, listened to the sound of far-off sirens, and caught a bus.

Half an hour later, she stepped off the bus and walked into a car park where she selected a car and fired the engine. Checking her rearview mirror, the woman dragged the wig from her head, shook free her real hair, and stuffed the wig beneath the car seat.

Guiding the vehicle out of the car park, she adopted a casual driving attitude and headed north for the motorway as she recalled the cryptic message written in the road atlas.

Shuffling his feet anxiously, Detective Inspector Bannerman studied the environment before him.

He took in Downing Street, Whitehall and the Cenotaph before turning to Detective Sergeant Terry Anwhari and the rest of the team saying, 'Lock it down! I want uniform search teams from here right across Westminster Bridge and beyond. Janice! Put a team together and secure all the CCTV on the route and any ancillary locations that might offer images of any kind. It should all be in the Base Delta response file.'

'Mine!' replied Detective Sergeant Janice Burns, a feisty scot of some repute.

'I want Martin to take control of the medical side of the forensics,' continued Bannerman. 'Ballistics, bullets, shells, cartridges, whatever is found. That includes bullets from the bodies of the victims. Catalogue everything! I want to be able to reconstruct the entire scene if needed. Harry Nugent to be the global exhibit officer.'

Harry nodded. It was what he expected to be doing and he replied, 'I'd like an on the ground video of the entire scenario and an aerial display from the sky.'

'Agreed!' replied Bannerman. 'Get the Air Support Wing involved and progress it.'

'Ballistic evidence!' remarked Martin Duffy. 'I have it.'

'Noted,' remarked Terry frantically making notes.

'Avoid speculation! Get the basics done first and get them done properly,' ordered Bannerman.

'And the investigation team?' proposed the sergeant.

'That will be our team in tandem with the Downing Street crew. Once you've got the ball rolling, I want a full history of the van used. I expect it's probably been stolen or fraudulently hired. Who knows what we'll find? Then I want…'

Taking command, securing crime scene evidence, thinking things through, Bannerman gradually managed and co-ordinated the police response to the Downing Street attack.

He had begun his career as a police officer in Cumbria but ten years later had transferred to the Metropolitan Police in London where he had eventually been drafted into the Special Escort Group of the Met's Royalty and Protection Squad. Recognised for his ability to adapt to fast-moving incidents, Bannerman had been seconded to the Special Crime Unit where he now held responsibility for bomb scene management and the supervision of major crime scenes.

His feet wore a size ten pair of shoes and stood six feet five inches tall inside them. Broad across the shoulders, he was quite muscular despite a slight paunch around his midriff. A chiselled square chin gave him the appearance of a man older than he actually was whilst a crop of microscopic ginger hair sprouted from a rounded skull and crept dangerously towards his ears. His mouth engaged in most of the action for at times he gabbled on endlessly about the most unimportant of things. From a distance, he looked almost bald. Up close, no one told him so. His friends called him 'the big man' but enemies called him 'the screaming skull'.

'You got it so far?' enquired Bannerman.

'Joe Harkness and Team Echo have just secured the monarchy and the prime minister as a result of direct contact from Commander Maxwell. They've doubled the guard at Buckingham Palace,' revealed Terry Anwhari chuckling.

'Very funny,' laughed Bannerman. 'I take it they've bolstered the teams and everything is as it should be at the moment?'

'Yes! No trojan horses! And Charlie Brown's team has deployed to Horse Guards Parade and is moving in to assist you.'

'Great! Thanks!' replied Bannerman. 'Okay, Ricky French to oversee all statement gathering and commence the investigation file. Uniform has set down a preliminary cordon to secure the immediate area. Locate the local Commander and double the perimeter of the cordon.

'The Borough Commander is setting up a computerised control centre,' remarked Terry.

'Good! Thank you, Terry,' replied Bannerman. 'Let's go to work. Rendezvous on foot on Westminster Bridge in one hours' time for an update. That's where you'll find me – at the scene of the beginning of the chase. What's the score with the police motorcyclist? Is he okay?'

'Possible fractured shoulder is all we know at the moment,' replied Terry. 'Ricky French to interview?'

'Yes, as soon as the medical authorities allow access please,' responded Bannerman. 'How many bodies in the van? Any descriptions? Any witnesses on the bridge? Same at the collision scene. I want answers to questions. That's the only way we're going to catch this one.'

'Got it,' noted Terry. 'I've also got the first two officers in the Downing Street Protection Team lined up to see you. They both engaged the van driver and returned gunfire.'

'Good! Let's have a word then. The next twenty-four hours are likely to be crucial to the end product. Just your best, please. That's all I ask.'

'When is the Commander back?' enquired Janice.

'Tomorrow hopefully!' acknowledged Bannerman. 'We'll brief him and Boyd as to what we've got and what we still need to do in the office. Now let's get the show on the road.'

As the team split up to begin their enquiries, Janice turned to Ricky and whispered, 'Och, the big man is on form today. It's the first major scene he's taken charge of and he's got the bit between his teeth, that's for sure. I don't envy him one little bit because this scene is likely to stretch right across London once we start putting it all together.'

'Yeah, but my shoe leather is running out. Can I get a new pair on expenses?'

'Nope,' replied Janice. 'But you can try.'

It was raining hard in Manchester when the train pulled into the railway station and gradually came to a standstill at the allotted platform. The doors burst open and the train discharged its passengers. Some ran, some walked, and others just ambled towards the ticket barrier.

A man in his forties stepped from the train, negotiated the ticket barrier, crossed the esplanade, and strolled into the street outside. Feeling damp, and slightly cold, he turned up the collar of his leather jacket and dodged the traffic as he made for the pub nearby. Entering The Star, the visitor bought a pint of bitter at the bar and took a seat near the doorway.

Supping his beer, he casually checked the surroundings and took in the people around him before easing the sunglasses away from the bridge of his nose for a moment.

Moments later, he dropped a few coins into an amusement machine, lost his money, but took the opportunity to check out if those present were the slightest bit interested in his movements. A television on the wall held everyone's attention when he left his drink on the table and entered the toilet block. In the gents, he removed a package from behind the cistern in one of the cubicles. Hiding it in his jacket, he quickly walked out of the Star towards a taxi rank close to the railway station.

The man jumped into the rear of the taxi and, a few moments later, it drove off into the city centre.

Two days later, Boyd sat in an office in the Special Crime Unit. He shook his head at the amount of paperwork that threatened to overwhelm the highly polished walnut desk that was now his bridge, his fortress, his base, his command post.

There was a knock on the door and Bannerman walked in saying, 'Pity they didn't have the decency to at least put a notice on the door indicating this is the Commander's office.'

'Well, that's how it is,' smiled Boyd. 'They couldn't afford a new nameplate for the door and there are more important things to consider. Are you ready?'

'Yes, whenever you are,' replied Bannerman.

'Thanks for looking after the shop,' declared Boyd. 'I never doubted your ability. It's not easy to take command of a major crime scene in a capital city.'

'There was more top brass there than soft Mick,' replied Bannerman. 'Even the Deputy Assistant Commissioner made an appearance.'

'Yes, that's usual,' remarked Boyd. 'The media is all over the top brass when things like this happen. Get used to it because it's the top brass that will look to you for all the answers.'

'Yeah,' grinned Bannerman. 'You can say that again. But we didn't end up with a prisoner.'

'I'm told you covered it well.'

'Thanks, Guvnor,' replied Bannerman. 'We're waiting for you.'

As Bannerman left the room, Boyd scribbled his signature over another document, placed it in the out tray, and then opened an envelope embossed with the Home Office stamp. Removing the innards, his eyes quickly scanned the documents and he realised it was a vetting form for Cornelius Webb, the newly appointed Chief Constable of Cumbria and the North West Counter Terrorism Command Centre.

'So,' he thought. 'The system entrusts a middle-ranking Detective Chief Inspector who doesn't even warrant an office nameplate with the fate of the nation? What is the world coming to?'

Boyd slid the document into his desk, locked it, and walked into the main office.

Bannerman stood at the front of the office in the Special Crime Unit and delivered his briefing to the teams gathered before him. To be more precise, he quickly explained where the enquiry had reached, and what was still to do as Boyd, Anthea, Antonia, and Commander Maxwell looked on. Coffee and tea were the order of the day as Detective Inspector Bannerman outlined the enquiry to date.

'To summarise,' explained Bannerman. 'We're looking for a tall, well-built blonde who was last seen entering a tube station at Kennington, South London.' Activating a video, he continued, 'And here she is. Local CCTV captures her abandoning the van outside the station, entering the concourse, and dropping the van ignition keys into a litter bin.' The video rolled on and Bannerman added, 'This shows her getting into a tube and, as yet, we've nothing more. I'm hoping we'll locate the station she left the train at but I don't need to tell you how long that takes and how many CCTV tapes we have to look through. I'll keep you all updated on that on the assumption it might actually lead us somewhere. Alternatively, it might lead us to the last time CCTV captures her.'

'What about the van?' enquired Anthea.

'Examination of the van reveals nothing that we can develop further than we already have.'

'As you've been on the ground with this one, Bannerman,' queried Boyd. 'The media have labelled the suspect as the Downing Street Assassin. But who do you think the killer was targeting? The Prime Minister and Cabinet Ministers or anyone who happened to be in the area?'

'Personally, I've no idea,' responded Bannerman. 'This has all the hallmarks of a terrorist-related incident, but it notably lacks any attempt at accreditation from ISIS. Not even an 'Allahu Akbar'. I've been advised by some government officials that this is because ISIS has been defeated and it's more likely to be some disgruntled political activist airing their grievances.'

'God! Give me strength!' replied Boyd. 'I thought we were dealing with a mass murderer, not a political activist! Sorry! Go on!'

'Yeah, we're dealing with weird people,' continued Bannerman. 'And some of them are in government. But here's the rub, the van is on false plates. It was stolen six months ago from Dagenham and there's no record of any sightings since. Furthermore, a forensic examination of the interior reveals quite a few fingerprints which we believe may belong to the assassin. There is no trace of any of these in the UK database.'

'Are we checking with European police forces across Europe and with the Americans and Canadians?' enquired Anthea.

'Yes, nothing stateside or Canada and zilch, so far, from our colleagues in Europe although we are still awaiting some replies. These things take time and involve various protocols, as well you know.'

'A foreign visitor?' suggested Antonia. 'If we're thinking ISIS should we not be checking for someone we know went to another country to join ISIS and then came back? We've possibly got a record of them already. Are they on our radar at the moment?'

'It's likely but not definite,' nodded Bannerman. 'But we've no fingerprint matches. It's hard to say but I wouldn't rule out the possibility of a foreign invader. The other thing is we have traces of her hair on the back of the driver's seat.'

'So we have a DNA contact?' proposed Boyd.

'No, we have synthetic fibres,' chuckled Bannerman. 'She was wearing a wig.'

The briefing continued as Bannerman brought everyone up to speed.

'A foreign invader,' mused Antonia as she stood up and walked towards a secure computer area. 'Excuse me,' she offered as she began closing the door behind her. 'Let me check something out.'

Eventually, Bannerman dried up, looked into Commander Maxwell's eyes and brought the briefing to a close with, 'That's us so far, Guvnor. How did I do first time out?'

Laying a hand on Bannerman's shoulder, Commander Maxwell replied, 'Very well, Bannerman. Very well indeed but I have to correct you on one point.'

'Which is?'

'As you are well aware, I'm no longer the Guvnor. I know some of you are aware and others might not be, but I can confirm that I'm off to Organised Gangs and Serious Crime as from tomorrow morning.'

Murmurs of disapproval were set aside when the Commander raised his hand and said, 'Boyd is now your Commander although there are no promotions to be had. The executive is still trying to make savings and balance the budget. But I leave you in excellent hands and would like to thank each and every one of you for...'

The Commander continued his emotional farewell but in an office down the corridor, Antonia Harston-Browne was tinkling the black and whites on a standalone computer that housed the highly encrypted state of the art Ticker Intelligence system.

With offices at both New Scotland Yard and the Security Services Headquarters at Thames House, Antonia was renowned amongst her male counterparts for her shapely legs and long red hair. Tall and slim, Antonia wore a dark blue, two-piece, executive-style suit set off with a silver brooch worn on the lapel. The neatly tailored skirt stopped short just above the knee. She called it her office uniform and wore it well. Antonia was one of those individuals who just didn't age. She thrived on adventure and tension. A child of the Sixties, she was every inch a lady: articulate, sophisticated, cultured, educated well above the national standard, and of the upper-middle-class bearing. Indeed, Antonia carried a highly polished professional demeanour wherever she went enjoying two honours degrees and playing a merciless game of squash. At the quintessential exclusive country club, she was in her element with the so-called 'county set'. Whilst in the oak-panelled corridors of Whitehall and the highfalutin financial offices of the City, she could wheel and deal with the sharpest of kids on the block. In the City, she wined and dined at expensive restaurants and wore long, flowing gowns that vitalised her sophisticated charms and discarded the I of her other life. She was privileged, virtually blue-blooded, the daughter of parents since departed: parents who had left her a financial legacy that revealed her to be of comfortable private means. In the City, in the country club, she had no enemies, save those who bitched at her pretentiousness. Moreover, Antonia had connections in every corner of society that one might imagine: the good, the bad, and the ugly. As a senior Intelligence Officer, she was a leading member of the controversial Special Crime unit and was in love with Phillip Nesbitt, Director General of the Security Service.

Her delicate fingers keyed in various instructions before a newsreel ran, at reading speed, across the computer screen. The system revealed live intelligence data which was being put into the Ticker system by authorised Intelligence officers from the police, military and intelligence services across the globe. Gradually, the ticker news system increased as Antonia keyed in more instructions.

'Nothing this month that suggests this invader is recent,' she thought to herself. 'But then again, who we are looking for may not be a foreign invader. Maybe I should recap the last few months on ISIS?'

Talking to herself, lost in her own mind, Antonia worked away at the multi-million-pound system thinking, 'Millions of pounds and it still doesn't recognise the words, SHOW FOREIGN INVADER. What other words should I use that won't bring back over twenty thousand suspected illegal migration movements?'

She clicked a switch on the machine and wondered how long it would take before the coffee was ready.

In Newcastle, the man wearing a black leather jacket hired a car. Unburdening a large canvas holdall from his shoulders, he packed it into the boot of the vehicle and set off from the west end of the city along the A69 towards Cumbria and the Roman Wall. As he drove casually west, he fumbled inside his jacket and removed a pair of black framed sunglasses which he carefully cradled across the bridge of his nose. Checking the rearview mirror, the driver smiled and realised how well the dark sunglasses complimented the black and grey bandana he wore on his head.

It wasn't long before the man was approaching Hexham where the North Tyne and the South Tyne rivers met and formed the River Tyne that flowed all the way to the northeast coast.

A mobile phone rang and he delved into his jacket pocket to answer the call.

'Speaking,' he said. Cruising casually on the dual carriageway, the man checked his rearview mirror and said, 'No! I'm clean. And you?' Listening to the caller, he offered, 'It failed because the target usually leaves number ten at the same time every day for Prime Minister's Question Time. Monday to Friday every week but today the time was slightly different and instead of waiting, you bottled it and were lucky to get away in one piece.' Removing the phone from his ear, he listened to a tirade of abuse before replying, 'Settle down! I don't know why the target didn't leave on time either, but you proved it can be done. What we didn't achieve today we can be successful with tomorrow. We'll shelve it for now. We only need to get it right once.'

The conversation continued before a hand adjusted the sunglasses and a voice growled, 'This is getting us nowhere. You're still in the game. Relax! Now tell me if you've had any problems since that I haven't read about or heard on the car radio?'

He checked the mirror again, listened, and then replied, 'Don't worry about it. You'll be fine. I'll be there in about two hours, but I might stop for something to eat on the way, probably Carlisle. We'll meet as discussed. Okay?' He smiled, let the caller finish speaking, and replied, 'Yes, I made the collection, but the beer was warm. Tell the 'Placer' to pick a better spot next time. The fewer people around the better. By the way, watch the news, my love. Diego has gone to work. We are not alone.'

The driver closed his mobile, fidgeted with his bandana, and then concentrated on the traffic as he headed towards a rendezvous in Cumbria

In the Special Crime Unit office, in London, Antonia was pointing at the computer screen saying, 'This is the nearest we've got, Boyd.'

'Surely it's Commander Boyd now,' suggested the Chief Inspector twisting a wry smile.

'No, it's Billy when we're off duty and Boyd in the office. Now shut up and listen,' chided Antonia.

Anthea and Bannerman grimaced slightly but Boyd remarked, 'What do we have on Ticker?'

'Sadly, not a lot,' declared Antonia. 'Well, other than almost three hundred possible suspects who have returned from various parts of the Middle East during the past six months.'

'Defeated ISIS soldiers?' suggested Boyd.

'Almost certainly,' replied Antonia. 'But I came across this reference to an attack on an ISIS convoy at Deir ez-Zor in Syria.'

'Oh yes, wasn't that once the oil capital of Syria?' queried Boyd.

'Something like that,' replied Antonia. 'An American air assault destroyed a convoy heading out of one conflict zone into another. After the attack, they sent a drone over to inspect the damage.'

'And got photographs?' proposed Boyd.

'Yes! Audiovisual actually!'

'Audio?' queried Boyd.

'Photographs of damage to the convoy,' stated Antonia clicking through to a video. 'And some people standing nearby. I'm presuming they are ISIS.'

Boyd and Anthea concentrated on the screen.

'Plus, we have some audio from the ground,' continued Antonia. 'The drone was blown from the skies, but its surveillance capabilities lasted for about forty-five seconds before the link was lost. It's not the best quality but someone down there calls himself Diego and tells the others that he's the Sultán of Spain.'

'Is the UK mentioned at all?' asked Boyd. "England in particular?'

'No, but did you know that a Sultán is someone who is a king or sovereign of a Muslim state,' explained Antonia.

'I thought a Sultán was a nut,' smirked Bannerman.

'Not quite,' replied Antonia. 'I think you mean a Sultána.'

'Oh, yes,' replied the big man smiling. 'Of course! A lady nut!'

'A Sultána is actually a female Sultán,' remarked Antonia as she continued to interrogate the keyboard.

'So, you are suggesting this Diego is the Muslim King of Spain?' chuckled Boyd.

'Well, I'm thinking out of the box,' answered Antonia. 'I'm trying to put myself on the ground out there and second-guessing the conversation they had. It's the only way to get into the audiovisual properly, and the minds of what is quite obviously our enemies.'

Boyd tapped his finger on the computer screen, listened to the audio again, and looked closely at those standing on the ground near to the burning convoy.

'I see tanks on fire and quite a few wagons,' revealed Boyd. 'Plus a male wearing a black and grey bandana and a cute pair of sunglasses like mine.'

'Like yours?' queried Anthea. 'You mean the bandana or the sunglasses.'

'Both!' replied Boyd.

'They well and truly made a mess of that convoy,' declared Anthea as she studied the footage.

'Antonia, if we were to go with your proposal,' suggested Boyd. 'Then one of these people is Diego.'

'Precisely!' acknowledged Antonia.

'So, if Diego appointed himself the Muslim King of Spain, who got the United Kingdom?' queried Boyd.

'No-one as far as I can tell from this limited coverage we have. It's not much to go on,' remarked Antonia. 'We're not mentioned and there's nothing concrete.'

'It's all a bit weak,' added Anthea.

'Pity,' nodded Boyd. 'I like that bandana. It reminds me of the one I wear when I go running across the moor at home.'

'Sultán!' murmured Bannerman. 'A King, is it?'

'I think so,' replied Boyd. 'Do some research on it and let me know what you find out.'

'Research?' queried Bannerman.

'Yeah! In this job you just never know what might happen. What is irrelevant today becomes relevant tomorrow when circumstances change. Check out criminal records for anyone with the surname or nickname Sultán. Then find out what the word really means. I'd like to know what the Islamic extremists think of the word as opposed to the Muslim people themselves.'

'I'll cover all the bases,' replied Bannerman. 'I'll ask a couple of Muslims I know what it means to them if anything. Presumably, they'll know about Muslim kings.'

'Me too,' nodded Boyd. 'You okay with this?'

'Of course,' replied Bannerman. 'Can do, but I think the Downing Street attack may well be more likely linked to a madman, the far right, or some outlandish cause yet to surface. No-one has claimed responsibility for the attack and they've had more than enough time.'

Bannerman took a seat at a neighbouring computer console and began interrogating data whilst asking, 'What do you think, Boyd? Any ideas who the perpetrators might be?'

'I'm not sure it's terrorism from ISIS,' revealed Boyd. 'Islamic State extremists have a history of remaining at the scene and taking as many people as possible with them during a terrorist attack. It's almost as if they were keen supporters of suicide but then, in their minds, they're going to a better place when they die.'

'The Downing Street attacker didn't hang around to discuss such a theory,' intervened Anthea. 'But that lady sure as hell showed us a clean pair of heels.'

Tapping on the keyboard, Bannerman remarked, 'We have some Sultáns on the criminal record database. Not one of them marked as of interest to us but here's the rub. It would be a generalisation for me to say that Sultán is mainly used as a forename – or title – in the east and a surname in the west. It's from the ancient French word 'Soudan' which in Arabic is pronounced Sultán and means ruler. It was originally given as a nickname to someone who behaved in an aristocratic manner but would you believe it was first recorded in the early thirteenth Century.'

'The Muslim Prophet and founder of Islam – Muhamad – was born in the fifth century,' observed Boyd. 'How come it took them eight hundred years to make Sultáns rulers?'

'No idea,' replied Bannerman.

'Find out why?' suggested Boyd.

'Will my expenses cover time travel?' enquired Bannerman.

'I'll authorise it,' replied Anthea. 'The new Commander just needs to justify it.'

'Just work on it,' sighed Boyd. 'And get onto the Centro Nacional de Inteligencia in Madrid. Have the Spaniards got anything on a Sultán Diego?'

'I'll do that,' replied Anthea.

'I'm drawing a blank,' remarked Antonia on the Ticker system. 'But if every Islamic fighter returning to Britain from the Middle East in the last three months is a suspect then we have at least three hundred problems to investigate, and I'll presume there's possibly more. We already have three thousand individuals on the Watch List. How long have we got, a year or two?'

Boyd stepped away and studied one of the blank screens situated in a corner of the room.

'It's switched off, Boyd,' explained Antonia. 'You can stand there all day, but it won't come on until I activate it through the Ticker system.'

Grinning, Boyd replied, 'Of course! It's so bloody obvious isn't it?'

'What is?' enquired Antonia. 'A blank screen?'

'What we need might not be on Ticker,' explained Boyd.

'Marvellous!' chuckled Antonia. 'The system captures virtually every piece of intelligence on the planet and you complain!' Then, more seriously, she enquired, 'What are you thinking? You're miles away again.'

'Precisely! Everything on the planet!' mused Boyd. 'But not in Space. I'm thinking there was an air strike on the convoy followed by drone surveillance.'

'Yes,' murmured Antonia slowly. 'So?'

'Someone knew where that convoy was located.'

'Obviously!' remarked Anthea exchanging glances with Antonia

'Antonia! Can you get your people to place a call with the National Reconnaissance Centre in America?' probed Boyd.

'Chantilly, Virginia,' nodded Antonia. 'Why?

'I'm thinking that if they knew the exact location to strike, and then sent a drone to capture the result, then they used satellite imagery,' explained Boyd. 'If that's the case, I'd like access to their database. I want to know if they've got any images on the group of Jihadis talking about Sultáns. They might have better photos than we have from the drone.'

'Good shout!' replied Antonia. 'I'll place the call.'

'Oh, by the way, Anthea' insisted Boyd. 'Go right to the top of that list of Islamic fighters returning to the UK and go down the list.'.

'I don't follow you,' replied Anthea.

'If the enemy has appointed a Sultán of Spain I want a line of enquiry on any possible Sultán of the United Kingdom. Commence a file, please. Restricted – Eyes only to members of this unit. Authorising officer myself and case officer myself.'

'Your first file as Commander,' remarked Anthea. 'Any reference or title?'

'My first one,' mused Boyd poignantly. 'Yes, call it THE SULTÁN please.'

'The UK underneath in brackets,' murmured Anthea. 'Do you want to open a file for the Spaniard link too?'

'Not at the moment,' decided Boyd. 'But push on with an enquiry on Diego, the Sultán of Spain. Is he someone we already know?'

'Let's see if we can find out, replied Anthea. 'And congratulations, Boyd. You're the first officer I've ever known who has opened a file on a Royal figure.'

'Royalty!' chuckled Boyd. 'Spanish Royalty! I wonder who he really is?'

*

4

Cordoba
Andalucia, Spain
The following day

'Situated in the centre of the autonomous region of Andalucia, Spain,' explained the well-spoken tour guide. 'Our charming city of Cordoba has a population of about 350,000 inhabitants.'

Absorbed by the guide's enthusiastic articulation, a small group of tourists followed the responsive lady as she fulfilled her duties.

'Historically, the city occupies a unique position in Europe. So grand is its significance that Cordoba is a World Heritage Site famous for the mixture of diverse cultures that it has experienced over many centuries. Indeed, there are very few places in the world that can boast to have once been the capital of a Roman province known as Hispania Ulterior. It was as also once the capital of an Arab State known as Al-Andalus and was the capital of the Caliphate of Cordoba. In modern times, of course, many of you will have heard of Andalucia which was once part of the larger area I have referred to as Al-Andalus. The term Al-Andalus translates from Arabic to Muslim Spain or Muslim Islam.'

A camera flashed and a strong Texan drawl interrupted with 'Well, I do declare this is some city. That's for sure. And there was I thinking Las Vegas was one hell of a place. What's it called again, Corleyoba?'

'Cordoba!

'Don't that beat all,' replied the American. 'Must be a Spanish name of some kind.'

'It surely is,' replied the extremely patient guide. 'Possibly because we are in Spain.'

Emerging from a shop door, Officer Santiago López waved a cheery goodbye to the shopkeeper and his wife, stepped onto the cobbled pathway, and took stock of the immediate area. He cast his eyes on the Texan drawler when the camera flashed again and he realised he had been photographed.

'Thank you, officer,' offered the American operator. 'That's some fine uniform you have there. I reckon with all those badges and medals you must be the Chief of the Corleyoban police.'

Officer Santiago was about to reply but the American denied any interchange by turning around and focusing on another target.

Turning to engage her audience, the tour guide nodded, smiled, and continued, 'Dissecting the geography of Cordoba brings us to the historic quarter where we are now situated. As you can see, it is a quite complex network of small streets, alleys, squares and whitewashed courtyards arranged around the world-famous Mezquita. The Mezquita is an eye-catching mosque that also houses a Christian cathedral. This truly matchless building undoubtedly reflects Cordoba's prominent place in the Islamic world during medieval times. The structure chronicles the diverse characteristics of a city that has undergone tremendous cultural changes over many centuries.'

A Muslim lady accompanying the guide adjusted her hijab slightly and asked, 'How old is that building?'

'It was constructed in 786 as a mosque,' replied the guide. 'The building was expanded several times under Cordoba's Muslim rule. You might be interested to learn that the Muslims ruled Al-Andalus, which at that time included most of Spain, Portugal, and a small part of Southern France, in the late 8th century. Historians believe that the Romans built a temple to the Roman god, Janus, on this site. The temple was then converted into a church by the Visigoths who seized Cordoba in 572. The church was converted into a mosque and then completely rebuilt by the descendants of the exiled Umayyads. They were the first Islamic dynasty who originally ruled from their capital Damascus. Following the overthrow of his family (the Umayyads) in Damascus by the incoming Abbasids, Prince Abd al-Rahman escaped to southern Spain. Once there, he established control over almost all of the Iberian Peninsula and attempted to recreate the grandeur of Damascus in his new capital, Cordoba. He sponsored elaborate building programs, promoted agriculture, and even imported fruit trees and other plants from his former home. Orange trees still stand in the courtyard of the Mosque of Cordoba, a beautiful, if bittersweet reminder of the Umayyad exile.'

'Thank you,' from a satisfied customer. 'It really has a complex story, doesn't it?'

Another voice asked, 'A mosque but Christian too! Two religions for the price of one! How diverse is that? But is there any evidence to reveal a stronger Christian connection?'

'When we eventually enter the Mezquita you will clearly see Jesus on the Cross as you do in many Christian sites. But search the red and white double arches and look for a section of black marble.'

'Why?' asked the tourist.

'There's a curious secret,' replied the guide. 'If you can find it you will discover a small, crudely drawn cross carved into a black surface. The age and origin are murky but according to one legend, the cross was created by a Christian man enslaved by the Moors during the time when Córdoba was the capital of the Caliphate of Córdoba. The man was supposedly chained to the column and used his fingernails to carve the iconic Christian symbol into the hard, unforgiving marble.'

'Chained because he was a Christian?' enquired a voice.

'Not necessarily,' replied the guide. 'The story goes that the Christian man had fallen in love with a Moorish girl who had agreed to convert to Christianity for him. On the night of her baptism, she was captured, killed, and her body was thrown into the river. The young Christian was taken into the Mosque-Cathedral and chained to the column where he remained exposed and vulnerable to the public's anger. When his captors realized the cross he had carved couldn't be erased, he too was killed and dumped in the river.'

'Mmm…How interesting.'

'Rather sad, I thought,' suggested the guide.

Approaching the area, Diego Rodriguez García wondered at the colossal size of the bell tower on the Mezquita's north side. The bell dominated the surrounding buildings and overlooked the network of alleyways and narrow streets.

As he closed with the gathering, Diego watched the tour guide turn to a couple of Jewish gentlemen in the multicultural ensemble and heard her explain light-heartedly, 'There's no synagogue, I'm afraid gentlemen, just the mosque and a cathedral.'

'That is fine,' replied one of the men smoothing the kippah on his head. 'Two out of three religions is good. Shabbat Shalom!'

'Pardon?

'It's Hebrew and means I wish you a peaceful Sabbath.'

'Yes, of course, it does,' replied the guide with an apologetic look. 'You must excuse me there are so many different religious beliefs to acknowledge in this place that I try to placate those who sometimes get upset because they have not been included.'

'There is no need to apologise. Please continue. I am enjoying your talk.'

'Thanks, yes, the current building is anchored in the 1600s when the present tower replaced a minaret that had previously dominated the site. Along the outside of the building, the wall resembles a fortress.'

A row of heads peered skywards towards the battlements.

'Yet there are no gun barrels or guards looking down on us today.'

There was a chuckle or two as the tour guide continued her lecture and led the group slowly through the tourist hotspot.

Officer Santiago rested the palm of his right hand on the butt of his holstered pistol as he strolled along his patrol route. The fact that the tour guide was on the same street was purely coincidental.

'She's pretty,' thought Santiago. 'I wonder what her name is.'

In the same area, a short distance away, Diego casually meandered through the narrow cosmopolitan alleyways occasionally pausing to read a restaurant menu or cast his eye on a bar or eating establishment. There were so many such places to choose from, and, as a Spaniard, Diego easily blended into the background as he gradually drew nearer to the Mezquita.

Spinning around suddenly, Diego studied the people behind him before turning back to his original route.

He strolled on with his camera bag hanging loosely from a cord around his neck and a rucksack slung across one of his shoulders. Eventually, shadows on the ground led Diego to glance skywards and realise he was almost directly beneath the famous bell tower.

Pausing outside a French bistro, Diego studied a wine list secured to the wall and then glanced inside. Smiling, he listened to the sound of diners enjoying their meal. It seemed a decent place, modest in its design, moderate in its prices, and with a quintessential Parisian flavour that stood out from its closest neighbours. The gentle sound of clinking glasses from a nearby table invaded his ears. Here, people were dining both inside and outside whilst enjoying the fine weather. There was a crush of people negotiating the immediate vicinity of this popular restaurant.

Casually, Diego removed the camera bag from around his neck and set his rucksack down on the ground before him.

Close by, a French waiter smiled at his diners as he presented the wine list and enquired, 'Vin rouge ou Vin blanc, monsieur ou champagne pour madame?'

'I think white with lunch would be most suitable. Yes, white it is then. I think a nice Chardonnay would be most acceptable, thank you.' A finger scrolled down a list and the voice added, 'A bottle of number thirty-six if you please.'

The waiter took the order, nodded, and withdrew politely.

Diego fumbled with his camera bag, set it to one side on the ground at his feet, and then hoisted the rucksack to his shoulder once more. As he edged slowly away from the restaurant, he slyly nudged the camera bag beneath a table and set his eyes on the route ahead.

The chatter of voices, the clinking of glasses, the murmur of people's voices died down as Diego strolled leisurely along the alley.

It was as if the whole world had turned up to pay homage to the mosque in Cordoba? Or was it the Sultán of Spain himself that was the unheralded attraction? He neither knew nor cared as he eyed the faces of those he encountered on his short journey. They were Asian, Indian, Australian, British, American, Canadian, Indonesian maybe even Russian, Chinese or of Middle Eastern extraction. Diego merely considered them to be unsuspecting witnesses to his presence, muted bystanders, blind eyewitnesses to what lay ahead. Their religion, culture or ethnicity were irrelevant factors in the game that he played. For in his mind, it was his destiny to wage war and, believers or not, such people were all expendable.

Shell-shocked, battle-hardened, his frazzled mind was fragmented by a complex Jihadi belief that waged war on those deemed to be enemies of the extremist version of Islam. Yet, for all that, it was within him to accept that often the good had to die to further the cause of the next Caliphate.

Checking his wristwatch, Diego reached a junction in the alley. He noted a tourist signpost and followed the route towards the Jewish Quarter. Looking back, there was no deviation and his eyes focused on a table and chairs where he knew his camera bag had been abandoned. Around him, the throng of holidaymakers, tourists, and locals alike grew as the sun climbed higher into the sky and the queue to enter the great mosque threatened to overburden the available space.

Spotting his next port of call, Diego allowed his rucksack to slide from his shoulder. There was a soft thud when it hit the ground and the top flap opened to reveal the contents.

The female tour guide and her small entourage came into view. Her voice declared a pre-defined script as a camera flashed and a jumble of varying languages tumbled out of the holiday group.

Kneeling, Diego Rodriguez García – self-appointed Sultán of Cordoba and the whole of Spain – glanced at his wristwatch, looked towards a camera bag about two hundred yards away, and murmured, 'Fifteen seconds!'

Officer Santiago, resplendent in his uniform, emerged from an adjoining alley. His eyes followed the attractive tour guide, a brash American cameraman, two Jewish gentlemen, a Muslim lady, and half a dozen others of various design and gender. Then he looked at Diego, glanced at the bag on the floor, and recognised the 'Shahada' when he heard it.

'Lā 'ilāha 'illā-llāhu muḥammadun rasūlu-llāh,' voiced Diego. 'There is no god but Allah, and Muhammad is the messenger of God.'

Above the narrow lanes and sights and sounds of Cordoba, the tongue of the bell, known as the clapper, swung eternally from its housing before colliding with the ancient metal.

The bell of the mosque at Cordoba rang.

Santiago's right hand dropped to the fastener on his leather holster.

In Cumbria, Boyd stood with an empty champagne glass as, all around him, the refined chatter of voices grew in crescendo as the invited guests gradually filled the room.

With tittle-tattle all around, Boyd yawned and forced a smile when two senior members of Cumbria's military garrison strolled by discussing the merit of their location. As Boyd considered the impressive uniforms of the Army and Air Force personnel, he realised he was not alone.

'More champagne?' enquired a polite uniformed naval steward hovering with the essentials.

'It's orange juice actually,' replied Boyd. 'I'm driving.'

'Canapes then, sir? A colleague will be along shortly with more soft drinks.'

'No thanks, I'm fine for the moment.'

The steward moved away as Anthea approached, took a drink from her glass and said, 'Of all the places to host a reception.'

'Mmm,' muttered Boyd with a wry smile. 'What a hostile enemy state would describe as a secret underground facility.'

'How far underground are we?'

'Deep!' replied Boyd. 'I counted twenty-five seconds in the lift to get here but I don't know what speed the lift travels at.'

'Quite fast, I thought,' offered Anthea.

'We could take bets in the office before we look at the plans. What do you think?' asked Boyd.

'I think the last two Commanders would have had your guts for garters for suggesting such a thing. Official Secrets Act, and all that.'

'Ah, yes, there is that to it.'

'I enjoyed the tour this morning,' declared Anthea. 'If anything goes wrong then at least we'll know what to expect.'

'Always nice to have a good look at a potential target,' proposed Boyd swiftly snaffling a full glass of orange juice from a passing waiter's tray. Settling his empty glass on a nearby table, he continued, 'If there's ever a problem here we'll know what the enemy is after and what security defences are in place. Commander Maxwell has already arranged for a map of the site to be delivered to our unit. I'll scrutinise it when we get back to London and get Bannerman started on planning the various responses we might need. He's good at that sort of thing.'

'Absolutely,' chuckled Anthea. 'Computer graphics or another wedge of paper? Either way, a whole bundle of whatever is about to hit your desk. You're the boss now, Guvnor. Your signature authorises everything we do, or don't do, as the case might be.'

'Tell me about it,' replied Boyd. 'I'm sinking under the weight of bureaucracy much faster than I ever imagined and that includes the computerised mail and stuff.'

'Here we go,' announced Anthea swivelling her head. 'I think the Chief is about to offer a vote of thanks to our hosts.'

On a stage at the front of the assembly, Cornelius Webb's presence dominated proceedings as he twisted one end of his meticulously combed moustache and shook hands with a Naval Commander before stepping onto a podium and beginning a speech with, 'It is my splendid duty, on your behalf, to thank the Royal Navy for their hospitality today and to congratulate everyone concerned in the inauguration of this thinly disguised nuclear waste store.'

There was an outburst of mild amusement before the Chief continued, 'Oh, yes. This facility does indeed store nuclear waste, but it also provides the nation with a discreet building platform for the next generation of mini trident submarines, powered by nuclear generators, and equipped with the latest high-tech missiles able to engage surface laser technology and a global defence system.'

'Or an attack system,' murmured a man in naval uniform.

There was an appreciative chuckle from the front row before Cornelius continued, 'I can only imagine what the site will look like when it is fully operational.'

'I can't hear him,' remarked Anthea. 'What's he saying?'

'Move down to the front,' suggested Boyd as the two senior detectives gently nudged their way forward. By the time Boyd and Anthea were in earshot of the Chief, he was in full voice.

'As the national lead in waiting in respect of counter-terrorism – as well being Chief Constable of Cumbria – I can assure you that the security of this establishment will be of prime concern to myself and the officers involved in its defence and security…'

The speech wore on as Boyd snaffled yet another glass of orange and listened patiently to Cornelius.

Leaning slightly towards Anthea, Boyd ushered her to one side and whispered, 'That reminds me, his security vetting forms are on my desk.'

'Then you'd better get them submitted,' murmured Anthea lifting her hand to stifle her voice. 'Otherwise, we'll both be out of a job. As I recall, the Special Crime Unit Commander is the last signature on the vetting document for the lead counter-terrorist job in the UK. I take it that's because of the level of access you now have?'

'Yes,' replied Boyd. 'I've gone from Blue to Violet.'

'Top Secret Omega Violet?'

'That's the one!'

'There's none higher!'

'Correct!' replied Boyd. 'None that I'm aware of that is. Unless Antonia springs me a surprise one day. It's the Security Service that set the goalposts and Sir Phillip of MI5 is one of the referees. The other one is Sir Julian from MI6.'

'Oh! I didn't know that,' whispered Anthea.

'I'll be doing yours soon since you are my deputy,' revealed Boyd. 'You'll be blue in due course provided you haven't gone over to the other side.'

'Of course not,' frowned Anthea. 'But I prefer the red. I've always been a Liverpool supporter. Actually, I'm beginning to ask myself if this is a vote of thanks from the Chief or an oration about the man himself.'

'As we have a senior military presence here from the north-west,' continued Cornelius. 'This is perhaps a good time to inform you all that the bulk of counter-terrorism work in this vicinity will fall upon my command in the north-west region. The days of asking for or expecting assistance from colleagues in London are numbered. An increase in armed officers will patrol the streets if the threat level rises and local detectives – who are trained to a high degree of professionalism in catching criminals – will be drafted in to counter the threat and ensure the safety of this and many other secure establishments here in the north-west. Most of you will know that Cumbria has the highest proportion of secret establishments than anywhere else in the country and it is my job to ensure we retain that security and enhance the nation's defence capability at the same time.'

'Did he just say what I thought he said?' murmured Boyd.

'He's planning to downgrade us completely,' whispered Anthea. 'There's an immense difference between a money-grabbing crook plotting a bank robbery and a dedicated terrorist intent on changing the world order. The two have different psychological profiles for a start. They're not even in the same class. What the hell is he thinking about?'

'A knighthood for taking the wrong route?' proposed Boyd.

'It's all me, me, me, isn't it? He's forgotten about the structure and make-up at the centre,' suggested Anthea.

'I don't know,' ventured Boyd. 'But I sure as well wish I had a brandy to put into this orange.'

The Chief droned on remorsefully enjoying every minute of his attention seeking thank you speech.

Boyd glanced at his wristwatch as the Chief finally drew to a close and the assembly began to break up and make towards the lifts that would take them to the surface and Cumbria's fresh air.

'Excuse me, sir,' offered Boyd. 'I get the impression you intend to use local and regional officers to counter an international threat, or am I mistaken?'

'That's my plan,' smiled the Chief. 'I believe policing responsibilities in respect of counter-terrorism should be decentralised now that the threat from Islamic State has been more or less eradicated. We spend far too much money at the centre and very little in the regions. Ladies and gentlemen, things are about to change for the better and the inspiration for that change is quite clearly this unique and stimulating complex which has the capacity to put the United Kingdom towards the front of the world order.'

A ripple of applause greeted the ending of the Chief's speech. Yet the atmosphere was one of incredulity as various defence chiefs and military personnel absorbed what had been said and its importance in the scheme of things. There was the shake of the head, a puzzled look, and an exchanged worried glance as the Chief smoothed his moustache and squared his tie.

Stepping down from the podium, Cornelius again immediately shook hands with the host Naval Commander who declared, 'Thank you for your kind attendance, Chief Constable. I thought it apt to make this ceremony specifically local in its being and have been proved correct in that assertion when I listen to your words. I wish you the best of luck in your endeavours.'

Cornelius Webb shook the Commander's hand vigorously as Boyd turned away and said, 'Am I missing something? He's taking the establishment with him on what appears to be a crazy journey.'

'Well, it's not just the banking crisis, government cuts, and austerity that have devastated the nation's police service,' remarked Anthea. 'Some of our top brass have become experts in absurdity.'

'Don't we know it,' replied Boyd. 'But to be fair, it's a speech. We'll know within a week or so what his real plans are.'

'You're sure?' asked Anthea.

'No! Just hopeful,' replied Boyd as he set down an empty glass on a table. 'Come on, let's go. I've had enough of this.'

As the two detectives made their way to the lifts, the Chief approached them and asked, 'Nice to see you both again. Have you enjoyed your day?'

'Up to but not including your speech, sir,' replied Boyd. 'But then, it was a vote of thanks, wasn't it?'

There was a sudden nudge in Boyd's ribs from Anthea.

'Indeed!' proposed the Chief. 'What did I say that upset you, Boyd?'

'You declined to admit that the battle against Islamic State will last at least another generation, sir.'

'I've heard the argument, Boyd,' replied the Chief who was obviously not impressed. 'But as the country becomes more diverse, multi-culturalism will defeat extremism. I don't subscribe to the gung-ho attitude of some of your counterparts. You would have us waging war for the next fifty years if you could. You see, Boyd, people like you have carved out a nice career making things sound a lot worse than what they are. Realistically, a change in direction is needed. We ought to embrace our people more rather than dissect them, put them into little boxes, and label them as good, bad or ugly.'

'I'd just point out that the Irish problem has never really gone away despite the Good Friday Agreement and the so-called peace process, argued Boyd. 'We still have live investigations regarding some subjects.'

'But not as many as before,' remarked the Chief.

'True! But places such as these will be of interest to the Russians and those nations who might not naturally favour the British way of life. The security of this establishment is a national responsibility, sir. Not a local one. Some of our enemies would give their right hand to have the technology hidden under this roof.'

'Well, we shall see,' pronounced the Chief. 'I'm sure we can manage security here without the abundance of defence and security advice that many will shower us with.'

'Do you actually have any experience of counter-terrorism or counter-espionage, sir?' enquired Boyd prodding and challenging Cornelius.

'Yes, of course,' snapped the Chief who suddenly began fiddling with something around his neck. 'I'm a bloody Chief Constable, you idiot!'

'Are you alright, sir?' enquired Boyd. 'Your neck?'

'I'm adjusting my crucifix if you must know,' barked the Chief. It's bloody warm in here.'

Anthea nudged Boyd's ribs again.

'Oh, I see. Forgive me! It's just that our paths haven't crossed before,' proposed Boyd. 'And that surprises me, sir. Do you know my good friend and colleague, Sir Phillip?'

'Of course!' replied the Chief tongue in cheek.

'He's a fine man and an inspiration to many. I think he will do well in the service, don't you think?' probed Boyd.

'Yes, I think so too,' offered the Chief weakly. The fingers of his right hand fumbled softly with the crucifix on his necklace. 'I'm glad we agree on something at last.'

'But it's not quite that simple,' proposed Boyd.

'Do I invade a coven of spies?' joked a tall dark-haired woman approaching the group. 'Am I allowed to listen to the great and good making decisions of wonderous importance?'

'Ah! My good lady wife,' smiled the Chief. A look of relief invaded his features. His hands dropped to his side when he continued, 'Allow me to introduce you to Divine.'

Taking in the fragrance of a strong perfume, Boyd swivelled his head to take in the delights of the female form.

'She is stunning,' thought Boyd.

'Divine by nature, Divine by name,' offered the Chief's wife with a beaming smile. She pecked her husband on his cheek and said, 'And who have we here, may I ask?'

Cornelius returned her smile and carried out the introductions as Boyd took in another lungful of scent and marvelled at the woman's figure.

Gesturing with his hand, the Chief finally reached Boyd and finished with, 'Not forgetting Detective Chief Inspector Boyd.'

Extending a limp hand, Divine Webb offered a weak beginning to a relationship strengthened only by the words, 'Mmm… Boyd! I've heard so much about you.'

'Really?' queried Boyd overwhelmed by her approach.

'Absolutely yes,' replied Divine simultaneously teasing whilst oozing sexuality. 'The new head of Diversity and Ethnicity. Superintendent Boyd! I'm so very pleased to meet you.'

Boyd's jaw dropped at the very words but he had no time to reply when the Chief quickly ushered Divine to one side saying, 'Well, we must be going. Our chauffeur is waiting. Good afternoon!'

The Chief and his wife were gone from the room in a matter of seconds leaving Boyd and Anthea nonplussed at the brief conversation.

There was the quiet electronic buzz of a closing lift heartened only in Boyd's eyes by the last view of a stunningly beautiful woman.

'When you manage to tear your eyes away from the Chief's wife, Guvnor,' offered Anthea. 'You might like to consider what she said. By the way, how is your wife?'

'Well!' growled Boyd. 'Meg and the kids are well, Anthea, as well you know. But Divine? Well, she is something else.'

'And you are the new head of Diversity and Ethnicity,' suggested Anthea. 'I didn't even know there was such a department.'

'Was that her idea of humour, or was it an unguarded moment?'

'I don't know,' replied Anthea. 'But the Chief whisked her away in quick time. What I do know is that you push some people too far. You're a Chief Inspector, Guvnor, not a Chief Constable. I suspect he thinks you are a cheeky bastard with a reputation for speaking out of turn and being well above your station.'

'Well, right now, Anthea,' snapped Boyd. 'My station, as you call it, is Commander and it's well above the actual rank that I hold. Speaking out of turn? Yes! Remind me of that next time we're running forward to an armed incident and he's pretending he knows everything about terrorism and espionage whilst sitting behind a desk. Are you with me, Anthea?'

'What do you mean?'

'He didn't pick up on the fact that Sir Phillip is the Director General of the Security Service and I truly believe he has limited knowledge of the subject he's supposed to be responsible for. Counter-terrorism? I don't think so.'

'Well, he's had a busy day. Perhaps he's just tired. Apart from that, Guvnor, you seem to have forgotten that very few people could actually name the Director-General, or the Chief of the Secret Intelligence Service for that matter. These posts don't sit happily with an advertising campaign. Only those who need to know actually know something about Sir Phillip and Sir Julian. You and I are in a privileged position. Don't forget that.'

'Yes, but I'd like to know what the hell his wife was doing here,' growled Boyd angrily. 'She's not service personnel and sure as hell hasn't been vetted to be in attendance at this location.'

'Oh!' exclaimed Anthea. 'Now who's upset about being mentioned as head of Diversity and Ethnicity? Rightly upset, Guvnor, but keen to bite back I see. Settle down, this isn't like you.'

'I don't care, Anthea,' responded Boyd angrily. 'She shouldn't have been here and he's not the right man for the job.'

'And you're hurt because he's downgrading the Special Crime Unit and putting you out to grass, and me for that matter. Am I right, Guvnor? Are you jealous, upset, or suddenly fixated by a woman you know you can't have?'

Boyd rounded on Anthea and barked, 'Are we getting the next lift or what?'

Twisting a healthy grin, Anthea replied, 'Put it this way, Guvnor. If Divine referred to you as a superintendent then it looks like promotion is coming your way at last.'

The lift doors opened, people filed in. Boyd paused and held his ground as he lost his place in the queue.

The lift doors closed and the quiet hum of the motor could be heard when the lift began its climb to ground level. Flashing lights on an indicator panel revealed what level the lift had attained.

Anthea moved in front of Boyd, looked deep into his face and said, 'What are you thinking?'

Boyd stood motionless before finally saying, 'He's going to try and buy me off with a comfy little number and a promotion to go with it. They call it career blackmail. A promotion and a convenient move in exchange for my silence on the matter.'

'Looks like it,' suggested Anthea.

'And you too, I suspect,' voiced Boyd.

Anthea considered the remark and replied, 'Are we getting the next lift or what?'

Stepping forward, Boyd pushed a button that would trigger the eventual downward movement of the lift.

With a glance at the clock above the lift, he ventured, 'Look at the time. We're going to be late.'

The noise of Cordoba's bell rang out across the city as the big hand on a small wristwatch face finally reached its destination and surrendered, its duty done. The mere touch of the big hand reaching the activation point resulted in the current from a tiny battery sending an electrical charge down a thin piece of wire that was part of a detonator.

The end of the detonator fused into a wad of soft and hand-moldable plastic explosive.

There was a flash, then a tremendous bang.

Diego's bomb exploded and in the split second that followed his camera bag ripped into a thousand pieces taking with it the street furniture under which it had been hidden.

The contents of the bag were nails, bolts and all kinds of jagged horrible pieces of metal that flew into the air slicing, cutting, maiming and injuring the bodies it came into contact with.

Almost simultaneously, a cloud of dust and debris rose into the air at the site of the discharge.

Diego saw the flash, heard the boom, relished in the dust cloud, and ignored the aftermath.

Stunned, shocked, appalled, Officer Santiago's jaw dropped when he witnessed the explosion and the immediate carnage.

A thinly disguised blast of air rushed down the alley and slammed Santiago back against the wall. His head clattered against the brickwork.

'Bomb blast!' he thought as he slithered to the ground.

Glass shattered everywhere, crashed to the ground, and showered those nearby with dangerously lethal shards.

A fracture in the building line appeared when the bomb blast tore into the ancient brickwork and threatened to destabilise the immediate environment.

Carnage followed in that split second when scores of people were blown against the walls, collided with each other, and then crashed to the ground either dead, dying, or seriously injured. Hundreds of ball bearings, nuts, bolts, screws, and jagged pieces of metal – propelled by the explosion – invaded the atmosphere. They found their mark damaging the human body whilst simultaneously destroying nearby buildings.

In the moments that shadowed the detonation, blood trickled along the ancient walkway then streamed towards the Jewish Quarter in a torrent of inconceivable horror. Dozens of tourists immediately stopped, turned around, and ran back towards where Diego and Santiago were located as all around the buildings shook and glass continued to crash to the ground.

Snatching an AK47 assault rifle from his rucksack, Diego pointed the automatic machine gun at the mass of people running towards him and let rip. He couldn't miss.

The constant noise of gunfire dominated the Mezquita when Diego took scores of people to the ground.

Laughing! Mad! Insane! A megalomaniac at play!

Unzipping a compartment in his rucksack, grabbing a hand grenade, Diego shouldered his weapon for a moment and threw the grenade into the panic-stricken crowd. Retreating slightly, he again dug deep into the bag and threw more grenades into the throng.

A succession of explosions followed as the grenades rolled into the crowd. They stumbled, fell, crawled, and died on the streets of Cordoba from the bullets and bombs of the Sultán of Cordoba.

Retreating to safety now, still laughing, Diego abandoned his empty rucksack as he stepped backwards covering his escape with more gunfire from the lethal Kalashnikov.

A tangled brain guided a withered hand which reached around a trouser belt to a leather holster and the butt of a gun. The hand withdrew the gun from its holster. Two eyes squinted and sought their target. A finger curled around a trigger. A shot rang out.

The bullet penetrated Diego's shoulder and spun him around him to face Officer Santiago lying on the ground bleeding from the back of the head.

Santiago took another deep breath, denied the pain in his skull, and pulled the trigger in rapid succession.

Another bullet struck Diego in the thigh, another in the stomach, and another in the forehead.

Crashing to the ground, Diego set his eyes on Santiago as he mouthed, 'Yo soy el ultan de Córdoba. Allahu…'

There was an agonizing grunt before another shot rang out and struck Diego directly between the eyes.

'Not anymore, you're not,' managed Santiago as he dropped back against the wall, exhausted, and badly injured.

Diego twitched, a hand reached out, and his life ebbed away on the streets of his hometown.

With every ounce of strength that remained in his body, Santiago pulled the trigger once more. The dull click confirmed the gun was empty. Santiago had run out of ammunition. His eyes closed and his head drooped onto his chest.

The Sultán of Cordoba was dead, along with a hundred victims of his mindless violent attack.

A thin stream of deep red blood trickled from the bodies of humankind when the first sound of sirens filled the air and the twenty-first century finally collided with the ancient cultures of Cordoba and the unwanted evil beliefs of Islamic State.

~

5

The Special Crime Unit
Ticker Intelligence Cell
The Following Day

A sign on the door merely revealed the unforthcoming letters TIC, which stood for Ticker Intelligence Cell, but the importance of the room was otherwise. The ability to enter the room was restricted to Special Crime Unit personnel armed with top-secret palmprint access facilities supported by an encrypted digital system. The door itself was said to be bombproof or, to be more precise, blastproof.

The cell housed a cyber software package valued in excess of five million pounds. No-one in the unit really knew the true cost – not even Boyd – but they did know that the computer was equipped with a state of the art anti-hacking system supported by a high-performance single-tenant infrastructure that was located in an unknown underground location. Computer experts might have described the system as 'standalone' but that was not quite the case.

Ticker used crystal technology which uniquely enabled it to share data with other trusted tenants who enjoyed access subject to their individual levels of security. It was exclusive in many ways since it was able to adopt a multi-tenant infrastructure in a secure controlled environment when directed to do so. The system was universally flexible and highly secure.

The Ticker Intelligence Cell also possessed the capability to covertly interrogate any known network on the planet. A secure web syndication package allowed the system to retrieve data from one source, store it, and send it to another when interrogated.

Ironically, despite the cost, the command system ran from a single manned desktop computer which transmitted a controlled feed to various screens around the office.

Various transparent screens and allied display technology received the data and converted it to an interactive display on the transparent surface glass. This revolutionary display allowed users to view what was shown on a glass video screen while still being able to see through it.

Underpinned crystal technology was the biggest secret in the unit.

'One hundred and four dead,' stated Antonia flicking her red hair as she read the screen. 'And over eighty seriously injured. The numbers are still rising.'

'Cordoba?' enquired Boyd. 'I watched the news report on television last night. I understand the offender was shot by police.'

Tapping on the computer keyboard, Antonia replied, 'Confirmed! Yes, Boyd! The offender was shot by a policeman who sustained a serious head injury during the attack and has been hospitalised for treatment.'

'I hope he makes it,' proposed Boyd. 'The world is short of real heroes.'

A finger pressed a key and the corner of a transparent screen burst into life when Antonia declared, 'I think you'll want to regularly refer to this so I've created a separate file entitled DIEGO. On screen now. You'll find it much more informative than the television.'

Closing with the screen display, Boyd perused the report and deliberated aloud, 'Local man recently returned from Syria. Apparently, he went to Istanbul for a holiday a few years ago and never returned home. Intelligence here suggests he went to Turkey before joining ISIS in the desert where he was trained in bombmaking, close quarter assassination and guerrilla warfare.'

'Guerilla warfare?' chuckled Janice. 'That sounds like Glasgae on a Saturday night.'

'Or the west end of London,' remarked Ricky. 'Pub fights are much more refined in London than in Glasgow.'

'You mean they use plastic bottles instead of glass?'

'Oh get you two,' remarked Martin.

'Sounds familiar,' frowned Anthea as she set down a tray of hot drinks. 'What else do we know, Guvnor?'

'He's a Spaniard and he's been identified as Diego Rodriguez Garcia. He has previous convictions for minor theft and burglary in Cordoba.'

'Diego?' mentioned Anthea.

'Identified by fingerprints?' suggested Bannerman.

'Correct!' confirmed Boyd. 'According to the Spanish Intelligence Service, Diego was recruited by Aishah and Ahmed Abdi. They are two brothers from Belgium. According to the FBI, they are long-established ISIS soldiers. They're both wanted in connection with bomb attacks on American targets in Beirut, Syria and Ankara. Apparently, the FBI has fingerprint traces at the scene of various crimes.'

Antonia looked up from the Ticker computer and said, 'The system also tells me they are well known in some circles. We even have photographs of them both. Transmitting! Standby! On screen now.'

'Can you do known associates too?' asked Boyd.

'Sure!'

Transparent interactive screens updated.

'Where are Aishah and Ahmed now?' enquired Boyd.

'Not known,' replied Antonia scrolling the computer log. 'Ticker tells me they are believed to be in the Raqqa area of Syria but – wait a minute – that was eighteen months ago. They could be anywhere now. I'm doing a person search – air travel, sea-going travel, port movements, anything recorded… Standby.'

'It doesn't matter how good Ticker is,' remarked Boyd. 'If people don't submit intelligence reports and stuff we want is not computerised then the system is not as good as it could be.'

'You play that thing like a piano,' suggested Martin Duffy. 'You've got the fastest fingers in the west.'

'Well, thank you, young man,' replied Antonia. 'Sadly, my brain isn't as fast as Ticker.'

'This is my first time in the cell,' replied Martin. 'It's amazing.'

As Martin strolled around the room checking various screens and display units Boyd revealed, 'Martin Duffy – From special escort group to Special Crime Unit. You've earned it, Martin. You all have.

Janice – From an expert driver and surveillance officer to covert burglar and pickpocketer extraordinaire. Terry Anwhari – One of the best detectives from the West Midlands who speaks various dialects including Farsi, and Ricky French – Ex Flying Squad, currently studying for a masters in criminology, a 'gizmo' man skilled in technological surveillance. You should all be pleased.'

'What did we do wrong?' asked Detective Sergeant Terry Anwhari.

'Nothing,' replied Boyd. 'I just thought it was a good time to say thank you. That's all. We've come a long way since the very beginning.'

'We certainly have,' agreed Bannerman.

'Okay!' continued Boyd. 'Let's look at what we've got and what we need to do. Any luck, Antonia?'

'System still searching, standby, Boyd.'

'Aren't we forgetting the obvious about Diego, Guvnor?' enquired Anthea.

'I know what you're thinking,' countered Boyd. 'The audio-visual from Deir ez-Zor?'

'Precisely,' offered Anthea. 'Antonia, tell me you have dozens of Spaniards jumping out of the screen at you.'

'They're everywhere,' joked Antonia. 'But the audio-visual keeps coming into all my search equations.'

'Can you bring up the visual from the Deir ez-Zor incident and then compare it with the photos we have of Diego Rodriguez Garcia, the Diego mentioned in the footage, plus Aishah and Ahmed Abdi?' enquired Boyd.

'One moment,' replied Antonia concentrating on the computer. 'I'll do better than that. I have a result coming in from the Americans in Chantilly. Wait one. It's decoding itself.'

'Satellite imagery? It was that easy?' enquired Boyd.

'I think Phillip masterminded an exchange protocol with the Yanks some years ago,' revealed Antonia. 'Everyone wants a bit of the doughnut if you remember?

'GCHQ in Cheltenham?' nodded Boyd. 'Most advanced countries have a national cybersecurity centre but ours is a global leader. No wonder the Americans love it.'

'It's tit for tat,' nodded Antonia. 'We scratch their back. They scratch ours. Stand by… Loading… No travel movements recorded on the Abdi brothers and no travel movements recorded on Diego Rodriguez Garcia. Wait one!'

The team moved closer to the display screens as Antonia continued her electronic research.

In other areas of the room, the remnants of three other Special Crime Unit teams could be seen. Jackets, pens, pencils, notebooks – various odds and ends left by those either off duty or out on a job somewhere else.

'Remind me to tell the other teams not to leave so much junk behind,' declared Boyd. 'I like clean tidy spaces.'

'We know,' murmured Anthea. 'Leave it with me. I'll speak to them.'

'Bingo!' exclaimed Antonia swivelling in her chair. She smoothed her trouser suit down and pointed to an interactive screen on the wall.

'The audio-visual shows the product of the drone overfly and reveals a group of men talking to each other. One of them calls himself Diego, the Sultán of Cordoba and the whole of Spain. Then we have the man with sunglasses and a bandana standing with a group of assorted odd bods. Then we have this from satellite imagery courtesy of the Americans.'

Scores of enhanced images from satellite surveillance booted up onto the screen.

Antonia hit a button on the keyboard and added, 'And this is a photograph of Diego Rodriguez Garcia who was shot dead by the police following the attack on the Mezquita in Cordoba. Question – could these images be one and the same man?'

'Close,' replied Boyd. 'Very close, but how close do you all think?'

'It's a pity about the camera angle,' remarked Ricky French. 'The drone is looking down on the man who might be Diego and only

83

catches a brief side view of him. The satellite ones are very similar. Wrong angle!'

'The hair is the same,' suggested Martin walking along the full length of the long screen. 'Same colour, same style and that nose is bent slightly.'

'Och, it's him alright,' offered Janice walking to the screen. 'I'd say that was the wee ferret we've been looking for. For my money, the man in the drone footage and the satellite imagery is the man responsible for the attack in Cordoba.'

Boyd joined Janice, pointed to the screen, and added, 'If we accept that hypothesis then Diego is down and out and no longer a target for us to chase. That said, these two here – on the drone footage – are the Abdi brothers. They're standing back a little from the centre of the image so the facial capture is pretty good. I agree with you all. The Diego mystery is solved as well as it can be at this time but tell me, Antonia, can we find any known associates that might match the man with sunglasses and a bandana? He's the one that really puzzles me. Is he the Sultán of England and the United Kingdom?'

'I'm flat out on Ticker,' replied Antonia. 'It's going to take some time trying to compare real photographs that we have on file with all the footage we've got.'

'Thank you,' replied Boyd. 'How long before we have a national facial recognition package ready for use?'

'Soon!' replied Antonia. 'The present system on trial needs upgrading. The problem is that practically it can be done to some extent but not to the magnitude that I would personally like to see in our Ticker system. That said, any basic package can be enhanced once it is put into daily use and the techies work on improving it. We need it to find the baddies, not the goodies. The problem for many will be that all the lefties and do-gooders will jump up and down and argue against its very existence.'

'I can understand that,' responded Boyd. 'It needs an accountable procedural and legally approved protocol to go with it before every unscrupulous Tom, Dick and Harry in the private sector gets their hands on it and uses it for their own good.'

'Well, you can wish,' frowned Antonia.

'Guvnor,' probed Anthea. 'There's nothing on that drone footage that suggests anyone is the Sultán of England. One man claimed to be the Sultán of Spain. He's dead now. Where do you get your ideas from?'

'Just a gut feeling,' frowned Boyd. 'I can't prove it. You're right but I when I put myself in their position, I see it all.'

Shaking her head, Anthea said, 'You've lost me! Explain!'

'To clarify my own thought pattern,' offered Boyd. 'I'm one of them. I'm standing on a desert road following an attack on a convoy that I've been part of. We've been defeated. I've lost friends and comrades in the battles that I've fought. Everything around me is on fire and my reason for being there has been rocked to its very foundations. I am virtually destroyed. I want revenge.'

Anthea nodded as the team listened to their newly appointed Commander.

'If you're the man on the desert road,' suggested Bannerman. 'You'll have worked out that the Caliphate is never going to happen. ISIS has been busted on the battlefield'

'And that's why I want to take the battlefield to the city streets,' enlightened Boyd. 'Where no-one knows me and where I'm not going to get attacked by a squadron of aircraft, a tank, an infantry regiment, or a drone from above. So when Diego – a comrade in arms – tells me he's going to Spain to exact revenge and continue the fight, I'm on his side. I'm going back to England to do the same. I want revenge too. Does that make sense?'

'Your mind is out of the box,' interrupted Antonia. 'As usual!'

'You've no evidence,' suggested Anthea. 'Just a list of those who went out to join the Jihadis years ago but nothing to say your bandana and sunglasses friend is a threat. Part of me wonders if you've conveniently jumped to conclusions because a certain Chief Constable has indicated he's taking the axe to the department and you're looking for something to fight his argument and get back at him. So far, I just see a product of your fertile imagination and I wonder if it's based on reality or resistance to what lies ahead for us. Do proposed cuts in the unit make you think this way?'

Boyd shrugged and turned away saying, 'I thought you of all people would support me, Anthea.'

'I will support you, Guvnor,' she replied. 'You know that and you know how many times I've followed you when you've flown by the seat of your pants and nothing else. But, I'm your deputy now, the Deputy Commander. I've got to take the harder line. I can support you only when I'm convinced.'

'I didn't realise you'd become a snowflake, Anthea.'

'You mean someone more prone to taking offence and less resilient than previous generations, Guvnor,' challenged Anthea. 'Someone perceived by others to have an inflated sense of uniqueness or an unwarranted sense of entitlement, or to be over-emotional, easily offended, and unable to deal with opposing opinions.'

'Well, I..'

'Remind me that I'm a snowflake the next time I'm standing in the bow of a boat on the River Thames and manage to shoot dead the killer who is pointing a gun to your head. This snowflake never existed, Guvnor. Or has your memory gone?'

'No, it's just that… Look, I'm sorry, Anthea,' apologised Boyd. 'Really sorry.'

'You'd better be,' snarled Anthea. 'You made me a DI, not a bloody snowflake.'

Boyd winced, hit squarely between the eyes by his deputy, and one of his closest friends.

'I'm with you, Boyd,' declared Bannerman with a slap on the back. 'And I've been meaning to tell you what a Sultán is.'

'Go on,' replied the deflated Chief Inspector.

'Okay! Basically, a Sultán is not a King even though he is a ruler. The term is restricted entirely to Muslim countries so if the audio-visual in the desert is correct then Diego has overstepped the mark by declaring himself Sultán of Spain because Spain is not a Muslim country.'

'Which would be irrelevant to him if my thought processes about them wanting revenge is correct,' professed Boyd.

'Agreed!' nodded Bannerman. 'The word is used, however, historically, to signify the title of certain rulers who claimed sovereignty in practical terms. By this, I mean that they never considered themselves to be the top man. In the region they existed, they were the ruler but never claimed to lead the Caliphate. Mind you, it has a religious significance because the holder of the title is there to uphold Islamic values.'

'That sounds quite complicated,' proposed Boyd. 'In a nutshell?'

'I'd say it meant the holder was responsible for a given area or region without ever expecting to be the overall leader of the global Caliphate because he is one of many leaders in a nominated geographical area.'

'Regional representatives?' questioned Boyd.

'Exactly,' nodded Bannerman. 'A bit like Chief Constables responsible for geographic areas. They know they'll never be the top boss but are happy to rule over their own patch until someone emerges to take overall command.'

Nodding, more assured now, Boyd considered Bannerman's response and replied, 'Thanks! But in my experience, some of our bosses would crawl over broken glass to get to the very top no matter what it cost.'

'Well, there is that to it,' agreed Bannerman.

'One particularly comes to mind,' muttered Boyd before raising his voice and asserting, 'Now you can see why I want to be sure that our little group of defeated ISIS soldiers all agreed to return to their various homes and cause mayhem for everybody. Anthea?'

'I understand what you're saying, Guvnor,' replied Inspector Adams. 'I just want the evidence that regional rulers exist.'

'There isn't any yet,' replied Boyd. 'Nothing concrete! But if ISIS has fragmented and shared out parts of Europe amongst its members then we need to know. Anyway, that reminds me, I need to clear some paperwork from my desk. There's a document from a regional ruler that

I need to sort out. Thanks, everyone. Antonia, let me know how you get on re those associate photographs.'

An icy stare flew across the room when Antonia ceased tapping on the keyboard for a moment and said, 'I know my job. I work for the Security Service. It so happens that I know this machine inside out. That's why I'm in the Ticker command seat. Why don't you go and do your job? I'll be in touch when I need to be.'

Her fingers re-engaged the keyboard and Boyd replied, 'Ouch! I'm gone. I think I just had a bad day at the office.'

Moments later, in Boyd's absence, Anthea murmured, 'You can say that again, Guvnor.'

'What's eating him?' enquired Bannerman.

'Something is troubling him,' replied Anthea 'He's not his usual self. Every time he opens his mouth he puts his foot in it.'

'No change there then,' chuckled Bannerman.

'Give him time,' suggested Antonia. 'He's the Commander now. It's a whole new ball game for him.'

Moving closer to the redhead, Anthea adopted a low tone and asked, 'Do you think he can do it?'

Without looking up from the keyboard, Antonia replied, 'Yes! Of course, he can. Boyd is special. He's not the Commander of the unit. He is the unit. Always has been. But don't forget he's now responsible for four teams and direct interface with everyone on the inside and the outside. Boyd is a doer, a leader, but not necessarily a manager. There is a big difference between the two. The sad thing is the arena he is now working in is rammed pack full of critics and talkers who've never stepped up to the mark.'

'It's that bad?' remarked Bannerman.

'He's actually doing the work once done by his Superintendent – Sandra – as well as Commander Maxwell,' continued Antonia. 'The practical side won't bother him, Anthea, but the paperwork for four teams is colossal. Then there's the diplomacy of command and everything it entails. That's where my worry lies.'

'Me too,' added Anthea. 'Sandra hoovered up paperwork as a woman possessed. How the Guvnor will cope is another issue altogether.'

'Normally I'd say fingers crossed,' responded Antonia. 'But I'm too busy selecting photos for comparison. Screen three, check these out.'

A new batch of images came to life on a transparent screen. The research continued as a host of images flashed across the screen and the team tried to put names to faces.

Meanwhile, the dark grey waters of the Irish Sea splashed noisily against the vertical cliffs of one of Cumbria's most beautiful sights: St Bees Head, or to be precise, North Head.

North Head is the most westerly point of Northern England and is the site of St Bees Lighthouse.

Here, close to the cliffs, a solitary woman unpacked her hackneyed holdall. She removed a clear plastic box containing an apple, a chocolate bar, and some sandwiches, and set them down next to a vacuum flask full of black coffee. Eventually, she withdrew a collapsible easel and carefully erected the apparatus. Then the artist set out her canvas and unpacked a container of watercolours, pencils and brushes as she prepared to capture an image of the St Bees lighthouse for posterity.

She began sketching lightly on the canvas and then carefully made ready her paints and brushes as she focused on what colours might best represent her intentions.

A number of smaller buildings clustered around the former World War Two radar station which she had cleverly placed in the forefront of her work. Angled, and in the background, the artist intended to capture the decommissioned foghorn building which lay slightly to the west of the lighthouse. Such an action truly represented the independent characteristics of the individual concerned since she sought to capture her own interpretation of the scene.

The immediate area was a nature reserve managed by the Royal Society for the Protection of Birds. It was a nesting site for herring gulls, guillemots and razorbills. Popular with birdwatchers, the site enjoyed three formal observation points that covered various parts of the headland. Only one discreet post covered the area occupied by the artist.

Inside the nearest observation point, a tall middle-aged man ignored the seabirds and adjusted his binoculars to focus upon the artist.

Studying his subject, the watcher confirmed the artist was alone. There was no-one in sight on the footpath that skirted the area.

'What a truly divine view,' murmured the artist. 'Just what I need at this precise moment. Some private time to consider things and decide what I'm going to do as I capture this one for my collection.'

She leaned outwards, peered towards the lighthouse, and then focused on the canvas as she lightly brushed the first stroke of the day.

The watcher swivelled his shoulders slightly and re-focused on the other two observation cabins. They remained empty. Only a pair of herring gulls disturbed his vision when they momentarily came into view.

The woman continued painting as the image took shape and a hint of colour found itself daubing the canvas.

A seagull of some kind flew low across the headland causing the artist to follow its flight with interest.

Observing the scene, the spectator allowed his binoculars to drop slightly and focus upon a clear plastic box and a vacuum flask. Then he suddenly ceased his observations, checked his wristwatch, and shuffled impatiently from one foot to another as the artist gradually covered her canvas with a backdrop of blue-grey.

A thin paintbrush dabbled in a splodge of questionable blue and embraced an artist's painting when another pair of gulls flew low across the clifftops squawking noisily in their graceful flight.

The birds disappeared from sight as the artist concentrated on the painting and the unknown watcher rubbed his eyes before using his binoculars once more.

Scanning his office computer, Boyd was soon hard at work checking files, documents, emails, expense sheets, leave requests and various reports from the four teams that made up the unit.

Opening an email, he read a message from the Assistant Commissioner responsible for leading counter-terrorism policing nationally. The message indicated that a staffing review into the unit was to be undertaken following a request from Chief Constable Cornelius Webb: Counter Terrorism Command, North West.

The communiqué confirmed Boyd's worse fears. Cornelius Webb would soon supersede the present incumbent to become Head of Counter-Terrorism in the United Kingdom.

'No!' murmured Boyd. 'He's the wrong man.'

Squinting his eyes, Boyd shook his head when he realised it was a wave of acute despondency that had infiltrated his mind and body.

'But then I have to prove it because no-one else will,' pondered Boyd. Alone with his own thoughts, Boyd mused, 'The world is full of snowflakes and most of them don't even like me because I say it like it is. My problem is I don't conform to the status quo. I have an attitude that is not always acceptable in the scheme of things.'

Reading further, the current structure of the unit was revealed. Boyd was required to justify his staffing levels which ordinarily should have been – one Commander, one Detective Superintendent, one Detective Chief Inspector (him), plus four Detective Inspectors each in charge of a team consisting of two Detective Sergeants and ten Detective Constables. The usual complement of officers was in the region of fifty-five of the most highly trained detectives in the UK. They were the sharpest tool in the box and the elite part of Counter Terrorism Command.

Boyd realised he was being instructed to make a case for the retention of the unit since Cornelius had proposed the Special Crime Unit might be disbanded since ISIS was no more.

'Reading this, we're two officers short in the manpower stakes already,' muttered an annoyed Boyd. 'A Commander who has been transferred and a Superintendent who died very recently. That leaves me the Detective Chief Inspector in charge but we do a damn sight more than chase after ISIS.'

Boyd re-read the email and formed the opinion that it was worded in a way that suggested he needed to argue his case for retention professionally, as opposed to emotionally, and that the Assistant Commissioner might actually be on his side if the argument held.

'I'll not count on that though,' thought Boyd. 'But then this is not for today. Our friend Cornelius is merely laying down a marker with the top man that he's going to be a pain in the arse. I'll leave this one for a while before I reply properly.'

Boyd tapped an acknowledgement on the keyboard. The words read, 'Sir, Content acknowledged. Reply under consideration. Signed Boyd, Det Ch Insp SCU.'

He reads the words, deleted Det Ch Insp SCU and amended them to read, Boyd, Commander Special Crime Unit, Counter Terrorism Command.' He pressed send and watched the email disappear into cyberspace.

Closing the email system down, Boyd opened the locked drawer of his desk and removed a bundle of vetting documents. Finding, Anthea's paper, he read the document from start to finish, noted the signatories and sources involved, and then signed off her security clearance at the increased level of Top Secret Omega Blue.

'Signed William Miller Boyd, DCI, Commander SCU,' voiced Boyd aloud. 'Last week I was number three in the unit now I'm number one. It's a joke. The job has gone to hell in a handcart. More for less?'

Rummaging through the papers, Boyd found the document entitled Cornelius Webb: Positive Vetting Top Secret (Verification Document) and duly opened it.

Half an hour later, Boyd was still reading the various reports, transcribed interviews, letters and findings by individuals who were part of the vetting verification system. He even read and considered ancient references dating back to when Cornelius had first applied to be a police officer. Boyd traced Webb's career then turned to more recent information relevant to financial status, sexuality, personality, and a whole host of other matters relevant to a position carrying such an important responsibility.

Noting the positions and signatures of those involved in the verification process, Boyd knew that he would be the last to sign the document due to his current command position. It would go directly from him to the Assistant Commissioner responsible for national counter-terrorism – a position that Cornelius Webb was waiting in the wings to take.

'To verify or not to verify, to recommend or deny,' mused Boyd. 'Will it make a difference what I say or do when my rank doesn't equate to the burden of responsibility I now hold? Am I a Commander and if so what of, or am I merely the instrument of a shower of manipulative misfits that have lost all sense and understanding of police management and leadership?'

Boyd's fingertips rattled the keyboard, kickstarted the computer into life, and guided him to the remote access button for Ticker as he told himself, 'Is this new job a step too far for me? I'm doing more for less if I'm two ranks down on the previous postholder.'

Unlocking a desk drawer, he removed a bottle of Bushmills, broke the seal, and poured himself two fingers of solitary relaxation.

'Let me think out of the box,' voiced Boyd to an empty room. 'Cornelius Webb! Ticker, tell me what you know.'

Sipping his Irish whiskey, Detective Chief Inspector Boyd – de facto Commander of the Special Crime Unit – watched the screen come to light and reveal all that was known of the subject under review.

'Birthdate, birthplace, gender, parents, school history, examinations, qualifications, teen images, adult images, religion, employment history, police career, hobbies, financial disposition, sexual orientation, criminal record, political allegiances, club memberships, association and organisation membership, awards nominated and awards given, sports played and teams supported, marriages, extended family, persons of interest associated to subject,' voiced Boyd quietly. 'Just the usual stuff. No wonder he's got this far. Ticker! Take me where no-one has been before.'

Boyd entered 'ENHANCE SEARCH,' and waited.

Taking another sip of his Irish spirit, he watched the screen flicker slightly as it went into overdrive.

The words, 'ASSOCIATES: UK, EUROPE, The AMERICAS, AUSTRALASIA, ASIA, FAR EAST, MIDDLE EAST, RUSSIA,' appeared on the screen.

'Jesus!' mouthed Boyd carefully downloading data to his screen.

Draining his glass, Boyd read the detail and noted that it was a duplication of what he had already seen – except for Asia, the Middle East, the Far East and Russia.

'Brilliant,' chuckled Boyd as he worked through the list. 'No traces anywhere. Russia, are you the same? Or have I wasted my time.'

'ENTER CLEARANCE LEVEL CODE' instructed Ticker on the screen.

'Oh well, there's a first time for everything,' replied Boyd tapping the keyboard.

'ENTER PASSWORD'.

Now vetted and cleared to Top Secret Omega Violet, Boyd entered his password and waited.

A document folder appeared on the screen and Boyd clicked into it.

Written in plain English, in Microsoft Word, the document detailed the attendance of a Mr Cornelius Webb, of England, at a hotel hosting an International Food Fair in St Petersburg, Russia. The address of the hotel was close to the airport and the dates and timings of the event were signified.

Holidaying there in his younger days, Boyd knew that St. Petersburg was once dubbed the 'Capital of Crime' and that it was a Russian port city on the Baltic Sea. It was the imperial capital of the country for over two hundred years and had been founded by Peter the Great in 1703. With a population of slightly over five million people, St Petersburg was Russia's second city. The location was now regarded as the country's cultural centre since it hosted such famous places as the Mariinsky Theatre where opera and ballet were prominent. The State Russian Museum was also domiciled in St Petersburg and showcased various forms of Russian art.

Scanning the bottom of the document, Boyd looked for an accreditation. There was no author's signature to be seen, no department claiming responsibility for the input to Ticker, nothing that might signify the source of the report other than the letters OSM/7 faintly typed in the bottom right-hand corner.

Puzzled, Boyd examined the report and noted that it was written in English (United Kingdom) not English (United States of America).

'Interesting,' he thought. 'Microsoft applications always default to English (United States of America). The writer has gone to the trouble of deliberately selecting English (United Kingdom). This suggests to me that the source is English, not American. But who the hell is OSM /7 and why haven't they used the proper authentication procedure?'

Boyd closed his eyes and considered the problem for a moment.

'Because I'm in enhanced search, that's why,' thought Boyd. 'The system has drilled all the way down to the roots it would seem. Boyd poured a smaller shot and pondered, 'Why would a Cornelius Webb travel all the way to St Petersburg for a food fair? And is it our Cornelius Webb? I wonder.'

Working the keyboard, Boyd recapped what he had previously read about Webb. There was not one iota of information suggesting that Cornelius Webb was a 'foodie' of any description.

As Boyd scribbled down the dates of the Food Fair, and its location, he wondered how many Cornelius Webbs had ever been born in the UK and visited St Petersburg.

The telephone rang and disturbed his thought pattern.

'Boyd!'

'Ah, Chief Inspector,' bellowed a voice on the 'phone. 'It's the Commissioner's Office.'

'Of course,' replied Boyd. 'And what can I do for you?'

'The Commissioner has been called to a meeting with the Prime Minister and the Home Secretary in Downing Street. The Commissioner needs to know the up to date situation and when an arrest is anticipated. Please advise, Chief Inspector Boyd.'

Shaking his head, Boyd bit his tongue for a moment and then replied, 'Does the Commissioner want this information before the staffing review or after the unit has been disbanded?'

'I beg your pardon,' came the reply.

'Not your problem,' replied Boyd awkwardly. 'You probably don't even know what I'm talking about. Okay! You can report that we have no suspects at the moment and I'm not planning to make any arrests in the foreseeable future. I do, however, have a mountain of paperwork to administer, three hundred suspects to investigate, and a smaller department than existed yesterday with which to do it. My compliments to all concerned but the official line might be we are diligently pursuing numerous avenues of enquiry. The bottom line is that we are well behind this one and have not yet been able to get a feel for who we are after. Will that do you?'

'Well, I'll..'

'Thank you,' replied Boyd placing the 'phone on its cradle.

'Don't bother me again,' he murmured as he punched the buttons on his 'phone, waited for a few moments, and then said, 'Bannerman! Drop everything. I want you to chase something down for me as soon as possible.'

'Where are you sending me to?' asked Bannerman.

'Just the office, maybe the Baltic!' replied Boyd. 'It depends what you find out. I want you to trace the author of a document for me. What's more, I want you to find out when and where it was written, why it was written and…' Boyd removed another glass from the desk drawer, poured a tot of whiskey, and said, 'Pop in. I'll brief you. It might be a blind alley, or it might be an eye-opener, but I need someone I can trust.'

'Give me ten minutes, Guvnor,' replied Bannerman. 'I'm nearly finished here.'

The paintbrush gently prodded into a globule of grey-blue that the solitary artist had mixed to represent the sky above. Relaxed, totally lost in her own world, the thinly bound bristles surrendered and allowed themselves to be soaked in paint. She gazed upon the canvas as she guided the damp paintbrush towards her picture.

Sitting back, she moved from side to side in order to view her painting better. Straining her neck, she angled her face seeking a new perspective on her work. Eventually, the artist stood up, stepped backwards, and studied both the view ahead and the painting on the canvas.

'Go on!' whispered a male voice from the interior of an observation point. 'Get on with it for God's sake.'

The artist reached down and opened her plastic sandwich box. She took a bite, devoured the rest within seconds, and then reached for her vacuum flask.

Inside an observation post, a pair of binoculars swung into position when the observer took a step forward.

She unscrewed the cap.

He held his focus and took in her flowing hair, that gorgeous figure, and those long legs that seemed to last forever. Swallowing, he moved his sightline slightly to take in the shape of her breasts pushing against her top and stretching the fabric to its limit. Then he re-focused, sighed, and captured her face.

She poured the thick black liquid into the cup.

The voyeur's chest heaved up and down as he tried to secure his binoculars with the excitement of it all. He feasted his eyes on the woman before him.

She took a drink.

More seagulls rushed across the clifftops when the artist sat down, set down her cup, and resumed painting.

The door of the observation cabin drew shut behind the man carrying a binocular case in his right hand.

There was a soft rustle of shoe leather parting the grass as the mysterious voyeur began his approach to the solitary painter.

'There, at the bottom of the page, OSM/7,' pointed Boyd. 'What does that mean to you? Oscar Stephen Miller or Olivia Stephanie Masters?'

'Who?' queried Bannerman entering the office with Antonia in tow.

'OSM/7,' snapped Boyd. 'I need to find out who he or she is.'

'Calm down, Boyd,' advised Antonia. 'You'll have a heart attack if you're not too careful.'

'Not before I bottom out OSM/7,' retaliated Boyd.

'Oh, I see what you mean,' replied Bannerman reading the document. 'It's not very clear is it.'

'Exactly,' replied Boyd. If OSM is the acronym of someone's name, then I want the full details. Chase it down as soon as you can please.'

'Do you want me to go to St Petersburg?' probed Bannerman.

'St Petersburg! Russia! Why?' queried Antonia looking over Bannerman's shoulder.

'Something I'm working on,' replied Boyd.

'A hotel list from St Petersburg,' offered Antonia.

'Correct!' replied Boyd. 'I thought you were searching Ticker?'

'I was,' explained Antonia. 'I came to update you but OSM isn't an acronym. It's an initialism.'

'A what?' queried Bannerman.

Shaking her head, Antonia looked at the two detectives and said, 'The difference between an acronym and an initialism is that the abbreviation formed with the initials OSM is not pronounced as a word. For example, the FBI is the Federal Bureau of Investigation, the CIA is the Central Intelligence Agency. They are initialisms because we don't use them as words. On the other hand, NATO – the North Atlantic Treaty Organisation – is an acronym because we use it as if it were a proper word.'

'Thanks for the grammar lesson,' offered Boyd. 'So, whatever OSM/7 is will remain a mystery.'

'Open source material,' replied Antonia. 'O for open, S for source and M for material.'

Exchanging confused glances with Bannerman, Boyd closed his eyes for a moment before replying, 'Of course! Of course, it is. I'm losing my marbles. It's the basics and I forgot the basics. Remind me about the oblique seven?'

'Not sure,' replied Antonia. 'Could be the seventh list, the seventh week, the seventh month. Why don't you ask?'

'St Petersburg?' queried Bannerman glancing at Boyd.

Antonia checked the document again and said, 'No need. That's an international hotel chain you're looking at. Their headquarters is in Bayswater. I'd try there first.'

Dropping some folders on Boyd's desk, Antonia said, 'Message from Anthea, Boyd. Charlie Tango Charlie is ready for deployment. Tried, tested, ready for use, and the latest department toy. She thought you'd like to know.'

'Toy!' snapped Boyd. It's hardly a toy, Antonia.' Pointing to the folders, Boyd continued, 'What you got there?

'These are print-outs of the three hundred primary suspects on our radar. Three hundred pieces of paper that will give you a quick idea of the calibre of the people under investigation. Selected bullet notes for a quick read. More in-depth intelligence is on Ticker and we have just under five hundred secondary targets.'

Turning to leave, Antonia paused, looked at Boyd and asked, 'I couldn't help but notice that your St Petersburg enquiry seems to put a Mister Cornelius Webb of England on your radar, Boyd. Can I ask why?'

'You can,' nodded Boyd. 'But I haven't got an answer yet.'

Antonia smiled and replied, 'Keep me informed. Russia is my patch, not yours. Stick with Bayswater and you won't get lost.' She nodded to Bannerman as she left saying, 'But if it's the Cornelius Webb we all know and love then it's your problem and not mine.'

'That's what I want to find out,' replied Boyd. 'And that's why you didn't hear what I just said. In fact, you're not even here right now, are you?'

'Mmm...' murmured Antonia. 'I'm sorry. I didn't quite hear you.'

'Good,' responded Boyd.

Smiling, Antonia remarked, 'Be careful boys. Play nice.'

The door swung shut behind her when Bannerman sat down, took a sip of the whisky Boyd had poured, and said, 'Remarkable!'

'Which!' replied Boyd. 'Antonia or the enquiry I've just given you?'

'Both,' chuckled Bannerman. 'Bayswater here I come.'

A hand reached out for the easel, but her fingers began to tremble. Her face became drawn and anxious as her body temperature plunged downwards. Suddenly, she felt cold and clammy and was aware that her pulse was rapid and feeble

'I don't understand,' she mumbled. 'What's happening to me?'

Her upper eyelids dropped and began to flutter uncontrollably as her body entered a state of shock. Then her jaw dropped.

The artist's hand eventually found the edge of the upright easel. Her eyes tried to focus on the image she had painted. Without warning, her vision became blurred. She began squinting and shaking her head in a bid to rid her body of this temporary invasion. Her pupils dilated and her heart began pounding.

The paintbrush dropped to the ground as she fell sideways and crashed into the easel with her respiration system faltering and her body shaking as if she was experiencing a tremor of some kind. Gradually, she drifted towards unconsciousness with the soft green grass of St Bees beneath her and a blue-grey sky above. Then her heartbeat began to go into spasm. Her chest heaved as her lungs fought desperately for oxygen. Within seconds, her heart was wavering.

Angry waves crashed against the bottom of the nearby cliffs and the gulls squawked in bizarre protest as a tall man carrying a binocular case approached.

Withdrawing a piece of black cloth from inside the binocular case, he looped the material around her neck. Kneeling in front of her, he pulled it tight and crossed the ends over in a loose knot.

As if kick-started back to life, the artist's eyes opened wide and a brief contorted smile invaded her cheeks.

The assassin then strangled her even though she was on the verge of certain death, and then let go leaving the cloth in place. Motionless, the woman's face looked up at her executioner with a fixed inexplicable smile as the skin distorted and her heart gradually stopped when paralysis took over the workings of her body. The killer gently eased the torso from her belongings and walked away carrying a vacuum flask.

A flock of seagulls gathered.

The artist's easel remained still. A paintbrush dried in the sunshine and a breeze blew the canvas from its resting place towards the edge of the cliffs and then into the depths below.

Strong arms gathered the woman's body, dragged it to the edge of the cliffs, and then rolled it over the edge.

A short time later, a car engine roared into life and a set of tyres sought purchase on the gravel as the vehicle drove away from the scene.

Passing Buckingham Palace, Bannerman was down Grosvenor Place and into Marble Arch with the Dorchester behind him and the Bayswater area ahead of him.

The drive from the Special Crime Unit only took him half an hour.

Finding the headquarters of the hotel group, Bannerman slid the car into a convenient space opposite Hyde Park and made his way into the reception area. He introduced himself, flashed his warrant card, and asked to see someone in senior management regarding a confidential police enquiry.

Five minutes later he was shown into a lavish office on the fifth floor where he displayed a copy of the hotel list to the Senior Operations Manager – a Mister Donald Anderson – and enquired, 'Thank you for your time, Mister Anderson, can you tell me who the author of this document is? It can be attributed to your hotel chain, I believe.'

'Possibly,' remarked Anderson seizing the document. 'Tea or coffee, Inspector?'

'Coffee would be nice,' replied Bannerman towering over his subject.

'Or perhaps something stronger?' suggested Anderson as he scanned the paper.

'Coffee will suffice.'

'Then take a seat, why don't you?' insisted Anderson.

'Thank you,' replied Bannerman sinking into a deep purple velvet armchair.

Adjusting his spectacles, the slimly built middle-aged manager stood up and walked casually over to a perpetual coffee pot. Glancing over his shoulder, Anderson studied Bannerman for a few seconds and asked, 'An important enquiry that you're involved in is it, Inspector Bannerman?'

'Yes, that's the nature of my particular job, Mister Anderson. I'm trying to locate the author of this document. It's signed or referenced OSM/7.'

Pouring two cups, the hotel group's senior manager handed one to Bannerman as he remarked, 'A list of hotel guests. How strange. Why do you want to know?'

'I'm not sure a hotel list is strange, Mister Anderson. It's just an enquiry I'm involved in,' responded Bannerman. 'I'm sure you're aware that police officers often make enquiries about hotel guests. There is a need to combat fraudulent behaviour by those who give false details and leave without paying. Sometimes we find people on the run that way. In some countries collecting details of people who stay in hotels is quite common.'

'Of course,' replied Anderson. 'Fraud, you say?'

'No, not on this occasion but it's of a serious nature that is confidential at the present time,' imparted Bannerman.

Nodding, the manager stared at Bannerman and challenged him with, 'Can I see your warrant card again?'

'By all means,' replied Bannerman producing his credentials once more. 'Is there a problem?'

'I wondered if you were legally obliged to require me to give you details of hotel guests, that's all?' responded Anderson looking directly into Bannerman's eyes.

'All serviced and self-catering accommodation premises must keep a record of all guests over the age of sixteen, Mister Anderson,' declared Bannerman. 'You'll find it under the Immigration Hotel Records Order of 1972.'

'Really?' challenged Anderson. 'I thought it was on the list to be repealed.'

'It is,' confirmed Bannerman. 'But it's still law until it is repealed.'

'This list does not originate in the UK, Inspector,' revealed Anderson. 'Your law is obsolete in…'

Anderson paused for a second before Bannerman said, 'Russia? And to be precise, Mister Anderson, I asked you if you could tell me who the author of the document is. Not who is on the list.'

Examining Bannerman's card, Anderson probed, 'I see you're attached to the Special Crime Unit. What is so special about the unit?'

'It's just a department that deals with specific crimes, that's all. There's no need to concern yourself, Mister Anderson. We deal with a wide variety of enquiries. Some of them link to national security which is why I hope you understand how discreet I need to be in talking to people. I do hope you can see your way to assisting us but I'm afraid I can't give you any details of my enquiry.'

'If a stranger knocked on your door at home would you tell him all your secrets?'

'Probably not,' admitted Bannerman. 'But then a stranger rarely calls with a warrant card in one hand and the business of the nation's security in the other.'

'Russia! Strange place,' grimaced Anderson. 'You need a visa to get into the country and then you must register it within seven days of arrival. I take it you've been to Russia before, Inspector.'

Bannerman skewed his reply with the comment, 'As you probably know, Russians need a visa to enter our country too.'

'Have you ever had a visa for Russia, Inspector?' persisted Anderson.

Bannerman made no reply.

'Your silence reveals you can neither confirm nor deny the matter of you ever having visited such a wonderful country,' persuaded Anderson. 'Did you know that in St Petersburg visa registration is usually completed by hotels and agencies through an online computer system?'

103

'I wasn't aware that was the case,' replied Bannerman. 'But I don't think it will hurt to tell you that this document was recovered from the internet.'

Donald Anderson nodded gratefully and continued, 'In St Petersburg, we advised regular guests to keep any original registration slip from their previous city of stay rather than handing it into the St Petersburg authorities. In that case, you should hand in both original slips at the border on leaving Russia. The author of your document – if British – would quite obviously have needed a visa, Inspector. Unless he was an illegal immigrant or member of the diplomatic corps.'

Momentarily confused, Bannerman suggested, 'St Petersburg interests me, Mister Anderson.'

Anderson removed a slimline phone book from an inside pocket in his jacket, flicked through the pages, and then set the book down on his desk.

Bannerman eyed Anderson as he sipped his coffee.

'Perhaps you should leave then,' suggested Anderson. 'I'm not sure that I'm authorised to help you. You're talking about Russia, but we are in England. I'm sure you've heard of the Data Protection Act.'

Standing up, Bannerman found himself towering over the smaller man. He glowered at the man and proposed, 'Perhaps you'd like to 'phone my boss in Scotland Yard? You seem to be unsure of me and my motives. I assure you I am above board.'

'I will make a 'phone call if you don't mind,' suggested Anderson.

Bannerman relaxed and took a sip of coffee whilst Anderson dialled a number and eventually said, 'It's Donald. I have a Detective Inspector Bannerman with me. He tells me he's with the Special Crime Unit.'

A friendly smile was offered whilst Anderson listened to his 'phone and simultaneously studied Bannerman.

'He's asking about OSM/7,' proposed Anderson. 'I thought you'd like to know.'

Bannerman's cup connected with the saucer when he suddenly realised that Anderson was not speaking to Boyd. The manager was speaking to someone else when Bannerman stared lividly into the manager's eyes.

Anderson listened, took instructions, and said 'I understand. I'll pass the message on.'

The phone landed on its cradle.

Placing his cup and saucer on the desk, Bannerman leaned across and challenged Anderson with, 'No disrespect intended but I'm a very busy man and I'm tired of politely chinking cups and saucers as you ring all and sundry telling everyone you've been invited to a murder mystery weekend at a cottage in the countryside. What the hell is going on, Mister Anderson?'

'I needed authorisation before I could speak to you about the matter,' explained Anderson. 'Are you interested in the hotel or a name on the list?'

'Both,' snapped Bannerman. 'Who were you speaking to?'

'Settle down, Inspector! You may be extremely tall and well built but I'd rather you didn't have a heart attack in my office. Thank you!'

Holding his hands up, Bannerman replied, 'Fine! My apologies but who was that on the 'phone?'

'A contact of mine who once told me they worked for a branch of the Department of Trade and industry,' revealed Anderson. 'He was lying.'

'The DTI?' queried Bannerman.

Anderson poured them both more coffee as he enlightened Bannerman with, 'I think you will know them by another name. Their office is in on the banks of the Thames at Vauxhall. I can't tell you anything else about my contact there, but I am authorised to inform you about OSM/7.'

'Vauxhall?' probed Bannerman. 'MI6 Headquarters?'

Nodding, Anderson regained his seat and said, 'As you know, one of our hotels is in St Petersburg in Russia. Indeed, it is the hotel you have expressed an interest in. Some years ago we became aware that the conference centre inside the hotel was being used by the Russians to invite British businessman to the area under various guises.'

'What do you mean by that?' probed Bannerman.

'They were hiring the conference facility under the pretence of presenting antique fairs, food and catering conferences, advanced technology lectures, and various events connected to tourism,' explained Anderson. 'We had no idea at the time that they were using such events to recruit people into the Communist Party.'

Nodding, Bannerman drained his cup and said, 'You mean British people, I presume, not Russians but British businessmen? They would be more likely to stay in a British-owned hotel rather than a Russian-owned hotel.'

'Precisely, Inspector Bannerman.'

'Would you call it a facility that would enable the Russians to recruit British people into the world of spying?' queried Bannerman.

'Possibly,' replied Anderson. 'But then I've never recruited a spy. I always thought that was an individual thing. Getting people to join a political party or ideological movement is surely much easier? The spy thing might come later if they proved to be good party members. I don't really know. I'm a bit rusty.'

'Rusty?' queried Bannerman.

'Nothing meant by that, Inspector. Just an irrelevant comment.'

'How did you find out the Russians were working in such a clandestine manner?'

'A gentleman from the British Consulate approached me one day and asked if he could examine the hotel's register in much the same way you have requested information about the OSM/7 document.'

'How do you know this, Mister Anderson?'

'Because I was the manager of the hotel in St Petersburg at the time. I remember it well. It was just before the fire.'

'The fire?' probed Bannerman.

'You mean you didn't know?' retaliated Anderson.

'I've never been to St Petersburg, sir,' revealed Bannerman. 'Tell me about the fire please and what that has to do with the hotel list marked OSM/7.'

Anderson poured more coffee, offered milk and sugar, and explained, 'When the chap from the British Consulate came, he explained that the Russian Commercial Tourist Board purported to be the hosts of these events, but this was a cover for their intelligence services. I eventually realised my visitor from the consulate was much more than a diplomat or messenger boy.'

'The DTI obviously,' smiled Bannerman.

'Yes, our man in St Petersburg,' replied Anderson. 'I agreed to provide MI6 with a list of people staying at the hotel whenever the Russians were hosting these particular events. It was quite easy really. Most of our staff at the hotel were Russian. Whenever visas were declared to us as part of the Russian visa travel procedures, I arranged to receive copies from our computer desk. I explained that such a course of action would assist the Russians authorities if we ever had a computer malfunction. St Petersburg is a magnet for holidaymakers from around the globe. Visas were declared almost every day. I just carried on regardless and said nothing at all to the representatives of the so-called Russian Commercial Tourist Board. Of course, my target was not holidaymakers. The target was British business people attending these clandestine cover events arranged by Russian Intelligence. They were the visa extracts I deliberately curated for MI6. I never said a word to anyone else working in the hotel. It was a secret between me and the MI6 officer from the consulate. The Russians seemed to organise a lot of antique fairs when I come to think of it. Anyway, the man from the consulate asked me to deliver the details to the British Consulate in Lafonskaya Street near the Neva river.'

'Rather than send details by email?' queried Bannerman.

'No, personal delivery of hard copy only, Inspector,' explained Anderson. 'I suspect the man from the British Consulate presumed our computer system might have been compromised by Russian Intelligence due to their activities in the hotel.'

Offering chocolate biscuits, Anderson continued, 'I agreed to help and wasn't particularly surprised at his approach. He knew all about me. The man had done his homework. Anyway, I did some research through the hotel registers and began to pick out the dates as well as the type of events he was interested in. The first one I delivered was OSM/1. The seventh one was OSM/7. Those in between were number

2 to 6 as you can imagine. Number seven was the last one just before the fire.'

'No, I don't see,' replied Bannerman as he snaffled a biscuit from the plate offered. 'What has the fire to do with all this?'

'Whenever they booked the conference facility for an event of some kind – usually an antique fair – I delivered the details of those who attended to the consulate. Sometimes I was able to deliver CCTV of the people who went to these things and on one occasion I allowed our MI6 man access to the conference room with some equipment.'

'Covert equipment?' probed Bannerman.

'I can neither confirm or deny that proposition, Inspector,' frowned Anderson. 'You'll have to ask them. Anyway, everything went wrong. I think the Russians got suspicious.'

'You're actually telling me that you are OSM/7 and that you were an agent for MI6, Mister Anderson. You do realise that, don't you?'

'Agent? Perhaps an occasional asset might be more accurate, Mister Bannerman but they paid well and I understand my contact is speaking,' he checked his wristwatch and continued, 'To his contact in the Special Crime Unit at this precise time.'

'Why are you telling me all this?' enquired Bannerman. 'You've gone from mistrusting me to pouring your heart out.'

'Because I have been authorised to do so and that, Mister Bannerman, speaks volumes of how your particular unit is looked upon by my masters.'

Pausing for a while, Bannerman considered the conversation and then gradually continued, 'A few moments ago you used the word rusty. What did you do before you went into the hotel business?'

'I was an officer in the British Army.'

'In which mob?' probed an intrigued Bannerman.

'The Intelligence Corps. I was a Major but took early retirement in order to travel the world. I didn't get very far. The chap from the consulate had obviously made enquiries about me and my position at the hotel made me an obvious choice to help.'

'The Intelligence Corps, you say,' nodded Bannerman. 'Manui Dat Cognitio Vires.'

'Indeed,' replied Anderson. 'The motto is in Latin. Aren't they always? Knowledge gives strength to the arm are the words you're looking for.'

'Okay,' mused Bannerman. 'Tell me about the fire.'

'There was a poisoning in Salisbury, Wiltshire. Two Russians visiting England were targeted and your people pointed the finger at Moscow.'

'Yes, I remember,' replied Bannerman. 'It's not that long ago actually.'

'There was a massive fall out between the two governments which led to the expulsion of diplomats in both countries. As senior operations manager for this company, I toured our sites supervising various aspects of hotel management and presentation. I decided to go back to St Petersburg. In Moscow, the Russians expelled twenty-three members of staff working at the British Embassy. The consulate in St Petersburg closed down. I was advised to leave by my contact but before doing so I collected the last papers that I'd found from earlier visits. They were from years ago and before I had been promoted to my present position. I wondered if I should burn all the hard copies and knew that if Russian Intelligence found the bundle OSM/1 to OSM/7 that it wouldn't take them long to realise those particular lists referred to their attempts to recruit people into the Communist Party.'

'Or worse,' remarked Bannerman.

'Your paper – OSM/7 – is from one of the very first antique fairs the Russians held,' continued Anderson. 'Anyway, we were short of time. I went into panic mode and blasted everything onto the computer system and let it rip. I took the OSM/7 paper with me. It was my last document. I think it referred to a fair some fifteen or twenty years ago. The date should be in the document.'

'So it is,' confirmed Bannerman. 'This would mean that the document wasn't filed on the internet until recently. The data in the form is twenty years old but the actual transmission across the internet is less than six months old.'

'Correct!' confirmed Anderson. 'It's a duplicate transmission because I wanted to be sure our people had received it. I shovelled everything onto the internet that day and sent a ton of paperwork off about the Russians I had met over the years. I thought I was stupid to do it but then I thought I was a bit of a James Bond hero. Either way, my emotions got the better part of me. How times change, Inspector. The internet went live in 1991 so the first OSM transmissions were arguably when the internet had not fully caught on across the globe. But I digress. Back to St Petersburg. That night a fire broke out in the hotel kitchen and by morning the hotel had suffered extensive damage.'

'Was the fire an accident or deliberate?' queried Bannerman.

'Take your pick,' replied Anderson. 'Our company investigated but couldn't find any reason why it had started. There was no malfunction in any of the equipment. We considered it a mystery so you can make your own mind up on what really happened in the kitchen. The head chef was French but there were a dozen or more Russians employed in the kitchen.'

'I see.'

'I took it as a message from the Russians. Get out! So we did! The hotel is due to reopen soon having been sold recently to a company from Dubai. To be honest, I didn't hang around to find out much about the fire at the time, but I think the Russians had discovered that we had rumbled them. I was on the next plane out. It took me to Paris where I walked into the embassy there and delivered OSM/7 and a ton of other hard copy to the military attache's office.'

'How interesting,' remarked Bannerman. 'I don't suppose you have access to copies of OSM/1-6.'

'No,' replied Anderson. 'But now you know who has them and why.'

'Yes, thank you,' smiled Bannerman. 'Just one thing before I forget.'

'Go on.'

'Why were the papers, or lists as you call them, marked OSM?'

'In the world of intelligence, Inspector Bannerman, information useful to an enquirer or research analyst is often referred to as Open Source Material because it is easily obtainable from public sources. It is open meaning it is not closed off or secret to anyone. It's in the public domain and anyone is entitled to read it if they are interested.'

'Yes, I'm aware of that,' offered Bannerman.

Anderson continued, 'My contact instructed me to mark the specific papers of interest with OSM so that if it were ever intercepted then it would clearly be seen as open source material and not anything secret. Hotel guest lists may be confidential, but they certainly aren't secret. My contact was just trying to protect me, that's all.'

'Of course,' smiled Bannerman. If you don't mind, I'd like to use your telephone and make a call.'

'Be my guest. I assure you there is no recording device on it.'

Bannerman took hold of the handset and paused.

'I jest, Inspector Bannerman,' offered Anderson. 'Now let me get you a drink. I think I have more to tell you about the kind of people who visited the hotel and it may be possible to produce some CCTV from long ago showing the people signing the register. Who knows? Some of the digital data is here, by the way. Now then, vodka perhaps?'

'I'll stick to the coffee, Mister Anderson, thank you. I'm driving. By the way, despite the anxious, panic-stricken circumstances you found yourself in, I think you're a bit of a James Bond hero. Rightly or wrongly you knew you were in possession of information that MI6 was interested in. You made the right decision.'

Anderson beamed a huge grin of satisfaction, attended the perpetual coffee machine, and replied, 'Which name are you interested in?'

'The seventh down,' replied Bannerman as he dialled Boyd's office. 'Nothing to get excited about, I can assure you, and another coffee would be well received, but please – no vodka. I can't stand the stuff.'

'Vodka!' replied Cornelius Webb as he unwrapped a litre bottle of the clear Russian spirit. 'What a marvellous present. That's so very kind of you, my friend. So very kind.'

'I thought it would be a change from that horrible Scotch Whisky you seem to enjoy.'

'Ah! The single malt! Well, the Scots are brilliant whisky makers but vodka? Well, as we know, Mikhail, vodka is in a class of its own. Will you join me in a glass?'

'Why not!' replied the Chief's visitor sliding a brown envelope across the table. 'Your home in the country is lovely but tell me, how is that gorgeous wife of yours by the way?'

'Absolutely fine,' replied Cornelius opening a drawer and sweeping the envelope into it with his free hand. 'She is beyond comparison.'

'No problems there then?'

'None whatsoever!' revealed the Chief Constable with a slight croak in his voice. 'Should there be?'

'No, no reason.'

'Good! You always seem to be interested in what she is doing. Any particular reason?'

'No, just making polite conversation, my friend. That's all.'

The seal on the bottle was broken and two glasses produced.

'Did you know that vodka is basically a distilled beverage which is composed primarily of water and ethanol? Traditionally, vodka is made through the distillation of cereal grains or potatoes that have been fermented.'

'Yes, I knew it was made from potatoes,' remarked Cornelius as he held the bottle up, studied the clarity of the liquid inside, and said, 'The Irish make potcheen from potatoes too. It's not dissimilar in taste.'

'I disagree completely,' replied the Chief's guest. 'According to legend, around 1430 a monk named Isidore from the Chudov Monastery inside the Kremlin made the first ever vodka. He was skilled in the science of distillation apparently and became the creator of this wonderful drink. They called it bread wine to begin with. For many years, it was produced exclusively in the Grand Duchy of Moscow. Now its popularity is worldwide. Comparing it with Irish potato juice is an insult, Cornelius.'

Pouring two shot glasses full of vodka, Cornelius pushed one across the table saying, 'They could make it out of seawater for all I care. It's just a great taste. To what shall we drink, Mikhail?'

'You have something for me, I believe?' ventured the Chief's guest.

'I was nearly forgetting,' replied Cornelius rummaging in the desk drawer. He found a white envelope and handed it his visitor saying, 'My apologies but this ought to make things right. My latest holiday snaps as promised.'

'Wonderful!'

Opening the lid of his laptop computer, the Chief's guest soon rattled the keyboard and negotiated his way to a website.

'What are you doing?' enquired Cornelius.

'Keeping things up to date,' replied the man as he tapped the keys. He continued, 'It's important to make sure one's investments are current and up to date.'

He swung the laptop around and showed it to Cornelius who leaned forward, smiled, and replied, 'Lovely! Thank you! Same time next month?'

'Why not? A different brand of vodka as well perhaps?'

'That would be most acceptable. Now, to whom shall we drink, my friend?'

'The Mother Country?'

'Of course,' replied Cornelius raising his glass. 'The Mother Country.'

Two shot glasses gently collided. The liquid was drunk.

'Na Zdorovie!'

'Na Zdorovie!' replied Cornelius as he replenished the glasses. 'To the Irish and their Potcheen and the Scots and their Scotch. Na Zdorovie!'

'Na Zdorovie!'

The vodka flowed from the neck of the bottle.

Meanwhile, slightly over a hundred miles to the north, the Strathclyde Grain distillery went about its daily business. Located in the Gorbals district of Glasgow, Scotland, it is a famous Scotch whisky distillery that originally manufactured gin. It has never produced vodka.

Equally well-known in Glasgow lies Her Majesty's Prison, Barlinnie. The premises are less than four miles from the Strathclyde distillery and close to the M8 motorway.

6

Riddrie
Glasgow, Scotland.
The following day.

In the language of Scottish Gaelic, Riddrie is written 'An Ruadh Ruigh' and signifies that this particular area has been around for a long time. It is a mainly residential area of northeastern Glasgow, Scotland lying on the A80 Cumbernauld Road. Riddrie consists mainly of 1930s semi-detached houses that were originally built as council housing but are now largely privately owned. The former Monkland Canal to the north was filled in during the 1960s and is now the M8 motorway which skirts Riddrie.

The neighbourhood is the site of Barlinnie Prison.

Threading through the run-down housing estate, the mousey brown-haired lady driving a white Transit van noted the number of three and four level housing units that had been built to accommodate flats and apartments in the area. Then she turned from the main road and began to drive casually through the estate roads where the semi-detached houses competed for the best-looking garden with the neatest grass and the cutest rose bush. There was a bump where the remains of an old tram line caused the suspension of the Transit to react and shake her into the present day. Changing down a gear, she checked her mirror, listened to the radio frequency scanner lying on the front passenger seat, and headed towards the prison.

The local criminal population that lived in Glasgow and the wider area of Scotland knew the prison well. It has many names, the most common is the Bar-L. Her Majesty's Prison, Barlinnie is operated by the Scottish Prison Service. Sometimes known as The Big Hoose, or Bar-L, the prison first opened in 1882 and consists of five accommodation halls named A, B, C, D and E. They were built between 1882 and 1897. Each hall held approximately two hundred inmates and it is to this location that the blonde guided her vehicle.

On the side of the white van, a logo read, 'Riddrie Laundry', and there was a local telephone number printed beneath the wording.

She reached the approaches to the building and turned into a driveway leading to the main entrance whilst simultaneously listening to the radio frequency scanner. The scanner stopped at a frequency, delivered a speech from two men talking to each other, and then continued searching for another frequency to key into. The woman reached over and entered a frequency into the device thereby manipulating the scanner to report on her preferred target. The scanner went silent and merely sounded a low electronic buzzing presence as it waited for more product.

The largest prison in Scotland regularly held about twelve hundred prisoners even though the design capacity was one thousand and eighteen. The building housed prisoners from the courts in the West of Scotland as well as retaining male prisoners on remand and prisoners serving less than sentences of four years. At times, it also allocated suitable prisoners from its convicted population to lower security prisons at nearby HMP Low Moss and HMP Greenock. It also held long-term prisoners in the initial phase of their sentence and prior to transfer to long-term prisons such as HMP Glenochil, HMP Shotts, HMP Kilmarnock or HMP Grampian. In addition, the prison also held a small number of female prisoners on remand.

The driver slowed to a crawl and withdrew a mobile 'phone from her anorak pocket. Punching in a number, she waited for a reply.

Her scanner suddenly burst into life with the announcement, 'Zone Three has a disturbance in the exercise yard. Response officers to attend.'

The mousey brown-haired woman smiled, parked the van, set the handbrake, and got out of her vehicle carrying the radio scanner. Clipping the scanner to her belt, she walked to the rear of the van, opened the door, and withdrew a large laundry bag.

Moments later, the female set down the bag beside the prison wall and stepped away. Wiping perspiration from her brow, she then checked her wristwatch and held her mobile 'phone close to her ear.

'Speak to me,' she pleaded.

A voice from the radio frequency scanner clipped to her belt boomed, 'Central control has a female standing at the northwest wall making a telephone call. She looks quite tall and is well built. There's a white Transit van close by. Dog handler to attend.'

A voice suddenly responded to her mobile call and said, 'Allah be praised. We are with you.'

The female interloper noted the reply on the scanner and reached into the laundry bag. Activating the device therein, she stepped away.

'Two minutes,' replied the woman walking quickly towards her vehicle.

In the distance, a prison dog handler came into view and began walking towards the scene.

'It's a laundry van,' from the scanner. 'Is that one of ours? I thought we had an in-house facility.'

'We have! Stand by!' from the scanner.

The woman walked on, reached the rear of the van, and opened the door wide.

'Stand well back,' she mouthed into the 'phone.

'Central CCTV, alert status two. Female subject has placed a holdall next to the northwest wall. Dog handler approaching. Suspect drugs incursion. Anticipate drone activity in the immediate area. I think she's trying to activate a drone delivery. Activate interior lockdown.'

An alarm sounded inside the prison building.

The rattle of cell keys competed with the heavy thud of boots running down corridors and across a metal gantry as staff began the procedure to secure inmates in their cells.

In the exercise yard, more male prisoners joined a developing disturbance as a fight began to grow out of control. Suddenly, prison staff were faced with the obvious dilemma as resources were stretched. It was difficult to lock down a prison when a group of prisoners were preparing to fight each other.

A punch to the jaw resulted in one man falling to the ground only to be jumped on by others.

Outside the prison wall, the dog handler appraised the situation and grew more anxious.

'Make alert status one,' radioed the dog handler. 'Looks like she has two 'phones and that laundry van has no business parked where it is. There's not a drone in sight.'

'Central! All received. Alert Status One!'

More alarms sounded. A loud klaxon dominated the environment.

She made the Transit, fired the engine, laughed, and reversed saying aloud, 'Dogs, drones and drugs my arse!'

'Stop!' shouted the dog handler now standing at the driver's door entrance. 'Switch off the engine and get out of the vehicle.'

In the microsecond that followed, the deadly assassin snatched a handgun from her belt and drilled two bullets into the guard's forehead.

He fell back onto the grass verge, released his dog leash, and knew no more when the Alsatian reacted by merely scampering backwards.

She watched the dog running away then checked her wristwatch.

Worried, she glanced at the laundry bag.

'Come on! Come on!' she pleaded.

Then there was a huge explosion. An avalanche of bricks, mortar, dust and debris blew into the air before cascading down on the grass verge next to the next van.

The bomb had blown a hole in the prison wall.

Emerging from the cloud of dust, two escapees ran towards the laundry van.

'Quickly!' she screamed. 'Run!'

Covered in dust and debris, the two absconders propelled themselves into the back of the van as it took off at speed with its tyres squealing on the dry tarmac and the woman wrestling with the steering wheel as she tried to keep the vehicle under control.

'Not you!' screamed one of the men as he suddenly threw the other against one side of the interior of the vehicle.

The Transit reached the first junction and cornered on two wheels with the rear doors flapping on their hinges and one of the fugitives inside striking the other violently on the head.

Klaxons and alarms from the prison reached fever pitch as the clamour of voices heard on a radio frequency scanner dominated the driver's compartment.

'But I helped you...' pleaded a voice in the back of the van.

There was the crunch of bone striking metal when an escapee of Asian origin grabbed his colleague's head and thumped it harshly against the van's side.

'Not any more, my friend,' from the aggressor.

'Hang on!' screamed the van driver as she clutched the steering wheel and slammed her foot to the floor.

Reaching down, the Asian antagonist hurled his colleague from the rear of the van and watched him bounce lifelessly along the tarmac as the van tore away from Bar-L at scorching speed.

'Officer down!' from the radio scanner.

'What's that in the background?' shouted the absconder.

'Dogs barking,' from the driver.

'Mad dogs!'.

Laughter from the driver's voice as she hurtled through Riddrie and the fulfilment of an escape plan.

'Mustafa!' she yelled. 'Are you with me?'

'Inshallah! Inshallah! I am blessed that Allah has sent you to save me from a life of worthlessness,' replied Mustafa as he dusted off the dust and debris of the prison. He climbed through an opening into the driver's cabin, slid into the passenger seat and said, 'My friend who helped me was a kafir. He is no longer a friend. He has gone. In truth, he was only ever a friend of convenience. Are you the one they call Yvonne?'

'Yesterday I was Yvonne. Today I am Yasmin. Tomorrow I will be someone else,' laughed the woman. 'What's in a name? I am the messenger. You are free!'

'Freedom!' bellowed Mustafa. 'The Prophet Muhammad has liberated me from the burdens and shackles of subjugation'

Yasmin snatched a lower gear and turned off down a side road saying, 'Muhammad was the messenger. I'm just the driver. Buckle up and shut up! You talk too much.'

Within a short space of time, the sound of prison klaxons, alarm bells, and barking dogs had been replaced by the sight of blue lights and police sirens heading at speed towards Barlinnie.

On a layby on the outskirts of Riddrie lay an abandoned Transit van fitted with false number plates and a tear-off plastic logo indicating ownership to a laundry that didn't exist.

The body of a prison inmate lay on the tarmac half a mile from the scene of the prison break. Freedom for one had meant death for another.

Slightly to the east, a man and a woman made good their escape in a dark grey Range Rover.

'La Bomba!' yelled Mustafa enthusiastically. 'You do not look like the kind of woman who would know anything about bombs. Where did you get that wonderful device?'

'El Sultán,' she explained. 'What kind of woman did you expect to be carrying a bomb, Mustafa? One with two heads and six legs or a crazy female Jihadist the like of which you have never met before?'

Mustafa suddenly adopted a more conciliatory tone when he remarked, 'I was thinking more of the wig that you are wearing. It has slipped to the side with the excitement of your madcap driving. Your ginger locks are showing.'

Moving her right hand from the steering wheel, the woman took hold of a handgun secured beneath her right thigh.

She pointed the gun at Mustafa and said, 'What ginger curls?'

Dry-mouthed for a moment, Mustafa nervously responded, 'Perhaps it is just the sunshine dancing on your hair. I see no ginger.'

'Good!' pronounced the driver lowering her gun. 'The less you see and remember the better. I have a job to do and that is to transport you to a place of safety. If you cause me problems, I will not hesitate to kill you and dump you on the roadside in the middle of nowhere.'

Peering into her eyes, Mustafa then glanced out of the window and said, 'A thousand pardons, whatever your name is. My mind is alive with new-found freedom. Can you tell me where you are taking me?'

'Falkirk,' explained the wig-wearing driver.

'Falkirk!' queried the escapee. 'It is in Scotland. Yes? No?'

'To a farm near Falkirk. It's in a remote part of the Scottish countryside actually,' she explained. 'Then south into England when it quietens down. Meanwhile, I am to give you this. These are your instructions from El Sultán. You are to follow them to the letter. Understood?'

Mustafa accepted a white envelope from the woman. He ripped it open and removed a typed note, some banknotes, a copy of the Quran, and a small piece of paper on which was printed a map of the northeast of England.

'Some money to be going on with,' remarked the prison escapee. 'And what appears to be details of a target.'

'Enough,' snapped Yasmin. 'That's your expenses for the days ahead. You are El Sultán's chosen one. I'd rather not know what the target is until we get to the farmhouse. Read and commit your instructions to memory. When you're satisfied, you'll find a cigarette lighter in the glove box. Burn the note and the map, pocket the money. You'll need that later. Now shut up and learn the script.'

They drove in silence as Mustafa concentrated on his instructions.

'When do we move?' queried Mustafa.

'When I receive my orders from El Sultán,' replied the brown-haired woman. 'All you need to do is keep your head down and get some sleep.'

'I am honoured to be the chosen one of El Sultán. He has the blessing of Allah. I can only wish you a thousand thanks as I dream of the virgins that await me in the weeks ahead.'

'You keep dreaming, Mustafa,' chuckled the driver. 'You just never know your luck. But please don't litter the van with bodies next time.'

'Bodies!' laughed Mustafa rattling his hands on the dashboard like a drummer in a band.

'Who was he?'

'A worthless infidel!'

'You mean you only found one kefir in the whole of that prison?' jested the driver.

'Just the one, my lovely,' laughed Mustafa. 'Just the one like your bomb. Viva El Sultán. Viva La Bomba!'

The driver checked the interior mirror and resettled her headpiece as Mustafa settled down and turned the first pages of the Quran which he began to read.

Glancing at her ebullient passenger, she remarked, 'I can't imagine what El Sultán has got lined up for you, Mustafa. I can only guess.'

*

7

Cumbria
Later

When two energetic corgis had raced along the thin pebbled beach chasing a rubber ball, the female dog walker did not expect them to come scampering back dragging the remains of a canvas painting that had been abandoned on the shoreline.

Shaking her head, chuckling, Monica tousled the head of both dogs before sending them away again to find their ball.

Monica lifted the canvas into a position where she could appreciate the painting. She held it out before her and realized it was an unfinished work. There was a gentle rattle from the pebbles when she threw the broken canvas onto the beach from where it had come.

The tide was outbound leaving various items on display at the foot of St Bees cliffs. Strolling on, enjoying the sunshine and the breeze, she noticed that the corgis had stopped at a pile of debris that been deposited on the beach by an earlier inbound tide.

One of the corgis ran off down the beach. The other sprinted to her side and began jumping up and down. Mystified, intrigued, she approached the pile of debris, pushed away a layer of sand, and realized she was looking down at what appeared to be a mass of some kind. A black cloth fluttered across the top part of the entity.

Withdrawing the cloth, Monica realised she was looking down on the body of a female. Stepping back, shocked, Monica held her hands to her face and then moved closer.

She removed a mobile 'phone from her jacket pocket, dialled 999 and waited for a response.

It wasn't long before a significant police presence attended and set up a cordon in the immediate area.

Once the tall and thin Detective Chief Superintendent Raymond Cullen had arrived, he took over management of the scene and examined the corpse.

'When did you find her, Monica?' enquired Cullen.

'About an hour ago,' she replied. 'I haven't touched anything other than a half-finished painting on a canvas. I threw it away over there.' She pointed along the beach and continued, 'I think I've seen her before. Not sure but she reminds me of a lady who often comes and sits on the clifftops painting the lighthouse.'

'You live locally, I presume?' queried Cullen.

'In the village. It's only a five-minute walk. Can I go now?'

'Soon,' replied Cullen. 'One of my officers will need to take a statement from you but what else can you tell me about the woman you think it might be?'

'She's an artist – a painter – you know,' replied Monica. 'She's not from around here though. Penrith area, I think.'

'Well, I can see paint on that smock she is wearing but what makes you think she's from Penrith?'

'I stopped to talk to her once. She told me painting was her way of finding private time to think things over. I think she had a troubled marriage but I'm just guessing.'

'Why?' challenged Cullen.

'Call it woman's intuition,' smiled Monica. 'Can I go now?'

Cullen nodded towards a colleague and replied, 'Of course! Thank you! One of my officers will take you home and take a preliminary statement from you but we'll probably need to speak to you again in due course.'

'I understand. I'm on the 'phone if you need me. Has she been murdered?'

'She's been strangled with a cloth or towel of some kind,' replied Cullen.

'Oh dear, I thought she might have fallen from the cliffs,' suggested the dog walker.

'Too far away,' suggested Cullen.

'The tide will have caught her and deposited the body here,' voiced the woman.

'Yes! Yes, that's possible,' replied the detective.

As Monica was escorted away, she gathered her dogs close to her whilst Cullen knelt down by the body to take a closer look.

'Excuse me, sir,' said a uniform sergeant stepping forward. 'If it is murder then we really need to talk to that woman properly and at length. If she recognizes the deceased then what else does she know? When did she last see this woman and who was she with? She could even be the murderer. Where has she been for the last twenty-four hours? Would you like me to go and fetch her back?'

'And you are?' challenged Cullen.

'Lowther,' sir, Sergeant Lowther.'

'What gives you the right to determine what I should and should not do, Sergeant Lowther?'

'Twenty-five years' service, sir! Ten as a detective before I was promoted.'

'Really? And you expect to make inspector by criticising your superiors?' ventured Cullen.

Short and sturdy, Sergeant Lowther took a step back and said, 'Never had a superior officer, sir. Always had a supervisor really. Just my thoughts, that's all. How do you think she died?'

Cullen replied, 'I'm sure the doctor will confirm my suspicions when he arrives but at the moment, I see we have a badly injured corpse that bears suspicious marks in the throat area.'

'Strangulation?' queried Lowther.

'Well, she has a ligature tied around her neck and isn't breathing. I'd say she's been strangled and that's precisely why you're a sergeant and I'm a chief superintendent,' responded Cullen with a sarcastic twist.'

'Her tongue isn't sticking out,' pronounced the Sergeant. 'That's why I'm querying it. That facial expression looks odd to me. Anyway, I've arranged for the cliff area above to be cordoned off. This is the scene of the body, but the scene of the murder might have been on the cliffs above.'

'Cliffs! Cordons! Murder!' snapped Cullen. 'Don't you go jumping to conclusions and making such decisions without reference to me in the first place.'

'What's that?' enquired Sergeant Lowther pointing to the corpse.

Lowther knelt down and examined a black cloth tied around the neck of the body.

'Careful,' snapped Cullen. 'Don't go upsetting my crime scene.'

Leaving the cloth tied to the body, Lowther allowed the remainder of the cloth to unfurl in the breeze.

'I don't believe it,' he gasped.

'What?' queried Cullen.

Sergeant Lowther gazed at the black standard and read the Arabic writing before remarking, 'No disrespect intended, sir, but aren't you one of those direct entry individuals that have just joined.'

'After extensive training and a lot of interviews, yes. I also have a degree in Policing and another in Greek Mythology,' replied Cullen proudly.

'Wonderful,' muttered Lowther. 'That explains everything. Your first murder then?'

'Not if you include the twenty or more murder scenes at the training school. By God, they put you though it there you know.'

Sergeant Lowther shook his head, looked Cullen deep in the eye, and replied, 'I don't think a Greek God is responsible for this otherwise you'd have cracked it by now. May I suggest you contact Counter Terrorism Command, Mister Cullen. This lady has been strangled with what appears to be the black flag of the Islamic State of Iraq and Syria. I've seen this flag before on the telly. I'm pretty sure that when forensics remove this ligature, they'll see it's an ISIS flag. Look, you can see most of the writing. They've left their calling card at the scene of this one.'

'ISIS!' exclaimed Cullen shaken and unsure of what to do next. 'ISIS!' he repeated. 'You mean we have an international terrorist attack on a beach in Cumbria? We're in the middle of nowhere, for god's sake.'

Looking towards the clifftops, Sergeant Lowther then eyed Cullen and suggested, 'I don't know, sir, but we'll find out if we do the job properly. As a reminder, and just for your information, sir, Sellafield is less than ten miles up the road.'

'Sellafield?' queried Cullen.

'A nuclear site, Mister Cullen,' advised Lowther. 'Where they reprocess fuel from nuclear reactors, apart from decommissioning and a ton of other stuff. The lads in my local call it a nuclear dustbin.'

'Dustbin! Yes! Yes, of course! I know all that! But it's my first murder scene,' spouted Cullen. 'And I end up with an international terrorist attack in Cumbria. How lucky am I?'

'Lucky!' challenged Lowther. 'Whichever way you read it, Mister Cullen, you might reflect on the proposition that this lady – whoever she is – didn't have any luck on the day she died. I'll make the call for you.'

'Luck! Call!' faltered Cullen. 'Yes! Yes! I was miles away. Sorry! Make the call, Sergeant Lowther. Counter Terrorism Command! Yes, they'll need my help on this one.'

Shaking his head, unsettled by it all, Sergeant Lowther stepped away and made a phone call on his mobile.

'My first ride in the new response vehicle,' remarked Boyd as he climbed aboard and buckled up.

'Welcome to Charlie Tango Charlie,' announced Antonia. 'Please stow your luggage in the overhead locker provided and ensure that it is safely secured. Handbags and briefcases should be stored underneath your seat when not in use and during take-off. Switch off all mobile phones and ensure all laptops are in flight mode. Our staff will be moving along the aisle shortly with a display of drinks, duty-free, complimentary newspapers and a variety of perfumes which are available to purchase during your flight. I personally recommend a particular kind of very expensive perfume only to be accompanied by a bottle of equally splendid champagne. May I wish you all a relaxing journey. Just sit back and enjoy.'

'Sit down, Antonia,' laughed Boyd. 'It's a response helicopter not a holiday flight to the Canaries.'

'Yes, but it is the maiden voyage,' chuckled the redhead.

'Stand by for take-off,' from the pilot's intercom.

Charlie Tango Charlie uniquely represented the call sign of the new Counter Terrorism Command helicopter and would hopefully soon catch on as the team's airborne callsign.

'As if we didn't have enough to do,' remarked Bannerman fixing his seatbelt. 'I'm still smarting over my trip to that hotel chain in

Bayswater. Guvnor, what did you make of my conversation with Donald Anderson a.k.a James Bond a.k.a. our man in St Petersburg?'

'The hotel boss?' queried Boyd. 'Interesting!'

'And?' frowned Bannerman. 'Surely not just interesting?'

'You and I have a meeting arranged with the Chief of the Secret Intelligence Service, Bannerman. We were lined up for today, but this incident has cancelled that out. One thing at a time, I'm afraid.'

'Do you think he will either confirm or deny that what Anderson told me is true?' proposed Bannerman.

Chuckling at the remark, Boyd revealed, 'The request for a meeting came from Sir Julian himself.'

'There are protocols to observe,' intervened Antonia in a scolding manner. 'What you perceive to be straightforward may not be as cut and dried as you think. I'd say play nice, boys and follow the rules.'

'You know something, don't you, Antonia?' probed Boyd. 'You're always one step ahead of the game. What do you know that we don't? Come on! You can tell us. We're all on the same side.'

There was a swish of red hair that sliced through the atmosphere when Antonia swung her head away and remarked, 'There are protocols in play. I'm not at liberty to say.'

Boyd and Bannerman exchanged quizzical glances before Boyd announced, 'Of course, protocols. You can't beat them. Everyone should have them.'

There was a slight shudder when the helicopter lifted off.

The Agusta 109 specially adapted helicopter had a maximum speed of 180mph. It boasted six passenger seats. Three white leather seats backed onto one side of the vessel and they faced the other three on the opposing side. The maximum range of the helicopter before it needed refuelling was 500 miles and it was designed to carry elements of the team from A to B as swiftly as possible. The vessel was equipped with various gizmos which inclued, but were not limited to, infra-red surveillance cameras, radio frequency monitoring devices, jamming technology, and a computer station for use by the passengers.

The front cabin was occupied by a pilot and his co-pilot from the Police Air Support Unit.

Boyd, Bannerman, and Antonia knew they'd be at the crime scene in slightly over two hours. On arrival, the trio would touch down on the clifftops. The helicopter would subsequently refuel and then head to the Barlinnie area where it would discharge Detective Inspector Anthea Adams together with Sergeants Terry Anwhari and Janice Burns.

As the flight gathered speed over London, the team got to work instructing stop and interview cordons to be put in place. The details of everyone passing through the cordons were to be recorded. Experience revealed these tended to be local people and the hope was that they might recall something out of place over recent days. In addition, an instruction was given to seize and secure all CCTV within five miles of the two scenes. It was the team's starter for ten. It often took days, weeks, or months to work through the data collated but that was the way a needle in a haystack might be found. The local police surgeon and a forensic pathologist had been called to St Bees. A bomb disposal team and a bomb scene management team were on route to Barlinnie Prison. Boyd had instructed the area be made safe from other devices before the bomb scene management team began collecting the debris that might one day be used to recreate the bomb set down by the blonde.

'Anthea,' instructed Boyd. 'You take Barlinnie and we'll do St Bees. Ring me every hour with an update. I want to know if they are connected in any way. Likewise, if we get a break, I'll be on the 'phone to you pronto. Understood?'

'As ever, Guvnor,' nodded Anthea. 'Janice will take the scene. Terry will take the exterior and surrounding area. I'll do the interior of the prison, the relevant inmates, and background on the two escapees. I've already asked for an updated list of stolen Transit vans to be recirculated and sent to us for examination. Companies that hire out vans are also under scrutiny as we look for anything untoward or out of place. I'm about to inform the Border Force so that a nationwide warning can be circulated. I'll back this up with the necessary information as it becomes available. I need to alert the Scottish airports as soon as possible. If the prison escape has been designed to get someone out of the country, as well as their cell, then I want to be sure our border controls are aware.'

'Excellent,' remarked Boyd. 'Local assistance is already on scene. Touch base with the Borough Commander on arrival.'

'Agreed!' replied Anthea holding her right index finger to her ear. 'Although I don't think Scotland has any Borough Commanders like they do in London. By the way, I'm hearing the body of one of the escapees has been found on the highway not far from the prison. I'll pick up on that when we arrive in Glasgow.'

'Dead, alive or injured?'

'Deceased!'

'One less to recapture,' remarked Boyd.

The tapping of keyboards and air to ground radio communications filled the time and it wasn't long before Charlie Tango Charlie made its first touchdown on St Bees cliffs.

Detective Inspector Ronnie Pitt stepped forward as soon as the helicopter landed. Approaching the trio as they walked across the clifftops, Pitt extended a handshake and introductions followed in rapid succession.

'There's been a development and I think you should know about it right now,' stated Pitt

'Tell me!' replied Boyd.

'I'm the local DI on my rest day. I turned out to the scene when my Sergeant rang me. He's an ex-jack with a decade of experience and he asked me to attend. We've got man-management problems at the scene which you'll see for yourself shortly. I recognized the deceased immediately. The others didn't know her, but I'm newly transferred from Penrith. I knew who it was right away.'

'You have a positive identification already?' queried Boyd.

'Yes, sir! It's Divine Webb. The deceased is the wife of Cornelius Webb who is the Chief constable of Cumbria.'

Stunned for a moment, an open-mouthed Boyd stood on the clifftops and eventually replied, 'Yes! Yes, I know Cornelius. Are you sure?'

'As sure as I'm standing here and you're standing there.'

'Not enough,' ventured a thinking Boyd. 'Evidentially, I mean.'

'Divine Webb always wore a particularly nice necklace, Mister Boyd,' revealed Pitt. 'I used to see her regularly in Penrith. I remembered her and recalled the necklace. They were both unique. I'm not mistaken although I accept there are other identification protocols to follow. Dentistry is the obvious one in due course and I'll stand corrected if I need to be. Trust me on this one, Mister Boyd.'

Nodding and understanding, Boyd asked, 'Okay. I'll go with you. Tell me, Mister Pitt, has anyone told the Chief his wife might have been murdered?'

'Not yet, sir,' replied Pitt.

'Have these cliffs been searched?' asked Boyd.

'No! Detective Chief Superintendent Cullen is waiting for you to take charge.'

'The scene should have been protected from the word go,' snapped Bannerman. 'What the hell is going on?'

'Mister Cullen is new to the job,' revealed Pitt. 'I didn't say this, but he'll get there in the end. He just needs a ton of experience as soon as possible.'

'We're used to not hearing things,' suggested Antonia. 'Don't worry and thanks for the heads up.'

'That response from the senior investigating officer is unusual,' remarked Boyd. 'They usually want to keep everything to themselves. That scene should have been cordoned off and worked on by now. Look, I know this is your rest day, but do you want in on this? It's your patch.'

'Absolutely! What can I do?'

'Place a hold on the victim identification procedure for now. I'll personally deliver the death message to the Chief once I've identified the body myself.'

'Absolutely!'

'Can you organise a fingertip search of the clifftops and a forensic search of those observation cabins over there. We've nothing to lose and everything to gain.

'They are RSPB observations points,' replied Pitt. 'I'll contact them if we need to gain access. Leave it with me.'

Boyd pointed as he continued, 'Is that lighthouse manned or automatic? When was it last occupied or visited by a human being.? And take us to the body. It's on the beach I believe.'

'Yeah,' replied Pitt. 'I'll do the checks, but the lighthouse is automatic so it's unlikely anyone has been looking out of the window at the time of the murder.'

'What about a window cleaner?' proposed Bannerman.

'I hear you,' nodded Pitt. 'I won't take anything for granted. I'll get a team together and make a start. By the way, she's been strangled with an ISIS flag, but I expect you know that already since that's why you're here. Chief Superintendent Cullen is at the scene. I think it's his first murder. Did you know her? Divine, I mean.'

'I met her very recently and for only a short time,' replied Boyd. 'But a new Chief Superintendent on his first murder is just what we need. Tell me he's a direct entrant with a degree in....?'

'Greek mythology!'

'Wonderful!' gasped Boyd shaking his head. 'I thought you were joking for a moment. Okay, let's go and take a look. Is the Professor of Pathology here yet?'

'You'll be pleased to know they sent Professor Frazer. He arrived about ten minutes ago,' revealed Pitt. 'Follow me. The route to the body along the beach is cordoned off and there's a uniform guard on it so that we can preserve any evidence. The only way you can get to the cliffs is from a car park at the end of the footpath.'

'At least he got one thing right,' responded Boyd as the trio of detectives made their way to the scene.

'That said,' revealed Pitt. 'The beach is about two hundred yards from the foot of the cliffs. The distance between the foot of the rocks and the sea is usually no more than twenty yards.'

'Not wide enough for beach volleyball,' joked Boyd.

'Not at all,' admitted Pitt. 'It's more rock and pebbles than sand in some places. Hardly a walker's paradise so we're quite fortunate that someone actually found the body so soon.'

'Yeah, the location looks bleak,' nodded Boyd. 'What do we know about the person who found the body?'

'Not enough,' replied Pitt. 'Local woman walking her dogs. Probably alright but more enquiry needed.'

Nodding, Boyd added, 'Does anything else strike you about the scene that I should know?'

Pitt paused and said, 'Take a good luck at the beach. It's thin, rocky, desolated, and rarely used by anyone other than a handful of locals. It gets broader as you move away from the cliffs towards the rest of the world. My gut feeling is the victim wasn't killed on the beach. I think she was murdered on the cliffs and was then thrown onto the rocks below. The tide washed her along the coastline and deposited her further along the beach closer to the village.'

'Any proof?' probed Boyd.

'Not yet,' answered Pitt.

'Antonia!' remarked Boyd. 'Tide times? Ebb, flow, strength direction of tidal movements? Can you help please?'

'I'll start with the local harbour master at Whitehaven,' advocated Antonia. 'Then I'll speak with the UK Hydrographic Office.'

'The what?' ventured Boyd.

'The Hydrographic office in Taunton, Boyd, I have an uncle who is a rear admiral there. I'm sure he'll point me in the right direction.'

'You and your uncles,' ventured Boyd. 'What's his speciality?'

'Hydrography, of course,' chided the redhead. 'The science of surveying and charting bodies of water, such as seas, lakes, and rivers.'

'Ouch!'

'Depth of seabed, rock formation...'

'Times and flow at this stage, Antonia,' interrupted Boyd.

'I'm on it,' replied Antonia engaging her mobile.

Charlie Tango Charlie lifted into the air as Boyd, Bannerman and Antonia took over the crime scene.

The helicopter flew towards the sea initially, overflew a line of officers searching the beach, and turned north towards the Solway Firth.

Five minutes later, the group were assembled beneath a canvas tent which protected the scene from the elements whilst simultaneously providing dignity to the deceased and privacy to the forensic examination taking place.

Introductions complete, Chief Superintendent Cullen pointed to a black flag tied around the neck of Divine Webb, looked at Boyd and asked, 'I'm told this is Arabic. What does the writing on the flag mean?'

'There is no god but Allah. Mohammad is the messenger of Allah,' delivered Boyd. 'Don't remove it. Photograph the knot and bag and tag the ends to prevent any loss of evidence.'

'Evidence? Such as?'

'DNA, chemicals, after-shave, perfume, anything on that cloth might give us the clues we need.'

'It's definitely an ISIS flag then?' enquired Cullen.

'Yes!' nodded Bannerman. 'The phrase is a declaration of faith used across Islam. It's known as the shahada. Beneath the top writing is a white circle emblazoned with black writing which means Mohammed is the messenger of God.'

'It reminds me of what Officer Santiago heard in Cordoba just before he shot that terrorist,' suggested Antonia. 'But then, when I think about it, that's what all these Islamic terrorists shout.'

'Bit of a difference in location,' suggested Boyd. 'Professor! My apologies! Remiss of me but this is Detective Chief Superintendent Cullen!'

The two men shook hands.

'What do you make of this so far?' probed Boyd.

'I'm not sure,' puzzled the middle-age bespectacled Frazer. 'A post-mortem is obviously needed but I can tell you the body temperature suggests to me that death occurred about twenty-four hours ago and she might have been strangled.'

'Any water in the lungs?' challenged Boyd.

'Yes,' replied Frazer. 'I'll be able to report in due course how much. I'm not convinced she drowned.'

'Are you sure?' asked Cullen.

Frazer ignored the interruption and continued, 'Strange one! I'm also thinking she's had a heart attack. Her tongue isn't sticking out of her mouth as is sometimes the case and that facial expression just doesn't seem right. It's almost a smile as opposed to a look of deathly horror.'

'What do you make of it?' asked Cullen.

'Well, when the tongue sticks out it generally means that the victim is in a state of shock from the initial attack,' explained Professor Frazer. Adjusting his spectacles, he continued, 'By that I mean the victim is suddenly compromised by a stranger and, in the moments of death, the tongue enlarges and often protrudes. That didn't happen here. It's almost as if the victim is laughing at the killer.'

'You're surely not suggesting the victim knew the killer?' probed Cullen.

'Absolutely not,' responded Frazer. 'I'm merely trying to make sense of what I see before me. I'll know better when I've examined the body properly on the slab. Right now, it's a bit of a mystery. That's why I'm here. Or to be formal and use some police speak, Chief Superintendent – it's too early to say and enquiries are continuing. We are keeping an open mind and working with our partners in a multi-agency approach in order to produce the best carrots in the field.'

Deadpan, Cullen nodded.

'And there's this,' declared the Professor. 'She's also wearing a silver necklace around her neck. There's a crucifix on the chain and on the reverse side, you'll find the name Divine inscribed in the silver. She's Divine but sadly no longer divine in so many ways.'

Again, Cullen remained unfazed.

Frazer squinted over his spectacles and advised Cullen, 'You are allowed to smile, chuckle or laugh, Mister Cullen. This is not the classroom.'

'You remember me from the training course then?' enquired Cullen.

'Yes, I do,' replied Frazer. 'Raymond isn't it? Raymond Cullen? Weren't you in Lancashire?'

'That's me! I transferred on promotion.'

'Of course, you did,' reasoned Frazer. 'How could I forget you, Raymond? I recall you had no sense of humour in the classroom either but now that you're out in the field I suggest you find one or this job will destroy you. Loosen up!'

Cullen studied the body and then Frazer before gradually letting go with, 'Yes, thanks! Yes, I'm sorry to be a pompous ass. I promise you I will learn.'

'You certainly will on this watch,' intervened Boyd.

'I'll try,' from Cullen. 'Headmaster permitting.'

Engaging Frazer, Boyd proposed, 'Has the homework class ended? If you two have quite finished, and if it's not too much of an inconvenience, Professor, could you enlighten us regarding defence marks?'

Lifting the corpse's hands, Professor Frazer said, 'Look, Boyd! I've already carried out a brief examination of the body in order to answer your anticipated question. Check this out!'

With his audience engaged, Frazer examined her fingertips and knuckles, checked the fingernails, and then scanned her knees and elbows as he spoke into his personal tape recorder and delivered, 'Note to initial assessment file - A second examination of all limbs present indicate no obvious defence marks in being. A further microscopic study will be made in the lab.'

'Nothing?' queried Boyd.

'Doesn't look like it at the moment. There are no signs of resistance, struggle, or self-defence but I'll do a microscopic search back at the lab. No knife marks! No bullet marks! No scrapes or bruises other than some minor abrasions to the heels?'

'The heels?' queried Boyd.

'The heels, Boyd,' repeated the Professor. 'I'll need soil samples from the cliff tops where I suspect you might find drag marks in the grass. This is consistent with the body having been dragged from the scene of the killing and then thrown onto the rocks below. I wonder if the murderer thought they were throwing her into the sea or onto the beach? Interesting when the sea isn't as deep as you think it might be. Anyway, Boyd, I see nothing obvious underneath the fingernails that might suggest scratching or defensive gouging. Yet there's just something about this one. I can't put my finger on it at the moment.'

'Am I right in thinking the offender is male if it's strangulation?' proposed Boyd.

'Almost certainly,' nodded the Professor as he continued the examination. 'A male gripping the female from the front usually means the male is more dominant – stronger, possibly of equal height, probably much taller. But this might have been done from the rear. Needs more work, Boyd.'

'In what way, Professor?' queried Boyd as Cullen looked on.

Making a cursory examination of the body, Professor Frazer addressed his audience with, 'I like to think that strangulation can be bunched into three different classes. There's strangulation by hanging – usually suicide or homicide - where the weight of the body plays an important part in the process of death. The jugular vein and carotid arteries are starved of blood which can eventually pool in the lower limbs of the body because there is no circulation taking place. People who are hanged have necks that are usually marked with furrows where the ligature has constricted the neck. The tongue usually protrudes because of the pressure on the jaw. I could go on, but this woman has not been hanged.'

'I thought not,' remarked Cullen.

'Manual strangulation is throttling with the hands, fingers, or blunt objects, such as sticks or batons that are applied forcibly to the throat. The airway is compressed and the larynx is usually damaged. Imagine if you were being strangled. You'd kick, scratch, punch, spit, bite, gouge, even headbutt to protect yourself. I cannot see any defence marks.'

'Interesting,' noted Boyd.

'Very!' mimicked Cullen.

'Getting you a weather report for this area over the last seventy-two hours,' revealed Antonia on her mobile 'phone.

'Another uncle?' probed Boyd.

'Not at all,' twisted Antonia. 'The radio, of course! Whatever made you think that?'

'Oh, nothing,' nodded Boyd with a smile. 'You're ahead of the game as usual.'

Antonia smiled a reply as Professor Frazer continued, 'Then, lastly, we have ligature strangulation. This occurs when a cord, rope, wire or other ligature is used to fully encompass the neck. Most ligature strangulations are carried out by males on women, children, and the elderly. If I'm being honest, I can't rule out that she tied the cloth around her own neck, tightened it, and then strangled herself.'

'You're joking?' remarked Boyd.

'Thinking aloud, Chief Inspector,' replied Frazer. 'I'm going through the various stages of examination that my brain is instructing me to take. Then there's that necklace to consider.'

'Necklace?' queried Boyd.

'Yes,' replied Frazer. 'The victim wore a crucifix on a silver necklace. That suggests she may have been religious.'

'Or just a lover of fine jewellery,' proposed Boyd.

'I'm trying to help by thinking like a detective for you,' remarked Frazer.

'I'd better stand back then,' suggested Boyd cheekily. 'Anything might happen in the next half hour.'

Kneeling by the body, Professor Frazer examined her throat and neck in detail and eventually revealed, 'When someone is hanged the ligature mark is nearly always found at the top of the neck below the jaw. This lady has been strangled from the front, I would say.'

'How can you tell?' enquired Cullen.

'The ligature mark is located in the lower area of the victim's neck and the knot is actually a crossover which ties at the front of the throat,' explained Professor Frazer. 'Had a person strangled the victim from the rear, it would be much more likely that the knot would be at the back of the neck.'

'That would depend on the circumstances of the attack,' suggested Cullen. 'Whether it was planned or spontaneous, for example.'

'It would,' admitted Frazer. 'You're absolutely right, Raymond. But I'm trying to give you an early appraisal at this stage and I can best accomplish that by using previous experience with regards to the number of homicide scenes I've visited. After thirty years of examining dead bodies found in suspicious circumstances, I can give you percentages of what is usual and what is abnormal. That's all. It's not perfect and probably never will be.'

'Why did you mention a heart attack?' questioned Boyd.

'The skin is ashen, quite pale and the blood flow has responded to the cessation of the heart. Livor mortis is present. The top part of the body is turning to a pale colour while the bottom parts have turned to a mottled, purplish-blue from the pooling of blood.'

'I thought you said that pooling blood in cases like this usually mean death by hanging,' from Cullen.

'I did but forensically speaking there are differences relevant to blood volume, transmission, and a host of other things that an internal examination will reveal. Externally, there's no evidence present that this body has been hanging around for some time. I also note the ends of the ligature are not torn. This is a gut feeling, Raymond.'

'For which we are eternally obliged,' remarked Boyd.

'Raymond, please note,' suggested Frazer. 'I've known Boyd since he was a youngster in Carlisle when he first began his job. He was a constable then and I was an NHS sprog. Rank and ability should not be confused. There are few detectives to whom I would impart my early beliefs. I understand Boyd's hunter instincts and he understands that an early prod from me will help him on his way but may or may not be substantiated in written form. The end result is no more than proven scientific academia. The conversation we are having is between working professionals. It's what is called a working relationship.'

'You're very kind,' said Boyd.

Cullen, puzzled to some extent, nodded.

'One last thing, Boyd,' stated Frazer. 'Your killer is likely to be left-handed.'

'And I can see why,' remarked Boyd. 'We've been down this path before. Most of the times you've been proven right, other times – wrong.'

'Some people are ambidextrous, Boyd,' counselled Frazer.

'Given that 90% of the population is right-handed that is a crucial nod in the right direction,' revealed Boyd. 'Pardon the pun! Listen to this, Mister Cullen, you are about to hear from the maestro himself. Go on, Professor. Would you be kind enough to harken back to the days of my youth and explain to the next generation of policing the percentages and common-sense approach as opposed to the academia?'

'You still haven't learnt to control your mouth, Boyd,' chuckled Frazer. 'But it's as simple as this, Mister Cullen. Look at the knot on the victim's throat. It's really no more than a double twist of the flag. When the right hand is dominant, there is a tendency to hold the flag in the weaker left hand and use the right hand to loop, create the knot, and pull tight by using the stronger right hand. The result you need to consider is not the knot. It is the length of cloth now held in the right hand. It's longer than the cloth in the left hand because of the dominant strength of the right hand. Now consider the left hand is dominant. It holds the flag in the left hand and replicates the methodology of strangulation that I have previously described. The length of cloth in your left hand is now longer than the other strand because of the dominance of the hand strength.'

Cullen looked on and said, 'That's not the science you taught me. It was never mentioned at the training school.'

'No, it wasn't,' replied Frazer. 'It's a percentage find that is useful. It's like fingerprint evidence that suggests you are on the right track but the number of proven points on the fingerprint evidence chart doesn't match the required legal standard. It's what I call a heads up to Mister Boyd. I will confirm the finding in my report whilst indicating it is inconclusive. It will be challenged in court if the offender is left-handed and pleads not guilty.'

Cullen bent down, studied the ligature, and replied, 'Left-handed but only by an inch or so.'

'I can hereby rule out 90% of the population,' chuckled Boyd. 'Thanks for the tip.'

Professor Frazer announced, 'I'm going to stand back and let your people take some more photos before I get stuck into the harshness of forensic examination. I'll have a preliminary report for you by lunchtime tomorrow subject to the availability of my secretary and her computer keyboard.'

'One last thing before I go, Professor,' suggested Boyd. 'Do you see all the hallmarks of a terrorist-related murder?'

Frazer glanced at Boyd, shook his head, and intimated, 'I think we both know that's not the case but then my work is about the cause of death. Yours is a whodunnit and the obvious clue before you is the flag.'

'I'm thinking about the flag, Professor,' nodded Boyd.

'The flag, Boyd! The flag doesn't fit. So sayeth the humble voice of an ageing Professor of Pathology who has always secretly wanted to be a murder squad detective stood in a canvas tent on a bloody windy beach in the middle of nowhere. The tide will come in and bring the rain with it and I'll get soaked to the skin before I allow this one to be carted off to the morgue.'

'The incident wagon is parked up top and has a heater in it, Professor,' replied Boyd. 'We can have the heater here for you in no time at all. What do you say?'

'You haven't got long on the beach, Boyd. Use the time well. This is a 'lift and carry' very soon. I don't want the heater increasing the temperature of my corpse. It's cold. It's always cold. I'll get by.'

'Thanks for the early heads up.'

'My pleasure,' smiled Frazer.

'Strangled on the clifftops,' suggested Boyd. 'Suffered a heart attack during the assault and was then thrown from the cliffs onto the beach where the tide claimed her, drowned her, and then deposited her back on the beach when the tide changed.'

'Could be your starter for ten,' Professor Frazer agreed. 'Of course, it's all irrelevant hearsay at the moment but which one of those anecdotes is correct is for me to prove or disprove in a forensic manner. I'll keep an open mind as I work through my protocols.'

'Thank you, sir,' added Boyd. 'Protocols? Yes, they're all over the place today. I'll respect your findings in due course, and I'm obliged for the early intimations.'

'Would someone mind telling me what on earth is going on?' probed Cullen. 'This is my case.'

'We have, Mister Cullen,' explained Boyd. 'An unusual and suspicious death which is best described as a murder. Do you know who the victim is?'

'Not at the moment, no!'

'Divine Webb, Mister Cullen,' replied Boyd. 'The Chief Constable's wife.'

'What!' expressed Cullen. 'The Chief Constable's wife?'

'Precisely,' agreed Boyd.

'How do you know?'

'I recognise her and so does your Detective Inspector Pitt.'

'Oh, I didn't realise.'

'I think you had other things on your mind,' suggested Boyd. 'I'm going to leave Detective Inspector Bannerman here in charge of the scene with your DI Pitt. Thank you for arranging the search on the beach. There's another search taking place on the clifftops right now. May I suggest we pop down to the village, establish a command post of some kind – perhaps the local village hall – and we can discuss the way forward and how we are going to have the body formerly identified. There's a lot to do.'

'Yes, absolutely,' replied Cullen. 'Let's do that.'

As the two men stepped away from the body, Boyd turned, winked at Bannerman and said, 'Catch you later. Antonia, care to join us?'

'But of course.'

'And you are?' asked Cullen.

'Cold and ready for coffee,' smiled Antonia as she led the way across the beach. 'Sometimes I even double as Boyd's secretary.'

'Ahh! A civilian,' replied Cullen. 'What an interesting job you have. I presume you must love working in the CID. Part-time or voluntary?'

'Oh yes,' enthused Antonia smoothing her red hair into a more disciplined position. 'It can be very interesting working for someone like Mister Boyd and, seeing as you asked, I'm fulltime salaried. I'm even allowed to claim expenses.'

'Really,' replied Cullen. 'That's amazing!'

Taking a sideways glance at Antonia, Boyd squinted and shook his head as they left the scene of crime tent.

It wasn't long before the village hall had been turned into an incident room and the murder enquiry was moving at the required pace. The next useful piece of news was in the form of Detective Inspector Pitt who informed the lead investigators that a couple of artist's paintbrushes had been found in the search on the clifftops. Nearby, an easel had been found and there was paint on the grass as well as scuffed grass indicating the body had been dragged from one place and then thrown from the cliffs.

Pitt argued that he had discovered the place where the deceased had been painting prior to her death and the killer was probably a strong man.

Antonia agreed and added to the situation by informing the team that twenty-four hours earlier the winds had been quite strong across the cliffs.

Bannerman revealed the nearby lighthouse and foghorn station were closed to the general public. The next maintenance visit was scheduled in six months' time. There had been neither visitors, maintenance staff, or window cleaners in the area during the time scale being investigated. He also added that an examination of the RSPB observation cabins was taking place and local enquiries were being made of people who regularly used the facilities there.

With the incident room now alive with officers engaged on various local enquiries, Antonia approached Boyd and said, I've arranged to link into Ticker and do the necessary.'

'The Watch List?' queried Boyd. 'And everything else including the Operations Centre!'

'Exactly!' replied the redhead from the Security Services. 'We have a link to Ticker and the Operations Centre courtesy of a portal via the Manchester office. I'll be looking for any connections that people have with Cumbria and that will include family, friends and associates. Anything that links anyone in Cumbria to Islamic extremism and the nation's Watch List.'

'Don't forget to claim the odd coffee on your office expense sheet,' winked Boyd.

'Cheeky,' winced Antonia. 'I might even claim a champagne dinner if you don't behave yourself.'

'Excuse me! Ticker?' queried Cullen.

'I'll tell you about it on the way to see Mister Webb,' responded Boyd. 'Well, Ticker that is.'

'Oh! Thanks!' replied Cullen somewhat confused.

'Boyd,' whispered Antonia. 'I told you this crime scene thing wasn't appropriate for me. I should have stayed in London at the end of the 'phone.'

'True,' voiced Boyd. 'I thought a break from the big city might do you good. But now that you are here you can link in with Glasgow if you don't mind. We're behind the game in so many ways at the moment. We need a result and soon.'

'One thing,' challenged Antonia. 'Why are you going to see Cornelius Webb? Even I know there are more ways to identify a body than confront the husband of the deceased in the way you seem to be going.'

'What do you mean by that?' asked Boyd.

'The unit knows the man is under your skin at the moment, Boyd. Don't go off half cock and arrest him just because he's the deceased's husband.'

'What if he's left-handed?' proposed Boyd.

'Boyd!' snapped Antonia.

'Don't worry,' replied Boyd. 'You do Ticker. I'll do the rest. I'm not wearing my stupid head today.'

Boyd and Cullen readied themselves to set off for Penrith with the intention of delivering a death message to Cornelius Webb when Antonia quietly advised, 'That makes a change. Play nice, Boyd. You're going about this the wrong way and just might get yourself into a heap of trouble if you're not careful.'

Grinning, Boyd replied, 'As you are apparently my secretary could you book a table for four at that Saudi restaurant in the West End.

The name of which escapes me for the moment. You, me, Meg and Phillip?'

'Shakshouka?'

'That's the one,' nodded Boyd.

'You're being adventurous,' ventured Antonia smoothing her jacket. 'Your new friend if I remember right.'

'It's time to be adventurous,' smiled Boyd. 'You know what I mean. Plus, he's more than a new friend.'

'The man is weird,' observed Antonia.

'He is not weird,' countered Boyd. 'People are just like wine to him. Some he loves, some he hates. You just don't understand him, that's all. He is beneath your level of comprehension.'

'Well, the pair of you talk in code,' revealed Antonia. 'You need a victualler's handbook to understand the conversation between you.'

'My weird friend, as you call him, is ideally placed,' proposed Boyd.

'I'll make the reservation,' remarked the red-head. 'I'll leave the rest to you.'

The car doors banged tight and there was a sudden screech of tyres when Cullen and Boyd set off.

'All for poached eggs,' remarked Boyd.

'Pardon?' queried Cullen.

'Nothing,' replied Boyd. 'Just a meal with friends.'

As they travelled the A66 from Cockermouth towards Penrith, Boyd's mobile sounded. It was Anthea.

'We're all systems go here,' revealed Anthea. 'We've hijacked a school near the prison and the incident room is alive. Two men escaped from the prison. One is a well-known paedophile serving time. Well, to be precise, he was serving time. Not now! We've traced some CCTV from a speed camera showing him being thrown from the rear of a white Transit van. The Transit has the logo Riddrie Laundry on the side and it was used in the prison break. He was dead on arrival at the local casualty department and the van has been recovered in a layby a few miles from the M8 motorway.'

'You now have a murder scene by the looks of it,' suggested Boyd.

'Janice Burns has the bit between her teeth, Guvnor. A homicide team from Police Scotland is in charge and Janice is working with their commander whilst keeping our interests at heart. The vehicle used was stolen, fitted with false plates, and there's no such laundry in Riddrie.'

'Great, the Scot will be in her element, and she knows the language. What about Terry?'

'Sergeant Anwhari is with me,' replied Anthea. 'The other escapee is a Mustafa Abadi. Thirty years of age from Sana'a.'

'A Yemeni?' queried Boyd as Cullen snatched a lower gear and overtook a slow-moving wagon on the dual carriageway.

'That's right. He's on the Watch List that Antonia produced for us recently. Currently doing six months for benefit fraud but he's recently been listed for deportation by the Secretary of State.'

'Why wasn't he deported on arrest?' probed Boyd.

'He was in possession of what turns out to be a false passport. The man was arrested, convicted and imprisoned in the wrong name.'

'You mean there's been an almighty cock up in the criminal justice proceedings,' ventured Boyd. 'His fingerprints should have been checked against the system before a court appearance.'

'Absolutely,' agreed Anthea. 'I've lodged a formal complaint and instigated an enquiry with the prosecutor as to why the recognised protocols weren't followed. By the way, Mustafa is his real name and not the name he was convicted in. According to our records, he's on the Watch List because of his allegiance to Al-Qaeda. We have his life story on Ticker. The bottom line is that he's a gunman suspected of murders across Europe.'

'Shootings?'

'Cold-blooded,' replied Anthea.

'Long range rifle or close quarter handgun?'

'Both! It looks like he's a quality marksman of the unwanted kind.'

'And we missed him because everyone took his word for it and no-one checked his details out,' proposed Boyd.

'Correct, not until his fingerprints were checked and his passport was sent to the Passport Office by which time the local Justices had sentenced him.'

'Brilliant!' mused an annoyed Boyd. 'The van?'

'We have a two-second burst of CCTV at the same speed camera complex that captures the victim being thrown from the back of the van. It shows the vehicle being driven by a seemingly blonde woman who is the spitting image of the Downing street assassin.'

'Probably wearing a wig then,' proposed Boyd.

'Agreed,' replied Anthea. 'She fits the bill for the woman spotted in the CCTV at Kennington tube station. We'll need forensic image analysis in due course.'

'The Downing Street assassin! Just what we don't need,' suggested Boyd. 'Anything else?'

'We're all over the van at the moment,' disclosed Anthea. 'It's been found abandoned. Forensics at the scene. Question for you?

'Go on?

'National appeal on television or police circulation only?'

'I presume we have Mustafa's photograph on file?' probed Boyd.

'Yes! It's fairly recent and shows him with a beard which I understand from the staff here has been shaved off since.'

'Good! Put an artist on that. I want a realistic draft of what he would look like without a beard,' proposed Boyd.

'Already actioned,' replied Anthea 'I'll have something within the hour.'

'Great! But the appeal to the public?' mused Boyd. 'We're damned if we do and damned if we don't.'

'True!' agreed Anthea.

'Right! Police circulation only at this stage – with the beard just in case he grows it again,' ordered Boyd. 'Difficult one, Anthea. If we blast their faces all over the media, they'll probably go into hiding and we won't get a sniff.'

'They're probably already in hiding now,' proposed Anthea. 'Or making for the ports and the quickest way out of the country.'

'He's already on the Watch List so that's covered,' remarked Boyd. 'Let's sit on it for a while and see what enquiries and search reveal. Question for you, Anthea?'

'Go on.'

'Why did the Downing Street assassin break a known killer out of prison?'

'Doesn't bear thinking about,' ventured Anthea. 'But I think we both know why.'

'Full alert to JTAC, please. The Joint Terrorist Analysis Centre need to be aware of at least two Islamic assassins on the loose. It's up to them if they increase the threat level. One more thing comes to mind, Anthea. All stolen and…'

'Hire vehicles! Yeah, Guvnor. We're already down that street.'

'Good,' chuckled Boyd. 'What about the bomb scene?'

'I have a team at work sweeping up all the debris and doing a fingertip search. Hopefully, we'll recover enough to identify bomb parts and reassemble the bomb. That might lead us to the bomb-maker.'

'Months down the line! Anything else?' probed Boyd.

'Not at the moment,' replied Anthea. 'I'll get back to you in an hour or so.'

Cullen drove around a roundabout as Boyd quickly updated Anthea on the St Bees murder.

'Where are you now?' asked Anthea.

'About to the break the news,' revealed Boyd. 'Good hunting!'

An Arabic radio station provided the music for two of Britain's most wanted.

'Careful!' advised the blonde.

'If you want to be useful, look out of the window or make me a drink,' remarked Mustafa. 'Just don't tell me how to do my job when my music is on. It reminds me of the Gulf and my home and helps me relax at times like this. You should remember that I was taught by the best. Go away. I'll tell you when I'm ready.'

'You've done it before then?'

Mustafa's eyebrows shot up and a look of scorn filled his face as he replied, 'Turn the music up.'

She did as she was told and saw him smile.

'Allah tells me that I should never answer to the lady who has no name. You said you would keep a lookout in case we had an unexpected visitor. Can I rely on you or not?'

Nodding, the blonde replied, 'Okay, okay. Get on with it. You just make me nervous, that's all.'

Threading a crucially thin wire through the handle of a shopping bag, Mustafa then inserted one end of the wire into the face of a wristwatch near the timing area which was governed by the movement of the brass hands. He then secured the watch in the bottom corner of the bag by using a hefty piece of bluetac which he covered with a pair of heavy duty gloves. Reciting the Quran as he worked, he then threaded the other end, upon which there was a detonator, through a hole in a plastic box before burying it deep inside a wad of plastic explosive.

Securing the plastic box, Mustafa said, 'Another one done. I need to attach it properly to the timer when we're ready.'

'Can you leave it that long? Shouldn't you do it now?' she asked.

'Well, if I activate the timer now the entire connection will go off within the hour and we'll both be fried. Why don't you just keep your nose out of my business and I'll keep my nose out of yours?'

'I'm just trying to keep you right, Mustafa.'

'You don't own me, woman,' snapped Mustafa.

'No, but the Caliphate does. Are you happy with the devices?' queried the blonde peering through the window.

'We're not in the desert where the enemy uses technology to defeat us. This is easy, basic, and covers my brief. These little soldiers will do exactly what is required of them. Any movement out there?'

'You're joking,' muttered his host. 'Even the clouds aren't moving. We're in the middle of nowhere and as safe as houses.'

The farm was slightly over five miles from the Clay Shooting Centre at Jawcrag, near Falkirk. There wasn't another vehicle or house anywhere to be seen. The only link to the outside world was the narrow tarmac lane that ran from the main highway three miles away and a never-ending line of electricity pylons that dwarfed their hideaway.

The blonde stepped away from the window and began checking the mechanism of various weapons as Mustafa placed the shopping bag on the table next to a collection of letters.

'When do we post our little surprises?' asked Mustafa.

'Once you've bought the stamps.'

'Very funny,' snapped Mustafa. 'I'll use the expenses you gave me. I don't want to fall out with you but when do we post our little demons?'

'When we're told,' snarled the blonde. 'Meanwhile, eat, drink, and help clean these weapons.'

Mustafa cast his eyes on the farmhouse table, counted the assault rifles and pistols, and enquired, 'Do you have an army for this lot?'

The blonde smiled but did not reply.

Opening the pages of the Quran, Mustafa took up his reading once more. He loved the Book, worshipped the content, believed passionately in what he read, and understood it to be his life.

Her mobile buzzed. She turned the music down and answered the call. 'Yes, we are all ready. Are you, my Sultán?'

The woman listened, scribbled some notes, closed her mobile and said, 'Now!'

The oak-panelled office was dominated by the biggest walnut desk that Boyd had ever seen in his life.

Looking down on the highly polished walnut, Cornelius Webb stared at his own reflection as he listened to Chief Superintendent Raymond Cullen deliver the bad news.

There was a sharp intake of breath when Cullen stopped speaking and the Chief wiped a tear from his eye. Taking a deep breath, Cornelius began inhaling and exhaling in quick time. The shock seemed to seep into his bloodstream when he suddenly clenched both fists and banged them hard on the desk.

Moving to a bar cabinet lodged in the corner, Boyd opened a door and scanned half a dozen bottles of Russian vodka before removing a bottle of whisky. He poured a tot, approached the Chief Constable and said, 'I see you have a desk twice the size of your predecessor, sir. Yet the bar remains in the same place. Sorry!' Boyd chuckled and immediately added, 'Rude of me I know but I know this office well. Forgive me, but I don't think banging on the desk will do you much good at a time like this. Perhaps you could do with a stiff drink. It might do you good.'

Cornelius Webb nodded and buried his head in his hands once more.

Glancing around the office, Boyd caught sight of a crucifix on the wall immediately behind where Cornelius sat. Measuring about six inches in length the wooden cross bore an old brass depiction of Jesus on the cross. At the top of the cross, the letters INRI were inscribed in a small brass plate.

'Perhaps the Lord will comfort you,' suggested Boyd. 'What do the letters INRI on the crucifix stand for, sir?'

'It's from a Latin phrase that means Jesus of Nazareth, King of the Jews,' replied the Chief. 'It's the notice Pontius Pilate nailed over Jesus as he lay dying on the cross. I take it you're not religious, Boyd?'

'Not really,' replied Boyd. 'Here! Knock this back.'

Sobbing uncontrollably for a moment, the Chief ventured, My wife! Are you both absolutely sure?'

'Sadly yes,' replied Boyd handing the glass to the Chief. 'I met her at Sellafield, as you know, sir. The local DI also recognised her from his days in Penrith. On the way here, a vehicle registered to her has been found in the St Bees area and a mobile 'phone in her possession has been proven to be hers. There are other connective issues that force us to come to you with this news. Indeed, DI Pitt was the first to alert us as to her identity. There's no doubt in our minds but we would, of course, like you to attend the morgue in due course.'

The Chief took the glass in his left hand and nodded his appreciation.

'Merely as part of the evidence chain,' interjected Cullen. 'A formal identification! You are the next of kin and her legal husband, I presume.'

'Yes! Yes, of course,' nodded the Chief sipping the whisky. 'I understand perfectly. Had she been painting?'

'Why do you say that?' enquired Boyd moving the bottle to the edge of the desk.

'It was her favourite place,' replied the Chief. 'She's painted that lighthouse a hundred times.'

'Yes, we've recovered her last painting from the beach,' revealed Boyd. 'There is, however, something you should know.'

'What do you mean?'

'We're treating your wife's death as suspicious,' imparted Boyd. 'Indeed, sir. I regret to inform you that we are following homicide procedures.'

'Murder?' queried Cornelius.

'Possibly terrorist-related,' added Cullen. 'We've found terrorist paraphernalia at the scene. Hence my request to Mister Boyd to help me with that side of the enquiry.'

Boyd threw a sideways scowl at Cullen and continued, 'I have an open mind at the moment. We're at an early stage in the investigation and it won't be long before I'm in possession of a forensic report detailing the cause of death.'

'I see,' considered the Chief. 'I'm afraid I'm not going to be much good to you, gentlemen. I'm shell-shocked at the moment. What will I do without her? I mean… I just don't know what I'm going to do. It's… It's…'

'When did you last see your wife alive,' sir?' probed Boyd.

'A couple of days ago, why?'

'Didn't it occur to you to report her as missing from home, sir?' questioned Boyd.

'No, it never occurred to me,' replied the Chief. 'Indeed, it wouldn't occur to me because she would often spend a night or two away when she was painting. Did you know she has her own website selling her wares? She's a professional artist. St Bees, Loch Lomond, and the Solway Firth were amongst her favourites. She'd book bed and breakfast somewhere and stay the night if she needed to.'

'I see,' nodded Boyd. 'I'm so very sorry for your loss, sir.'

Shaking his head, the Chief lifted his hands and began rubbing his forehead. Gently massaging his brow, he fought to hold back the tears before reaching for the bottle of whisky situated on the edge of his desk.

'No!' admonished Boyd gently. Resting his hand on the bottle, Boyd continued. 'I'm sorry but one drink to kill the mental shock is one thing but I have questions for you and I'd rather you were sober than under the influence.'

Cullen immediately announced, 'I'm sure such questions can wait until tomorrow, Chief Constable. They are not that important. We can only offer our sincere condolences. At times like this one seldom finds the right words. We are all quite devastated at the news, sir.'

Cornelius Webb glanced at both men before snatching the bottle from Boyd and rasping, 'It was you who got the whisky out, Boyd. Why don't you leave me alone for half an hour? Can't you see I'm upset?'

'Yes!' replied Boyd. 'And you know that the first forty-eight hours in any murder enquiry are often the most crucial. I need to know about friends, family, enemies, clubs, associates, shopping habits, her lifestyle – and yours. Sorry, but that's the way it is.'

'Tomorrow and not before,' argued the Chief.

'Fifteen minutes of your time now, sir,' proposed Boyd. 'It's important. You can help us clear some wood from the trees. Tell us about her movements. Why did she regularly go to St Bees? Did she ever meet anyone there that she told you about? Was she always alone? Who else knew of her journeys to that location? You can also assist us with links to people on her mobile phone, surrender her computer so that we can examine it, hand over any diary she may have kept. Was she under pressure from something or someone? You know the procedure, sir. These things need to be done. Perhaps I haven't presented things as well as I might or in a more timely and convenient manner to you, but I'm focused on the task ahead. It's all part of the job when you're a detective.'

'I'm not a detective. I'm a Chief Constable, Boyd.' Webb's left hand reached towards his neck and he began feeling the crucifix attached to a necklace. 'Cut me some slack and get off your high horse. I'm not a terrorist.'

'No, but I see you are left-handed,' remarked Boyd.

'Ambidextrous actually,' barked the Chief as he removed the bottle top with his left hand and then poured with the right. 'What's that got to do with it?'

'Nothing, just an observation.'

'Any other observations you'd care to make?' growled the Chief.

'Are you wearing a crucifix, sir?'

'Yes,' replied the Chief. 'Why?'

'Your wife was wearing one too.'

'Is it identical to this one?' enquired the Chief unbuttoning his collar to reveal a silver crucifix dangling from a silver chain. 'It should have her name on the back of it.'

'Yes,' confirmed Boyd. 'It's identical!'

'It's definitely Divine then,' remarked the Chief. 'We bought each other matching crucifix some years ago. Any other observations?'

'Just that we have politely informed you that your wife was found in a deceased condition, but you have never once asked how she may have been killed.'

'I'm still taking things in, Boyd. There's a lot to take in and my mind is not quite with me at the moment. They call it a shock. Now, if you don't mind, I'd like to make some telephone calls and tell a few friends about this.'

'No family to tell, sir?' probed Boyd. 'I mean your wife? Does she have close family other than yourself, sir? Perhaps a brother or sister? Cousins, nephews or a niece, for example?'

'Cullen!' barked the Chief. 'This is your case. Sit down. I'll be with you in a minute. You can fill me in on the detail.'

'Of course,' nodded Cullen rather exhilarated by the prospect.

'Boyd! Get out!' snapped the Chief. 'Your attitude stinks and I'm in no mood to answer your stupid questions at this precise moment.'

'I'm investigating a terrorist-related incident and I have national responsibility for such cases. With respect, I am the senior investigating officer in this case, not Mister Cullen.'

There was a quietness that descended on the three men before Cornelius Webb eventually broke the silence with, 'Only until I'm sitting in the national chair, Boyd, and thereafter, be assured, you will be out. We need people with a common-sense approach not a gung-ho charge of the light brigade attitude.'

'The charge of the Light Brigade was a success,' revealed Boyd. 'It only took a short time to reach its target.'

'But it was the wrong target, Boyd,' declared the Chief. 'From the very outset, it was the wrong target. Someone sent them the wrong way, and they paid very dearly for that mistake. Very dearly indeed! Do you understand what I'm saying, Boyd?'

'Oh, I hear you,' replied Boyd. 'Loud and clear, but tell me, did either of you have clandestine relationships with other people?'

'Boyd!' snapped Cullen. 'That's not appropriate.'

Ignoring Cullen, Boyd focused on the Chief and probed, 'A common question, sir. Were either of you having an affair with someone else? Was it a good marriage?'

'Very! Now please note I am complying with the investigation and will answer only to Mister Cullen. You may supply him with a list of questions, and I will provide him with the answers. I don't like you, Boyd. I don't like the way you carry out an investigation and I don't like the way you frame your questions. It is a choice I care to make. Meanwhile, your presence is excused. You wouldn't want to fall from your high horse whilst charging into the valley of death, would you?'

'You do realise this will put your application for the other job back?' suggested Boyd. 'It wouldn't be right to promote someone into one of the most important policing jobs in the UK when they are...'

'Suspected?' interrupted Webb.

'I was going to say suffering from shock,' replied Boyd.

The phone on the desk rang and the Chief reached out to answer it with his right hand as Boyd walked out of the room.

Closing the door behind him, Boyd felt the solid woodwork against his back when he leaned against it and exhaled deeply.

'The right target or the wrong target,' muttered Boyd. 'And how long before I reach the end of the charge down the valley floor?'

The Chief Constable's secretary approached and asked, 'Are you okay, Chief Inspector? You look as white as a sheet.'

'I'm fine, thank you, Jean. Just fine. I just have a gut feeling, that's all.'

Boyd stepped away and made towards the exit with his mobile in his hand talking to Bannerman.

'Bannerman! Chase up the work on Divine Webb. I want everything and I want it yesterday. Likes, dislikes, mobile phone contacts, email contacts, recent texts – make that all texts in the last twelve months – spin the deceased's drum and turn it upside down. Stocks, shares, finances, banks, boyfriends, foreign holidays, foreign contacts. Everything!'

'Does the Chief know about her death?' queried Bannerman.

'Oh yes,' replied Boyd. 'He knows now but he's not exactly helpful.'

'Are you sure it's not you and your overzealous approach, Guvnor?'

'Could be,' admitted Boyd. 'But there's something nagging at me, Bannerman. It's like sniffing in the air and knowing you're onto something but you don't what, why or when you're ever going to make a breakthrough.'

'You've got detective's fever, Guvnor,' suggested Bannerman.

'The key is Divine,' declared Boyd. 'But I don't know why.'

'I've sent you an email about the current state of the enquiry. What we've done, what still needs to be done, and some background. Leave Divine with me. I'll give it my personal attention.'

'Thanks, Bannerman,' replied Boyd. 'I need you in London with me tomorrow morning and I need an update from Anthea today. I'll ring you with the arrangements later. That reminds me, I have a date with Meg tonight. I'll hitch a ride back later today in Charlie Tango Charlie.'

The airwaves busied themselves as Boyd punched the buttons on his mobile and sought the team at Barlinnie.

Gliding to a halt next to a letterbox, the blonde driver looked across at her passenger, pulled the handbrake on, and said, 'This one will do. I can't see any CCTV in the area. Quickly now, we have a long way to go.'

Carrying a holdall, Mustafa stepped out from the dark grey Range Rover and looked about him. A moment later, he began feeding the post box with letters.

The car door banged shut when the vehicle drove smoothly away leaving the town of Berwick on Tweed in its rear-view mirror.

Later that night, Shakshouka was on the menu at an Arabic-designed piano bar in the west end of London. It had become a favourite for Boyd over recent months and it was to this establishment that he guided Meg, Antonia and her fiancée: Sir Phillip, the Director General of the Security Service. Within a short time, the group were seated in a private cubicle in a quiet corner of the establishment. An order for shakshouka was taken and polite conversation finally surrendered to shopping and fashion for the ladies and the latest good wines for the men.

'Remind me again,' probed Meg. 'What have we ordered?'

Boyd took a deep breath and replied, 'Shakshouka: A dish of eggs poached in a sauce of tomatoes, chilli peppers, and onions, commonly spiced with cumin, paprika, cayenne pepper, and nutmeg. Some Tabasco sauce and a smidgen of honey are also used. Or so the owner told me once. It became popular in Israel when the Jews were escaping from the Persian wars and the fall of the Ottoman Empire. Basically, they brought it with them to the west.'

'Poached eggs with bits,' nodded Meg. 'That's fine with me. Protein whilst on a diet is good. Hey! That's the same name as the restaurant.'

'Did I tell you my Arabic is improving,' announced Boyd. 'Shakshouka actually means a mixture of something.'

'I'd stick with learning about wine,' suggested Meg. 'There are too many spices to mix in this at home.'

'Whatever you say,' laughed Boyd. 'Wine it is then.'

157

'It doesn't matter how rich you become,' advised Sir Phillip. 'The best wine you will ever taste will be exactly as your palate dictates. In my case, it will be less than a twenty-pound per bottle palate even if I win the lottery tomorrow night.'

Chuckling, Boyd ran his finger down the wine list and settled on a bottle priced at £18. 'Okay with that one?'

'Of course,' nodded Sir Phillip. 'You can't beat a nice Barsac at any time of day.'

'Barsac!' lilted a friendly voice with a Turkish accent. 'Perhaps too sweet, gentlemen?'

'It will be fine, Yusuf,' indicated Boyd. 'Just the two glasses, please. Or are the ladies joining us?'

'Not for me,' replied Antonia. 'I'm driving.'

'Or me,' smiled Meg.

'You are well, Mister Boyd?' enquired Yusuf, the owner.

'I am,' replied Boyd. 'And yourself?'

'I am good. We are all good,' ventured the owner in a conspiratorial fashion. 'Despite all the bad news that I hear.'

'Bad news?' queried Boyd frowning.

Scribbling details of the chosen wine, Yusuf tucked the pen into his jacket and bent down saying, 'The Caliphate is not dead, Mister Boyd. It is just resting.'

'They tell me old wine rests,' suggested Boyd in a manner indicating he was sharing a secret with Yusuf. 'In fact, my friend, I'm told that the Caliphate is defeated. The wine, if it is a wine, has no life and soul. It is finished for the foreseeable future.'

'Only until the new wine arrives,' remarked Yusuf. 'And I hear it may already be here with others coming soon.'

Stepping away, Yusuf selected a tray, covered it with lace, and then engaged the wine collection.

'Wine?' queried Sir Phillip as he studied a suddenly concerned Boyd.

'A friend,' replied Boyd, his eyes narrowing. 'He tells me much about wine and has been proven to be correct on more than one occasion.'

'But not just about wine,' proposed Sir Phillip quietly.

'No, but the conversation is mature,' declared Boyd. 'As is the grape he speaks of. His vineyard has credentials.'

'I see,' frowned Sir Phillip. 'You've drunk from the well before then?'

'Yes,' replied Boyd. 'On a number of occasions recently.'

'I may well learn something then,' smiled Sir Phillip.

'Perhaps!' nodded Boyd before becoming a tad sarcastic in replying. 'Do you need to know? It may just be tittle-tattle or it may be something that you don't need to know. I mean, can you either confirm or deny that you really need to know about mature wines?'

Sir Phillip's hand rushed to cover his face and stifle a smile as Yusuf returned with the bottle, uncorked it, and at Boyd's invitation poured a taster for Sir Phillip.

A smile and a nod from Sir Phillip followed.

'Can you tell me about the old wine?' probed Boyd. 'Such things interest me as well you know.'

Yusuf gently stood back with the wine and routinely mentioned, 'Abu-Al-Ghamdi is dead. He is no longer one of the leaders in the wine industry, Mister Boyd.'

'He was killed in an airstrike,' replied Boyd softly.

Yusuf poured Boyd a taster.

'You are well placed to know such things, Yusuf.'

Yusuf nodded and remarked, 'There is a very old wine still in circulation, my friend. It's called Aishah and Ahmed. They are both trusted leaders, but they are also very scarce at the present moment.'

'From the Abid vineyard?' probed Boyd.

'You are also well informed, Mister Boyd.'

'But not as well as you,' replied Boyd.

Sir Phillip took a sip of wine as Antonia's alert system upgraded itself and she tried to listen to two conversations at once.

'Aishah and Ahmed Abdi,' she recalled. 'Two names from a convoy attack in Syria.'

'Both wanted for global terrorism,' remarked Boyd.

'The old wines need not be of interest to you, Mister Boyd. They are still in the Middle East resting in the caves, recovering from the sun, cooling their temperatures.' offered Yusuf. 'The wine will remain there, I assure you.'

Another waiter walked by and Yusuf pointed to the wine list, adopted a formal attitude, and advised, 'As I say, lovers of fine wines looking for an emerging adventure from the Middle East would do well to watch for wines from both Israel and Lebanon. They tell me there are some new Cabernet Sauvignons coming along nicely in the Bekaa Valley.'

'Yes, I read about that in the Times recently,' added Sir Phillip judiciously.

The waiter moved out of earshot allowing Yusuf the opportunity to turn the wine list towards Boyd and ostensibly advise, 'But I would beware of the new wine, Mister Boyd. When uncorked, it may well be not what you expect.'

'Jewish or Arab?' queried Boyd. 'I refer, of course, to Israel and Lebanon.'

'William,' spouted Meg with a chuckle. 'I did not know you were such a wine expert.'

'I'm learning,' replied Boyd with a smile.

Antonia's foot connected with Meg's toe. She pressed down.

'Ouch!' mouthed Meg.

'Leather!' ventured Antonia. 'I came across the most wonderful leather coat the other day…'

'You are interested?' continued Yusuf as he twisted the bottle and finished pouring the Barsac.

'I am always interested, Yusuf. But why do you tell me such things?' probed Boyd.

'Do you love your country, Mister Boyd?'

'Yes, of course.'

'And I mine,' replied Yusuf. 'Yet the lands of my father are nothing more than a billion acres of blood-soaked sand on which there stands hundreds of years of broken promises, decaying buildings, and war-torn lives destroyed by people who would sink lower than an emaciated scorpion lying under a rock waiting to kill the first non-believer it meets.'

Using a napkin, Boyd brushed his lips and tried to respond appropriately when he replied, 'I thought you were Turkish, Yusuf?'

'I was born in Syria but brought up in Istanbul, Mister Boyd. I have journeyed across the sands of time.'

'So, I hear,' replied Boyd. 'We could take a stroll in the park and sort the world out. Perhaps take some fresh air?'

'I have your number from last time, Mister Boyd. I will use it only if the scorpion threatens the wine.'

'Do you think that will be soon?' pushed Boyd

'I think it is now, my friend. A wine that has not been uncorked before in this country is making the rounds. It is very volatile, I understand.'

'Do you know its name?' questioned Boyd. 'Does it have a vineyard? Is there just one or are there others? How did you hear about the movement of such wine?'

'I know these things from listening to my contacts,' replied Yusuf.

'Contacts in your mosque presumably?' quizzed Boyd.

'Some, but mainly from those I meet regularly in the musalla,' explained Yusuf. 'In the musalla, I listen to those who think they would make a better Iman than the one who currently stands before us in the mosque. You know how it is, Mister Boyd. In the mosque, we listen to the Iman but outside in the musalla we use the shelter to gather, to talk, and to discuss the world around us. Here, in the prayer halls and gathering places where business between us is regularly discussed, we talk family, friendship and politics. Some of the younger ones talk about their favourite football teams and the best bands playing at the local music hall. We have singers, dancers, musicians as well as people house hunting or job seeking. I tell you this, there are a lot of normal people in my community, Mister Boyd. People who mean you know harm despite their differences in culture, religion and opinion. But I caution you, Mister Boyd, it is in the musalla that I hear talk of extremism from those who have wider contacts than I could ever imagine. Of course, we use the musalla to pray but we always find someone who has a better opinion, is wiser and wants to be heard by those who would follow and listen to the idiots amongst us. Privately, I call them 'mouths that talk with no brain'. They talk about a great Sultán coming to deliver the Caliphate soon. I laugh up my sleeve because my normal friends, as I have described them, have no interest whatsoever in the Caliphate. They just want to get on with their lives and be happy. Don't we all?

'Yes, we probably do,' agreed Boyd. 'The Sultán, Yusuf! Tell me what you know about this man they call the Sultán.'

Shrugging his shoulders, Yusuf responded with, 'He has been sent by the new leader – Aishah. Such people who talk in the musalla are not my friends. You must understand that, Mister Boyd. We are not all bad people.'

'The Sultán?' probed a galvanised Boyd. 'What do they say about him?'

'Not a lot,' replied Yusuf. 'Sometimes they make stories up in an effort to entertain us. I'm not sure if such a person exists, but I continue to listen.'

'To the people who have friends and family living abroad?' enquired Boyd.

'Precisely!' replied Yusuf.

'Do you get involved with them?' probed Boyd.

'No, I listen and remember,' replied Yusuf. 'I smile and nod and tell them that I am only a common café owner earning a living by selling shakshouka to the non-believers who live amongst us. I tell them that I fleece you of your money in return for eggs that were laid by a wretched chicken that died a week ago. They laugh at me and with me.'

'I bet they do,' chuckled Boyd. 'But do they know the prices you charge?'

Yusuf frowned but replied, 'I am nothing to them, Mister Boyd. They love it when I listen and nod in agreement with their words because they think I am a simple man who was born to follow the likes of them without question.'

'You are far from a simple man, Yusuf,' ventured Boyd. 'You are a very independent individual.'

'I try my best to change the world. One day, perhaps, things will be better for all of us.'

'I have an odd question for you, Yusuf,' indicated Boyd. 'I presume that the only people in the musalla are Muslims?'

'Of course,' frowned Yusuf.

'Do you know what I mean by Far-Right terrorism?' probed Boyd.

'I know that right-wing terrorists would like to overthrow the government and replace them with nationalist or fascist-oriented governments, Mister Boyd. Are you talking about neo-fascist skinheads, hooligans, youth sympathisers and those intellectuals who believe that the state must rid itself of foreigners like ourselves in order to protect the so-called rightful citizens of this country?'

'Yes,' nodded Boyd. 'I ask because both ISIS, the supporters of the Caliphate, and the Far-Right all have one thing in common. They all want to overthrow the state so that they can take power.'

'As I said, most of my contacts in both the mosque and the musalla are normal people,' replied Yusuf. 'Yes, they are Muslims, but they are not extremists like the ones you describe. Only a handful in our mosque is of concern to me. I cannot understand why you are asking me about the Far-Right though.'

Boyd feigned a slight smile and replied, 'Because experience tells me that some people who crave power will do literally anything to achieve it. They'll even get into bed with their enemy if it guarantees success. Some of them describe themselves as Christians but I might describe some of them as violent extremist Christians. I just wondered if there was anyone on the periphery making approaches to your group? It's unlikely, I know, but those who plan war often get their weapons from the same sources irrespective of their beliefs in Islam, Christianity, Communism, Nationalism, or whatever. They'll try and acquire their weapons from anyone in the business of selling. I'm just covering all the bases, Yusuf. That's all.'

'I'll bear it in mind.'

'Thank you,' said Boyd.

'News will come to me one day soon,' revealed Yusuf. 'I will hear something. I merely advise you to be on your guard from those who profess themselves to be from the religion of peace but are actually warmongers who see no value in a prolonged and lasting peace between our competing religions. I tell you this, you need to be very careful of the wine, Mister Boyd.'

Looking deeply into Yusuf's eyes, Boyd probed, 'Are we talking about a middle eastern wine?'

'From Syria is all I know,' whispered Yusuf. 'But it has a domestic flavour.'

'Meaning the grapes might be originally grown here but used elsewhere?'

'It would seem so.'

'You know more, don't you?' quizzed Boyd.

'No, but when I do, I shall let you know that the wine has arrived in London and is ready for tasting, Mister Boyd.'

'Thank you. It is important that the temperature of the wine is watched lest it becomes too warm and explodes in its bottle. Too volatile and the whole cellar will explode. We need to keep things as cool as possible,' ventured Boyd. 'Stay safe and stay in touch, Yusuf. And if you hear anything about a Sultán coming to town, please let me know right away.'

Nodding, Yusuf withdrew saying, 'Who knows? If the stories are true, there may be a connection.'

When they were briefly alone once more, Sir Phillip took a sip of wine and said, 'Some of your friends are quite interesting, William. Ahh! Here's the shakshouka at last.'

The waiters arrived and served hot dishes as Antonia glanced at Boyd and Meg before saying, 'Weird? Not weird, but it puzzles me that he's never asked for any money.'

'And probably never will,' replied Boyd. 'He loves to speak in code too. He's the owner of this restaurant by the way. It's certainly not a café when Barsac is eighteen pounds a bottle. I suspect Yusuf enjoys that deep inner feeling of being a spy of his own making and realising that everyone around him has absolutely no idea of his treachery.'

'As simple as that?' queried Sir Phillip. 'I think not.'

'And you would be right,' declared Boyd. 'From my seat, and his, he does not see himself as treacherous in the way that his culture might imagine. In his way, he is still fighting a battle for his father and his father's father. Deep inside his mind, he rejects the ideology of his previous upbringing and adopts a newer fresher ideology that he has chosen to embrace.'

'Such people are invaluable,' declared Sir Phillip. 'They are driven to do what they do because of their beliefs, their ideology, sometimes their revenge. I have met such people before. They are, as you say, independent in their mannerisms and way of life.'

'You mean he's with us now?' ventured Meg.

'Yes,' replied Boyd. 'He's changed sides. He's happier now.'

'It's equally important, Boyd, that we have investigators who are able to get inside the mind of the subject and recognise a potential that can be developed,' suggested Sir Phillip.

'I think it was you who lectured me in how to penetrate the target, Phil,' offered Boyd. 'It must have been a good lecture.'

'A lecture!' grinned Sir Phillip. 'Surely not!'

An egg fractured and a yolk spilt yellow across the brilliant white plate when Antonia remarked, 'Let's hope he stays onside then.'

'If the wine arrives, we'll make sure of that,' declared Sir Phillip. 'Keep me in the loop, William.'

*

8

SIS Headquarters,
Vauxhall, London
The following day.

Sir Julian Spencer K.B.E - Knight Commander of the Most Excellent Order of the British Empire - acknowledged the introduction of both Boyd and Bannerman when they were escorted into his office on the banks of the River Thames.

Six feet tall, the dark-haired Chief of the Secret Intelligence Service exuded supreme confidence aligned to a quiet air of mystery. He wore a dark grey suit, pristine white shirt and dark blue-grey tie.

'Good to see you again, Boyd,' remarked Sir Julian. 'And a pleasure to meet your Inspector Bannerman. Tea or coffee?'

'Coffee for me,' replied Boyd.

'And me,' added Bannerman.

The pleasantries continued for a short time before Sir Julian guided them into an area furnished with armchairs, a sofa, and a circular coffee table.

Finally seated, their host came quickly to the point.

'When Bannerman spoke to Mister Anderson recently a telephone call was made to this office. I took that call, Boyd. Prior to reaching the dizzy ranks of my current office of employment, I was stationed in the former Soviet Union. I monitored the recruitment and handling of British agents working against the Russian target. One of my agents was a Mister Anderson to whom Bannerman produced a document marked OSM/7.'

'Thank you for that,' nodded Boyd. 'Hence your request for this meeting.'

'Correct!' replied Sir Julian. 'It might seem unusual to you, Boyd but I am aware that you are currently investigating the terrorist-related murder of Divine Webb and, as a result, I drew the conclusion that you may be interested in the name Cornelius Webb which appears on the OSM/7 list.'

'It does indeed,' agreed Boyd. 'Your information is impeccable. May I ask who the source is?'

'No, you may not,' replied the host.

'Am I to presume therefore that our unit is bugged?'

'Don't be ridiculous, Boyd.'

'Okay! I think I can guess where this came from,' proposed Boyd. 'Tell me, is there anything we should know about the name? Have you convened this meeting to tell us about the Cornelius Webb we know or the Cornelius Webb that appears in the list? Are they both the same man, Sir Julian?'

'Ah! That is indeed the question, Boyd.' Sir Julian checked his wristwatch and added, 'Sherry? Either of you? It makes a nice accompaniment to coffee and we need to break the ice, I sense.'

Bannerman followed Boyd's lead when the head of the Special Crime Unit nodded and Sir Julian poured sherry.

Placing the drinks on a table before them, Sir Julian asked, 'What did you make of Anderson, Mister Bannerman?'

'Helpful,' replied Bannerman. 'Eventually.'

'No disrespect, Sir Julian,' intervened Boyd. 'But why have you really invited us here?'

'Do you have information that a man using the name Cornelius Webb was recruited by Russian Intelligence to work for them against this country?' probed Sir Julian.

'Do you realise,' countered Boyd. 'That you introduced the conversation with Divine Webb's death and intimated our enquiry into the OSM/7 document was kick-started by her murder. That is not the case, Sir Julian, and you must know that our interest in OSM/7 precedes the death of Divine Webb. We're supposed to be on the same side but right now we're not even on the same wavelength. What's this all about?'

Studying Boyd quizzically for a moment, Sir Julian leaned back, grimaced, and replied, 'Donald Anderson is strongly suspected of being a double agent. Now, bearing in mind what I am about to tell you, I must remind you both that you are signatories to the Official Secrets Act and…'

'Do us a favour,' interrupted Boyd. 'We handle secrets every day of our working lives – as you do. Tell us about Donald Anderson, Sir Julian. That's really why you wanted us here, isn't it?'

Smiling politely, Sir Julian took a sip of sherry, returned his glass to the table, and said, 'You really are a hardboiled hardnosed individual, aren't you, Boyd?'

'If that's what you've heard,' remarked Boyd. 'I acknowledge that your sources are impeccable.'

'My problem is that I know that you are the last signature required on a certain vetting form,' revealed the SIS Chief. 'Once you have signed that form it will be rubber-stamped and you will kickstart a very short procedure that will ultimately see a certain individual becoming the national police lead for counter-terrorism in this country. That postholder will immediately have access to matters that originate – not only in our own country – but in America, Australia, Canada, Europe and elsewhere. I don't need to tell you, Boyd, that counter-terrorism and counter-espionage work are often closely related to each other depending on where the target is located. And that's where I come in, Boyd. This organisation has a remit to watch over matters developing on the global horizon. Hence, my interest in the candidate.'

'Cornelius Webb, once the current post-holder moves on and I believe that is soon,' nodded Boyd.

'Sooner than you think, Boyd,' revealed Sir Julian. 'The present incumbent tendered his retirement papers a week ago and Sir Edward, the current leader in the North West who was expected to step up to the mark, has decided to take early retirement due to concerns about his personal health. Your Chief Constable – Cornelius Webb – has jumped from the third horse in the race to the only horse in the race and he is about to become the national lead as a result.'

'Provided I sign his vetting form and you don't want me to do that, do you, Sir Julian?' quizzed Boyd. 'Otherwise, we wouldn't be having this conversation in your office where it is easy for you to indicate we were discussing all manner of things – not just Cornelius Webb. The alternative, of course, is that I am conveniently removed from office but then I know too much, Sir Julian, and you know my pedigree inside out.'

'It's not my job to do your job, gentlemen, and I have no formal remit to advise you on such matters, but it's like this,' explained Sir Julian. 'What Anderson told you was true but then again it might have been a pack of lies.'

'He seemed quite intent once he had permission to speak to me,' related Bannerman.

'Yes,' replied Sir Julian. 'And I note that when I asked you before you told me he was eventually helpful.'

'He was.'

'The full story is as follows,' intimated Sir Julian. 'It is true that Donald Anderson was the manager of the hotel in St Petersburg. It is also correct to say that we recruited him so that we could use his position to access the hotel, the hotel guest list, and the profiles of those Russians who visited and worked in the hotel. Matters were of specific interest to us when we blew the KGB's cover story and learnt that those conferences had nothing to do with antiques, travel, technology or whatever. We are aware that over a dozen such conferences were held and that they were hosted by senior officers from Russian Intelligence. Their motive was quite simple really. They set up the conferences in order to recruit British people into the Communist Party.'

'To spy for Russia?' queried Bannerman.

'I'm sure that was the eventual goal,' suggested Sir Julian. 'It would be a sensible thing to recruit people into the party whilst they were in Russia and then move closer to them once they had been assessed. We are aware that some of those at these conferences subsequently joined the Communist Party and at least two of them then began giving information to the Russians.'

'It's not illegal to join a political party,' remarked Bannerman.

'Correct,' agreed the host. 'But our colleagues in MI5 have always been concerned by the threat of Communist and Trotskyist subversion. The government are more concerned when their policies are attacked by people whom they label subversive. It's no secret that British Intelligence has often disagreed with the government over the meaning of subversion. Political parties in power in Britain often presume that subversion equates to activities which threaten a government's policies. That is not the case at all. Subversion is a systematic attempt to overthrow or undermine a government or political system by persons working secretly from within.'

'Are you saying that the Russians in St Petersburg were recruiting people to subvert the government?'

'It may seem so,' admitted Sir Julian. 'But there were no government members in attendance at these meetings.'

'The Latin root of subversion,' explained Boyd. 'Is subvertere, which means to turn from below, or in such cases of real subversion – from within.'

'Precisely,' acknowledged Sir Julian. 'And that brings me to the problem facing us. OSM/7 names various people as staying at the hotel and attending a conference.'

'Did that include our Cornelius Webb?' probed Boyd.

'His name is on the list but the true answer is yes and no!' pondered Sir Julian. 'Donald Anderson told you that he sent us twenty years' worth of documents. Actually, he sent the last OSM/7 only a couple of months ago.'

'I hope you are going to tell me that an agent – or a double agent – did not access the Ticker Intelligence system in order to upload OSM/7,' probed Boyd.

'No! Certainly not but our authorised Ticker handlers did. We wanted to watch for a reaction from various quarters including the Russians. My problem is that it purports to be twenty years old. I am not in a position to verify that fact. We believe the details of those who attended may be false. You see, gentlemen, I am suggesting to you that a double agent – like Donald Anderson – has deliberately fed you, and us, wrong information. In a convoluted way, he has attempted to mislead you. It is a possibility that he has set us all up to believe that people on the list he has provided either harbour subversive tendencies or are spies working for the Russians. I put it to you that his masters are using him to deliver false information to us.'

'How do you know it's wrong?' probed Bannerman.

'Because over the years we have fed Anderson with false details ourselves. Using other methods and sources, we eventually learnt of his misgivings and moved to the belief that the Russians had recruited him to work against us whilst he was in St Petersburg.'

'The insanity of complex espionage,' remarked Boyd. 'What a mess!'

'Absolutely,' agreed Sir Julian.

Boyd took a gulp of sherry, pointed at the bottle, and said, 'May I?'

'Please do,' replied Sir Julian who promptly topped up their three empty glasses.

Looking deeply into the amber coloured sherry, Boyd heard Sir Julian remark, 'Talk to me, Boyd. I'm turning the box inside out on this one. What do you make of it all?'

'It would be quite easy for someone like Anderson to feed you with false details,' considered Boyd. 'But it's not as if the Russians would know that years later Cornelius Webb might end up as Head of Counter-Terrorism in the UK. If you are sure the latest papers purport to be twenty years old but have actually been falsified by the Russians recently then it looks as if Donald Anderson is in a whole lot of trouble. Are these papers properly dated and audited digitally?'

'No,' admitted Sir Julian. 'That is one of our problems. Anderson's method of transmitting stuff to us is fraught with irregularities. One of which is that his digital mail went through a Russian-based server and his hard copy deliveries may not be as authentic as we would wish for. It's quite possible the Russians were monitoring the hotel long before we developed our interests there. They may well have manipulated some of the data and deliberately placed false information in the lists without his knowledge.'

'In which case, Donald Anderson might not be a spy but may well be a pawn in a game that he is not even aware that he is a part of,' suggested Bannerman.

'It's possible but I prefer to think unlikely,' replied Sir Julian. 'Another obvious problem that we see is Russia itself. The whole country has been controlled by the state security apparatus for decades.

Firstly, we experienced the KGB before a name change to the FSB. They can titivate it any which way they want but the reality is State surveillance is a fact of life. In every company, office, shop, block of apartments, housing complex, beach, park or street you'll find someone who works for the Federal Security Service.'

'I thought communism in the Soviet Union ended with Gorbachev?' queried Bannerman.

'It did and arguably things improved slightly for us under Yeltsin. But there's a lot of evidence to show that the bully boys from the KGB merely tweaked their operations and moved into organised crime, cybercrime, drug smuggling and fraud. You'll find many of them now in senior government posts running the country.'

'Including the current President,' argued Bannerman.

'Yes,' agreed Sir Julian. 'The point is the Russian State purports itself to be all lovely and fluffy to its people whilst the situation is quite different. They still ration food and shortages are commonplace. Only the powerful and elite are above all this. State surveillance continues unabated and it's an almost unplayable ground for us. The enemy is everywhere. In London, if you hear a Russian voice you'll probably just walk on by. On the streets of Moscow, and anywhere else in Russia, an Englishman is likely to be stopped, checked, harassed, and put under surveillance. That, gentlemen, is the truth of the matter and why what appears to be an amateurish way of obtaining intelligence in a hotel in Russia is a proven operational pathway. We are not blind in Russia but it is a dangerous park in which we play.'

Bannerman nodded his understanding and replied, 'We've got it quite easy here, haven't we!'

'Yes, we have,' agreed Sir Julian.

'Thinking alternative patterns,' probed Boyd. 'It may be the case that Cornelius Webb did indeed visit such a conference twenty years ago and Donald Anderson merely sent you a list of names that was actually correct. The Russians may not be up to speed on the fact that our Cornelius Webb is in line for the top job. Come to think of it, how would a hotel manager know that the likes of Cornelius had applied for the top job in counter-terrorism? Furthermore, I presume you've looked into the possibility of some kind of relationship between Webb and Anderson?'

'Yes, we have. There's nothing to report on that front.'

'How interesting!'

'Do you understand why I arranged this meeting?' enquired Sir Julian.

'Oh yes!' chuckled Boyd. 'It's the spying game alright and there are numerous motives for each of the patterns in play. I think I'd rather try the Rubik's Cube puzzle. It might be easier to understand.'

'Hence my problem, gentlemen,' surrendered Sir Julian

'Why not pull Donald in and question him?' suggested Bannerman. 'There's enough to haul him over the coals for an espionage offence surely?'

'Because we feed him with false information which goes back to Russia – either intentionally or unintentionally - and we need him where he is. It's a game, gentlemen and it's played out across the globe on a regular basis. The spying game, as you say, and the team who think they have won have often in reality lost.'

'And everyone in the world of espionage plays it,' acknowledged Boyd. 'Realistically, you don't really know if Anderson is in the Russian camp or not, do you?'

'The jury might be out on this case,' admitted Sir Julian. 'Personally, I think he's with the opposition.'

Boyd stood up and wandered to a row of photographs that were displayed on the Chief's wall. Each photograph depicted the image of a historic Chief of the Secret Intelligence Service.

'I wonder what they would make of it all now,' voiced Boyd as he perused the images.

'Things have changed?' suggested Sir Julian.

'No, they'd tell us to do what we do best,' countered Boyd.

'We do a lot of things well, Boyd.'

'I know you do. I have impeccable sources too. But these people are telling me there is one way to move things along,' revealed Boyd still staring at images from the past.

'Such as?' probed Sir Julian.

'Cornelius Webb himself.'

'What do you mean by that?'

'Who is he really? What makes him tick? What does he bring to the table that no other person of his apparent calibre does? Where is he now and what is he doing?' queried Boyd. 'I think it's time I opened another file.'

'Boyd!' whispered Bannerman. 'We haven't established whether or not the man on the list is our Cornelius Webb. It could be anyone or no-one at all. You're moving too fast and too far.'

'Or not far enough and fast enough?' proposed Boyd. 'The matter seems to have reached the dizzy heights of a complicated puzzle.'

'Dizzy heights? That reminds me,' observed Sir Julian. 'Your new helicopter, are you happy with it?'

'Yes! Why?'

'Marvellous view from such an aircraft, Boyd. Absolutely awe-inspiring. But let me show you a little toy of mine. It's a fly with six legs.'

'You're going to tell me it can tap dance,' chuckled Boyd

'Oh, no! it does much more than that,' revealed Sir Julian rummaging in a desk drawer.

'Where did you get it? Or is that a stupid question?' asked Boyd.

'From a toy shop, of course. Where else?'

'I was just wondering,' remarked Boyd glancing at Bannerman. 'This building is much more than just a collection of offices.'

The SIS man withdrew a mechanical device from a matchbox-sized metal box. He placed it on the fingernail of his index finger. Then, with a small and compact control unit in his other hand, he switched it on and announced, 'This is my latest little friend. It looks just like a dragonfly and I call it Odonata. It is so named because it is based on an insect belonging to the Odonata family.'

'Odonata!' queried Bannerman glancing at Boyd.

'A carnivorous order of insects which includes dragonflies,' explained Sir Julian.

'An elongated fly?' suggested Boyd.

'A fly has two wings, Boyd,' revealed Sir Julian. 'Dragonflies have four wings. This one uses two to fly and two to listen. Sound in stereo, would you believe. It's never been used operationally yet and it is earmarked for use against particularly difficult targets.'

'Fascinating,' remarked Boyd. 'But never been tested?'

'You never know when an opportunity will arise,' indicated Sir Julian.

'What range has she?' probed Boyd.

'Extensive,' replied Sir Julian. 'It can be activated up to three hundred and fifty miles from its target.'

'Why on earth would you want that?' queried Boyd.

'So that we can penetrate a hostile enemy state without ever stepping foot in it.'

'Of course,' replied Boyd. 'That's quite amazing.'

'Here, let me show you how it works,' offered Sir Julian.

As Sir Julian arranged his display, Boyd excused himself for a moment and used his mobile 'phone. He selected 'encrypt' and instructed the registry to open a file on his behalf.

'Restricted,' ordered Boyd. 'Omega Violet Eyes only. Non-digital. Authorised by myself. Case Officer myself.'

'All received,' replied a voice on the 'phone. 'And the title, sir?'

'CRUCIFIX. I'll provide content in due course,' replied Boyd. 'Whilst I'm on I need to draw SHEPHERD from the archives. I also need updated one-time passcodes for the Operations Centre. Can you assist?'

'Just a second, sir,' from the registry. A few moments later, the registrar replied, 'You have a security clearance but it's HAND CARRIAGE ONLY for SHEPHERD, Commander. Your requirements can only be accessed in the archives under standard security conditions. Passcodes for the Operations Centre will be personal issue on arrival.'

'Thank you,' replied Boyd. 'I'll be over shortly. Have a good day.'

Boyd terminated the call and turned his attention to Sir Julian and a device called Odonata.

'I wonder if this little thing would ever reach Cumbria?' suggested Boyd.

'There's only one way to find out,' proposed Sir Julian. 'Do you have a pilot's licence.'

'Not yet,' replied Boyd. 'But I'm keen to fly.'

The A1 was busy with traffic when Mustafa and his blonde driver headed south towards England. They were through Alnwick, Morpeth and entering Newcastle without a hitch and not a care in the world.

'How far to England?' asked Mustafa.

'This is Newcastle,' replied the blonde. 'We're already in England.'

'Newcastle!' remarked Mustafa. 'Then we're nearly there.'

'Not far to go,' replied the driver.

'I don't like big cities,' declared Mustafa. 'They're far too dangerous and it's never easy to get out of them if anything goes wrong.'

'Is that because you're wanted in Beirut, Syria and Ankara?'

'But they never knew about Nairobi,' laughed Mustafa. 'No, they hadn't a clue about Nairobi. But I still hate cities.'

Mustafa's chauffeuse studied the traffic ahead and replied, 'Take it easy, man. You can hide a thimble in any city and it will never be found. Relax, man. El Sultán told me you were one of the best and could be trusted to get the job done.'

'I am the best,' replied Mustafa. 'But I always get nervous just before the start of things.'

'Is Allah with you or not?' challenged the driver.

"Of course," barked Mustafa angrily. 'Allah is oft forgiving and most merciful. Peace be upon Him.'

'Good! Although I don't expect many disbelievers will appreciate the oft forgiving and most merciful.'

'Then, as the Book says,' offered Mustafa. 'We shall fight those who disbelieve him. Indeed. Allah does not like transgressors. We shall transgress against the transgressors.'

'Sounds right up my street,' revealed the driver. 'We'll be crossing the River Tyne soon.'

'The Tyne is a river, yes?' quipped Mustafa. 'Is it bigger than the Gulf of Aden? Or is it just a trickle of rainwater drizzling into the sea?'

'You'll see soon enough, Mustafa. Get your mind into gear. Life is nothing more than a theatrical performance and you're on next.'

'I'm on next,' chuckled Mustafa nervously. 'Nairobi! Did I ever tell you about Nairobi, my lovely? Now there's a story to tell. It all began…'

In the south of England, the drive to the home of SHEPHERD took Boyd slightly over an hour and a half.

Reaching the north Kent coastline, he guided the black Porsche Cayenne from the A299 and arrived at a detached bungalow standing in its own grounds on the outskirts of the town of Whitstable.

Boyd parked the Porsche and heard the soft rub of gravel beneath his shoes when he got out and turned to look at the grey swell of the North Sea in the near distance.

'William!' boomed a voice from the direction of the house. 'You're late. That's not at all like you.'

'Commander!' replied Boyd turning to greet the man. 'I'd recognise that voice anywhere. But the beard and moustache! You look younger than when you retired, boss.'

'I decided to shave,' chuckled retired Commander James Herbert: founder and first Commander of the Special Crime Unit. 'And I'm not your boss anymore. Everyone hereabouts calls me James.'

'Your family, Commander, are they all well?'

'Extremely! Thank you. My wife is looking forward to seeing you again. She's preparing a light meal before your return to London. But your phone call disturbed me, William. I'd prefer to walk and talk if you don't mind.'

'Of course not,' replied Boyd. 'You never did like conversations that might be interrupted. To the promenade, I presume or along the beach?'

'I take it you've never visited Whitstable before?'

'No, I haven't, James,' replied Boyd.

'There's no promenade, William, just a pleasant footpath to walk along. The beaches are very shingly here but there are some sandy areas close to the harbour. That's where most of the sunbathing takes place when the weather is good. Out there…' The host pointed out to sea. 'There are half a dozen second world war sea forts and further out you can see an offshore wind farm.'

'Plenty to take in,' remarked Boyd.

'And not the reason you came to see me,' ventured James. 'You pulled my file and that means you must have been promoted since I retired. Is my past in a blue box and am I still coded the shepherd?'

'You were always our shepherd, James,' smiled Boyd. 'And your blue box is huge. How are you coping with the stress of living anonymously?'

'Much better than I anticipated,' replied the retired Commander. 'You know the story I presume? The Security Service gifted me anonymity on retirement as they assessed the likelihood of an attack on my life was high. It won't be a surprise if I tell you that I accepted it for personal security reasons.'

'I tried to find you before I gained access to your file,' responded Boyd. 'But you've been rubbed out. You're not in the telephone directory. There's no trace of you anywhere, not even a passport or a driving licence. You've no national insurance number. No medical records. Nothing! I turned the haystack upside down and nothing fell out. You don't exist, my friend.'

'Oh, I assure you I do,' replied James. 'I have all the necessary documents with which to live. They're just in another name. The Service rubbed my previous identity out, as you say, to protect me from those who would like to say thanks for disrupting their lifestyles.'

'Terrorists, megalomaniacs, master criminals, fraudsters, assassins, killers, murderers! Yeah, I get the picture,' chuckled Boyd. 'Plus a few rogue States and a score or more terrorist organisations and organised crime syndicates from Colombia to Clapham and everywhere in between who would like to get their hands on the man who made it all happen.'

'Oh, no,' replied James seriously. 'I only guided everyone along the path. You people did the hard slog.'

'You are conveniently forgetting that you dreamt up the Special Crime Unit, argued for it, staffed it, and then went out and dragged in every professional crook and scumbag you could lay your hands on to make it work. Not content, you then developed the unit into what it is today. Have you any idea how many people you put away and organisations you destroyed? No wonder the State decided to protect you.'

'Well, I don't cost them anything now,' chuckled James. 'Only my family know the score and we're happy to live out the later years of our lives in relative anonymity. That said, we've discreetly made trustworthy friends in the area and things are well. We fill our days sailing around the forts or walking along the coast enjoying life in our late seventies. But I know what you mean, William. There are no public links to me in existence and hardly any private ones. I love being rubbed out.' He laughed but continued, 'If the truth be known they've just made it almost impossible to find me through public records.'

'You can say that again,' grinned Boyd. 'Anyway, boss. It's absolutely great to see you looking so well.'

'Before we start, William, I presume you are now Commander and I would like to offer my congratulations to you. I'm sure it is well deserved. If I learnt anything in the unit it was always to try and select the best and I think I achieved that when you joined us. Now tell me, are you enjoying opening these 'eyes only' files in the registry?'

'Thank you,' replied Boyd. 'I've not been in the Commander's chair that long and they didn't promote me. They're in the process of some cutbacks in the unit because Islamic terrorism has apparently been defeated on the battlefields of the middle east. I was a convenient option for the post of Commander when Superintendent Sandy Peel died suddenly and Commander Maxwell was transferred to Organised Gangs and Serious Crime.'

'Edwin has been transferred!' exclaimed James. 'I recommended him as my replacement and as for Sandy, I must confess I never knew her.'

Boyd shook his head and continued, 'Yes, that took us all by surprise, sadly. So I end up as the Commander of convenience but obviously not the choice of many it would seem.'

'Ridiculous in one way,' remarked James. 'There may not be a need to devote the same military resources if ISIS has been defeated but surely that needs a common-sense review of the situation. I'm out of the game, William so I wouldn't really know about the ins and outs of it all. That said, such top-level decisions should have more to do with the unit's workload rather than political or economic expedience. I do watch the News and have to say ISIS seems perfectly capable of mounting attacks throughout Europe. Did they imprison or liquidate everyone in ISIS? Did they seize their bank accounts and all their weapons? I think not. If not, where are they now? Who on earth makes these decisions concerning the Special Crime Unit?'

'A government living in cloud cuckoo land,' revealed Boyd.

'Yes, but they are usually inspired by an individual or group that are opposed to the normality of things,' suggested James. 'Do you have someone in mind or is there a subversive group in play that is working the puppets from the sidelines?'

'That's why I pulled the SHEPHERD file,' admitted Boyd. 'What I think about the matter is not generally supported by those with whom I work. They think I'm out of order and upset because I'm expecting to be recalled to Cumbria where they are going to promote me to Superintendent in charge of 'Ethnicity and Diversity.'

'A department which does not recognise your undoubted talents and ability to penetrate the target,' observed James.

'Something to do with community cohesion apparently, if ever there was such a thing. Anyway, I came to you for advice and guidance, Commander,' ventured Boyd. 'I have a conundrum for you. What I would like to discuss is such that I have no one to bounce off in the office now that you are gone. I can't slide into your office with two cups of coffee and go through a dozen different scenarios because you're not there. I need good counsel and I hope you don't mind.'

'William, it's James, not Commander but I take it you have opened a restricted file relative to this conversation in which you will record details of why you sought this counsel and what led you to me?'

'Not yet,' admitted Boyd. 'But I am aware that all restricted case files at Commander level contain the thought processes of the

Commander and why they reached the decisions they did in the operations they were responsible for. It's an individual dairy for every case really. It was your idea all those years ago and we still keep to it. Transparency and reflection in decision making, that's the way I understand it.'

'Good!' smiled James. 'You know the score in that respect so we can have an off the record chat about things until such time as you commence that file.'

'That's all I ask for,' revealed Boyd. 'I have two files I want to run by you. One is coded SULTAN and the other is CRUCIFIX. They are both conundrums I could do without.'

James Herbert – codename SHEPHERD - pursed his lips, looked at Boyd, and asked, 'Interesting! Or should I say puzzling? Your call mentioned a colleague I might know. Come on. Let's stretch those legs.'

The two men crossed the road and began walking towards Herne Bay as the sea churned against the military forts and an ocean-going vessel appeared on the horizon.

Smiling, James guided Boyd from the footpath onto the shingles. They walked along the beach as James remarked, 'Sultan?'

'It's the codename we have given to an ISIS fighter that we know was in Iraq. I believe he may have returned to England and has been appointed by ISIS as their regional commander. Alternatively, he may have appointed himself as the regional commander with the intention of inspiring returning fighters to band together and continue the fight on the streets of England. We really don't know what his true position is.'

'Ah! Sultan equals regional commander. Okay! Who is he?' probed James.

'We've no idea,' admitted Boyd. 'All we have is a grainy photograph from a drone overfly. Yes, we have odds and sods here and there but the bottom line is we are going nowhere with the enquiry and even if we had a name connecting him to recent events the available evidence will not be easy to tie him in.'

'Is he linked to the woman on the News? I see there is a search on for what they have dubbed the Downing Street assassin.'

'Not known at this stage although part of me is suspicious since she appears to be responsible for breaking a terrorist out of Barlinnie prison.'

'Liberated to order?' quizzed James.

'Possibly,' nodded Boyd. 'And more likely if there really is an ISIS regional commander now at work in the country.'

'I see,' replied James. 'Now tell me about Crucifix? Who and why?'

'Cornelius Webb! He's the current Chief Constable of Cumbria and is almost certain to be appointed as the National Head of Counter-Terrorism Policing in the UK.'

Stopping in his tracks, James remarked, 'Cornelius Webb! Who is the senior vetting officer? Who has the last signature on the vetting folder before it goes to the Commissioner and then to the Home Secretary for rubbing stamping? Is it still the Special Crime Unit Commander?'

'Yes! Me!' replied Boyd. 'Once it would have been yours.'

'If you have concerns about any matter why don't you take it up with the Commissioner? Surely that is the right route and not this one. All you've found here is an old-timer seeing out the rest of his days walking up and down the beach whenever it takes his fancy.'

'It's not that easy,' suggested Boyd. 'Let me tell you the whole story about both these investigations.'

'Do you really need to?'

'I'd like to because if I've worked out everything correctly in my mind then there are some big stepping stones ahead. That said, I might have got it all wrong. Only time will tell.'

'I see,' offered James. 'Let me see if I can help you then. Fire away!'

The two men turned, strolled aimlessly along the shingled beach, and felt a cold wind moving in with the new tide as Boyd recounted recent events concerning his appointment, the Divine Webb murder, the mysterious man in a drone photograph, and the future he was considering.

Half an hour later, turning, the two men made their way towards the house with James advising, 'To summarise, William, I knew him only when he was a Detective Inspector in Hackney. His team did not like him although, to be fair, they always responded with good results. I did not take to him, Boyd. For me, Cornelius Webb was a rubberstamp armchair warrior who took all the credit when something went right and was the first to criticise anyone and everyone if something went wrong.'

'A growing breed?' suggested Boyd.

'I'm sure he wore hobnail boots at times, William. Handy for trampling over people. Yes, I fear there was something amiss but I never knew what. He was more interested in himself than others but that is not unusual. I think he was less capable than many around him considered him to be. He was one of those who seemed to get on in the job because successive department heads didn't take to him and moved him on with recommendations for further development. You know how it is. You never want to lose your best but gladly recommend those you want to get rid of. It's the oldest management trick in the book. I suspect Cornelius Webb was clever enough to transfer this bad management tactic into promotion capability when being formally interviewed for higher status jobs. I don't really know. It's just a thought that occurs to me.'

'How about religion? Did he have any strong beliefs in that field?'

'Not that I was aware of but, come to think of it, he always wore a crucifix around his neck. Yes! Yes, of course. That's why you named his file CRUCIFIX, isn't it? Well, I do recall that his parents were devout Catholics. His father was initially an Anglican priest who converted, after marriage and the birth of their only son, to Catholicism. His mother eventually took holy orders later in life. That will be in his personnel file surely.'

'Yes, it is, but did he ever mention Russia?' queried Boyd.

'You mean is he loyal to his country?'

'If that sounds better, then yes,' replied Boyd.

'Not sure,' replied James. 'I say that because I was never aware of his political views and have no evidence, either way, to sway you on that one. I once heard that he had shares in a few Russian oil companies but that was just tittle-tattle in the Officer's Mess and it's not illegal to make such investments.'

'A holiday in Russia perhaps?'

'Not that I know of Boyd.'

'Divine, how did he meet her?'

'I've no idea,' replied James. 'But that won't take you long to find out by normal investigative methods. I'd suggest he met her on the social circuit such budding senior officers seem to somehow latch onto as they progress through the job. The majority of Chief Constables, for example, attend some kind of social function on behalf of the job three or four times a week. I presume there's a marriage certificate in being somewhere?'

'I'll know the answer to that one soon,' proposed Boyd.

On reaching the house, Boyd joined James and his wife for a short refreshment period before continuing his journey.

Later, as Boyd bid farewell, he said, 'Thank you, James. It's been lovely to see you and I am grateful for your counsel.'

They shook hands but former Commander James Herbert held onto Boyd's hand a moment longer and said, 'The Sultan! To catch this man you may need to think like him and connect the Downing Street woman to the suspect in some way. From what you tell me there is bound to be a connection of some kind between the two. For too long, we have paid far too much credence to the computerised intelligence system. There are times when we need to step back from the computer and think outside the box. You should never follow the computer records blindly. You were a detective before you were a reader of computer screens. Never forget that, William. Once, you worked things out by good old fashioned policing without a computer being anywhere in sight. Perhaps you need to pretend there is nothing to help you. Where would you start? Secondly…'

'Go on,' replied Boyd. 'I'm listening.'

'Earlier, you asked me about loyalty to one's country.'

'Yes, I did,' nodded Boyd.

'Do you recall the old motto of the Anti-Terrorist Branch, William?'

'The bell, book and candle?'

'Yes, that one,' nodded James. 'It traces back to a method of excommunication from the Catholic church for one who had committed a particularly grievous sin. It involved a Bishop with twelve priests reciting an oath to an altar.'

Boyd continued, 'We separate him, together with his accomplices and abettors, from the precious body and blood of the Lord and from the society of all Christians. We exclude him from our Holy Mother, the Church in Heaven, and on earth. We declare him excommunicate and anathema. We judge him damned with the Devil and his angels and all his reprobate to eternal fire until he shall recover himself from the toils of the devil and return to amendment and to penitence.'

'Then the Bishop would ring a bell to evoke a death toll,' continued James. 'Close a holy book to symbolise the excommunicate's separation from the church and snuff out a candle or candles knocking them to the floor to represent the target's soul being extinguished from the light of God.'

'I never could fully understand it and always got shivers all the way up my spine when I read it,' grimaced Boyd. 'Why do you ask?'

James grinned and ventured, 'It took only the Bishop to end things.'

'To end things? Oh, I see,' puzzled Boyd before his face cracked a huge grin. 'I guess I will have to be the Bishop then. Well, I must be going. Take care and stay safe.'

Moments later, Boyd fired the Porsche and headed east towards Canterbury.

Simultaneously, a blonde-haired driver and her male passenger pulled into a lock-up garage in the north east of England. She shut off the car engine and walked to a brick wall at the far end of the building. There, the woman perused the various tool racks and wooden cupboards that adorned that part of the building. She used a key in her possession to open a locked metal box fixed to the wall. Reaching inside, she withdrew a thin notebook and flicked through the pages.

'Phone numbers,' she remarked. 'We're another step closer.'

'That close,' mused Mustafa. 'We're going to be busy, my lovely. Very busy! By the way, how many wigs have you?'

'Enough to change regularly,' voiced the blonde. 'If we were ever discovered on CCTV, Mustafa, it will slow the police down when they are looking for a blonde, then a mousey dark brown-haired woman, and now...' She donned an auburn coloured wig and offered, 'Another one. If I were a Christian, I would tell you that I am Jacob with a coat of many colours, or to be precise, a head of many colours.'

'You crack me up,' offered Mustafa. 'Have you got a spare?'

'No!'

In London, a grey Mercedes Benz bearing diplomatic plates pulled out of the main gate of the Russian Embassy situated in Kensington Palace Gardens and turned north. A nearby remote covert camera relayed the image of the vehicle and its driver to MI5 headquarters. The details were logged along with all the other movements of diplomatic vehicles of interest in the capital. The Mercedes travelled north towards the M1 motorway. The vehicle contained one male driver who was known to the Security Services as Mikhail Korobov: an officer who was suspected by them as being a member of the GRU – the foreign military intelligence agency of the General Staff of the Armed Forces of the Russian Federation.

Posing as a trade and industry diplomat, Mikhail Korobov was said to be 'of interest' to the Intelligence Community.

When Boyd skirted Canterbury, he had the cathedral in sight but chose to navigate inland to where only a handful of small villages clustered together.

Checking the satnav, Boyd braked and turned left down a nondescript narrow tarmac lane. He noticed that the hedgerow to his nearside had eventually petered out and had been replaced with a double palisade metal fence that stood over twelve feet high. At the end of the fence, a secure gateway beckoned.

Boyd slowed to a standstill, lowered the car window, and presented his security clearance card to the digital monitor. A green light flashed, and Boyd tapped a sequence of numbers into the control monitor.

Moments later and the gate opened allowing Boyd to enter the complex.

Driving slowly forward, Boyd took in a selection of half a dozen antennae that sprouted from the roof of a building before him. The anomaly was that his location was the same height above sea level as the antennae.

The road swung left into a hairpin bend and descended below ground very swiftly. Within seconds, Boyd found himself at another security gate which was monitored by CCTV and a similar entrance methodology. It was dark and lit only by one spotlight which focused on the vehicle and driver. Scanning his card, using a different set of numbers, Boyd unlocked the security system and gained access to the underground facility. Parking close to a lift, Boyd soon found himself descending further. The lift opened and he stepped into a corridor.

'Welcome to the Operations Centre,' voiced a middle-aged man dressed in trainers, denim jeans and a denim shirt. 'Your first visit and I have to say much sooner than your two predecessors managed.'

'Good to see you, Reg,' said Boyd extending a handshake. 'I've heard so much about this place but never knew your location. Now I know why.'

'We're a top-secret telephone interception unit, Boyd,' replied Reg. 'It's the location that is top-secret not necessarily the job we do. Everyone who has ever read a spy novel knows about telephone tapping. A quick tour before we discuss the reason for your visit?'

'Sounds great,' replied Boyd. 'How do you know I have a specific reason to visit today?'

'I don't,' replied Reg. 'I just know that the Operations Centre comes to the fore when a problem arises and someone wants the impossible done. Come on!'

Accepting a guided tour, Boyd stepped in line with Reg and strolled to an observation platform where he took a seat.

'This is the Operations Centre, Boyd. Here, under Home Office warrant, we listen in real time to both landline and mobile telephone conversations that we know belong to our various enemies. Espionage or terrorism today, Boyd?'

'Terrorism!' replied Boyd.

Reg pointed to a sizeable part of the Operations Centre below them and continued, 'I currently have three team leaders and thirty operators intercepting slightly over three hundred telephone lines or mobiles in the UK, Boyd. They listen in real time, record everything that is heard, and are even able to rerun tapes seconds after the initial recording in case they experience simultaneous calls.'

'So, you haven't got three hundred people listening to three hundred conversations all at the same time?' probed Boyd.

'No, but technology allows us to cover three hundred conversations in as real-time as you could ever imagine, and that number is increasing all the time. Before you ask, Boyd,' remarked Reg. 'We have your Watch List covered and each section has a case officer who, when appropriate, has a direct link into your office and the Ticker system.'

'Yes, I know about that,' acknowledged Boyd. 'Your unit is a crucial part of our operation, but your location is secret and I can see why. There is, however, one thing I want to know.'

'If I can help you, I will,' ventured Reg. 'But are you sure you have the right place and not GCHQ in Cheltenham?'

'They can of course help in a big way, Reg but you guys are in real time and live. They're not sweeping stuff out of cyberspace and analysing it at the same time. Your section is able to define a specific area – such as London – and monitor it in real time. Cheltenham has slightly different protocols. I think the Operations Centre is exactly what I want.'

'Okay, what can we do for you?'

'I want to know if you recognise call patterns,' explained Boyd. 'Who talks to who and when? Who makes most calls and who seldom calls? I want real-time analysis for an operation I'm planning. Does that make sense?'

Reg turned to a computer console and rattled his fingers over the black and white keys before pointing to a larger screen fixed to the wall.

A video recording began.

'Yesterday's call patterns,' explained Reg. 'Each white dot represents a target on your Watch List. Each yellow directional line is a call from one target to wherever. Each red directional line between the white dots is a call between two targets. I can use the system to tap into anywhere on the map and it will bring me a recording of the conversation plus the names of the targets we are interested in together with a link to an intelligence report submitted by a case officer. Does that help?'

Boyd stood up, studied the flashing images before him, and said, 'You bet it does. I didn't know you could do that. It's mind-boggling and it actually reminds me of one of those sci-fi films where a nuclear war breaks out and the computer shows all the nuclear strikes in play.'

'Pretty cool analysis,' admitted Reg. 'Most of the time these people of interest are merely that – just of interest and no more. Most of them live insignificant lives whilst others have more enthusiastic lifestyles. They're not planning war every day of the week. You get to know about the ones our in-house case officers raise to you. It's all about intelligence gathering and sharing, Boyd, and fortunately, the Operations Centre has always had a good relationship with your unit.'

'Pleased to hear it,' replied Boyd. 'How long do you keep the recordings?'

'Twelve months initially and then the case officers prune them in or out. It really depends on the severity of the case, how interested we are in the targets, and what the content is. Some of our files go back more years than I care to mention. We try to apply common sense whenever we can.'

'Great stuff,' remarked Boyd. 'Now tell me this. A new player is about to arrive and disrupt your video presentation. He's not on the Watch List and we don't know who they are or where they are. What we do know is that our man has a list of people he is going to activate in the war that he plans.'

'My God!' exclaimed Reg. 'Armageddon?'

'How do we stop him?'

Reg stared at the screen searching for an answer.

'I'll put it another way,' suggested Boyd. 'Hypothetically speaking.'

'You're not famous for the hypothesis, Boyd,' frowned Reg. 'Give me the worst-case scenario.'

Boyd pursed his lips and said, 'I'm feeling this in my bones, not working it out with evidence. Hence, it's hypothetical but I need the answer. How quickly can you notify us that specific targets – your white dots – are all receiving telephone calls from the same would-be master of a self-proclaimed Armageddon who is not known to us? He's about to raise his army to take part in an all-out attack on London?'

Reg stared directly at Boyd, studied the screen, and proclaimed, 'I think I need to write a new computer program, Boyd.'

On a lay-by close to Police Headquarters in Penrith, Cumbria, the driver of a mobile home stood at the rear of the vehicle manipulating an electronic console as he studied the skies above.

A police patrol car pulled up and two male officers got out of the vehicle and approached the man.

'Is that a drone you're controlling?' asked the older officer brusquely.

'Why do you ask?' replied the man politely.

'Because you are parked next to a complex where the police, fire and ambulance services operate, that's why. Drones have a bad habit of interfering with radio communications apart from invading secure areas to which they are not welcome. Let me see that console?'

The man flicked a switch on the device and said, 'This? Oh, I see what you mean, officer. No, it's not a drone flight controller. I'm a radio ham. You know - an amateur radio enthusiast.'

'No way,' voiced the younger officer. 'I've heard about people like you but never met one.'

'Well you have now,' replied the radio ham with a huge grin. 'Did you know that right now I'm listening to the pilot of a British Airways aeroplane who is flying at close to thirty thousand feet above us. He's about to contact the tower at Glasgow. It's the evening flight to Aberdeen. Listen!'

The device spewed out a deluge of electronic cackle before a sharp yet relaxed voice radioed, 'Bravo niner-sierra-papa, heading two-seven-zero, cleared to Aberdeen and maintaining twenty-five thousand feet. Entering your control area and wishing you a good evening.'

'Good evening, Bravo niner-sierra-papa. Maintain course and altitude...'

The conversation continued and the younger police officer looked to the heavens and said, 'Up there?'

'Do you see it?' probed the radio ham.

'What else have you got in your vehicle, Mister Radio Ham?' inquired the older officer. 'I want to know what you're doing here.'

'It's just about to break cloud cover now,' replied the radio ham ignoring the remark. 'Over there.' He pointed to the south and continued, 'You can just make out its flashing lights.'

Peering skyward, the younger officer replied, 'Yeah! Yes, I see it. You're not chasing it to Aberdeen, are you?'

A chuckle followed by, 'No, not in this old jalopy.'

The older policeman strolled beside the van and asked, 'Is that a computer console you have in there?'

Detecting that the more experienced officer was being nosy, the radio ham slid the side door open and said, 'Yes, it is. Take a look if you feel the need. I do podcasts for an aviation website. Once I've recorded a few of these conversations between pilots and air traffic controllers, I'll transmit the results to the audience. You'd be surprised how many people listen to my stuff online.'

'Really?'

'Yes, really.' The radio ham reached inside the vehicle and removed a selfie stick and camera before suggesting, 'Hey! Great idea! Can I take a photo of you both with the police car in the background?

'Well, I'm not sure we ought to do that,' from the older one.

'Absolutely...' from the younger one. 'Will we be in the podcast?'

'Of course, you will.'

'Me! On the internet?'

'Yes!' replied the radio ham. 'In fact, all three of us and the police car if we can use this selfie stick the right way. Come on. This is going to be fantastic. The podcast could go global with you guys involved.'

'I'm not so sure,' decided the older officer warily.

'It will take two minutes and then I can get back to listening to my aeroplanes and preparing my podcast. It will be a massive audience tonight. You can be sure of that. What do you think?'

The younger officer began to pose but his colleague realised he was losing the thrust of the conversation and announced, 'No way! Come on! We're done here. Just move your wagon elsewhere.'

'You're a spoilsport,' quipped the younger policeman.'

'Shut up and get in the car, junior. You're driving.'

The radio ham lowered the selfie stick before placing the equipment inside the caravanette. He laid the selfie stick and phone camera on a table next to a well-thumbed paperback book, a pair of sunglasses, a wallet, a bandana, a copy of the local newspaper, and an empty coffee mug that was crying out for a good clean.

'Look,' explained the radio ham. 'I'm here for the night listening to the pilots. It's my hobby and I love what I do. If I'm in the way I can soon move to the caravan park in Eamont Bridge if you'd prefer.'

'Would you mind?'

'Of course not. I'm used to you guys asking questions about drones and stuff. The radio receiver is just a mobile device that is tuned into the aviation frequencies but it's quite powerful and completely legal. Give me a couple of minutes and I'll take off. Well, not take off,' he chuckled. 'As you can see, I'm no pilot, but I once flew economy class to Paris for the weekend. No, I'll move to another patch and then everyone will be happy.'

'Fine! That's fine!' nodded the officer. 'Have a good night and thank you.'

The police happily returned to their patrol car as the radio ham closed down his electronic device and slid the doors on the van closed.

The police patrol car drove off.

Fifteen minutes later, the radio ham swung his vehicle into an all-night caravan park on the road to Ullswater. There, he recommenced operations away from the prying eyes of the local police force.

In a sorting office in Berwick on Tweed, John McCorrie: a postal worker, emptied a sack of letters onto a table where the mail was separated into various postcodes for further delivery.

Hundreds of envelopes fell onto one another and spilt from a growing mail mountain towards the end of the table.

One letter slipped to the floor, began to discolour, and seemed to be alive.

Bending down to retrieve the item, McCorrie realised there was something wrong when the envelope gradually charred, turned black and began to burn.

'What the hell!'

There was a sudden flash when an unidentified chemical inside the envelope interacted with a corrosive substance and exploded inches from John McCorrie's face.

Blown upwards for a moment, McCorrie collided with the underside of the table, fell forward, and inadvertently upset the contents of the sorting table onto the floor.

Within moments, Guy Fawkes arrived in Berwick on Tweed when dozens of letters caught fire and immediately engaged their nearest neighbour in an attempt to increase the growing turmoil.

There was another flash, followed by another when a score of envelopes containing hazardous substances reached a certain temperature and added to the fire.

Outside, egressing the car park, a large Royal Mail postal van entered the traffic and began its long journey. In the rear of the van over fifty bags of mail were on route to a sorting office in the south.

The postman was running late.

*

9

The Special Crime Unit
London
The next day

Approaching London his mobile 'phone rang. Handsfree, he recognised the number and answered with, 'Boyd!'

'I have the murder weapon!' announced Bannerman. 'How long will you be?'

'Half an hour!'

'Great! Don't be late, Guvnor and whatever else happens today, don't have your coffee from a vacuum flask! You need to watch what you are drinking.'

The phone went dead. Moments later, it rang again.

'Gelsemium! I've found Gelsemium in Divine Webb's cell membrane.'

'Bannerman?' queried Boyd. 'Is that you? What's going on?'

'No! Professor Frazer, you idiot,' snapped the Professor of Pathology. 'Gelsemium!'

'Gelsemium!' queried Boyd. 'What the hell is that?'

'A poison,' declared the Professor. 'I knew there was something strange about this one. That's why I've taken so long to determine my findings and get back to you. I like to be absolutely certain, Boyd.'

'Yes, I understand,' quipped Boyd. 'What have you got for me, Professor?'

'I've concluded that she was administered a high dose of Gelsemium just prior to her death. Essentially, Boyd, our murderer is a very clever individual.'

'In what way?' probed Boyd.

'The murderer poisoned the victim and seconds before she died strangled her with an ISIS flag so that it would look like it was a terrorist-related killing. The killer wants you to think she was strangled by an ISIS supporter. She wasn't. Divine Webb met her death at the hands of a poisoner trying to fool us all. My report will be with you very shortly.'

'Yes! Yes, of course,' ventured Boyd trying to take it all in. 'I'll read your paper and then get back to you. Gelsemium, you say. Where would you get that?'

Professor Frazer became annoyed with Boyd and snapped, 'Don't you read any of the academic papers I send you? Of course, you don't. You're always telling me you don't have time. Well, Boyd, if you go back to the 2012 papers, you'll find that Gelsemium is a toxic compound concentrated in its roots and leaves. The Chinese strain is particularly virile. It's a yellow coloured flower that has a fast-acting poison which causes a storm of seizures and convulsions before it paralyzes the spinal cord and lungs. Ultimately, it leads to asphyxiation. Gelsemium has been suspected of several despicable deaths, including the 2012 demise of a Russian chap who was alleged to have been killed by the Russian State as part of a conspiracy to cover up the theft of $230 million from the Treasury of Russia. It's all in my report, Boyd. Why don't you read it? See the addendum regarding the use of Gelsemium as a poison.'

'Will do and thank you,' replied Boyd. 'Professor Frazer!'

'Yes, Boyd!'

'Nothing,' ventured Boyd gradually. 'Nothing! Russia again! That's all. Just a great big thank you from me to you.'

'How kind,' chuckled Frazer. 'I can tell you are a happy man. May I ask why?'

'Soon,' replied Boyd. 'Soon!'

Entering the innards of the capital, Boyd closed the phone down as his mind went into overdrive and he pondered the days ahead.

Moments later, the phone rang again.

'Guvnor! It's Anthea. I'm moving the Barlinnie team to Berwick on Tweed. We have confirmed reports of letters exploding in the sorting office. Janice is on site and organising things. She's asking for CCTV coverage from the area. It's on the News. I'll get back to you later today.'

'Nothing to link the prison break with Berwick yet?' queried Boyd.

195

'No, but it's only a question of time before we make a connection. The coincidence is too much to ignore.'

'Agreed! Good luck!'

Boyd closed the phone down and drove into the unit's car park.

The deep aroma of coffee invaded Boyd's nostrils when he entered the main office and met Antonia.

'I want a word with you,' frowned Boyd. 'Sir Julian! That's all! He knows too much.'

'Yes,' replied Antonia. 'He's awfully good at reading other people, don't you think?'

'Well…'

'And I spoke out of turn. I apologise. Before you go any further, talk to Bannerman. He has a minor breakthrough in the Divine Webb case.'

'So do I,' declared Boyd. 'Professor Frazer tells me she was poisoned with Gelsemium It wasn't a heart attack and it wasn't strangulation. This turns the enquiry upside down.'

'Indeed, it does,' enthused Bannerman engaging the conversation. 'The vacuum flask, Boyd. So bloody obvious and we missed it the first time around.'

Sliding his briefcase onto the desk, Boyd ventured, 'What have you discovered?'

Shaking a bundle of papers in his hand, Bannerman revealed, 'The team in Cumbria interviewed scores of people who walk those clifftops where Divine Webb was murdered. DI Pitt, Chief Superintendent Cullen, and I, all missed the obvious. It's here in the statements. I could kick myself.'

'Please don't,' chided Boyd. 'You'll hurt yourself.' Boyd poured coffee from a jug, handed it to Bannerman, and said, 'Now tell us what you've found before you have a heart attack.'

Taking the cup, Bannerman put the statements down on the desk and explained, 'When the murder scene was examined there was no trace of a vacuum flask or a sandwich box. Not even on the beach.'

'Go on,' replied Boyd. 'We're all ears.'

'So, the team do house to house in the area, turn the village upside down, talk to everyone in the vicinity and then cast the net to include everyone who regularly walks the cliff paths. What would you expect them to discover?'

'Those who remember Divine painting on the cliffs,' suggested Boyd.

'Exactly!' professed Bannerman. 'And here in these statements, you'll find more than a dozen people who stopped to talk to the woman painting. She was friendly. The victim didn't know them, and they didn't know her, but she always shared the contents of her vacuum flask with them each and every time she was there. One thing stands out above everything else. We never found the vacuum flask. Why?'

'Because it was the murder weapon,' speculated Boyd. 'Of course! The killer didn't strangle the victim. They made it look as if she had been strangled by a terrorist with an ISIS flag but actually, the killer poisoned her by adding poison to whatever the drink was in the vacuum flask.'

'It fits,' smiled Bannerman. 'It's been going through my mind all night. I couldn't sleep. Poison! I kept thinking to myself. It has to be arsenic or something.'

'And now Professor Frazer tells us it was Gelsemium,' confirmed Boyd. 'You were right all along, Bannerman.'

'The poison was in the vacuum flask,' acknowledged Bannerman clapping his hands. 'Therefore, we can assume the killer was at the scene at the time of her death. It also suggests to me that the killer knew Divine, had access to her vacuum flask and knew she would take it with her when she went painting. I think we know who the chief suspect might be here. Oh yes, I can see it in my mind. The killer is lined up in one of those RSPB cabins watching the victim paint and waiting for her to take a drink from the vacuum flask. Eventually, she does and the killer knows that she has only minutes to live. On the point of death from the poison, the killer strangles her and then walks away with the murder weapon – the vacuum flask containing the poison – and takes it who knows where? Or does the killer throw it in the Irish Sea along with the body of the deceased? The murderer made it look like strangulation, but the reality is she had already been poisoned. It was all set up to throw us off track and persuade us that we were looking for some ISIS terrorist who had turned his hand to killing locals in the middle of nowhere.'

'Except it didn't work,' observed Boyd. 'It didn't feel right from the start, did it? That said, well done, Bannerman. We're starting to make sense of it all now. Tell me, is it worth doing another search to see if the tide has returned the vacuum flask to the beach?'

'Why not?' proposed Bannerman. 'I'll get onto the DI up there and see if he's onside. I'm sure he will be.'

'Thanks!' nodded Boyd. 'If we can trace the vacuum flask, we might get some evidence that directly links the flask to the killer. You never know but I agree, Cornelius Webb is well and truly in the frame.'

'I think so too but Divine Webb!' announced Bannerman. 'You wanted her life story.'

'And?'

'I'll cut to the quick,' revealed Bannerman. 'I did a full financial enquiry on the subject. She has shares in various companies of interest and, before you ask, so does he – Cornelius Webb. And nothing adds up between them.'

'There's nothing wrong with holding stocks or shares unless you're going to confirm my suspicions,' probed Boyd.

'No trace of company ownership via stocks but plenty of evidence that she has multiple sources of income through various shareholding facilities.'

'I see,' replied Boyd. 'Go on.'

'Her income is derived from the sale of paintings. Hence her hobby which is actually an income stream.' Bannerman paused before continuing, 'But she also receives regular share dividends from a dubious finance house based in the Channel Isles.'

'Offshore banking?' quizzed Boyd.

'Correct!' agreed Bannerman. 'And it's the same with Cornelius. So far, I've unearthed one joint account that seems to be used to pay off all family related things such as utility bills and the like but, in addition, they each have their own private accounts. One thing standing out in their accounts is that every three months he deposits a shedload of money into her account and has done every quarter for the last five years. Then, approximately a year ago, the electronic transfers stopped. No more money goes into his wife's account. His account just grows like there was no tomorrow. Her account remains fairly static but continues to grow via interest rates. Between them, they've more money than they know what to do with, and I'm talking seven figures. It's just not right, Guvnor. Their savings and investments from offshore banking exceed the chief's salary and her income. Something is badly amiss here because they have more to their name than they earn. It's damn near criminal.'

Boyd chuckled, began reading the documents that Bannerman had prepared for him and remarked, 'Crooked even.'

'It's not actually illegal to make money from good investments,' suggested Antonia. 'Or bad ones for that matter. In any event, as we all know, the value of shares goes up and down like a yo-yo at times. The market can be a bit of a rollercoaster but if they have made good investments and the return is high then that might explain what you have discovered. Similarly, if the interest rates paid by the bank are high and the administration fees low then another reason for their wealth is apparent.'

'Yes,' agreed Bannerman. 'But the number of shares they hold continues to increase. Where do they get them from? At the moment I'm inclined to call it untold wealth because I might only be scratching at the surface.'

'There's no record in these documents of either Divine or Cornelius Webb buying any shares,' observed Boyd. 'So, as you rightly ask, where did they get them from?'

'Inheritance? Gift from parents?' suggested Antonia. 'Or have you thought of the possibility that they were bought years ago for pennies and are now worth pounds?'

'It's a possibility,' admitted Boyd.

'Except to say that an online examination of both parties reveals that the shares they hold are from oil companies based in Russia, gas facilities in Ukraine, construction companies in Syria, Iran and Iraq, and consumer-based electronic services in China, Japan and various parts of Asia.'

'Interesting,' noted Boyd. 'But we will need to get hold of the actual share certificates or secure authorised copies from the financial authorities to prove the transactions.'

'Of course,' fielded Bannerman. 'It's when you discover that their broker only deals with UK companies and the Far East that things get interesting. He doesn't deal with Russia or the Middle East for a host of reasons. One of them being, he explained, that cybercrime was rife and often traced to these countries. He steers well away from them.'

'Yet they have shares in Russian interests and that includes Ukraine,' mused Boyd.

'Ukraine's natural gas is one of the reasons Moscow annexed the Crimea,' explained Antonia. 'It wants the gas as well as the deep-sea ports the Crimean Peninsula provides for its Black Sea Fleet. I'd say the Ukrainian shares are from a company controlled by an entity somewhere in the Russian Federation. The other thing that strikes me is that Syria, Iran and Iraq are the very places where current Russian foreign policy is concentrating. They're making friends in the Persian Gulf. It's what we call making geopolitical alliances.'

'Jeez!' shrugged Boyd. 'This is getting deep.' Scanning the documents again, he added, 'If their broker is to be believed then it looks like these UK and Far East shares were originally bought over two decades ago at a very low share price. All he's done is to manage the account and report annually on the value of the holdings. There's no indication their broker bought the shares from Russia and the Middle East on their instructions. In fact, if I'm following these documents correctly, Bannerman, there's nothing to connect their broker with the purchase of these dubious shares. Maybe it's me but I find all this very…' He struggled for words.

'Questionable, controversial, and worthy of further investigation?' suggested Bannerman.

'They could be a gift of thanks for services rendered?' ventured Antonia.

Boyd allowed the crease of a thin grin to invade his face when he said, 'Converted? Are you reading my brain cells, Antonia? Are we thinking the same thing about Cornelius Webb?'

'I doubt it,' returned the redhead. 'I happen to agree with Anthea.'

'In what way?' probed a disappointed Boyd.

'I heard you were warned about putting the Chief Constable into the frame for the murder of his wife,' observed Antonia. 'You went off after him like a greyhound leaving the traps. There's nothing to directly connect the Chief at this stage other than your gut feelings. Yes, there's a lot of DNA and fingerprints here and there that connects him to the victim, but they are man and wife. What would you expect? And if you do find the vacuum flask, Cornelius is quite likely to turn around and say, yes, of course, it's ours. But that doesn't prove he put the poison in the flask. The Gelsemium and vacuum flask are interesting developments. Very interesting! They might load the dice in your favour, but you are still a long way off and, if you don't mind me saying, you need the killer bang to rights, as you detectives say. You may have an interesting story to tell, but we're not playing Cluedo, gentlemen. Colonel Mustard may have been in the library with his wife but you have no evidence that he killed her with a monkey wrench.'

'I didn't know you played the game,' ventured Boyd.

'I don't,' replied Antonia. 'You can get as excited as you want about the Divine Webb murder but there's nothing conclusive.'

'Not yet,' flared Boyd. 'But we're getting closer. Tell me one thing, Antonia.'

'Go on!'

'If you were running a Russian agent in Moscow and paying him for information how would you pay him?'

'In roubles, of course,' said Antonia.

'Provided the agent was going to stay in Russia,' ventured Boyd. 'If he was wanting out at some stage what would you do?'

'Pay money into an account in this country or…'

'Buy shares for the agent so that the income is not easily found?' ventured Boyd.

'There are dozens of ways of paying such people, Boyd and you conveniently forget that your restaurant friend gives you information for nothing,' argued Antonia. 'No disrespect but you are trying to make the circumstances fit your own thoughts. Unproven, Boyd. Unproven! Get some evidence that will stick.'

'Seriously?' quizzed Boyd.

'No further comment,' snapped Antonia as she answered the 'phone. She listened to the caller and then continued, 'Extensive and historic mobile phone scrutiny is underway. Both parties! I'll let you know the full results in due course. If you don't mind, Boyd, can you take a call from Janice in Berwick on Tweed? Just a minor case – a terrorist running amok in Scotland, England and who knows where.'

She handed Boyd the 'phone.

'Ouch!' wheezed Boyd.

Taking the 'phone, Boyd spoke to Detective Sergeant Janice Burns.

'Morning, Janice!'

'Morning, Guvnor! There's no more explosions or injuries at this stage but the main suspects have been caught on CCTV in the town centre. The coverage is from a shop near a post box, would you believe. How lucky were we? Anyway, we have Mustafa, the escapee, posting dozens of letters and a nearby blonde woman obviously in his company. She fits the bill for the female wanted for the Downing Street job. I'll throw my hat in the ring and say she's now strongly suspected of the Barlinnie break as well as collusion in these letter bombs. We just need to find them.'

'Any vehicle sightings?'

'Not at the moment but I've been onto the Commissioner's office and they're advising the government to inform all sorting offices to exercise extreme caution in handling suspect mail. I just hoisted the petard in a funny kind of way.'

'You might have just saved some lives,' remarked Boyd. Turning to Antonia, he asked, 'Any traces on Ticker that show an allegiance between Mustafa and a female of interest?'

'None!' replied Antonia.

'Okay, Janice, thank you,' from Boyd. 'Split the team and move south clearing the primary CCTV systems as you go. It looks like they are moving south. Chase on! Agreed?'

'On my way,' revealed Janice. 'By the way, when are we getting Ricky French back? Anthea tells me you called him away on a special assignment and we've not seen him since. Am I allowed to ask what the score is there, Guvnor?'

'Of course, you can ask,' replied Boyd. 'But you won't get an answer. He's busy right now. I'll be in touch.'

The 'phone call ended with Boyd easing himself into a seat next to the Ticker console. He fired up the screen and said, 'We're drowning in this quagmire. Do we chase the murderer or try and intercept the two terrorists?'

'We have one murder in Cumbria,' revealed Antonia. 'Multiple murders in Downing Street, a dead man who was thrown out of the escape van in Glasgow, and now injured people in the Berwick on Tweed sorting office and rogue letters flying all over the country. It's no contest, Boyd. The Webb murder goes on the back burner.'

'Yes, I agree,' ventured Boyd. 'Maybe we should have been circus jugglers.'

'You could make it three terrorists actually, Guvnor, voiced Bannerman. 'We still haven't identified the guy in the bandana and sunglasses – the so-called Sultán of England.'

'Don't I know it,' replied Boyd. 'But here goes. I've been meaning to do this since I met an old friend recently. I'll do it now before I forget.'

'What? Precisely!' enquired Antonia.

'Let us suppose that there is an individual who was born in England, or the UK, converted to Islam or was already of that faith, and went abroad to fight for the Caliphate,' proposed Boyd rattling the keyboards.

'I've tried all the connections,' declared Antonia. 'The photograph we have from the drone and the satellite imagery doesn't match anyone with a criminal record or an intelligence file. There's no trace with the CIA, the FBI, Canada, Australia, or any of our European friends. Furthermore, the images we have do not match anyone on our Ticker Intelligence system and they do not match anyone on the nation's Watch List.'

Concentrating on the screen, Boyd ventured, 'No, he won't be on the system because he's clean. He's not on Ticker because he's never come to notice previously.'

'Okay,' answered Antonia. 'In that case, he's not going to be of great concern to us. No previous history means no need to investigate!'

'You should never believe everything you read on a computer,' remarked Boyd. 'It's too easy to accept that if it's on the computer it's right, and if it's not on the computer it's wrong.'

'What are you getting at, Guvnor?' quizzed Bannerman.

'To catch a terrorist, you must think like one,' replied Boyd. 'For example, let's do this.'

'Explain, why don't you?' replied Antonia.

Boyd interrogated the computer, tapped the keys, and continued, 'On 30th June 2014 Islamic State – known to us as ISIS – declared the existence of the Caliphate in Iraq and Syria. I, being a devoted follower of the Book – the Quran – and fully engaged with Muhammad, Allah, and the entire Islamic religion live in England. I live inside the Book, worship it, know it from cover to cover inside out and outside in. My whole life is Islam. I pray each and every day. Never miss! My mind tells me the Caliphate is the way forward. I am not just an enthusiastic supporter of the idea. I am the Caliphate. It's in my blood. My endurance and intensity are such that I have to go and join ISIS to make this all happen and deeper inside, I hate those who aren't of my religion. To make it enduring and lasting. I will do as the Book says and in one place the good Book says, 'Slay them (the non-believers) wherever you find them, and drive them out of the places whence they drove you out, for persecution is worse than slaughter and fight them until fitnah (rebellion) is no more, and religion is for Allah.' Now before you go off on one, Antonia, I am well aware there are all kinds of interpretations of such words and sentences by various academics who have studied Islam and argue that this religion has as much love in it as any other but, for the purposes of me thinking liking a terrorist, and being a terrorist, I happen to believe in the extremist view. So, that means I'm reading the Book as a potentially violent extremist, not as an academic following a hundred different opinions. No, for my purposes, I'm sold. I'm joining the Caliphate.'

'Where is all this leading?' quizzed Bannerman.

'To me leaving England to join ISIS in the summer of 2014, or shortly thereafter,' proposed Boyd. 'I need a passport?'

'But you already have one,' contended Antonia.

'Yes, William Miller Boyd – me – has one, but I'm the English terrorist who wants to join ISIS and I don't have a passport. Follow me, Antonia!' pleaded Boyd. 'Let me see where this takes us.'

Tap! Tap! Fingertips bouncing from the keyboard.

'I'm stuck,' admitted Boyd. 'Antonia, how do I put up the drone image for comparison with the entire 2014 and 2015 collection of UK passport photographs?'

'Like this,' she revealed taking over the keyboard and stroking the black and whites. 'But Ticker doesn't carry such photographs.'

'I know,' replied Boyd. 'But I need a driving licence too. Can we access the UK driving licence database?'

'Okay,' nodded Antonia. 'Here goes but it won't be that easy.'

'Try it please,' instructed Boyd.

Making the necessary digital strokes, Antonia eventually pointed to one of the transparent screens and said, 'Screen three shows the best of the drone images of the man we've dubbed the Sultán. Screen four shows photographs of the driving licence images used in the 2014 and 2015 timeline.'

'Facial recognition technology?' enquired Boyd.

'Soon,' replied Antonia. 'It's coming through, but the program is slower than we would wish for because you are searching thousands of photographs and comparing them with the best we've got.'

'Time!' ventured Boyd. 'Give it time.'

Thirty minutes later, and two more coffees later, the screen remained blank.

'No show,' suggested Boyd. 'Let's try the same again with UK passports.'

205

The same procedure was repeated once access to the UK Passport Office had been established.

Antonia rattled the keyboard, entered the necessary protocols, and waited.

More coffee.

'Boyd!' snapped Antonia.

Closing with the image on the screen, Boyd spoke aloud.

'Angel - Edward John Angel was issued with a passport in July 2014. Date and place of birth shown and a reference to a Pat Ann Angel in the emergency notification area. That tends to suggest he had applied for the passport prior to the June declaration date and if that is right then it suggests to me that he either went and queued for the passport which he needed quickly, or he had prior knowledge of events and applied for the passport before June 2014 so that he could get hold of it as soon as possible and from July onwards.'

'Can't help you there,' explained Antonia tapping the keyboard. 'But I'm accessing the 2014 street indexes system and electoral roll for more. Stand by.'

'Bannerman, what do you think?' enquired Boyd pointing at the screen.

'I'd say your Edward John Angel has a remarkable resemblance to the man in the drone photograph. But then I'm asking myself if that's what I want to believe or is it true.'

'I've got more,' revealed the redhead. 'An address which appears to have since been condemned and knocked down plus a Pat Ann Angel of the same address. I'm presuming they are man and wife or brother and sister. She is the only name listed in the 'emergencies' page at the back of the passport. The one where you can denote the person you want to be informed in the event of an emergency.'

'The passport was issued in July,' noted Boyd. 'Same date as Pat Ann Angel. Image?'

'On screen,' replied Antonia. 'No trace of either on the Watch List. No trace of either name on the Ticker Intelligence system. No trace criminal records. But the photographs…'

'The photographs tell a story,' argued Boyd. 'She's tall, well-built, has ginger curly hair and hasn't aged a bit. Bring up the Downing Street assassin photos. There's one of her at…'

'A tube station,' intervened Antonia interrogating the keyboard. 'Here she is.'

Images flashed on the screens. Bannerman shook his head in disbelief. Boyd smiled and Antonia sat back and said, 'Why didn't we do that earlier?'

'Because we have convinced ourselves that what we want to know is inside a multi-million-pound computer system that mainly stores intelligence and criminal records,' contended Boyd. 'We've forgotten to think like detectives and investigators. We press a button, run a name, and expect a result. Somewhere we lost the ability to step back and make a list of enquiries we should make. We stopped thinking because the computer just needs a name and it will do the rest. Wrong! So very wrong!'

'But you got there in the end, Guvnor,' suggested Bannerman. 'A hard lesson and an acknowledgement that we went off the tracks.'

'True!' murmured Boyd.

'The result is we now have names, ages, addresses, and photographs revealed Bannerman. 'We have ourselves two targets just because one of us started to think like a detective and not a computer operator.'

'Let's tidy this up,' suggested Boyd. 'Utility bills, credit cards, bank accounts, driving licences, gun licences, library cards, NHS cards, any kind of card or account you can think of that once belonged to an Angel or two. Let's make a list and tidy this up. Let's go for gold. Turn it upside down. It looks like an angel is a sultan.'

'How did we miss out on the obvious?' asked Antonia.

'Because we've no time to investigate properly anymore,' remarked Boyd. 'There's not enough of us and the computer button is the easiest to work, not the brain. But today, we stopped juggling and started detecting. Angels! Would you credit it? We're looking for bloody angels killing people. Hit those buttons, make those calls. Let's tidy these two up before we call in the dogs.'

'I wonder when they returned to the UK?' asked Bannerman.

'I'm still thinking like a terrorist,' ventured Boyd. 'If I returned using the same identity as when I went out then I know that when I present myself to the arrivals desk in the UK, I'm going to be refused entry unless I submit myself to interview and enquiry by the Security Services. I'll be interrogated at length, tell them the whole story or else, and probably go to prison for being a member of a terrorist organisation, or some other such terrorist-related offence. No, I don't want that. I want to come back here to continue the fight so I came back on a different passport or no passport and I didn't travel back with Pat Ann Angel. In fact, Bannerman, if I survived and did become the Sultán of England, then I'm no longer Edward John Angel and she's no longer Pat Ann Angel. They are just shadows in the night, irretrievable in the scheme of things, nonentities on a computer system. They no longer exist. They've rubbed themselves out.'

'We're looking for the devil,' suggested Antonia. 'Two of them. One using the name Pat, I'd say.'

'There's one thing we can do right now,' decided Boyd. 'Get those angelic photographs circulated to every member of the Special Crime Unit now.'

'How about nationwide circulation to every officer in the UK?' proposed Bannerman.

'Tempting!' replied Boyd. 'But as my dear friend, Antonia, recently reminded me today, we need hard and compulsive evidence if they were arrested. Photographic evidence is strong on this one, but we all know that standing alone it's not usually enough to secure a good conviction. As Antonia says, we need to catch them bang to rights nowadays. Put simply, the legal system has always been a game between good and evil. I think the score is 50-50 in favour of no-one. It's unlikely to change in the foreseeable future. So I find myself in the Command Post making a command decision that will see me damned if I do and damned if I don't. I'm juggling again. Thinking like an Islamic terrorist, I'm not reading the Book. I'm just a killer hellbent on doing away with the non-believers. I know that if I'm caught, I will kill anyone who gets in my way. Yet my inner soul that believes in the extremist elements of the Book knows that I must not be caught because if I am arrested the Caliphate will take a little longer to happen, and I want it to happen on my watch. I won't be revered by the faith, not spoken of at salat (prayers), not mentioned by the Iman who promotes extremism. No, I will be either dead – killed by law enforcement at the scene of an attack – or imprisoned for the rest of my life in a hell hole where only the ants survive.'

Bannerman rested his hand on Boyd's shoulder and said, 'I never quite thought of it like that.'

Swishing her red hair across her shoulders, Antonia voiced, 'Boyd, you are in command. You are the Commander of this godforsaken, irrelevant, soon to be disbanded outfit. Make a decision. You are who you are. Be who you are.'

Nodding, scratching his nose that didn't need to be scratched, Boyd replied, 'Make it three. As Bannerman reminded me, it's a trio of trouble we're looking for. Add Mustafa Abadi to the list for circulation. Circulation to Omega eyes only. That means the Special Crime Unit and all authorised counter terrorist detectives in the UK. No-one else. No national circulation, no planned leaks to the media, nothing. In house only. Photos of Mustafa Abadi, Pat Ann Angel and Edward John Angel. I have a plan to counter the Armageddon that I think might befall us. I just pray I have it right.'

'Your prayers, Boyd!' quizzed Antonia. 'Are you still praying as a terrorist or as yourself?'

'I have no religion, Antonia. My job is my religion. I believe in it. Let's do it.'

Pursing his lips, Bannerman considered Boyd's reply. Moving closer to Boyd, he said, 'I remember you as a sprog PC on the streets of Carlisle. A nobody who became a somebody when he began to fight for those who couldn't stand up for themselves. Are you sure, Billy? If we catch them soon, you will be a hero. We'll all be heroes. If you make the wrong decision and people get hurt, or worse, because you made the decision to tell only a few, then they will lynch you. You will be finished. You know that, don't you?'

'I'll write up my thought processes in the Sultan file, my friend. It will be there to see and ponder upon in the years to come. What do I know? It might rain tomorrow. Then again, the sun might shine. It is what is. We live and work in the shadows. It's where we are strong. We cannot see the enemy. They wear no uniform. They are in the shadows too. It's where the war on terrorism is fought – in the dark corners and recesses of the world where the shadows lurk. We shall stay there and leave only when we need to win. I have made my decision.'

'Then I shall stand by you,' replied Bannerman.

'Thank goodness for that,' remarked Antonia. 'I'll order a cake from the canteen.'

Bannerman and Boyd exchanged surprised glances as Antonia placed a call for refreshments.

'Chocolate I hope,' suggested Boyd.

'Or those vanilla things,' proposed Bannerman.

She placed the order, slammed the 'phone down, and hit the keyboard saying, 'I changed my mind. Chocolate digestives!'

Grinning, Antonia began the process of circulating the trio of photographs to the selected few.

The hunt was on.

Anthea, Janice and the team raced south from Berwick on Tweed liaising with local counterterrorist units on the way. The instruction was easy to follow but much more difficult to carry out. Monitor CCTV for Mustafa and the Angels at places of public resort.

'Well, that covers most of the country,' sighed Anthea. 'At least it's a start. We have names and photographs for the armed patrols.'

The couple were laden with shopping bags. They carried two each as they wandered through the streets looking in the shop windows, chatting to each other, and acting like ordinary shoppers in the area. They turned a corner and approached the monthly continental market that was in full swing.

Popular, and attracting lots of day trippers from the North East, the market featured traders from around the world who offered all kinds of goods from quirky craft items to tasty hot food treats. A lot of the stalls provided food and there was a number that had been set up to offer fine ales, beers, and wine.

'These bags are heavy,' remarked Mustafa as he came to standstill.

Stooping, he reached into both shopping bags and primed the explosive device therein before standing tall and saying for the benefit of others nearby, 'That's better. It must be old age creeping up on me.'

An old lady passing by smiled and replied, 'You need to rest now and again when they are too heavy. But you can carry mine if you like.'

Mustafa returned the smile but was soon off again. This time he carried the auburn-haired woman's bags and, after a hundred yards or so, he feigned tiredness again, bent down to the bags, and primed the last two devices.

They walked on mingling with the crowds, filling their nostrils with the odours of German sausage, French onion soup, Chinese fare from a huge wok, and Spanish paella. Loud voices from the stall holders promoting their bargains and best buys constantly filled the air as the couple sought to negotiate the throng of shoppers in Sunderland's Market Square

Mustafa paused at one of the stalls, set down a shopping bag on the ground, and then discreetly pushed it underneath the stall with his foot.

Likewise, his lady friend, now identified by the Special Crime Unit as Pat Ann Angel, sauntered to a nearby food stall, briefly examined the display, and similarly placed one of her bags beneath the stall.

She checked her watch and remarked, 'Fifteen minutes?'

Mustafa acknowledged her with a nod and replied, 'Casually in and casually out. We've plenty of time.'

Linking arms now, the couple strolled towards the exit, a car park, and the getaway they planned.

The old lady who had spoken to Mustafa watched them go, realised they had left a shopping bag beneath a stall and shouted after them. 'Hey! Your bags. You forgot your bags.'

Far enough away not to hear the call, Mustafa and Pat walked on, slowly increasing their speed.

'Officer!' remarked the old lady as she approached two armed policemen patrolling the market. 'That couple…' She pointed. 'They've left their shopping bags. Look!' She pointed again. 'I know the man said they were heavy, but they had four bags and they've left them here.'

The couple were gone from sight.

Jim, one of the armed officers, set off in the general direction of Mustafa and Pat, the other, Brian, engaged the elderly lady in conversation, asked more questions, and then approached the nearest shopping bag to him.

'A man and a woman, you say?' queried Jim.

'Oh yes, mind you,' whispered the old lady, 'He was one of them foreigners and she has short auburn hair.'

Removing a set of photographs from his breast pocket, Jim asked, 'Did they look like these people by any chance?'

The old lady rummaged in a handbag for her spectacles, perched them on her nose, and looked at the images.

'That's the foreigner, the man. He's…' She looked around before cautiously whispering, 'Coloured. Not black but kind of brown.'

'And the woman?' quizzed the officer.

'No, she has auburn hair, but she does have the look of her in the photograph,' declared the witness. 'Maybe she dyed it. But him? Oh, yes,' replied the lady. 'Nice smile he had. Nice smile.'

Cautiously, Brian used the tip of the barrel of his Heckler & Koch MP5SFA3 semi-automatic carbine to slide one of the shopping bag handles to one side. He peered inside, nudged a parcel to one side, and then bent down to see what he had uncovered.

'Shit!' he mouthed before standing up and shouting, 'Stand back everyone. Move away from the stall. Quickly now!'

It's a bomb, he thought, or it looks like one. Time to juggle. What do I do now? I found one. She said four. Where are the other three? Do I join Jim and rush after the couple this old lady thinks put it down or, do I shout 'Bomb', cause widespread panic, and clear everyone away from the area? Should I use my radio because if the device is set

212

off by a radio signal from the bomber my signal might override his and set the bomb off? Is this the only bomb? I wonder how much explosives are in this particular bomb? Should I move this bag? Will it go off right away? Is the witness right? Is it really two of those circulated earlier today? Where's the third one? I don't know which order to do what. I'm damned if I do and damned if I don't and I need to decide what to do in the next few seconds.

Engaging his radio, Brian updated his control room with the situation ending with, 'Confirming, subject Mustafa Abadi and one unidentified female sighted in Continental Market. Two Suspect devices found. Two suspect devices still to locate. Assistance required pronto.'

His heart was beating at twice the speed when he shouted, 'Jim! We've got a live one. Mustafa Abadi positively identified! One unidentified female with him could be the Angel woman. Assistance on route. I'm clearing the area.'

Finding a dustbin at the rear of the trader's stall, Brian promptly turned it over, emptied the contents onto the floor, and shoved the shopping bag away from the immediate area. He then placed the dustbin over the bag, hoped it might cushion an explosion, and said, 'Move away, please. No need to get excited. Just a precaution.'

People stepped back. Shoppers expressed concern at what the policeman had done. A trader pointed to another bag secreted beneath his stall.

'Is it a bomb?' someone asked.

'Bomb!' was repeated and the seed of panic began to feature throughout the market.

Brian approached the second bag, checked the inside, realised it was identical to the first and then forcibly shouted, 'Everyone! Move away now. Move away from the market. Now!'

Mustafa and Pat were in the car park. They mounted the Range Rover. She fired the engine, selected a gear, and drove away.

Jim approached the entrance to the car park, saw the Range Rover approach, and stepped into the middle of the road to stop the car.

The woman driver slammed her foot to the floor and accelerated as fast she could.

Jim took aim and shouted, 'Stop! Police!'

Mustafa pulled a pistol from his trouser belt, wound his window down, and pointed his pistol at the officer.

'Stop! Police!' shouted again. His feet firmly wedged to the tarmac beneath him. 'Stop! Armed Police!'

She swerved, forced the Range Rover into the offside of the road, missed the policeman, and mounted the pavement.

A gang of school children jumped for their lives. An approaching taxi hit the brakes and swerved the other way.

'Shoot!' radioed Jim. 'Bombs! They've just put down bombs!'

The Range Rover bounced from the pavement back onto the road with a taxi narrowly avoiding a collision and school children screaming at the top of their voices.

The policeman brought his carbine to bear. He found the trigger guard and aimed.

A careering taxi came into view, blotted his aim, and a school girl ran across the road to get out of the way.

'No clear shot!' he shouted. 'Get out of the way!'

The Range Rover swung from side to side as Jim charged down the road in hot pursuit with his weapon at shoulder height as he fought to ensure a positive shot.

Suddenly, a huge explosion erupted from the Continental Market when four bombs exploded.

The first bomb destroyed the fabric of the shopping bag, lifted the dustbin of the ground, but was somewhat suppressed by the metal container.

Remnants of rotten food and groceries flew through the air.

The second bomb had been pushed by the policeman beneath a tradesman's four-wheeled caravan trailer. It erupted and blew a hole in the trailer's floor but no more.

Two other shopping bags exploded when the devices inside detonated. The fabric of the shopping bag accompanied a terrible collection of nuts, bolts, screws, nails and jagged metalworks as the bomb set about harming all around.

Screaming! Maiming! Burning!

The brutal politics of a hate-ridden extremist group arrived in Sunderland. Sirens, blue lights, and a full response by emergency teams followed but the two evil maniacs in their Range Rover had escaped.

'To the pickup point,' remarked Pat. 'Time to dump this one, take the other, and south to the Sultán.'

'Do you think they got the car number?' enquired Mustafa.

'I hope so,' replied Pat. 'It will give them something to look for. We'll be in the van.'

'Good!' exclaimed Mustafa. 'Why Sunderland of all places? And why the market?'

'El Sultán made the decision,' replied the accomplice. 'Something from his past, that's all. Getting even, he told me. I don't know the full story.'

'I can't wait to meet the man,' ventured Mustafa. 'I'm going to tell him to stop wasting time on these market people. They are irrelevant.'

'True! They are,' replied Pat. 'Particularly the dead ones.'

They drove on, dumped the Range Rover in an out of the way layby, and drove away in a dark blue Transit van fitted with a logo on the side.

Two hundred and seventy-five miles away, a postman ambled down the footpath of the Office of the Secretary of State for the Environment. He shoved a letter through the flap of the door, retraced his steps, and whistled happily as he checked the envelopes he was carrying.

'Two doors down,' he mumbled to himself.

Inside the building, a clerk retrieved the letter from the carpet, walked back to her office, and began opening the envelopes with a thin knife.

'Haven't you seen the News? Bombs in Sunderland and they got away,' remarked a uniformed security officer.

'What's that got to do with it?' asked the clerk.

'Have you not read the memo? The newspaper thinks it might be the same people who did the letter bombs?'

'Of course, they would say that, wouldn't they? That's what sells newspapers, you idiot.'

'Yes,' argued the security officer, 'But the boss sent out a memo and you're expected to comply with it.'

'Really?' a nonchalant look from the clerk.

'Why anyone would pick this place out as a target is beyond me? Still, the memorandum says put it through the scanner before you open it.'

The clerk placed the half-opened letter on the table and switched the scanner on.

Intrigued, the security guard approached the letter.

A pungent smell escaped the envelope. There was a sudden flash when it exploded and filled the room with a caustic powder and a tongue of fire exploring the atmosphere.

The female clerk began screaming.

The security officer clasped his hands to his eyes and began shouting, 'I can't see. I can't see!'

A covert camera, hidden in the palm of the photographers' hand, clicked, captured the road sign, panned, and clicked again. The individual took images of the surrounding countryside before concentrating on the gated entrance to a secret underground facility. The installation was well-known as a nuclear waste repository, but it also provided the nation with a discreet building platform for the next generation of mini trident submarines, powered by nuclear generators, and equipped with the latest high-tech missiles able to engage surface laser technology and a global defence system.

Not known to the general public was the location where the photographer was deployed. Somehow, he had discovered the rear entrance to the installation, or had his intelligence sources guided him there?

It was not on the map. There were no signs to say what lay beyond the gated entrance. He could see a long tarmac lane that petered out in a left-hand bend and then seemed to drop downwards into the earth. By now, he knew the land, knew that it was over five miles from the main repository entrance, and knew he had made an interesting find for the Mother Country.

This is the entrance that needs watching, he concluded. Not the front which is well known. This! Here! Five miles away from the public eye where the secret materials and the finished product would be removed from the installation and taken into military possession. And a host of other issues filled his mind. This is my Bonanza!

It would be confirmed and developed by satellite imagery in the months ahead. He congratulated himself. It was one thing to have all the satellite technology in the world, but quite another to know where to point it and use it effectively.

Mikhail Korobov slid the camera into his pocket and casually fired the engine of his grey Mercedes Benz motor car.

Hours later, Mikhail would steer away from his normal route south and park the vehicle in the grounds of a Travel Lodge for the night. He had a meeting to attend and planned to wait patiently for the woman he loved.

Boyd's mobile sounded and he answered it with, 'Boyd! You have something for me, Ricky?'

'You're not going to believe this, Guvnor.'

'Right now, I'll believe anything,' replied Boyd. 'Shopping bag bombs in Sunderland, letter bombs In London. What else can they throw at us today?'

'A television programme!' suggested Ricky

'You're kidding me?' ventured Boyd.

'Well,' responded Detective Sergeant Ricky French, 'More of a fly on the wall documentary, I suppose.'

*

10

The Commissioner's Office
New Scotland Yard
London.

'I'm sorry, Chief Inspector Boyd,' revealed the Commissioner, 'But your authority to sign off Cornelius Webb – or anyone else for that matter – for the post of Head of Counter-Terrorism in the UK – is hereby revoked as is your level of security clearance. You are now Omega Blue downgraded from Omega Violet.'

Shocked, stunned, Boyd eventually replied, 'Why? What have I done wrong? By the way, you can't do that. The clearance comes from the Home Office, not the Metropolitan Police.'

'Can't I?' smirked the Commissioner. 'You will find that the Home Secretary – Maude Black - has complied with my request without argument. I believe you know her, Chief Inspector?'

There was an uneasy few moments as the overweight, fifty-something, Police Commissioner sat rigid in his high-backed chair and stared into Boyd's face.

'We are still investigating Cornelius Webb in relation to his wife's murder,' revealed Boyd.

'Yes, precisely!' announced the Commissioner. 'You ought to have replied to the effect that your team was still investigating the Divine Webb murder, not the individual Cornelius Webb. You seem to have set off from the very start with the intention of pinning this murder on Cornelius Webb and steamrollering anyone who got in the way. It is not the way things are done, Boyd. It's almost as if you don't want the man in Counter Terrorism Command under any circumstances.'

'I don't,' agreed Boyd. 'I consider him a dangerous liability and I've actually had a hunch about him right from the start. It's the way the investigation has shaped my views. My enquiries will be consolidated in due course and evidence will be forthcoming to you and the judicial system.'

'Why not now?'

Pausing for too long, Boyd replied, 'I can give you innuendo, circumstantial evidence, suspicion, some fact and…'

'Fiction!' interrupted the Commissioner with a confidence born out of a slow thinking Boyd. 'Look, Chief Inspector, it's an open secret that Cornelius Webb intends to develop your unit and restructure it accordingly. Isn't it time you thought about taking that nice chair-bound promotion in Cumbria?'

'Whoever told you that, sir, was also talking fiction,' argued Boyd. 'He's planning cutbacks, not development and evolvement.'

'That may be the way forward,' proposed the Commissioner as he smoothed his hand over a balding scalp. 'Simply put, Boyd, you have no hard evidence and your murder enquiry is wallowing in very deep water. You could get yourself into serious trouble if you persist with the current line of enquiries. Maybe, it really is time for you to relax, accept that promotion in Cumbria when it comes, and take up fell walking, lake swimming, or something like that!'

'Dog walking?' frowned Boyd.

'Even better,' smiled the Commissioner.

'I have no intention of taking early retirement from life, Commissioner,' contended Boyd.

'Furthermore, in respect of Webb's application,' added the Commissioner. 'I have to say that you have pussy-footed around with it for far too long and it is obvious that it is all too much for you. Sadly, I think the procedure we adopted to replace the last Commander with an individual of lesser rank was a mistake. It's obvious to me and my senior management team that we should have put an existing Chief Superintendent, at the very least, into the post. We didn't promote you because there were those amongst us who suspected you were not capable of holding the rank and accepting the responsibility. I accept that they were correct. You will need to know that the Chief Constable of Cumbria – Cornelius Webb – will commence duties as Head of Counter Terrorist Policing in the UK. He will oversee the Special Crime Unit as well as the many other Counter Terrorist Units throughout the UK. His appointment is effective one month today. His promotion will make him almost on par with myself as far as the rank structure is concerned. It's possible that in the future, he may become Commissioner of the Metropolitan Police – possibly when I retire in a few years' time. I want you to think about that, Boyd. Trying to mess about with the normal order of things is not good for you. Do you hear me, Chief Inspector?"

The Commissioner of Police for the Metropolitan Police Service seldom minced his words but, at times, he had a bizarre way of talking to people. Often, it was as if he were lecturing to them rather than engaging them in conversation.

Boyd supposed that the Commissioner had enjoyed a career that had been more about words than action. That said, Boyd sat at a much lower rank and lived and worked in a different world to that of the Commissioner and his senior management team.

Staring directly at the Commissioner, Boyd argued, 'Have you ever read my personal file, sir? Do you think I, and those in my team, received the Queen's Gallantry Medal for pushing pens across pieces of worthless paper? No, we were awarded that reward, and many more over recent years, for service to our country and bloody good police work. We kept the lid on things whilst others slept the night away.'

'Be that as it may,' ventured the Commissioner. 'But you should always remember that your team is actually my team since I have final authority in all such things here in London and beyond. Your CV and your various medals and commendations are all history now. Your contribution to policing is there for all to see and you should be proud of your achievements. However, the truth of the matter is that they are really all quite irrelevant since ISIS has been defeated and it is time to accept that and restructure our approaches to crime. Money is tight, Boyd. Knife crime is rocketing and murders in the capital are at an all-time high. The Home Secretary supports the creation of an investigative task force that can meet these challenges head-on. I have a budget to address, Boyd, and a victory over ISIS allows us room to manoeuvre in the financial sense.'

'Not you too,' remarked Boyd. 'Instead of continually making cuts why not argue with the Home Secretary for more resources so that such a task force can then be created?'

'Your unit is finished, Boyd. Whether you like it or not.'

'The point is that the culture and ideology that drives ISIS to want a Caliphate has not been defeated,' contended Boyd.

Raising his hand for a second, the Commissioner disputed, 'Are you becoming Islamophobic, Boyd?'

'Now that's for you to decide, Commissioner,' challenged Boyd. 'I'm told that Islamophobia is the fear, hatred of, or prejudice against, the Islamic religion or Muslims generally, especially when seen as a geopolitical force or the source of terrorism. That would mean that every counter-terrorist officer in the United Kingdom working against the ISIS target is therefore Islamophobic.'

'Or the definition is wrong?' suggested the Commissioner.

'We agree on something then,' smiled Boyd. 'It reminds me of the legal definition of subversion. If people speak out against government policy, various governments over the years have wrongly defined the speaker as subversive because the individual has a different opinion to that of government. Is it the case, Commissioner, that when Islam is upset because someone has an alternative or competing perspective, they – Islam, that is - consider themselves to be victims of Islamophobia?'

'I hear you, Boyd,' offered the Commissioner.

'The fact is the Caliphate is fourteen hundred years in the making and will take a damned sight more than fourteen months to destroy, sir. Look at the history of Islamic extremism. There have been umpteen attempts at creating a global Caliphate and it will continue until that unwelcome ideology is totally destroyed, not just an army of self-made assassins. The Caliphate is their dream and it has merely been suspended, not destroyed!'

'Another chink in your armour, Boyd. It pays you to argue that ISIS has not been defeated because you realise your unit is likely to become superfluous to requirements. Oh yes, I know ISIS hasn't completely given up, but they are not the force they once were. We need to adjust our response accordingly.'

'I don't agree with your opinion or your selection,' argued Boyd. 'In any event, I need extra manpower for an operation that is about to impact on London.'

'By God, you've no fear of senior rank have you?' scolded the Commissioner. 'I'll tell you this, I read your report. How many did you want again?'

'One thousand armed officers,' replied Boyd. 'I need one thousand armed officers for a seven-day period – twenty-four seven in fact.'

'Not going to happen, Boyd. We have two and a half thousand authorised firearms officers in the Met. They cover twenty-four hours every day of the week in eight-hour shifts, at the very least. You don't need to be a mathematician or a rocket scientist to work out how many are actually available at any time in the capital.'

'We could ask for mutual aid and bring in officers from surrounding forces.'

'We?' queried the Commissioner. 'I make the decisions. Not we! It's not going to happen, Boyd. And before you mention it, that's a firm no to the SAS. I've made my decision.'

'Pity! The SAS would understand the kind of being we're looking for. The fact is I'm hunting a man and woman who are led by an individual who is ruthless.'

'Really? Convince me, Boyd. Tell me about this man who is so ruthless that you need one thousand armed officers to take him out?'

Boyd scratched an itch on his nose and began, 'He is a strong leader, a convert to the faith, a true and trusted warrior who has proved himself on the battlefields of Syria, Iraq, Turkey, and probably elsewhere too. There's little doubt that he is a killer of men, possibly women and children too. The individual is not just a soldier. He is a hero to the people he represents. The man has no resources, no computer at his side, no staff with him, no senior management team from whom he can take advice. No files to study, no timescales, just patience, ability and a true love of the Caliphate. He carries his war plan in his head because if he can learn the Book inside out, he can sure as hell commit his battle plan to memory. This is a man for whom violence is commonplace. It's in his bloodstream. It's all he knows.'

'Potentially,' suggested the Commissioner. 'You are telling me he is a martyr who will take many with him.'

'Possibly!' nodded Boyd.

'Have you met him?' asked the Commissioner.

'No, of course not,' replied Boyd.

'Then how do you know so much about him?'

'Because it is my job to know about such people, Commissioner, and their culture and beliefs. People like this man — our target — live in the shadowy world in which we work. Such people live and breathe evil, think nothing of you, me, or the people with whom we live. We are their enemy. He is not planning to be a martyr. Our ultimate target is a leader of men. His soldiers are those who carry the bombs, wear suicide jackets, and cause mayhem throughout society. Leaders, such as he, harness their soldiers, convert them from warrior to martyr, convince them that Allah awaits the true hero, and persuades them how great a heroic death is in the world of Islam. I fear my man has many soldiers to call upon.'

'All pinned on a drone photograph taken in Iraq according to your report,' suggested the Commissioner. 'Supported by loose talk.'

'There is a fine line between intelligence and evidence,' proposed Boyd. 'But our intelligence sources are impeccable and of the highest quality.'

The Commissioner was visibly losing patience when he replied, 'Intelligence is not evidence. Factually, Boyd, not fictionally, we've had enough terrorist attacks in London over the years to write a book and a half about terrorists and their organisations. The last thing we need is another opinion on what you think a terrorist might be.'

'It's what I do,' declared Boyd. 'Some people learn a language. I learnt about an extreme culture that created an evil creature that we hunt every day. We chase and harrow such creatures all the time. Listen to me. I need one thousand officers to stop the Armageddon.'

'It's not going to happen, Boyd,' stated the Commissioner. 'Once again, I read a paper from you that is fictitious in nature. I agree that you have lots of signposts, some interesting ideas and visions of what might happen, but the reality is you are looking for at least two terrorists who are responsible for multiple offences. They appear to be led by one other according to your intelligence. Your primary reference appears to come from a source who says something is going to happen soon and when it happens, he'll let you know.'

'My source is of the faith. He is a follower of Islam and is proven to me. When he tells me there is a move underway to bring about an attack on London, I listen to him because I know he will be right. He is a good man.'

'Wrong,' argued the Commissioner. 'You listen to him because you are looking for a way to circumnavigate the Cornelius Webb issue and get your own way. Yes, you have evil people to find and arrest, but you do not need one thousand officers to do it. Request denied!'

'If it were only that simple,' suggested Boyd. 'Armageddon is coming, Commissioner. Of that, you can be sure.'

'Is there anything else you would like to tell me, Boyd?' enquired the Commissioner brusquely.

'No, sir. Just that I did not realise how wide the influence of Cornelius Webb had spread. Everyone loves him, don't they?'

'Enjoy your posting to Cumbria when it comes, Boyd,' fielded the Commissioner. 'It's time for you to move on and make way for the next generation.'

'Commissioner! Do you think a man who reads the Quran – the Book – is a man of peace?'

'Probably, why?'

'Do you think a man who wears a crucifix is, therefore, a Christian and a man of peace?'

'Highly likely in the scheme of things,' contended the Commissioner. 'Why the quiz?'

'I wondered if I was becoming more antichristian than Islamophobic, that's all. But then I was just thinking about how wrong people's perceptions of what they see can be. They see only want they want to see without ever looking beneath the veneer of things in order to determine the truth about an individual.'

'What are you trying to say, Boyd?'

'Do you know what this stupid misguided society is in danger of creating?' quizzed Boyd.

The Commissioner offered no reply.

'Then I'll tell you,' ventured Boyd. 'A terror state within the state.'

'Close the door on your way out,' instructed the Commissioner. 'I've had quite enough of this ridiculous conversation.'

A desolated Boyd tried to hide his emotions as he closed the door behind him and made his way to the Special Crime Unit office.

The Mercedes moved into the third lane and continued to gain speed as the vehicle climbed a long enduring ascent and the southbound carriageway of the motorway became clogged with heavy goods vehicles in the other two lanes.

Gradually, traffic reached the summit and headed downhill as the road ahead meandered slightly and a panoramic view of the Midlands lay before them. Soft music played from the Mercedes radio as the needle on the speedometer edged towards one hundred miles per hour and the driver gently tapped his fingers on the leather-bound steering wheel.

He checked his mirror, knew he enjoyed diplomatic immunity from all road traffic offences and criminality in the UK and squeezed the accelerator pedal further to the floor.

Oh yes, he thought, any such misdemeanour might result in me being expelled from the country, but we'll cross that bridge if we ever come to it.

Stretching his left arm out, he turned the volume up as a thirty-two-tonne articulated wagon edged into the fast lane partially blocking the Mercedes. There was a flash of headlights and a blast on the Mercedes horn as the car driver ploughed on relentlessly.

The wagon driver moved further into the fast lane causing the driver of the Mercedes to stand on the brakes and swerve violently into a crash barrier to avoid contact with the vehicle.

Crash!

There was the scrape of metal upon concrete when the front offside wing of the Mercedes collided harshly with the crash barrier in the central reservation. The articulated wagon continued unabated down the fast lane of the carriageway, its driver apparently unaware of the motorway mayhem developing to its rear.

The Mercedes driver wrestled with the steering wheel when the car rebounded from the central carriageway and spun dangerously into the southbound carriageway.

As the driver of the Mercedes looked to his offside, a white Transit van careering down the middle lane ploughed into the offside of the grey car and spun it around again. A look of total horror filled the Mercedes driver's face when he whirled around the carriageway having completely lost control. Another wagon, this time in the slow lane, smashed into the rear of the Mercedes causing it to roll over on its roof.

Like a rag doll, the driver lay upside down hanging from his seat belt as the Mercedes rolled over and over in the centre of the southbound carriageway.

Eventually, the grey Mercedes came to a standstill. Steam blew from its engine block, the windscreen and rear window exploded into a thousand pieces of tiny glass, and the bodywork mangled into a twisted, bizarre ruin.

Finally, when an austere silence dominated the scene, the rear diplomatic number plate clattered to the ground. A loose screw that had once secured the plate bounced on the tarmac and rolled towards the hard shoulder.

An hour later, alerted by the motorway police, Charlie Tango Charlie approached the scene of the accident with both Boyd, Bannerman and Antonia, looking down from the response helicopter on the wreckage below.

'Oh my God,' exclaimed a shocked Antonia. 'It looks like a war zone not the scene of a road accident.'

'Road collision,' remarked Bannerman. 'Apparently, the right description is road collision, not a road accident.'

'Whatever it is,' suggested Boyd. 'Be thankful someone reported the Russian diplomatic plates on the car to us. Bannerman, can you please search the boot? Antonia, take the rear passenger compartment. I'll take the front and the dashboard area.'

'What about the body?' enquired Antonia.

'I'll speak with the officer in charge,' volunteered Boyd. 'The motorway is closed so we have time to do what we came to do. Make a search of the diplomatic vehicle. Remember, the driver has diplomatic immunity, not the car. Let's do it.'

The response helicopter set down in the southbound carriageway and allowed the three investigators to walk towards the scene of the atrocity. Fire and Rescue personnel stood with police officers as the emergency services secured the scene and began their enquiries into how the incident had developed.

The body of the Mercedes driver lay on the tarmac having recently been cut out of the vehicle by the Fire and Rescue Service. It was covered with a blanket and a police photographer was busy taking an abundance of evidential photographs.

An undertaker sat patiently in his vehicle waiting to be called forward when the time was right.

Boyd approached an Inspector at the scene, introduced himself, and said, 'Thanks for the call. I appreciate it. If it's alright with you, we'll search the body and the vehicle for matters relevant to our sphere of responsibility in respect of diplomatic staff and their vehicles.'

'I thought you might be interested,' replied the officer. 'You guys don't always come to these incidents, but I suppose the Russian plates are of interest. My people have removed the property found on the body but if you'd like to do the car then be my guest.'

'Bannerman, Antonia,' remarked Boyd. 'As discussed!'

The Inspector guided Boyd to the rear of a police incident vehicle where property from the body of the Mercedes driver was displayed.

Boyd quietly inspected the deceased's belongings before picking up the mobile 'phone belonging to the dead man.

Flicking through the data, Boyd remarked, 'Why does a Russian diplomat have the number of the wife of the Chief Constable of Cumbria on his mobile phone?'

'Beats me,' replied the Inspector. 'Do you know the deceased? I mean his identity. Is he known to your mob?'

Examining documents in the deceased's possession, Boyd replied, 'My colleague will be interested in this. Thank you. According to his credentials, this is the body of Mikhail Korobov. Antonia, what do you make of this?'

The redhead approached, scrutinised the paperwork and said, 'Yes, we know him. Poor sod. What a terrible way to go. Such a cruel death on the roads of a foreign country.'

Bannerman joined them carrying an envelope containing some photographs and added, 'Look what I found.'

Perusing the images, Boyd announced, 'A personal one, I think.'

Bannerman replied, 'The deceased, Mikhail Korobov with his arm slid around the waist of Divine Webb. Both smiling. Don't they look happy?'

'They certainly do,' ventured Antonia. 'Very interesting indeed. Do we have another murder suspect? What on earth is he doing with Webb's wife? More worryingly, for me, what about these?'

A collection of photographs showing a gated entrance set in the country, a signpost, and more countryside came to light. Along with another sealed envelope.

Boyd broke the seal and removed more photographs. The images were of a partly constructed small nuclear Trident submarine.

Stepping away slightly for more privacy, Boyd said to Antonia, 'This is the very latest mini-submarine under construction. It's not even in service yet and the deceased has photographs of it in his possession. What the hell is going on?'

'Not sure,' replied Antonia. 'I'll show you something in a moment though. If it's what I think it is then all will be explained. Where were these taken?'

'I know this place,' announced Boyd. 'I've been there. This photograph was taken in a top-secret underground nuclear facility in

Cumbria. A tragic road accident on the motorway leads us to a Russian spy, espionage, a possible murder suspect, and who knows what else we'll find?'

The trio continued to search through both the vehicle and the body of the deceased.

A few moments later, the redhead lifted a box of matches from Mikhail's possessions and said, 'No cigarettes or cigars but a box of matches. What does that tell you?'

'He's a non-smoker,' chuckled Bannerman. 'Probably just given up. Or is he going to a bonfire celebration?'

'I don't think so,' proposed Antonia. 'Watch this.'

In full view of Boyd and Bannerman, Antonia palmed the box of matches and then squeezed it between the muscle at the base of her thumb and the base of her pinky finger.

The matchbox made a clicking sound which caught her attention. She then gently scratched the surface of the matchbox to reveal a tiny camera lens pressing through the thin paper covering. Antonia then prised open one end of the matchbox before removing a small compact digital camera. Flipping the camera over, she unclipped the back of the camera and removed a flat memory card.

'No match sticks,' smiled Antonia. 'Not a piece of sulphur in sight. Just a spy camera.'

Shaking his head, Boyd said, 'I've never seen a handheld that small before.'

'Oh, they come smaller than this,' revealed the redhead. 'But this is an intelligence officer's covert camera. The interesting thing is that you don't carry these around with you every day of the week. No, he's used this on an assignment very recently. It will be interesting to load the memory card onto a computer and discover what he's been photographing.'

'He might already have done that,' suggested Bannerman.

'Perhaps, we'll see. Still, it proves one thing,' proposed Antonia.'

'Meaning?' queried Boyd.

'Mikhail Korobov is not a diplomat,' declared the lady from MI5. 'We've suspected him of being a spy working out of the Russian

Embassy for some time. Getting it all tied up beyond a question of doubt for the authorities might not be that easy since the man is dead.'

Boyd smiled and said, 'You may have clever tricks to show us from the palm of your hand, Antonia, but I know someone who might be able to help us.'

'Who?' probed Antonia.

'Ricky French!' replied Boyd.

The conversation was interrupted by a call on Boyd's mobile. He glanced at the number and recognised it as Yusuf's.

'Hello,' stated Boyd.

'Mister Boyd,' replied Yusuf. 'The wine has arrived.'

'When? Where? How many cases?' enquired Boyd.

Moments later, Boyd pocketed his mobile and said, 'That was Yusuf. The wine has arrived. That means our trio of most wanted is somewhere in the capital. The show is about to start.'

'I'll finish searching the car,' replied Bannerman.

'I'll give you a hand,' proposed Antonia bagging the covert camera and the photographs. 'We'll take everything with us. Can you sign off the paperwork, Boyd?'

Boyd's mobile rang again.

'I'll take care of the paperwork,' replied Bannerman. 'Looks like the Guvnor is a popular man today.'

'That makes a change,' murmured Antonia.

Stepping onto the hard shoulder, Boyd engaged his 'phone and enquired, 'What you got, Reg?'

'I don't know, Boyd. It's very unusual, that's all I can say at this stage'

'Unusual? In what way?' probed Boyd.

'I wrote that new program you suggested,' revealed Reg. 'The lights in the Operations Centre are beginning to flash in earnest. There's much more traffic than usual but we don't have a fixed pattern as yet. It's just busier than normal but there's no primary contact as you had hoped for. If you are right about what you told me was going on, then there's something you should know about that little war you mentioned during your last visit.'

'Armageddon?' queried Boyd.

Deep underground, not far from the cathedral city of Canterbury, Reg turned to look at a series of lights flashing on a map of London. Every now and again, one light flashed and ran a line to another light. The traffic was one way. The board was busy.

'I think something is going on,' ventured Reg. 'Statistically, traffic is fifteen per cent higher than normal but with my own eyes I can see that most of the traffic is not two way. You wanted an early warning. This might be it. In which case your Armageddon theory is about to start.'

'Thanks, keep a close watch on it, Reg. I'll make the necessary response,' replied Boyd.

Closing down one call, Boyd rang Anthea.

'Guvnor?' she responded.

'Where are you?' quizzed Boyd.

'Southbound into London three hours behind the target.'

'How on earth do you know that?' probed Boyd.

'We've just recovered CCTV from South Mimms service station. Mustafa and Pat bought fuel there three hours ago. They're travelling in a Ford Transit van registration number…'

Boyd keyed the number into his phone and replied, 'Well done! Circulate details. No approach. All sightings to be reported directly to yourself.'

'Understood,' replied Anthea. 'According to the police national computer, it's an overdue hire van. I guess they'll dump it when they reach their destination.'

'Agreed!' remarked Boyd. 'I'm calling all units in for a briefing at 0600 tomorrow morning. It's time to swamp the playing field.'

'All four wings?' enquired Anthea. 'It's a first!'

'Correct! Everyone! You, me, four DI's, eight DS's and forty DC's. I asked for one thousand for this operation, but we'll have to manage on fifty-four detectives from all four units. I'll also be calling in another four units from the armed response teams of Counter-Terrorist Command. That makes slightly over one hundred officers. Operation Swamp is on!'

'You mean you're going to use one hundred armed officers to cover the entire Metropolitan police area. Are you mad or just a genius with another crazy plan?'

'One or the other, Anthea,' laughed Boyd. 'Ring me with any updates or sightings. Otherwise, I'll see you in the morning. Don't be late.'

Closing down the call, Boyd slammed the buttons on his mobile and said, 'Ricky! I got a job for you. I want you in the Ticker Cell monitoring a live feed from the Operations Centre.'

A short time later, the Agusta 109 response helicopter lifted off from the motorway and returned to its base in London.

Inside, Boyd updated Bannerman and Antonia as he rattled the keyboards of an encrypted computer and arranged briefing papers and photographs for his operational participants.

11

The Special Crime Unit Amphitheatre
London
The following day

In accordance with usual practice, Ricky French – the gizmo man - had electronically swept the room for bugging devices and then made sure that all mobile phones were switched off prior to the secure briefing. The protocols were long established and fully accepted by members of the unit.

Ricky dimmed the lights and prepared to run the video presentation that Boyd would use in his briefing.

There was a quiet unspoken covenant between those seated in the semi-circular amphitheatre and Boyd who took to the stage to deliver his message.

But it was different today. Word was out that things had not gone according to plan. Despite Ricky's best intentions with regards to security, an atmosphere of rumour, tittle-tattle and confusion, had seeped into the room and it was generally accepted that this would be Boyd's only appearance before the entire Special Crime Unit in the role of Commander.

A ripple of applause greeted Boyd before people in the front row stood up and began clapping in earnest. The ripple grew to a swell of respect and admiration as the unit welcomed their recently ridiculed leader. Nothing was sacred in the Met. Not even a conversation in the office of God and his deputies. The audience knew that the Commissioner had made mincemeat of their man and no longer supported them.

'This is my first ever briefing to the combined wings of our Special Crime Unit,' explained Boyd. 'It is also likely to be my last. Before I begin, I would like to thank each and every one of you for being you, your professionalism over the years, your loyalty, and your undisputed dedication.'

The applause broke out again, but Boyd raised his hand and remarked, 'But before I go, one more time. That's all I ask. Just one more time.'

Ricky nudged a switch and the video spurred into action as Boyd delivered his final briefing.

It was the way of Boyd, the style he chose to interact with the unit, and the manner in which he sought to draw out the best in everyone present.

Unfazed when it came to a confrontation with what he reckoned to be inevitable, Boyd told them all the story – so far – exposed the photographs, differentiated between intelligence and evidence, raised the possibility of some of the targets seeking martyrdom, and others craving power and dominance in the Caliphate they planned. Then, again, he praised those who had worked with him and supported him all the way. Finally, he told them he truly believed they were about to face a disjointed army of ISIS soldiers who had returned from Syria in the last twelve to eighteen months. They wouldn't be driving tanks or jeeps on the streets of London and wouldn't be manning machine gun platforms welded onto the back of a dozen different pickups. The army, said Boyd, would not line up with their flags, regiments, brigades and platoons. They weren't organised that way. Rather, they would be dressed in jeans and tee-shirts, hoodies and tracksuit bottoms, trainers and bandanas, and their colours would be undetermined. Probably black, possibly combat green, always mixed. They were from the shadows, explained Boyd.

And they were waiting for the call that his ridiculed mind had decided was on the cards. It is in the shadows they had been hiding. Now the Sultán would inspire them, call them forward, and expect them to reignite the desire for a Caliphate.

Oh yes, Boyd said. Many of them had been on the de-radicalisation programme. Some of them had actually repented and revised their lives, were doing well, might turn out to be useful citizens in years to come. Others had ticked the boxes, followed the agreements, and then abandoned the system. Some of them had just told blatant lies. Then, suddenly, Boyd was back to where he had started. He was alone on the stage and finished. His mouth was dry from the task.

In the Commissioner's Office, Boyd had been listened to and criticised. In the amphitheatre, he was believed because he did not need to convince anyone present of his understanding of the events unfolding. It's what they did, what the unit preached, and what the unit fed on – namely, the understanding of various evil and extreme cultures and beliefs that represented the unit's bottom line.

Boyd called it, 'The Basic Understanding of the Enemy's Objective.'

The temporary, unwanted, inappropriately appointed Commander, who would soon be on his way back to a cosy little number in the Lake District, was best described as a living legend in the room in which he delivered his only briefing.

They'd listened patiently to Boyd for almost an hour in the cramped confines of the amphitheatre. They'd drank their coffee, swallowed their tea, nibbled on chocolate bars, crisps, mints, and energy bars, chewed gum, made notes on everything from a well-thumbed notebook to the back of the hand, and studied the papers presented to them.

The questions had been asked, the answers were given.

Now they pocketed the photographs, harnessed their surveillance radios, and adjusted their body armour.

Very shortly, they would check their weapons and move out.

It was time.

'Ricky! Hand deliver the video briefing to the Commissioner's office at 9 am precisely, please. Then man the Ticker Cell until close down. Your incoming priority is Reg from the Operations Centre. Your outgoing priority is the nearest team to the information Reg will provide. By the way, don't wait for a reply from the Commissioner. Just tell him that we're on the streets of London doing what we do with what we've got.'

'Will do!'

'That's it,' announced Boyd. 'Good luck everyone. Remember, we're monitoring live calls. Keep your ear to the radio. Stay alert and watch your arcs of fire. We're all done here.'

Within the hour, the entire unit clustered on various streets in the capital. Boyd drove his Porsche into an area between the Tower of London and Canary Wharf and settled down with his crew to monitor the radio.

'Here,' he said. 'We'll make our stand north of the river.'

'Should I get out and plant a Roman Standard?' chuckled Bannerman.

'If I had one spare the answer would be yes,' replied Boyd. 'The Eagle of the Ninth would do.'

'I thought the Ninth Legion was destroyed somewhere in the UK,' ventured Bannerman.

'I believe so,' remarked Boyd. 'But not us and not today!'

Stationed in car parks, main streets, side streets, and off-street parking areas, the unit listened and waited whilst their armed uniform colleagues moved off to man their allotted public targets.

The seconds ran into minutes, and then hours.

In the Commissioner's Office, a video presentation was watched, considered, and thrown nonchalantly into the out tray before a scribbled note was made in a diary reminding the writer to call Boyd to the office at the soonest 'compatible time'.

Mid-morning arrived on the 'surveillance plot' with traffic moving freely through the city as more coffee was drunk, tea swallowed, and another energy bar slid its way towards an ever-growing nervous stomach.

A light flickered on a huge screen in the underground facility that was the Operations Centre on the outskirts of Canterbury. Two seconds later, the Ticker computer system relayed the identical data into the security office of the Special Crime Unit.

Ricky French lifted the 'phone, punched the buttons, and spoke to Reg. 'I have you in the Ticker cell. Confirming live receipt. Virtually simultaneous?'

'A two-second delay,' replied Reg. 'You should have Target 32 on your list talking to Target 19 and you should remember that technology is not always perfect. You are two seconds behind my live receipt determined by my instant transmission to you. So you might be five seconds or more behind if the truth be known.'

'Confirmed! Sounds good to me,' reported Ricky running his finger down the Watch List.

'They're talking about going to the supermarket. It's code. They are being switched on by another user.'

'Who? Where?' quizzed Ricky.

'We're working on it,' revealed Ricky. 'Programme running, stand by!'

'Acknowledged,' replied Ricky.

He flicked a switch on his radio and announced, 'Starburst control, we have our first real contacts. Targets 32 and 19. Take closer order. Move to stand by positions.'

The entire unit checked the numbers, fingered the lists, and reacted accordingly. The vast majority remained static.

Two covert patrols in the Croydon area checked the identified targets and aligned them to a map in their possession. They fired their salon cars and took 'closer order'.

Another signal, another light shone, and Reg watched an illuminated route journey to its partner.

'Copying,' reported Reg.

'Target 19 talking to Target 14,' radioed Ricky.

Two more patrols moved in. A car door closed quietly and a woman in jeans and a hoodie began to make ground towards a certain target address.

Moments later, 'Target 14 talking to target 38,' from Ricky. 'Now target 38 talking to target 266.'

More patrols moved closer to the target addresses. Some in vehicles, others in civilian clothing.

'Ricky?' queried Boyd. 'Where is the source? Who is kickstarting these calls? It's a domino message system. One calls another who calls another who calls another. Do you see it?

237

Moments later, from Ricky via Reg, 'Yes! Were on it! Stand by! Programme running!'

In Croydon, Omar pocketed his mobile and carried a short step ladder to the top of the stairs. He gained access to the loft, gathered a rucksack, checked the contents, and replaced the loft cover. He returned the stepladder to its place in the kitchen annexe and walked out of the back door into the streets of London.

Omar hoisted the rucksack onto one shoulder and eased a twelve-inch zombie knife into a more comfortable part on his trouser belt.

In Stratford, Sayid dismantled his mobile 'phone, threw the sim card in the fire, and left the house by the rear door. From a garden shed, he removed a machete from beneath a tarpaulin sheet on a workbench, placed it inside a sports bag with other weapons, and then opened a gate into a narrow lane at the rear of the house.

A female in pair of jeans and a hoodie clicked her radio twice and began to follow Sayid.

More lights. More routed calls as Reg watched the screen develop and Ricky tried to keep up with the movement of targets.

'Any luck?' probed Ricky.

'Not yet,' replied Reg. 'Source unknown. GCHQ downloading assistance data package. Stand by.'

'Another one,' noted Ricky. 'Starburst Control! Target 18 talking to target 97. They're meeting at the community centre.'

Another door closed behind another suspect as they made their way into the capital with their bags, hidden weapons, and wicked intentions.

Another squad car moved closer to the target as a complex attempt at surveillance of the many was carried out by the few.

Omar crossed the road, broke into a jog, and boarded a bus.

Sayid hailed a taxi.

'Heading into the city centre, towards Westminster,' from a lady in jeans and a hoodie.

'Same here,' from another member of the unit.

'All units, plot routes and report direction your target is taking,' ordered Boyd. 'Is there a common denominator?'

In East Ham, Barking, Dagenham, Croydon, Harrow, and Leytonstone – to name but a few boroughs - the Sultán's army obeyed the call, left their homes, and followed their orders.

The most complex surveillance operation ever mounted in the capital was underway.

Two more targets emerged from the electronic surveillance system inspired by the facilities of the Operations Centre. One made for a tube station, the other walked through a park and headed towards the mosque.

Detective Sergeant Terry Anwhari's team split into two and began following the latest targets on foot.

'Guvnor,' radioed Terry. 'We are running out of troops. I have nothing left for you.'

'Noted,' replied Boyd. 'Stand by!'

Boyd housed the radio and quietly thought, 'Shit! Now what I do. If I were playing fives and threes at dominoes, I'd be out of wood and knocking on my turn. Oh, for a thousand officers and a blankety-blank domino. There are going to be too many to take out if this continues the way I think it will.'

Ricky radioed, 'Guvnor, capacity approaching command overload. Permission to take control?'

'Agreed!' radioed Boyd. 'Starburst control takes the lead. Starburst has operational deployment control!'

Ricky French and MPS radio controllers took over the deployment of resources as Boyd breathed a sigh of relief and checked his firearm.

'Contacting MPS air support wing for assistance,' radioed Ricky.

Prayers were at an end.

Yusuf bowed to his closest friends, grasped many hands in the parting, and nodded to others as he gradually made his way out of the mosque and into the daylight.

Gripping his hands low across his stomach, head down, Yusuf negotiated the steps into a broad plaza and then strolled slowly towards the musalla and the circular pillars that supported a large shelter enough to house a score or more of men. There were no women present in either the mosque or the musalla. In this mosque, as was common in the majority of such places, women were not allowed.

Dressed in a grey coloured thobe, Yusuf's ankle-deep Kaftan was buttoned at the neck. Long-sleeved, there were four buttons that stretched in regular intervals to his chest. Here a breast pocket was available, and the garment was finished off unpretentiously with a flurry of grey-white needlework on his right shoulder. It was important to Yusuf to look smart but not stand out. Deliberately, he did not sport a colourful thobe. His drab kaftan met his requirements perfectly and was complimented by a matching skull cap (taqiyah) which was often worn during daily prayers.

Each step was carefully measured. Each pace carefully timed. Yusuf did not rush to the scene of those whom he knew would be dissecting the words of the Iman. He did not wish to be first at the opinion feast that would seek an alternative to the words he had heard in the mosque. Rather, he walked slowly intending to climb the two steps into the musalla and take his normal place towards the rear of the audience. Here, he would look, listen, and remember who was there and what was said between those he considered to be his enemies.

Finding a place in the shadows beside one of the circular stone pillars, Yusuf bowed to the speaker and then avoided eye contact with those who were taking things to heart.

The colour of his clothing blended admirably with the drab circular stones that encircled him and the grey ceiling that hung above him. With narrow eyes, he watched proceedings as the arguments and opinions of those disenchanted with an unpopular Iman sought to outdo each other.

'Never before have I heard such words,' said one. 'To suggest that women in the western world have jobs – status if you will – that in some cases makes them of a higher status than a male is abhorrent to me. Where does our Iman get these judgements from?'

'Agreed!' from a voice in the gathering followed by, 'Not in our faith. Allah - the one and only God, creator and sustainer of the universe - surely dictates that women are merely our servants and know their place in the scheme of things.'

'Precisely,' from another voice in the centre. 'The words we have heard today are misplaced, misguided, and cannot have come from the voice of Allah – Peace be upon him – in the way that the Iman has said. No! We all know what women are for and it is not their place to hold a higher status than men.'

'It is the Shayaatin (devils) that would have us believe women are such important creatures,' professed another. 'Denounce the Shayaatin.'

'The Iman's words are surely from those who are of the Scripture – the Jews and Christians – or any other disbelievers that should not be listened to when they suggest such ridiculous things. It is not the way of Allah who is All-Seer of what you do – Allah, Peace upon him.'

Yusuf joined in as those around him nodded vigorously in agreement.

One man stepped forward. He wore a blue kaftan and seemed to be instantly respected by those around him.

In a softer voice, he began to read aloud from the Book.

A mobile sounded somewhere amongst the crowd and to the left of Yusuf.

A hand slipped into a pocket and retrieved a 'phone.

Yusuf stepped to the side, moved closer to a pillar, and watched the recipient step away from the group to take a call.

Unusual, thought Yusuf. Prayers have just ended. Perhaps it is his wife.

The man engaged the 'phone. He was dressed in the colour brown, but Yusuf could not see all of him from where he stood. Yusuf listened and then stepped casually forward into the group when the 'phone was pocketed.

'And so it is written,' from the man in the blue kaftan who had captured the audience with a passage from the Book he intended to read aloud.

Yusuf turned his head to watch one of the followers leaving the group and making towards the main road. The man was wearing a dark brown ankle-length kaftan with a matching skull cap. He hurried along the pavement.

'Yes, that's him,' decided Yusuf.

Closing his eyes, Yusuf tried to remember the words he had heard during the telephone conversation and then stepped away from the musalla as he followed the man wearing a brown kaftan.

Elsewhere in London, the airwaves were in use.

'I'm following Sayid,' radioed DS Janice Burns. 'He's in a taxi registration number… and we're making towards Westminster. I'm in the taxi behind'

'Noted,' from Boyd. 'Stand by! With you shortly.'

Boyd hurtled through the London traffic, reached to the dashboard, and activated a siren.

'Now,' remarked Boyd switching lanes and gaining on the two taxis at speed. 'I have control,' radioed Boyd. 'Stand by, Janice. Stand By! Strike!'

Boyd hurtled past Janice in the first taxi, overtook the second, and then hit the brakes forcing the taxi containing Sayid to swerve to the nearside and stop.

Bannerman was out of Boyd's Porsche and running back to the taxi when Janice Burns beat him to it.

She reached the taxi door, pulled it open, and shouted, 'Police! Freeze!'

Producing a double-barrelled shotgun from beneath her clothing, she thrust the weapon into the rear passenger compartment and pressed it into Sayid's chest saying, 'Don't even twitch! Hands! Let me see those hands!'

'What the hell,' screamed the taxi driver.

'Easy driver,' counselled Bannerman. 'Police! It's all under control.'

'Hands up!' yelled Janice.

Sayid remained motionless.

'Excuse me,' ventured Bannerman.

Leaning into the taxi, Bannerman grasped Sayid by the collar and unceremoniously yanked him from the vehicle onto the footpath.

Clutching a sports bag, Sayid sprawled onto the pavement and tried to grab a machete from inside the bag.

A large round fist connected with his nose followed by Bannerman shouting, 'The lady said freeze!'

Sayid's nasal bone cracked and blood spurted onto the pavement.

Janice knelt on Sayid's back and prodded the end of her double-barrelled shotgun into Sayid's skull allowing Bannerman to upturn the sports bag.

A machete bounced onto the concrete followed by the rattle of two more long knives, assorted ammunition, two handguns, and two sawn-off shotguns.

'Well, thank the Lord for that,' pronounced Janice. Radioing Boyd, she revealed, 'One arrested in possession of knives and firearms. We have a positive find, Guvnor.'

A shrill whistle of relief filled a Porsche as Boyd stepped from the vehicle and acknowledged Janice with, 'Praise be! I'm calling all the Borough Commanders.'

Surrounded by a small crowd that had gathered, Bannerman handcuffed Sayid whilst Boyd radioed control with, 'One arrested Westminster in a covert operation designed to disrupt large-scale terrorist attack in Central London. Advise all Borough Commanders of incidents in progress. Also, inform the Commissioner's office of multiple incidents taking place. We are taking prisoners, but the city is under attack.'

'Bit heavy there, Guvnor,' suggested Janice. 'I only counted one arrest, or did I miss something?'

'I needed to be,' replied Boyd. 'We've got one in the bag but there's at least another twenty on the streets and I reckon they are all up to the same thing. I'm kind of hoping the message might kickstart the Commissioner. Does it matter? They want rid of us anyway. I've nothing to lose, Janice.'

Boyd's radio clicked and he leaned into the Porsche to catch the response from Met Control.

Simultaneously, a huge explosion occurred when one of the targets detonated his suicide vest at the entrance to a nearby tube station.

Glass shards tumbled from high buildings and the ground shook for a few moments as London's world took a turn for the worst.

'We missed something,' replied Boyd gently steadying his feet from the bomb blast that rocked the ground upon which he stood. 'It only takes one, Janice, and they've done it.'

Hauling Sayid to his feet as a police van approached, Bannerman stood him against the wall and enquired, 'Looks like a friend of yours as just gone up in smoke. Did you know him?'

Laughing, Sayid spat into Bannerman's face and said, 'And now he has more virgins waiting for him than you have hairs on your arse.'

'How many of you?' probed Bannerman.

'Too many for you,' chuckled Sayid.

Two officers arrived, opened the rear door of the police arrest van, and guided Sayid into the prisoner compartment.

'Book him in and I'll be along shortly,' instructed Bannerman.

A cloud of black curling smoke from the suicide bomb swirled brutally into the sky above the building line amidst a growing cacophony of blaring sirens and screaming people.

'We need to be there,' suggested Janice pointing towards the direction of the explosion.

'Damned if we do and damned if we don't,' voiced Boyd. 'Our job today is to try and stop the attacks. Leave it!'

'Breaking! Breaking!' radioed Detective Sergeant Terry Anwhari. 'I'm on a bus with target Omar. Urgent assistance required. He's bulky. I think he might be wearing a suicide vest.'

'Let's go,' ordered Boyd. Then radioing, he enquired, 'Location? Bus route? Top or bottom deck?'

'I'm there,' broke in DI Anthea Adams. 'Approaching fast.... Top deck... Location Covent Garden...'

Boyd's Porsche pulled away from the scene of the first arrest with the vehicle siren blaring and Bannerman and Janice hanging on for dear life leaving two uniform officers remaining on the spot to gather a sports bag full of incriminating evidence against Sayid.

Two more section patrol cars arrived to assist the uniforms as Boyd hurtled the Porsche towards Covent Garden.

A hand reached out of a car window and placed a magnetic blue light on the roof of Boyd's Porsche as he switched to main beam headlights and gunned his way towards the bus.

'Boarding at Temple Place,' bellowed Boyd on the radio.

'Sounds appropriate,' suggested Bannerman. 'Make haste, Guvnor. We don't want to miss the service. I've got my best bib and tucker on. Is it Holy Communion?'

'No,' bellowed Boyd. 'It's nearly Easter and time to stop a crucifixion.'

'Hot cross buns! Don't get cross, Guvnor. Get even!'

'Remind me to reboot you, Bannerman. You have the weirdest sense of humour in the unit.'

'Oh! At least I'm good at something then.'

On a bus in central London, Anthea bent low to the floor of the bus and then gradually slid beneath the first row of seats.

Terry Anwhari stood up and said, 'Please, don't do that. You don't need to do that. Really!'

Omar opened his anorak to display a foot-long jagged zombie knife stuck into his trouser belt. Above the belt, Terry Anwhari made out the unmistakable contours of a self-made suicide vest.

'Omar, isn't it?' probed Terry softly.

'Who are you?' blurted nervously by a frightened man.

'Don't be scared,' ventured Terry. 'I am of your faith. I can help you. Just do as I say and you'll be alright. You don't have to go through with this.'

'Who are you?' shrieked Omar at the top of his voice.

'Just a friendly policeman asking you not to do that, Omar. It won't do any of us any good.'

'It will take me to paradise and send you to hell,' voiced Omar.

Terry counted eight hand grenades and an explosive package hanging from the vest. They were all connected to one fuse wire that led to a handheld detonator under the control of the subject Omar.

Omar's finger rested on the top button of the detonator. The slightest pressure applied might blow them all to kingdom come.

'I don't want to go to hell, Omar,' insisted Terry. 'I have so much still to do with my life. And I am a man of peace. I just want you to disconnect that device you're wearing before anyone gets hurt.'

Anthea's stomach flattened as she crept beneath another seat. The smell of stale tobacco and abandoned litter filled her nostrils from the downtrodden floor of the top deck of the bus. Her long crawl continued.

The bus came to a standstill in Temple Place when Boyd slung his Porsche directly into the path of the vehicle and jumped from the driver's side.

'Temple Place!' radioed Boyd. 'It's going down now.'

'What's happening?' yelled Omar. 'Why have we stopped?'

'Just routine, I expect,' suggested Terry softly. 'It is a bus route after all. People get off to go shopping and others get on to go home. You know how it is, Omar. The conductor will be taking their fares on the bottom deck. Did you pay your fare, or should I pay it when we get off the bus? Are you coming with me, Omar? Death is short but a life well-lived can bring so much to one who has learnt how to love. Don't die today, Omar. Live!'

'Upper deck, row nine, I'm belly down and crawling,' whispered Anthea on her radio.

'Boarding,' replied Boyd as he and Bannerman jumped onto the rear platform and began to ascend the winding staircase.

Janice took control downstairs, updated the conductor, quickly ushered passengers from the vehicle, and then made her way to the front of the bus to speak with the driver.

The wireless was now full of call signs attending scores of incidents across the capital as Reg continued to rapidly feed the operation with live telephone data from across an operational screen originating from the quiet undisturbed suburbs of Canterbury. Ricky fielded the calls and deployed the sparse troops that were available, and Boyd learnt all there ever was to know about multitasking from the fourth step of a London bus staircase.

Less than two miles away, to the west, a rattle of gunfire filled the shopping complex near Clerkenwell when two names on the nation's Watch List unleashed the power of El Sultán's army on an unsuspecting crowd of shoppers.

Similarly, a man dressed in jeans and a tee shirt walked into a cinema in Marleybone, two miles to the east, and promptly produced an eighteen-inch zombie knife. He threatened staff briefly before being taken to the ground by the company's security staff, a veteran soldier, and a retired policeman from Devon and Cornwall who had been waiting in the queue.

In the Metropolitan Police Service (MPS) Radio control centre, the hand of the officer in charge reached a button on the wireless system and radioed, 'All units MPS, be advised all firearms units MPS now engaged at multiple locations. All Borough Commanders aware and military assistance now being sought.'

Located in secure army barracks in central London, a dozen blacked-out 4 x 4 multi-purpose, specially adapted, vehicles drove out of their depot and travelled at speed to a shopping complex in Clerkenwell. The driver wore a beret-sporting the cap badge of the Special Air Service.

Boyd emerged from the staircase and took his first step onto the upper deck.

'Easy!' whispered Boyd. 'Take it easy, Omar. I am a friend of Terry here. He is a good friend and a good man. Terry is good at helping people, Omar.'

'Stand still. Don't crowd me,' bellowed a frightened man called Oman who took a step to the side and then returned nervously to his original position.

'Who told you to do this?' probed Boyd.

Omar stepped to the side again, stood in the middle of the upper deck, between the rows of seats, and shook the detonator with his hand shouting, 'No-one! The Caliphate! The Caliphate will survive.'

'It was the Sultán, wasn't it?' quizzed Boyd discreetly releasing a handgun from a holster in his belt.

'You are both police?' probed Omar stepping back towards the front glass window of the upper deck.

'He is my friend,' revealed Terry. 'He has come to help. I call him Billy. Billy wants to know if the Sultán told you to do this.'

'The Sultán,' wavered Omar. 'Yes, the Caliphate and the Sultán. I am going to paradise. The Sultán promised me my life would begin in paradise. Praise be to El Sultán.'

'Did he telephone you?' enquired Boyd. 'The Sultán! Did the Sultán phone you, Omar?'

Omar shook the detonator again and said, 'It is written in the Book. It is the word of Allah – Bless Him and grant Him peace – I am called to defend the Caliphate by El Sultán and our leader Aishah.'

'You don't need to go anywhere,' softened Terry. 'Why don't you disconnect that, and it will be all over?'

'Disconnect?' muttered Omar confused. 'I cannot disconnect it. I have vowed not to disconnect the vest. It is my time. My time for the Caliphate.'

'Come to me,' pleaded Terry. 'I will disconnect you from the Sultán, the Caliphate, and all the hate that has been crammed into that confused, bewildered mind of yours. Trust me, Omar. Billy and I will look after you. You are not a terrorist of the truest kind. You are not like the bad people we find. Your mind is troubled and confused, Omar. Come with me and follow the way of peace with me!'

Terry Anwhari took a step forward as another bead of sweat trickled down his neck, his heart rate doubled, his blood pressure reached boiling point, and the adrenalin pummelled its way into every corner of his body.

'No! Never!' screamed Omar. 'I will be a martyr. Inshallah! If Allah wills it. Inshallah!'

Terry's short pace forward was enough to cross an imaginary line that separated truth from deceit, religion from fantasy, fact from fiction, love from hate, and sanity from disorientation. It was as if the line had been crossed and broken forever, as if Omar's mind had been taken over by an unseen being.

'On three,' whispered Boyd on the radio checking on the whereabouts of Anthea. 'One…' He moved the weapon's safety switch to 'off'.

'Allah may not will it,' voiced Terry.

'You are with them,' screeched Omar. 'Disbelievers! Shayaatin!'

'Two…' from Boyd, his finger stretching along the trigger guard and preparing to curl the trigger.

Omar stepped forward waving the detonating button in Terry's face, screaming more abuse, and then lifting both arms to shoulder height.

A mobile 'phone rang. There was a shrill note bouncing from the walls of the bus that was sufficient to distract Omar.

Turning, Omar swivelled his head towards where he thought the sound was coming from.

Anthea leaned upwards. Her face suddenly became visible to Omar.

He saw her outstretched hand and the firearm it held.

'Three…' from Boyd.

'Allahu Akbar…' loud and clear from Omar as the thumb on his right hand began to plunge the detonator and his eyes scanned the top deck of a London bus for a noise his bewildered mind could not establish.

The first two bullets fired from floor level by Anthea took a microsecond to travel not much more than a yard from the dirty downtrodden floor of the top deck to Omar's rear skull just above the top of the spine. Anthea's target was the top of the spinal cord where the central nervous system was located. A good shot on target might render the system instantly incapable of transmitting instructions to the rest of the body. The hope was that such a shot would prevent Omar from detonating his suicide vest.

Simultaneously, Boyd fired his Glock directly into Omar's throat hoping the bullets might hit the same bodily target from a different angle.

Terry Anwhari threw himself to the left and onto the floor at the same time that Bannerman pulled both triggers and felt two slugs rush down the tubes of his double-barrelled shotgun.

The suicide vest was ripped to pieces when Bannerman's slugs hit the target.

Thrown backwards at speed, Omar smashed into the back of a seat and then fell forward with the detonator fully depressed and a length of cord flapping carelessly in the chest area.

Anthea rolled over. Boyd ducked. Bannerman reloaded and stepped forward.

Impulse!

Omar's body was indeed shattered but not to the point where the thumb on his right hand had stopped working all together.

Repeatedly, his thumb plunged the detonator down. Repeatedly, nothing happened. Finally, he died.

Boyd reached forward, ripped the detonator cord from Omar's possession, and then pulled open the suicide vest.

'It's a dud!' realized Bannerman. 'The vest is faulty. The bloody vest is faulty,' bellowed Bannerman.

'Just as well,' snapped Boyd. 'What a bloody cock-up. We train every week. Anthea! A double tap to the central nervous system at point-blank range works. Not a shot from the bloody floor at three feet. Who taught you that one? You went from bullseye to a triple zilch in less than a breath. Not good enough!'

'The same training says switch your mobile off when engaged on trigger operations,' frowned Anthea.

'Point taken!' admitted Boyd. 'You're right.'

'Real life is never the same as the training ground, Guvnor. You know that.'

'Well, so much for the sodding training ground,' chuckled Boyd. 'Good work, Anthea. Terry! I feel for you. I thought you were going to get there. You really tried so hard.'

'Sad, Guvnor!' responded Terry. 'Some bastard of a Sultán deliberately picked a man with mental health problems and then convinced him to blow himself up.'

'And we were lucky the vest didn't work,' declared Boyd. 'Put the bus off the road. Call in the team and inform forensics and MPS control. The usual. Meanwhile, I need to make a call.'

Helping Anthea to her feet, Boyd said, 'Still a great shot though. Are you alright?'

'I'll survive,' replied Anthea. 'But my knees are as stiff as hell. It's cramped down there.'

'Walk around quickly,' advised Boyd. 'Get that blood pumping through your body.'

Stepping into a pool of blood escaping from Omar's body, Anthea remarked, 'Poor sod thinks he's in paradise now. How lucky are we? If that vest had been working properly…'

'Don't even think about it,' replied Boyd deliberately looking away from the body. 'Excuse me. I have that call to make.'

Boyd made his way down the staircase, found the missed call on his 'phone, and recognised the number. He rang Yusuf.

'Yusuf! What you got for me?' quizzed Boyd.

'I've just got off the tube at Finsbury Park, Mister Boyd,' revealed Yusuf. 'I've been following a man from the musalla. He walked, took a bus, walked again, and then got a tube. I'm sure he's taking me to your man, Mister Boyd.'

'What makes you think that?' probed Boyd.

'He took a call on his mobile in the musalla. I was standing close to him at the time. The caller told him it was time for prayers with

Aishah. Prayer time was over, Mister Boyd, and I know that Aishah is home in Syria.

'Are you sure Aishah is in Syria?' quizzed Boyd. 'Any mention of Ahmed – his brother?'

'No! None at all,' replied Yusuf. 'I think the Sultán has called my man forward. He's one of the extremists I spoke of. I do not trust this man I am following. He is evil.'

'Where are you now?'

'Walking towards Crouch End.'

'On your own?'

'Yes! My feet are tired and I do not know this place well.'

'Wait a moment!' remarked Boyd.

Gesticulating, Boyd signalled Bannerman to join him saying, 'Hand the scene over to the locals when they arrive. Get the team together. I have a tip coming in about the location of the Sultán. Prepare to move.'

'Will do,' replied Bannerman hastily engaging his radio to call reinforcements to the scene. 'It's fast move day and I'm not sure we can keep up with all this.'

'It's the job, Bannerman,' scolded Boyd. 'Crack it!'

As a number of emergency vehicles converged on the area, Boyd continued talking to Yusuf.

'Describe your man,' pleaded Boyd taking notes and eventually responding with, 'Okay, any chance he's seen you following him?'

Janice and Anthea joined Boyd as local officers arrived at the scene and were briefed by Bannerman.

'Give the man plenty of room, Yusuf,' instructed Boyd.

'He's got into a van,' said Yusuf. 'It's a red Mercedes registered number…'

'Which way is it travelling?' enquired Boyd.

'It's not. It's stationary,' revealed Yusuf. 'The vehicle is actually static on parkland adjacent to the roadside. There are a few vans parked nearby, Mister Boyd. Two white ones, a blue one and two grey ones. I don't know what makes they are.'

'What's going on?'

'It looks like a meeting of some kind,' advised Yusuf. 'Not prayers. Something else! I don't know what is happening, but they look as if they are all together.'

'How many vans have we?'

'Six,' declared Yusuf. 'What do you want me to do?'

'Absolutely nothing except stay exactly where you are,' ordered Boyd. 'I'll ring you back shortly.'

Ending the call, Boyd rang another number whilst walking to the Porsche and waving at this team to join him.

The call connected and Boyd said, 'Reg! Do you have any coverage on the Crouch End area?'

'One call fifteen minutes ago made from an unknown mobile to a mobile on our Watch List,' replied Reg checking his log. 'That's all. Why?'

'If the man we were looking for was constantly travelling, unknown to us, and had a clean previously unused mobile 'phone, the locations would change every time he made a call. Am I right?'

'Yes, Boyd, obviously,' revealed Reg. 'You've become a techie at last.'

'Do you have any traces of unknown mobiles connecting with known targets on the Watch List since our operation began?' enquired Boyd.

'Stand by,' from Reg perusing his log once more. 'No! Nothing untoward.'

'Are you sure?' enquired Boyd. 'How about you look at yesterday, for example. Anything interesting there?'

'Wait one!' from Reg followed moments later by, 'That explains it. I've two traces since the operation began and eighteen over the last twenty-four hours. Sorry, make that twenty, it's still updating.'

'All because we started monitoring calls this morning – mid-morning to be precise - but those calls from an unknown mobile all began yesterday, Reg. Am I right?' probed Boyd.

Reg worked his fingers across the keyboard, checked the big screens before him in the Operations Centre, and said, 'The basics! He nearly damn well beat us with the basics. Yes, you're right, Boyd. Most of the contacts from that unknown mobile to the known 'phones were made late yesterday evening. You know what that means if you're right. He's a day ahead of us. Your man called everyone yesterday. He's just tidying up his missed calls today. What I can see here, on the screens, is the domino factor.' His fingers went into overdrive on the keyboard and the processor approached overload before he continued with, 'Those he called yesterday all called someone else shortly after he rang or this morning. Good God, Boyd. It's a whole goddamned network he's in touch with.'

The Porsche engine fired. Boyd reversed, swung the car around, and headed off towards Crouch End with a blue light rotating from the roof, an engine roaring, a pair of headlights flashing wildly, and dozens of Londoners watching and wondering as some sought safety and others sought news.

'Can you identify that unknown number?' requested Boyd. Then turning to Bannerman, Boyd said, 'Yusuf gave me this van number. Who owns it?'

As Bannerman called MPS, Reg triggered another phase of the system and waited for an answer.

Meanwhile, Boyd weaved in and out of the traffic oblivious to the multiple assistance calls now filling the airwaves.

'Clerkenwell squad need back up,' from the radio. 'Terrorists taking hostages. Military engaging.'

'Two men armed with knives arrested Oxford Street,' from the radio.

'Gunfire and explosion Regent's Park area,' from the radio. 'Believed another suicide bomber.'

'Armageddon!' voiced Boyd. 'London is under attack and falling apart.'

A car ran a red light at a junction and Boyd slammed the car horn before swerving around the offending vehicle.

'Anthea!' shouted Boyd. 'Get hold of Ricky and update him. I want Joe Harkness and his team to join us. How many is that?

'Mick Turner, Hazel Scott, George Fish, Harry Nugent, Phil Charlton, Tom Richardson and Martin Duffy,' reported Anthea. 'That makes another eight.'

'Divert them to Crouch End pronto,' instructed Boyd. 'There's me, you, Bannerman, Terry and Janice. That's five making a total of thirteen.'

'Unlucky for some,' remarked Janice.

'Things could be worse,' argued Boyd. 'It could be Friday the thirteenth,' argued Boyd. 'We'll do what we can with what we've got.'

Stowing his mobile, Bannerman reported, 'The number of the Mercedes van doesn't exist. It's never been issued which probably means it's stolen or on false plates.'

Reg phoned and said, 'I have a trace on the unknown mobile. It's linked to a company based in Brussels which is on the Interpol 'suspicious enterprise' list. That means the company is flagged to law enforcement agencies as possibly involved in money laundering or some other kind of financial crime. It looks like you're onto something, Boyd.'

'Thanks, Reg,' replied Boyd. 'I owe you one.'

Bannerman gazed out of the window, glanced at Boyd, and enquired, 'Are you sure, Guvnor? Are we headed in the right direction? Okay, the 'phones in the area are red hot but the city is under attack and we're off chasing a mystery man who got into a suspicious red van. The world needs us. Is this right?'

'It has to be right,' professed Boyd. 'He's activated a small army that he can use to today and stand down until who knows when? There are others who can deal with those calls, Bannerman. Our remit is national security. No-one else has access to Reg's telephone monitoring system. I'm reading what's going on but I've no time to tell it to the world. In any event, I've already told the Commissioner what to expect. Do you want me to tell the whole world I told you so?'

'Of course not, but if we're on the wrong track, the Commissioner and every politician in the country will crucify us,' argued Bannerman.

'Well, what do you prefer?' enquired Boyd. 'Being closed down anyway or being crucified.'

'I'd rather go down fighting,' from Bannerman.

'Hear! Hear!' from Anthea. 'It's not every day you survive a suicide bomber.'

'Seeing as how it's our lucky day,' revealed Terry. 'What could possibly go wrong?'

'We need to catch the leader,' argued Boyd. 'The man who inspires the others, makes them martyrs, and causes mayhem. I know what you're all thinking. Should we be somewhere else trying to take someone else to the ground? The answer is no! Leave the dead and dying. Save the living!'

'My so-called weird sense of humour would like to suggest to you that someone somewhere would set up a five-year public enquiry into what you have just said,' offered Bannerman. 'And still have no answer to the problem other than to create a sub-committee to consider the problem before engaging a consultancy to prepare and submit a report on the subject.'

'Weird sense of humour! You've got five seconds max to decide on the future. With me or against me?'

'Always with you!'

Selecting a lower gear, Boyd threw the Porsche around a tight left-hand corner, carelessly bumped across a pavement, and said, 'Okay! This is what we're going to do. Copy it to Joe and his team.'

Forty-five minutes later, Boyd slid Yusuf into a squad car and removed him from the area to a secure police station.

By now, the two teams were dispersed into five squad cars operating on their own securely encrypted radio channels and each linked into Ricky French hoping for another telephone contact to the immediate area. The squad were plotted and watching the red Mercedes van and the other five vans that seemed to be connected.

Boyd radioed, 'I have control. I have the eyeball. We have bodies moving at the rear of a white van. Stand by.'

Through binoculars, Boyd zeroed in on a woman and man who were taking packages from the rear of the white van and putting them into one of the grey ones.

'Bingo!' radioed Boyd. 'Second opinion please!'

'Agreed!' from Anthea. 'Mustafa and the Downing Street assassin – Pat Angel – That's who I see. But what are they doing?'

'Not sure,' said Boyd. 'Joe! Can you take this gey van away when it moves and do a hard stop, search and report? I'd like you to confirm my thought patterns.'

'Will do, I'll take Mick and George with me. Three mobiles.'

'Stand by for movement,' from Boyd.

The team watched Mustafa and Pat Angel moving equipment from the van to another. Handshakes followed and then the grey van began to move away as Pat and Mustafa returned to the white van.

'We need to know what they are up to,' remarked Boyd. 'Better to be prepared and armed with some fact before we go charging in.'

'Please, no charges,' replied Anthea. 'My knees won't make it.'

'Stand by, target manoeuvring,' radioed Boyd. 'On the grass, moving to the road, headed your way, Joe. Two male occupants visible in the front of the van. Late twenties, I'd say.'

'I have all that,' from Joe. 'Target coming this way. Give it space, gents. I want it well out of the playground before the strike.'

The team acknowledged as Boyd turned his attention to the parking area and studied the red Mercedes van that interested him.

Five minutes later, Joe radioed, 'Take closer order. Come through Mick. Come through George.'

Joe's team closed on for the stop on the outskirts of Crouch End as Boyd's team listened to the commentary and watched the remaining vans on the parkland.

'You have control, Mick,' from Joe. 'You have control.'

As Joe remained at the rear of the grey van, Mick and George began overtaking the target van with Mick at the head of the convoy sizing up the traffic situation.

'Stand by…. Stand by…. Strike!' from Mick.

Immediately, Mick swung his squad car ahead of the van, braked, and forced it to slow down. Simultaneously, George drove closer to the offside of the van, reduced speed, and prevented an overtaking opportunity from appearing.

Joe drove hard up behind the van, prevented it from reversing, and waited for the van to stop.

'Metpol! Trigger! Trigger! Trigger!' radioed Joe.

The driver of the grey van had two alternatives. One was to put the foot down and barge out of the way, the other was to stop driving.

The grey van pulled into the near side of the road as George came to a standstill and Tom and Martin jumped from the vehicle with their weapons drawn. Moments later, Joe's team had pulled the two males from the van, taken them to the ground, and – under armed conditions – handcuffed the suspects. Pulling the van keys from the ignition, Joe stepped quickly to the rear of the van, unlocked the rear compartment, and climbed in.

'Shopping bags!' announced Joe rummaging through the contents. 'Not your usual kind.'

Tom and Martin glanced at the prisoners and then at Joe who was walking towards them carrying a shopping bag.

'Not yet primed, I'd say,' said Joe directing his remark to the cuffed prisoners. 'Gentlemen! Can I ask you why you are carrying a number of explosive devices in the back of your van?'

There was no reply save for Joe who nodded to his colleagues and said, 'It's a lock up. Do the business.'

Stepping away from the immediate area of the arrest, Joe radioed Boyd with, 'Guvnor! Hard stop complete! Two males arrested in possession of multiple shopping bags containing explosive devices. Sorry, but I can't leave this one. I'm calling in bomb disposal to make the scene safe.'

'All understood,' replied Boyd. 'Well done and thank you. Call in the locals as quickly as you can and deploy triggers when you can to this plot please.'

'Will do,' replied Joe. 'Good luck, Guvnor. 'We'll be there as quick as we can.'

'Suspicions and thought patterns confirmed,' remarked Boyd to his team. 'But we haven't got much time. That stop and the subsequent action it is about to create will be all over social media within five minutes.'

'And any one of them in those vans could be tuned in watching,' observed Anthea.

'Well, I'll be...' muttered Boyd. 'Who have we here?'

On the parkland, perhaps five yards from the highway, a man wearing sunglasses and a black bandana slid from the front seat of the red Mercedes and began deliberately stretching his legs. The man was tall, broad-shouldered, and swarthy in appearance. He was dressed in trainers, jeans, and a camouflage-coloured combat jacket.

'He's stiff too,' noted Anthea. 'And if I'm not mistaken that is our mystery man - one Edward John Angel.'

'The Sultán,' announced Boyd.

'All we really need now is for that man to get cosy with Mustafa and Pat Angel and we've got all three in the same area. I think that helps the evidence chain.'

'Just a bit,' chuckled Bannerman.

'He must have heard you,' offered Janice. 'Look!'

The woman in the trio was pouring a drink of some kind from a vacuum flask she was holding. She kissed Edward on the forehead before passing him a cup. Then she poured Mustafa one.

The team continued to watch proceedings as Janice loaded her shotgun, checked her handgun, and said, 'Are we invited to the tea party? The clock is ticking.'

'They're praying,' offered Bannerman. 'Look, the three of them are praying.'

On the grass, in the parkland, the wanted trio and their followers from the other vans, took up their positions and began praying in the Islamic tradition.

'We've three cars and there are eight of us with Hazel, Harry and Phil from Joe's team,' declared Boyd. 'If they're praying then they're not on the same wavelength as us. They don't smell a rat. We'll approach the plot casually and then at speed and hit them hard. Surprise and stealth ought to do it.'

'And some luck,' muttered Janice.

'I'm calling it in,' revealed Boyd. 'What was that about the training ground, Anthea?'

'Ordinarily,' explained Anthea. 'We should have at least one perimeter secured by armed officers to contain the situation and prevent escape but as I look around and see black smoke rising from various parts of the capital, I think there's more chance of getting a delivery of rocking horse shit.'

'Agreed!' ventured Bannerman checking his shotgun. 'I'll take out the tyres then. That should stop them.'

'Me too,' volunteered Janice.

Tapping buttons on his mobile, Boyd got through to MPS and reported, 'This is a Trigger message from Commander Boyd of the Special Crime Unit. An armed terrorist incident is in progress at parkland near Crouch End. We are moving in to arrest three persons who are wanted for multiple murders and terrorism in various parts of the globe. Please inform the local Borough Commander. Assistance required. Trigger operation in progress. Multiple targets with armed supporters. Ends.'

Boyd listened, waited, and then replied, 'Yes, another one. Pray for rain. That usually sends people home.'

A green Ford Escort suddenly screeched to a halt near the red Mercedes van. The driver got out and approached the trio. He pointed in the direction of Crouch End and became agitated.

'It's going down now actually,' said Boyd ending his 'phone call. 'That's blown it,' said Boyd. 'I'll bet that's one of the gang updating his mates about Joe and the hard stop on the van.'

'Let's do it,' from Anthea.

'All units,' radioed Boyd. 'Stand by! Strike!'

Three squad cars set off from different directions towards the temporary terrorist camp that had been set up on the edge of the parkland.

Slowly at first, and then Boyd slammed the accelerator and covered the last one hundred yards at high speed. The Porsche mounted the pavement followed by a Renault Megane and a BMW 4 X 4.

Slithering on the grass, Boyd brought the car to a standstill and realised that Bannerman and Janice were already out with their shotguns drawn shouting, 'Armed police! Everyone, stand still!'

A van's engine burst into life and then died just as quickly when Janice pulled the trigger and put two shotgun slugs into its engine block. Spinning carefully, she targeted the red Mercedes and shot out its tyres.

Equally, Bannerman rushed along the line of parked vans shouting, 'Stand still! Armed police!' as he pulverised the van tyres with shotgun slugs.

The driver of the green Ford Escort tried to jump back into his car but felt the butt of Boyd's handgun and promptly fell unconscious to the ground. An armed male, somewhere in his forties, stepped from a blue van and aimed a rifle at Janice. It was virtually point-blank range as his finger curled around the trigger and he began to apply pressure. Anthea raised her handgun and shot the man dead with two bullets in his forehead.

Janice nodded her thanks and reloaded.

The Sultán fired the engine of his Mercedes and tried to drive away. He felt the wheels dragging in the deep grass, couldn't find any traction and heard the engine block splinter when Janice disabled the van with another slug.

Suddenly, the Sultán was out of the van and running on foot towards a row of houses about two hundred yards away. He looked back to see Boyd chasing him on foot, withdrew a handgun, and pulled the trigger.

Throwing himself to the ground, Boyd felt the bullet whizz through the air above his head. Moments later, he was up on his feet giving chase and shouting, 'He's mine.'

Simultaneously, another 4x4 driven by Joe Harkness suddenly appeared on the scene with Martin Duffy. The vehicle mounted the pavement, dragged itself into the parkland, and swung around to face the row of parked vans.

By now, Terry was armed with and a handgun shouting, 'Armed police!' as he prodded the gun forward and aimed it at the occupants of the vans. Moving from left to right, he made sure everyone got the message.

Some of those present were bewildered and totally surprised at the speed of the unexpected attack. Others were much more switched on, full of street sense, and looking for a way out.

'Down! Down on the ground!' bellowed Bannerman as he joined Terry and swung his shotgun this way and that dominating the area with his size and determination.

A shot ran out and one of Joe's team fell to the ground.

'Hazel!' shouted Anthea.

'She's been shot!' screeched Joe.

'Officer down!' radioed Anthea.

'Do one if you dare,' screeched Bannerman as he gradually corralled the more compliant followers and forced them to the ground.

'Search and cuffs!' yelled Bannerman.

'My shoulder,' groaned Hazel. 'I took a round in the shoulder. One of them as a gun.'

Terry began searching the prisoners as Joe's team moved in to help in the arrest operation.

'Ambulance on route,' from one of the team.

A helicopter from the Air Support Wing appeared in the skies above as the Sultán's mini-army surrendered in the lush green pastures of the parkland of Crouch End. But the Sultán was long gone with Boyd doing his best to stay with him as they moved closer to the housing estate skirting the park.

Back at the park, Mustafa delved into his sports bag, withdrew two smoke grenades, and randomly threw them towards the detectives as he turned to the Downing Street assassin and snapped, 'Are you coming me with or going with your brother?'

Pat Ann Angel, sometimes Yasmin, often other names, wanted by the police as the Downing Street assassin, frequently a blonde, scanned the park and saw Boyd chasing her brother, Edward – the would be Sultán of England.

'You!' she yelled and yanked an AK47 from a holdall. 'Is that all you've got left? Smoke grenades?'

'Shut up, woman! Let's go!'

When the grenades detonated, a huge ball of black smoke discharged into the atmosphere and bit into the throats of those present. Bannerman and the team threw themselves to the ground and, in the seconds that followed, Pat and Mustafa ran through the confusion and into the highway heading for Crouch End.

'Run!' screamed Mustafa. 'Run!'

In the billowing murkiness of the smoke grenade aftermath, one of the camp supporters withdrew a huge knife from his belt and charged at Terry. Slashing like a mad man, he tried to sever Terry's arm and dislodge Terry's handgun.

'Nay lad,' bellowed Janice in her brief Scottish brogue. 'No today, bonny lad.'

Janice pulled the trigger and watched the knife fall harmlessly to the ground when a slug smashed into the attacker's chest. Coughing, Janice spat smoke-inspired spittle from her throat as she closed with the assailant and saw him reach for a handgun hidden in his trouser belt in the small of his back. Despite his serious injuries, he achingly raised the gun, pointed it at Janice, and began to pull the trigger.

He reeled backwards when Janice drilled another slug into him saying, 'I think I found Hazel's gunman.'

An array of liveried section patrol cars and two ambulances began to arrive at the scene. The area was soon filled with emergency vehicles, blue lights, sirens, and police responders who gradually moved in to assist the Special Crime Unit teams.

The helicopter circled and began to lose altitude as it sought to capture proceedings on its video system.

Anthea was on foot. Stiff or not, she was chasing after Mustafa and the blonde and using the trees for cover as the two escapees made towards the urban landscape.

'Two targets running towards the town,' radioed Anthea. 'Pursuing on foot. Anyone with me?'

'Coming,' from Bannerman, Janice and Terry.

'Where's the Guvnor?' from Janice.

Boyd was at full pelt across the park with his quarry fifty yards ahead of him just about to make the concrete jungle that was either

Harringay or Hornsey. He wasn't sure which. Underfoot, the ground was unpleasant, uneven, and so bad that Boyd lost his footing, his radio, and his sense of composure. He stopped, couldn't immediately lay his hands on the radio that had loosened from his body, and then looked again at the escaping terrorist.

'What to do?' he said aloud. 'My throat mic is no good without the other half of the transmitter system. Find the radio and call for assistance or press on?'

The gunshots and exploding grenades to his rear were still in Boyd's mind when he abandoned his search for the radio and set off once more.

Wearing a black bandana and a pair of sunglasses, Boyd's target was super cool. The Sultán was out of the parkland and into the housing estate striding out like an Olympic athlete with two handguns stuffed down his trouser belt and a foot-long knife resting in a thigh holster.

Boyd saw the traffic, saw pedestrians, and realised the thin grey line ahead of him signified the end of the grass and the beginning of the housing estate. He took a deep breath, implored those strong legs that had been honed to perfection on the Lake District fells, and then propelled himself faster and more determined than ever to take down his target.

'Boyd!' radioed Ricky. 'Guvnor! This is Starburst Control. Respond please.'

An Alsatian dog waddled by, paused in the grass, cocked its leg, peed on a highly encrypted secure radio, and then waddled on with its tail up when the dog walker tugged on the leash and brought the animal under control.

'Boyd?' repeated Ricky.

Turning to Antonia in the Ticker Cell, Ricky declared, 'I have to call it. He's lost radio contact. Or worse!'

'I'm on my way,' said the redhead. 'Call it, Ricky. I might not be part of the takedown squad today, but I am now. Call it.'

Nodding, Ricky engaged the wireless once more and radioed, 'All units, Crouch End. The Guvnor is out of the game. No response from his radio. DI Adams, it's your call?'

Anthea was on the street hiding behind a large recycling waste bin with her Gloch pointing skywards and her eyes following two targets making towards a taxi rank. Now she knew she had to step up to the plate as Boyd's deputy.

She engaged her throat microphone with, 'I have all that. All units, I have full unit control. Secure the operation. Hold and secure. Maintain operational strike. The Guvnor will have to wait. He is not the priority. Maintain strike mode. I say again, maintain strike mode.'

The radio was silent for what seemed an eternity before Janice intervened with, 'Where are you, Anthea? We must be getting closer.'

'Behind a bin near the taxi rank,' radioed Anthea. 'They haven't seen me yet.'

'We're closing with you,' radioed Bannerman.

'I don't like it,' replied Anthea. 'Too many people around.'

'You are in my sights,' radioed Janice.

'Spread out,' ordered Anthea. 'Split up and make yourselves harder targets. Understood?'

Bannerman and Janice acknowledged on the radio, followed instructions, split up, and began to jog towards the scene.

Terry Anwhari radioed, 'On foot! Making ground!'

Anthea stood up, used the bin for cover, and saw Mustafa looking over his shoulder towards the approaching detectives. Within seconds, Mustafa had dropped to one knee and was firing at Anthea. Next to him, Pat unleashed her AK 47 on the Detective Inspector. Within seconds, the recycling waste bin was a pepper pot and Anthea had scurried to the offside of the road where she took cover behind a parked car.

Popping up above the car roof, Anthea returned fire. Ran out of ammunition, reloaded, and fired again.

At the far end of the street, a red double-decker London bus pulled into the near side of the road and stopped.

Mustafa turned around, saw the bus, and began firing at the vehicle. Then he dropped his gun and removed a shoulder born rocket-propelled grenade launcher (RPG-9).

The bus driver pressed the emergency exit button and ushered the passengers out of the rear door an onto the pavement

Losing altitude, the police helicopter zeroed in on Mustafa.

A police transit van turned into the street with its siren blaring, blue light flashing, and headlights on full beam.

When Pat Angel realised the helicopter was a threat, she raised her AK 47 and deliberately let off a salvo at the helicopter.

Simultaneously, Mustafa twitched the RPG-9 two degrees left, fired, and watched the missile thunder through the air, obliterate the windscreen, and completely demolish the police transit van in a huge explosion. Glass, metal, equipment parts, blew into the air, landed on the pavement and hit some of the passengers who were running from the threatened London bus.

The police driver saw the attack coming and dived from the Transit in time to watch its destruction.

A bus driver ran from the rear platform and kept on running as he shouted at everyone, 'Run for your lives!'

The first half dozen 7.62×39mm cartridges fired from Pat's AK 47 flew beneath the helicopter as the pilot sought to gain height. The next score or more of cartridges peppered the pilot's cabin, tore into the control system, and wrecked the rotor system.

Grappling with the controls, the pilot gained altitude, lost control, steered away to his offside – towards the parkland – and began to radio, 'Mayday…. Mayday… Mayday… Going down Crouch End.'

Firing constantly at the helicopter, Pat hit the craft again and again as it faltered, surrendered, and sank almost casually to the ground in parkland no more than fifty yards from a row of terrorist-related vans. The pilot unhooked his seatbelt, threw himself out of the pilot's seat to the ground below, and bizarrely watched, from the corner of his eye, the helicopter rotor blades tear up the grass and soil of the park as the vessel died before everyone's eyes.

A spark ran from the rotor blades to the control fuse box to the fuel system. There was a colossal explosion when the spark ignited the fuel and blew the helicopter into a thousand pieces.

The Sultán had made the railway lines that signified the rail link between Harringay and Hornsey. Here, over twenty-five railway lines breached the land between Crouch End and Harringay and detailed the route north to King's Cross and onward to the East Coast mainline. The area was both an industrial estate and a rail hub that denied the wanted man an escape route to West Green and Tottenham where he had contacts. Unperturbed, he adjusted his bandana, reset his sunglasses, and ran parallel to the rail lines on the approach to Hornsey. He glanced behind, saw the buildings and businesses that made up the industrial park, and focused on the route ahead. There was no sign of Boyd.

Chest heaving, Boyd was at full length on the ground – hidden from view – watching his target's progress. Muddied, tired, yet still determined, Boyd reached for his Glock, checked the load, and then set off running at a crouch.

A train whistled past on its journey from Harringay and, on a road adjacent to the line, a delivery van pulled away from a retail unit.

Boyd ran into the road and stopped the vehicle.

In Crouch End, Pat and Mustafa stood back to back firing indiscriminately at their enemies. Bodies fell, killed by the assassins from Armageddon.

Reloading, Pat fired her assault rifle towards Bannerman, then Janice and Terry, and then Anthea. It was as if she were at a shooting gallery at a fair. She moderated her position, took a new footing, and fired again. Every shot counted. Every shot was carefully aimed, loud, penetrating, potentially destroying.

For Mustafa, it was simple. He reloaded his RPG, fired, totally obliterated the bus, a bus shelter, a sports shop, and an old car parked nearby. He was like a man possessed and glorified in the destruction he was causing when he felt the heat of the flames on his skin.

'I'm running out of ammo,' announced Pat.

'Me too,' replied Mustafa.

Bannerman was flat out on the ground praying, dodging a constant barrage of bullets, and returning fire when he could. Janice hid beneath a car, returned fire, but couldn't quite get her shots on the target. Terry hid behind a tree and returned rapid gunfire whenever he could.

No-one was going anywhere.

Mustafa and Pat couldn't break free and the detectives couldn't break the mould. All around people ran screaming, glass shards shattered to the ground, wooden doors and plastic building entrances collapsed under the sheer volume of gunfire. And a mannequin in a sports shop finally melted and fell from the window onto the pavement with a pair of very expensive trainers and sports apparel burning the dust on a London street.

The atmosphere was rich with the smell of cordite, dread, nervous tension, and pure cold fear.

Here and there, a motionless body lay on the roadside. Others lay near a bus or a shop and were obviously injured. They were mostly dead or dying from the relentless slaughter.

For the moment, they were the anonymous witnesses to a street battle inspired by an event in a cave fourteen hundred years ago when a man called Muhammad was allegedly visited by the archangel Jibrīl, (Gabriel for Christians) who revealed to him the beginnings of what would later become the Quran – the Book. The event took place in a cave near Mecca. Gabriel (Jibril for Muslims or Hebrew) appeared before him and commanded him to recite the first lines of chapter 96 of the Quran. Over the centuries, times had changed. Somewhere along the line, a so-called religion of peace had been shanghaied by those who planned nothing but war, violence, and the death of those who did not comply with the teachings of the Book in its extremist interpretation.

Out on the street, in the killing zone where life was less than a second away from death when the bullets whistled around, Mustafa said to Pat, 'It's our time.'

'For the Caliphate?' suggested Pat.

'For the Caliphate!' agreed Mustafa. 'By the way, I have two grenades left in my sports bag. Real ones!'

'By the way,' offered Pat with an approving smile. 'My brother Edward was right. You are the best.'

'For the Caliphate!' declared Mustafa.

Back to back, unafraid, committed, they loaded and waited.

An eerie silence befell the street. The remnants of a police van burnt merrily away, its blue light somehow still flashing, its plastic-coated police sign melting in the fire. A blaze engulfed the bus, glass cracked, fell to the ground, its tyres popped with the heat, and a bizarre puff of steam constantly escaped from the engine block. A retail unit burnt, its flames licking the floor above, and a couple of fire engines were held by hostile events at a safe distance – waiting to attend the fires.

At the other end of the street, a helicopter burnt remorsefully on the park. Its pilot severely injured, unable to be attended to by ambulance crews who had fled the area, but safe in the knowledge that he might live tomorrow if the violence ceased. And the vans were still in situ, some burning as a result of the helicopter crash, others sunken in the soil with shot-out tyres, and a few engine blocks steaming in their death throes.

The people had gone. They were no more. Only the emergency services remained in touch with proceedings, waiting, watching, wondering.

Stalemate!

'Terry!' shouted Anthea pointing to her Gloch. 'I need another.'

Sliding a Gloch 17 along the ground to Anthea, Terry replied, 'Take this. I'm locked and loaded and ready to go.'

The Gloch was two feet away, short of Anthea.

She reached out.

A range of bullets pounded the area, ceased, and allowed Anthea to quickly recover the weapon.

Anthea checked the magazine and then radioed, 'Okay! All units on me. Stand by... Stand by... Strike!'

Immediately standing tall, Anthea engaged the wanted duo on her own. She walked towards Mustafa and Pat with both weapons discharging continually and hitting the target.

There was a scream from Pat when one bullet hit her thigh, and a tremendous groan from Mustafa when a bullet tore his shoulder to pieces.

Bannerman and Janice reacted, joined the attack, and blazed away at the duo.

Step by step, yard by yard, Anthea pulled the trigger as she closed with the target, paused, reloaded, and continued her onslaught.

From the other side, Janice used her shotgun. Bannerman used his and the two detectives closed with Mustafa.

Pat took aim, missed, and took a hit in the chest from Anthea who just kept coming, just kept walking towards the most violent wanted criminals in the whole of Europe.

Anthea emptied her gun, stood unafraid, and fired again.

Pat fell to the ground.

Mustafa reached inside a sports bag, stretched towards a grenade, and pulled it from the bag. He began to unclip the device as Bannerman and Janice paused to reload and Terry suddenly let loose with a rifle and shot Mustafa squarely in the forehead.

The grenade fell to the ground, rolled a yard away, and stayed neutral when the pin remained lodged in its holding.

'Two targets down,' radioed Bannerman.

Anthea continued walking, kept on firing, oblivious to it all, denying everything that had happened, constantly pulling the trigger.

Click! Click! Click!

The hammer of the gun inspired the firing mechanism but there were no more bullets in the chamber.

Bannerman approached Anthea, put his hand across the top of her weapon, and said, 'Guvnor, it's over.'

Click! Click! Click!

Anthea eventually stopped pulling the trigger, held the gun still pointed towards the target, and then sunk into Bannerman's chest. She was spent.

'Easy, young lady,' remarked Bannerman. 'It's all over, Anthea. We're all done here.'

Sighing, collapsing, Anthea allowed the Gloch to fall to the ground and said, 'The noise! Did you hear the noise? My ears! I can't hear anything. Talk to me!'

'That was the bravest thing I've ever seen,' ventured Janice.

'Really?' quizzed Anthea.

'No, but your hearing is okay,' replied Janice with a slight chuckle.

'Where's Boyd?' enquired Anthea.

Eric Lisek was a Polish immigrant who had been living in England for the last twenty years. Married to his Polish sweetheart, they had raised an English-born family and worked hard to achieve their objectives. Eric was short and stubby and enjoyed a good command of the English language.

Today, Eric Lisek was station manager at Hornsey railway station.

He spent most of the day making sure trains were on time, scheduling staff duties, managing porters and ticket sellers, and making sure that the day to day operations of the station was in keeping with the traditions of an efficient rail system. Eric would be on the station platform for an hour before moving on to another station where he would carry out the same duties. A disciplinarian, the man did not suffer fools gladly and expected nothing but the best from his staff. Often, he would educate them in the ways of the world, remind them of the contribution the Polish Air Force made in the Second World War, and admonish them when they made fun of the government and politicians. So much so that Eric was often regarded as now more British than Polish.

Coming towards him, approaching the northbound platform from the railway lines, a tall, rugged man wearing sunglasses and a black bandana emerged from the area of the industrial park and made his way towards Eric.

The smaller stationmaster noted the man's trainers, jeans, and the camouflage-coloured combat jacket he was wearing before shouting, 'Hey! You there. You people from the business park have been told to use the proper route. Now kindly return the way you came and use the footpath provided.'

There was no reply.

A delivery van pulled up outside the station and parked next to a red Aston Martin.

The bandana and the sunglasses made the platform.

Eric stepped forward and lifted his hand saying, 'I said you, sir. You can't come this way. I presume you speak English?'

The Sultán pushed Eric away and ran along the platform towards the entrance.

Boyd and Antonia presented themselves on the platform blocking the Sultán's obvious route.

'Damned foreigners!' yelled Eric. 'Come back here!'

The Polish stationmaster set off in pursuit of the man he considered was invading his railway station.

'What kept you?' enquired Boyd.

'Nothing,' replied Antonia, settling her hair across her shoulders. 'I needed a breath of fresh air and my new Aston Martin needed a drive. That's all. You have a problem with that?'

'No,' offered Boyd. 'Of course not. I came by a delivery van. It was full of pet food.'

'I can smell it,' offered Antonia. 'You need a bath by the way.'

'Welcome to the club,' replied Boyd. 'Now look down the platform. Here comes our man.'

Fifty yards away, the Sultán jogged towards the exit with Eric Lisek on his heels shouting, 'Hey! Come back here.'

Boyd took a step forward, drew his Glock, and was immediately joined by Antonia. Together, they pointed their weapons at the running target.

Antonia coughed, removed the safety catch, and offered, 'I surely can't forget anything else today, can I?'

Breathing hard, the Sultán saw the man and woman standing in the entrance with their weapons drawn. He realised they were law enforcement and accidentally crashed into a large shelter used by passengers waiting for the trains.

'Got you at last,' bellowed Eric as he took hold of his man by the jacket. 'Now you will come with me and we'll phone your boss. This is not an acceptable practice for business park staff.'

It was then that Eric saw a knife in a thigh holster, and two handguns in the man's trouser belt.

'Back off,' hissed the Sultán. 'Or you just might die today.'

In shock, Eric's jaw dropped when the man pulled out the knife and held it to his throat.

'Did you hear me?'

Nodding vigorously, Eric swallowed hard and then felt a lump of cold steel resting against his Adam's apple.

Boyd and Antonia were stepping out finely towards the man that would be the Sultán of England. Guns drawn, they hammered down the platform towards their target.

The Sultán dragged Eric from the shelter with the knife held to his throat and his foot kicking the back of Eric's knee as he took him into a kneeling position.

Standing over Eric, his free hand withdrew a handgun and he shouted to Boyd and Antonia, 'No further or he gets it.'

Skidding to a halt, Boyd lowered his handgun, steadied Antonia who was beside him and replied, 'Don't do it, Edward. It's not worth it.'

The word 'Edward' seemed to resonate with the Sultán, brought him into the present day, and shook him to the core. He glanced around again. There was no burnt out truck to hide in, no irrigation ditch to drop into, no lizard waiting to be killed, and no convenient friendly mosque waiting to offer shelter in the desert lands of the Middle East.

'Oh yes, we know who you are,' revealed Boyd. 'Eddie is it? Do you prefer Eddie or Edward?'

Loosening the blade against Eric's throat, the Sultán glanced behind, then to his right and left, before pulling Eric to his feet and wielding the knife in a dangerous manner.

'You're not going anywhere, Eddie,' ventured Boyd. 'The station is surrounded. You'll never make the roadway.'

Moving towards the railway lines, the Sultán tried to step around Boyd and Antonia.

Boyd persisted with, 'Oh yes, we know who you are alright. Edward John Angel, I am arresting you for conspiracy to commit acts of terrorism in the United Kingdom and elsewhere. You're finished, Eddie.

The Sultánate you dreamt of isn't going to happen. In fact, Eddie, the Caliphate is finished and so are you.'

'The Caliphate will never be finished,' spat the Sultán.

'Oh, you can talk,' suggested Boyd. 'Good! Now put the knife down and drop the gun. It's all over.'

'Oh no it's not,' bellowed the Sultán as he drew the knife back, lifted it, and began to bring it down to bear on Eric's neck.

Two gunshots rang out when Boyd double-tapped the assailant hitting him squarely in the forehead directly above the bridge of the nose. A microsecond later, two more bullets raced down the barrel of Antonia's weapon and penetrated the Sultán's skull above his left eye.

The knife faltered, lost its strength, fell with a clatter to the ground as the would-be murderer let go of Eric Lisek and dropped to the ground.

Eric's hands rushed to his throat as he jumped out of the way and threw himself to the ground.

The Sultán's fingers twitched, slithered towards a handgun, and then ceased movement altogether when Boyd and Antonia each fired once more into the head of the terrorist.

'It's over now,' suggested Antonia. 'All over.'

'You got a radio?' enquired Boyd.

'Nope!' replied the redhead. 'I forgot to draw one.'

'A mobile 'phone?'

'No signal here,' replied Antonia.

Holstering his weapon, Boyd placed a hand around Eric's shoulders and asked, 'Are you alright?'

Shaking, unsure, stunned, Eric replied, 'I think so. He was going to behead me, wasn't he?'

'Yes, I think so.'

'What did you want him for? What did he do wrong?'

'He killed people,' replied Boyd. 'Could I borrow your 'phone please?'

'In the office,' suggested Eric. 'It's in the office. I'll show you.'

A small crowd gathered as Boyd removed his jacket and placed it over the top half of the Sultán's body.

'Make the call, Boyd,' suggested Antonia. 'I'll look after the shop.'

Fifteen minutes later, the railway station was temporarily closed when emergency vehicles, responders, and investigators descended on the station and began their enquiry into the incident.

That night, the sun went down over London. The smell of cordite still lingered in the nostrils, smoke from explosions and suicide vests still permeated parts of the atmosphere, and the flames from various buildings that had been set on fire could still be seen.

Over two hundred people had been killed in the last seven days, and as many again injured in over fifty pre-planned attacks that had been organised, inspired, and funded by El Sultán and his co-conspirators.

This was London.

An attempt to rename the capital Londonistan failed.

Midnight approached at Euston railway station.

Boyd met Ricky French at the ticket barrier and said, 'Thanks for coming so late at night. Have you got it?'

'All here,' replied Ricky handing Boyd a tablet computer. 'Everything you asked for.'

'Thanks! If the Commissioner wants me, Ricky, just give him this report and ask him to read it.'

Boyd handed Ricky a sealed envelope and said, 'Okay?'

'Yes, no problem. Is that everything?' questioned Ricky as he studied the envelope.

'It's the basics, that's all,' explained Boyd. 'All the Commissioner needs to know and no more. Some things are best kept in house.'

'Where are you going, Guvnor?'

'I'm invoking the Commander's privileges,' replied Boyd.

'What privileges?'

'It's time for a short holiday.'

'London is on fire,' argued Ricky. 'There's a mass of work to do and you're taking a couple of days off.'

'There's plenty of officers to get on with it apparently, and they've called in mutual aid from surrounding forces. I'm going to see the Chief Constable about my new job. I'll be in touch.'

Boyd turned and boarded the night sleeper as Ricky French watched him go and then turned to walk across the vast marble concourse that was Euston station.

*

12

The following morning
Police Headquarters, Cumbria

Boyd's taxi dropped him off at the entrance allowing the detective time to stroll through the complex and arrive at reception. A short time later, he was admitted to the senior officer's suite where he took a seat and waited to see the Chief.

'You don't appear to have an appointment, Chief Inspector,' ventured Jean, the Chief Constable's secretary. 'I do hope you realise he may not have time to see you this morning. He's a very busy man.'

'I'm sure he'll want to see me, Jean,' suggested Boyd. 'I'll wait if you don't mind.'

'As you wish,' replied Jean. 'Can I get you coffee or tea?'

'No thank you.'

'It's just that the Chief likes his coffee and a couple of chocolate digestives promptly at 10 am and prior to his meeting with the Command team at 10.30am.'

'No, seriously, I'm fine, Jean. Thank you!'

The intercom activated and was quickly answered by the lady who then turned to Boyd and said, 'The Chief Constable will see you now.'

She ushered him to the Chief's office as Boyd replied, 'Thank you,' and entered the lair of Cornelius Webb.

'Boyd!' declared Cornelius who remained seated. 'I presume you have come to brief me on yesterday's events in the city or ask about this new role I have planned for you. Or do you come to offer an apology for your ridiculous behaviour of late?'

'Perhaps?' replied Boyd as he glanced at the Chief's secretary. 'What I have to tell you might be construed as confidential at this stage, sir.'

'Of course,' smiled the Chief. 'That will be all, Jean, Thank you!'

'Excellent,' remarked Jean. 'I'll attend to matters relevant to your ten o'clock schedule, sir.'

The Chief's secretary closed the door behind her when she left the two men alone together.

'My sources in London tell me you are the flavour of the month after yesterday's operation,' remarked the Chief. 'I don't know whether to congratulate you for closing down what might have been a prolonged attack or admonish you for not bringing the matter to my attention earlier. I would have ensured a better national response which would have led to many lives being saved. You need to trust me, Boyd.'

'Trust?' queried Boyd. 'Actually, I've come to tell you about a surveillance operation in Cumbria, Mister Webb.'

'In that case, it can wait until tomorrow. Kindly book an appointment with me for late tomorrow afternoon.'

'I think not,' contended Boyd.

'I don't care what you think, Boyd. I'll see you tomorrow when I shall have your new job description ready. Close the door behind you when you leave. Thank you!'

The Chief turned his attention to some documents on his desk and ignored Boyd.

'I don't think so, Cornelius,' persisted Boyd. 'What I have to say is relevant to a covert surveillance operation and discreet enquiry which has been centred upon yourself, your wife, and a third party known to you. I suggest the way forward may be to listen to me or stand before a higher authority to hear a similar version of what I am about to tell you. It's your decision.'

'If you must, Boyd.' The Chief checked the time and continued, 'You have ten minutes and no more, but I warn you that the cosy little number I have lined up for you in Headquarters can soon be changed to a permanent night shift in – which part of Cumbria do you dislike most?'

Ignoring the remark, Boyd declared, 'In respect of your wife's murder, I now have evidence as to who the killer is. Cornelius, would you like to hear the case against the accused?'

The Chief became agitated and replied, 'Chief Constable or Sir will do, Boyd. We are not personal friends. You will refrain from the use of Cornelius.'

'Whatever you wish, Mister Webb. Allow me to present my evidence in video format.'

Boyd withdrew a tablet computer from his briefcase and switched it on saying, 'Of course, this is merely a brief summary of evidence but when presented properly in a court of law – with documentary evidence - it will totally destroy the accused, bring him into disrepute, and soil his name for decades to come. In addition, he will make a major contribution to the loss of trust in the profession of which he is currently a part. May I continue?'

There was no reply from Cornelius Webb just a brief but slightly nervous nod from the other side of the desk.

Swivelling the tablet computer around, Boyd selected a file and ran a series of images as he talked through the slides and – where appropriate – a video presentation.

'You wife,' indicated Boyd. 'A quite beautiful woman who was desired by many because of her good looks, her wealth, and her charisma.'

Cornelius nodded his agreement and began to smooth his moustache as he listened carefully to Boyd.

'She was an artist who loved to paint,' declared Boyd. 'Her favourite place was St Bees in West Cumbria. She painted there often and sold the product on her website. Divine made a lot of money from her paintings. Here, for example, Mister Webb, is a photograph of one of her bank accounts. It's an offshore account. Did she make all this money from painting?'

'You'll have to ask her,' suggested a perplexed Chief Constable, his fingers suddenly racing to a crucifix on a necklace around his neck.

'She was murdered by this man,' revealed Boyd.

A photograph of Cornelius Webb dressed in his Chief Constable's uniform standing next to the Home Secretary and the Metropolitan Police Commissioner appeared on the computer screen.

'Nice photo,' ventured Boyd. 'I wonder what his friends would think of him now?'

'You can't prove any of this, Boyd,' snapped the Chief, a bead of sweat appearing on his forehead.

'I can and I will,' argued Boyd. 'You murdered your wife on the St Bees cliffs with this.'

A photograph of a bright blue vacuum flask appeared on the screen.

Cornelius remained silent. For a moment, Boyd detected that the Chief was stunned. Like a child playing with his comfort toy, the Chief rubbed his crucifix as his moustache seemed to bristle in anticipation.

'You bought the vacuum flask three years ago from a mountaineering shop in Keswick using a debit card issued to yourself some two years earlier by your bank. Did you know that if you turn over someone's financial records you can find all kinds of incriminating evidence? Yes, my team have completed a full financial investigation in relation to yourself and your late wife.'

'Where did you find the vacuum flask?' enquired the Chief.

Boyd walked to the other side of the desk, leaned across, noticed the sweat forming on the Chief's brow and challenged him with, 'Find it? In order to find something, you must first lose it. Where did you lose the vacuum flask, Mister Webb?'

'I think there's been a mistake,' suggested the Chief.

'One of our team found it on the beach at St Bees. When you threw the vacuum flask away, after murdering your wife, you thought you were throwing it into the sea, didn't you?'

'Don't be preposterous, Boyd,' argued the Chief. 'If you continue like this, I will call security and have you removed.'

'Security?' chuckled Boyd. 'You thought your security was guaranteed when you walked away from the murder scene and then threw the flask into the sea. Your problem is that you walked too far, Mister Webb. Did you know you missed the sea? The tide was coming in but the flask was found on a pebbled part of the beach where the tide did not reach. It's amazing what you can discover when you put your mind to it. Marine scientists can tell you all about tides, tidemarks, the strength of ebb and flow, the direction of tidal movement – shall I go on?'

'Hypothetical!' muttered the Chief.

'Not when you recover the item from the dry beach and have it forensically examined. It has your fingerprints on it. They are the only fingerprints on the article.'

'You've never taken my fingerprints, Boyd.'

'No, but the police service did when you joined. You do remember giving consent to your fingerprints being taken when you joined, don't you?'

The Chief was sinking into his chair. A look of despair began to invade his cheeks.

'Back to your wife,' remarked Boyd. 'This is the reason you killed her.'

A photograph of Mikhail Korobov flashed onto the computer screen.

'He's a Russian spy, Mister Webb, and he worked out of the Russian Embassy in London. But you knew that all along because you've spent many years giving him and his friends information about political figures, persons of interest, and anything relevant to the nation's defence that you came across during your rise to the rank of Chief Constable.'

Cornelius Webb loosened his tie and undid his collar.

Boyd leaned over and forwarded the presentation to the image of a bank account in the name Cornelius Webb.

'You earnt a hell of a lot of overtime as a police officer, Mister Webb. So much that it actually exceeds your salary many times over and caused you to open an offshore account in the Channel Islands. You've also bought an enormous number of shares in foreign countries. Russia, for example, to name but one.'

Images of the accounts flashed across the screen.

'Where did they recruit you?' enquired Boyd. 'St Petersburg? Or did you volunteer?'

Silence from Cornelius Webb.

'No matter!' continued Boyd. 'The fact is that Divine found out about your affiliation to Mikhail, the spymaster, and that troubled you. It troubled you more when you realised she had fallen in love with Mikhail Korobov, your Russian handler.'

The Chief began to wipe his eyes when images of Mikhail and Divine together in romantic poses appeared on the tablet screen.

'She was highly skilled in deception,' suggested Boyd. 'But not clever enough to realise you had found out about their love affair. You do recall telling me that your wife often stayed overnight somewhere when she was painting, don't you, Mister Webb?'

'You have a story of pure fiction,' muttered the Chief. 'Just a story, that's all.'

'And then there's this,' revealed Boyd. 'Do you like dragonflies?'

The image of two dragonflies appeared on the screen.

'Not just dragonflies,' ventured Boyd. 'Highly advanced technically astute surveillance equipment the size of an overgrown dragonfly which we call Odonata. They were under the control of one of my technical officers who was briefed to penetrate the target. You were the target. Here, take a look.'

A video - taken from the perspective of the surveillance dragonfly – showed the fly approaching the Chief's detached home near Ullswater and then locking itself onto the lounge window. Another showed a different fly attached to a tree overlooking the front of the Chief's house.

'This is the surveillance product,' stated Boyd.

Images of Mikhail Korobov arriving in his car at the Chief's house appeared. Mikhail carried a bottle of vodka. He was greeted by the Chief and then escorted into the lounge. The two men were alone.

'The audio from Odonata is quite good,' declared Boyd. 'Listen to this.'

The audio ran on the tablet.

'Here, Mikhail hands you a bottle of vodka and you discuss how you are going to present it to the Home Secretary, Mrs Maude Black,' explained Boyd. 'You are plotting with the Russian spy and agree to deliver the vodka to her in the hope that she will enjoy it. Do you remember the conversation?'

The Chief nodded, stood up, and went to the cabinet behind him. He removed a bottle and a glass and prepared to pour himself a drink.

'It wasn't the first time Mikhail had given you Gelsemium to mix with vodka, Mister Webb. The audio tells us that you had been experimenting over the last three months with the dosage. You needed to make sure the mix wasn't too strong apparently. Why? Because the right dosage would return a colourless mix to the vodka. The wrong dose would make the vodka cloudy. So, you needed to practice for a while. Oh, don't take my word for it. Listen to the audio tape of you and Mikhail discussing how the poison works.'

The audio ran in as Cornelius Webb sank further into his seat.

'You decided to murder your wife, not Maude Black. You tried to fool us all,' revealed Boyd. 'You hoaxed us with what appeared to be a terrorist inspired murder by strangling Divine with an Al-Qaeda flag. Did you do that because you wanted those in authority to think you were a target, particularly as you were in for the top counter-terrorism job? You wanted to feel important, didn't you? Even in murdering your wife, you had to show how important you were.'

'I… I…' the Chief could find no words.

'Rather than use the Gelsemium on the Home Secretary, you used some of the poison given to you by Mikhail and mixed it into the vacuum flask that Divine took to St Bees. The poison delivers an extremely hard to detect kickstart to what becomes a heart attack. You knew that because Mikhail told you and he repeats his briefing to you in the dragonfly video you are watching. Just prior to the point of death, you leave your hiding place on the cliffs and strangle your wife. Actually, you know she's having a heart attack. You are just trying to fool us and push us towards a terrorist murder that never happened. Do you still have any Gelsemium left or have you used it all? Where is it, I wonder? No doubt a search might uncover the remains.'

A substantial silence followed as Cumbria's Chief Constable and designated head of counter-terrorism in the UK stared at the tablet computer screen, watched the video play out, and then recap the highlights before ending.

'It's as simple as that, Mister Webb,' ventured Boyd.

Cornelius Webb broke down, placed his head in his hands, and began to sob.

'Sorry for doing what you did, or sorry for being found out?' probed Boyd.

'What will happen to me?' asked the Chief.

'That's not for me to say,' replied Boyd. 'It's my job to investigate, detect where I can, and deliver miscreants to the legal system whenever I can.'

'Prison?'

'Probably,' agreed Boyd. 'I'd say definitely.'

'I'd be cannon fodder in a prison,' offered the Chief. 'Used and abused because of the position I once held.'

'Perhaps you should have thought about that earlier,' suggested Boyd.

'Disgraced! Finished!' ventured the Chief. 'A bloody carbuncle on the nation's backside. They'll talk about me, write about me, and abuse me forever and a day. I'll die a broken man in a stinking cell somewhere in the hell that awaits me.'

'Probably?' contended Boyd. 'Get your coat on, Mister Webb.'

'Is there another way?' probed the Chief a look of surrender on his face giving way to a glint of hope.

'That's a matter for yourself, Mister Webb,' said Boyd. 'You are a national disgrace. A carbuncle we could do without. The Chief Constable who became a spy, a money-launderer, a fraudster, and a murderer. I don't think we've ever had one of them before. I thought it would be easier and quicker to show you the result of our enquiries on the tablet. Now it's time for you to decide on the next step. Do you fight the accusation or accept it? Think about it. I'll be outside waiting for you.'

Boyd closed the tablet and walked towards the door where he turned and said, 'You were a bad shepherd who decided to look after your own interests instead of those of your flock. I was just one of the team who spends his life picking up sheep shit for a living whilst being stepped on from those above. It's a long road, Mister Webb. Why not have your last sip of vodka before you go? It's your choice.'

Boyd closed the door behind him, held it ever so slightly ajar, realised the Chief's secretary was still away making the Chief's coffee, and leaned back against the door.

'What have I done?' thought Boyd. 'Oh, my God, what have I done?'

Ostensibly resting against the door, Boyd listened via the slight gap that he had manipulated with the not fully-closed door.

Silence for a few minutes.

The thin sound of a glass clinking against a bottle inside the Chief's office could be heard.

Boyd closed his eyes and listened intently.

The top of the vodka bottle was removed. Boyd heard the faint sound of the vodka filling the glass and then there was a silence that followed. He thought he detected the sound of swallowing but couldn't be sure.

Time moved on.

The clock on the wall above Jean's desk eventually made a sudden sound when it reached three. It was a quarter past ten.

Moments later, the sound of glass hitting the highly polished wooden desk could be heard, followed by the roll of a bottle across the desk, a short silence, and then the sound of a bottle smashing on the floor.

A thin groan from the Chief's voice could be barely heard but to Boyd, it was the sound of thunder in a storm.

Something fell onto, or from, the desk inside the office. Boyd did not know which. He remained motionless, listening to the sounds, thinking, wondering, and with his eyes closed tight.

A silence reigned. Boyd opened his eyes and looked up to see Jean carrying a tray of hot drinks and biscuits into the office.

'Can I help you?' offered Boyd.

'Oh no, I'm fine,' replied the Chief's Secretary. 'On the basis that you might still be here, I made you a coffee. If you don't want it just leave it.'

'Very kind of you,' remarked Boyd. 'Yes, I'll enjoy that, thank you.'

Jean gathered some mail from her desk and said, 'I'll be back shortly. I'll just attend to the Chief.'

A number of uniformed and plainclothes officers entered the senior officer's suite. They were led by the tall thin Detective Chief Superintendent Raymond Cullen who recognised Boyd and said, 'Ah! The new diversity boss, how are you, Mister Boyd?'

Jean approached the Chief's office door which Boyd opened for her.

Taking his coffee, Boyd sat down on a couch, nodded politely at the group of senior officers who had joined him, and replied, 'Very well thank you, and yourself?'

'Good! I am good!' replied the Chief Superintendent.

Moments later there was a scream from inside the Chief's office when Jean found the Chief Constable slumped over his desk apparently having suffered a heart attack.

In the rush that followed, Boyd's coffee tumbled to the ground as Chief Superintendent Cullen charged into the Chief's office to find Cornelius Webb motionless with his head and shoulders lying on the desk.

Cullen lifted the Chief back into his chair, felt his pulse, tried to sense a breath coming from the Chief's mouth, and finally declared, 'He's dead. Good God, man, the Chief is dead. Look, he's undone his collar and tie. Obviously felt an attack coming on and taken a drink to try and help. Do we need a doctor?'

'Yes! Yes, of course,' someone said. 'I'll phone for one.'

'Are you alright, Jean?'

'No! No!' cried Jean. 'This can't be happening. He was such a nice man.'

A uniform cradled Jean in his arms and gently escorted her from the office.

'A heart attack?' queried Boyd as he moved almost surreptitiously through the group and reached the Chief's desk. 'Are you sure?'

'Look at his face,' advised Cullen. 'And he obviously felt unwell and loosened his collar and tie. Poor chap. Far too young!'

'Yes! Yes, of course,' whispered Boyd. 'I'm so sorry.'

The group gathered around the Chief fussing and talking as Boyd quietly picked up a bottle of vodka from the floor and poured the remaining contents down the hand basin.

'What are you doing?' enquired Cullen.

'No disrespect intended, gentlemen,' offered Boyd. 'But the last thing we need others to think is that the Chief was on a bender with a bottle of vodka on the day he had a heart attack. Let's keep it tidy.'

'Good idea!' replied Cullen. 'Yes, terrible way to die but if a man has to go then let him go with dignity. I'll get a cloth and tidy this desk.'

'What a clever idea,' ventured Boyd.

'Leave it to me, Boyd,' ordered Cullen. 'I'm used to these things by now.'

'Of course,' murmured Boyd retiring. 'I'll get out of the way. I don't want to intrude any further.'

As Boyd stepped away from the office, the senior officers took over the scene.

By mid-afternoon, the local media were reporting the death of a Chief Constable who died from a sudden heart attack whilst working hard on a range of policing documents that required his expert attention.

*

13

Later that week
The Special Crime Unit,
London Office

Halfway down the corridor towards his office, Boyd encountered Anthea who greeted him with, 'The Guvnor is back at last. No more privileges then?'

'Not today,' replied Boyd with a smile. 'Any word on Hazel?'

'Bullet went straight through the shoulder. She's going to be off a while but it's not serious and she'll come back strong.'

'Excellent! Can you make arrangements for you and I to visit her one day this week?'

'Will do,' replied Anthea adding, 'Bad news about Cornelius Webb.'

'Very sad,' offered Boyd as the two walked towards Boyd's office.

'All that work and no court proceedings,' ventured Anthea.

Pausing for a moment, Boyd offered, 'These things happen, and in the circumstances, it's perhaps best there were no court proceedings.'

'I'm told some people are heartbroken at the loss of Cornelius Webb,' revealed Anthea. 'I'm also hearing what really happened, Guvnor. Apparently, he had a heart attack, but a medical report suggests he took a small dose of Gelsemium prior to his death. He poisoned himself in the same way that he poisoned his wife.'

'Tragic,' suggested Boyd.

'Did he have any help, I wonder?' ventured Anthea.

'I think he managed it all by himself,' offered Boyd.

'Yes, I believe so,' replied Anthea. 'Not even with the help of a passive witness?'

'As a I said,' responded Boyd. 'These things happen, and in the circumstances, it's perhaps best there were no court proceedings.'

'You've been flying by the seat of your pants again,' suggested Anthea. '

Smiling, Boyd replied, 'I do appreciate the ongoing support, Anthea. The most loyal and trusted of friends and colleagues have a habit of hanging onto those pants whenever they catch fire.'

'Good!' replied Anthea. 'Thank you!'

No,' frowned Boyd. 'Thank you! Anyway, what's on the cards today?'

'Lots of catching up still to do. By the way, the Commissioner sent this for you.'

Accepting a bottle bag, Boyd withdrew a bottle of Spanish brandy and chuckled, 'Wow! Does this mean we are back in the good books?'

'Don't know,' offered Anthea. 'You tell me, but for your information, I got a bar.'

'Which one? The Eagle around the corner?' probed Boyd. 'The drinks are on you.'

'No, a bar to my QGM. What does that mean?'

'It means they have awarded you with the same medal again and you will be presented with a bar that signifies that fact. You are a holder of the same medal on multiple occasions. It has an asterisk beside it when it's written down. You know, one of those starry things (*) for each bar.'

'Oh! Well, I'm not the only one then,' replied Anthea. 'While you were away, this memo arrived.'

Boyd read the memo. It was a long list of medals and commendations for Anthea, Janice, Boyd, Bannerman, Antonia and others in the unit.

'Wonderful!' smiled Boyd. 'Do me a favour, Anthea. Ring the Shakshouka and book a table for the entire wing. A celebration will not go amiss and it will be a good way of saying thank you to Yusuf.'

'Will do, Guvnor.'

Boyd walked along the corridor wondering if he should open the bottle of his favourite Spanish brandy. How did the Commissioner know it was his favourite, he wondered? Is someone constantly watching me or is it just me in need of a proper holiday and a getaway from this stress-filled place? That reminds me. I must ring Sir Julian.

Delving inside the bottle bag, Boyd recovered an envelope which he tore open to reveal a handwritten note.

On reaching his office, Boyd paused to read a new nameplate that had been affixed to the door.

He read aloud, 'Superintendent William Miller Boyd. QGM**. Commander. Special Crime Unit.'

Shaking his head, Boyd unfolded the letter which read, 'Dear Commander Boyd, congratulations on your well-earned promotion to the rank of Superintendent and Head of the Special Crime Unit. The Commissioner's protocols over-rides other considerations such as formal promotion interviews. The protocol is hereby exercised. I trust you will find your new nameplate satisfactory. You are formally reinstated to security clearance Omega Violet with immediate effect and as authorised by the Home Secretary. Your proposed transfer to Cumbria is withdrawn. Many thanks. Indeed, my personal thanks. (signed, the Commissioner)

'About time too,' thought Boyd picking up the telephone and dialling a number. 'Meg, we've been promoted…'

Fifteen minutes later, Boyd phoned Sir Julian in MI6 and after the usual pleasantries revealed, 'Odonata crashed and burnt. Both of them, but thanks anyway.'

There was a slight pause on the 'phone before Sir Julian returned, 'These things happen, Superintendent Boyd. By the way, congratulations, a source in the Home Office confirmed the situation a short time ago.'

'Your sources remain impeccable, Sir Julian.'

'I knew if I gave those dragonflies to you we would get a true evaluation. Now I know they don't work, we can forget all about them. Between you and I, Boyd, I don't have a record of my little dragonflies ever having existed. Why on earth we would use something that doesn't work is beyond me.'

'The less people who know about such secrets the better,' proposed Boyd.

'Absolutely,' countered the MI6 Chief.

'A little bit like sudden or unexplained death, Sir Julian, even murder,' suggested Boyd. 'You can point someone at what is there to be discovered but they don't always see it. They only see what they want to see. Sometimes, it's because that's what they really want to see and sometimes it's convenient for those who prefer to take the easy way out.'

'I agree,' replied Sir Julian. 'If I can ever help in the future, Boyd?'

'I'm sure you'll be in touch,' ventured Boyd.

Boyd chuckled slightly before replacing the 'phone on its cradle. He stared at the 'phone and thought back to the Odonata project and how well the electronic dragonflies had worked, and how well Sir Julian knew they worked.

'Did I make the decisions or did someone else guide me unconsciously towards them?' pondered Boyd. 'Am I my own kind of man or am I merely the instrument of those who seek to control me?'

Standing, Boyd strolled to the window and looked out across the London skyline.

'What a wonderful view,' he decided. 'But somewhere out there lies the enemy. Or is God and all those competing religions the real enemy? Funny that I believe in the Loch Ness monster, extra-terrestrial life, and the possibility of life forms in the deepest parts of our unexplored oceans, but I can't believe in God as much as I should. Maybe it's something to do with who I trust in the telling of such things.'

An aeroplane flew over the capital inbound for Heathrow.

'Who is the enemy?' wondered Boyd. 'The misguided misinformed Muslim who clings to the idea of an unnecessary Caliphate that will take society back fourteen hundred years to a violent and potentially evil time? Or is the real enemy a bunch of corrupt, overzealous and dishonest capitalist-thinking Christians who would rather run things their own way without any specific thoughts for the rights of others? The Sultán or the crucifix? As individuals, they were both regional commanders in their own different ways, and they were both wicked men with evil intentions. How far should an individual go to preserve the peace, protect the public from evil, practice the art of national security, and walk that thin line between right and wrong in order to preserve such beliefs?'

'How far?'

Boyd returned to his desk and removed the files SULTAN and CRUCIFIX from a locked drawer.

'What have we here?' mused Boyd. 'An evil mix of Islam and Christianity.'

Filling his fountain pen, Boyd decided, 'It's all about who you trust in the scheme of things, I suppose. Trust? A dangerous potion that knows no boundaries or a complicit element in the scheme of life. That said, I think I'll cross reference these two files and begin them with unit's remit which is 'to police and defend the freedom of the nation and its people.'

Opening the bottle of brandy, Boyd thought, 'Should I take a drink from one who once chose not to trust me? Is it really brandy? What was that about trust? Is it allied to leadership and ability or is that just a fallacy?'

Smiling to himself, he raised the brandy glass and said, 'I suppose this brandy is a bit like life itself since it has a deep amber colour that is tainted with golden highlights. I wonder if Commander Maxwell is still enjoying his retirement walking along the beach at Whitstable? Strange how it all turned out. My old boss - the Shepherd - told me that only the Bishop could end things. Some things are best done by yourself, so I suppose I turned out to be the Commander's Bishop. I'll drink to that. In fact, I'll drink to the Shepherd; a Bell, Book, and Candle, and a Bishop who ended it all?'

Boyd took a sip.

The Ticker Intelligence Unit continued to chatter away with dozens of various pieces of intelligence being presented for recording and analysis.

Telephones in the office continued to ring as the pressure of insufficient staff continued to tell.

An unknown man with evil intentions clung to the underside of a wagon as it crossed into the United Kingdom at the Port of Dover.

Donald Anderson became a target of MI5 and was placed under long term surveillance.

A series of interactive red and white dots blinked away in an underground facility near Canterbury known as the Operations Centre.

Another car bearing diplomatic plates left the Russian Embassy and journeyed into England's heartland.

The first mini nuclear submarine was finished in Cumbria and safely taken out of the rear entrance of an underground facility. In the skies above, there were no enemy satellites looking down on proceedings and no agents from a hostile enemy state anywhere to be seen.

Life in the unit went on.

The end, until the next time…. Almost

Author's Notes

Sultán

I took Sultán from the Arabic language, its culture, and its history. I found that it had a powerful and far-reaching meaning best understood by placing the entire concept in a global setting.

The word has several historic meanings worthy of mention. Originally, it meant strength, authority, and rulership and it is derived from the verbal noun 'sulṭah', which means authority or power. Over time, it came to be used as the title of certain rulers who claimed almost full sovereignty - in practical terms – over certain geographic areas. The commonality exists that such rulers, or sultans, lacked dependence on any higher ruler or powerful governor of a province and seldom claimed the overall Caliphate. The adjective form of the word is 'sultanic', and the dynasty and lands ruled by a sultan are referred to as a sultanate.

The term is distinct from the king, despite both referring to as being a sovereign ruler. Sultán is restricted entirely to Muslim countries where the title carries a lot of religious significance. Comparatively, the word 'king' is much more secular and is used in both Muslim and non-Muslim countries. By the way, references to the word 'secular' mean not relating to or believing in a religion.

A feminine form of the sultan, used by Westerners, is Sultana or Sultanah and this title has been used legally for some Muslim women monarchs and sultan's mothers and chief consorts. The female leaders in Muslim history are correctly known as 'sultanas'.

In recent years, Sultán has been gradually replaced by the king by contemporary hereditary rulers who wish to emphasize their secular authority under the rule of law. A notable example is Morocco, whose monarch changed his title from the Sultán to king in 1957.

To reveal how deep and far the word (and culture therefrom) surrounding the existences of 'sultanates' extends, consider that my research has identified approximately two hundred Sultanates across the planet. They are found in Asia, the Levant and Arabia, the Middle East, the African continent, Indonesia, Thailand and the Pacific Islands.

There is an obvious commonality in these positions across the world. The Sultan enjoys religious power whereas the prime minister and government enjoy political power. In only a few cases does one individual enjoy both the power of being both religious and political leader.

Where a global or geographically confined Caliphate sought to deploy a religious belief to all, it would only be a short time before political and government power fell to the Caliph

There has never been a sultan in any part of the United Kingdom.

* * *

The Crucifix

A crucifix is a word from the Latin 'cruci fixus' and means the one who is fixed to the cross is identified as Jesus on the cross, as distinct from a bare cross.

The crucifix is a principal symbol for many groups of Christians, and one of the most common forms of the Crucifixion in the arts. It is especially important in the Latin Rite of the Roman Catholic Church but is also used in the Orthodox, Oriental Orthodox, Assyrian, and Eastern Catholic Churches, as well as by the Lutheran and Anglican Churches. The symbol is less common in churches of other Protestant denominations, which prefer to use a cross without the figure of Jesus. The crucifix emphasizes Jesus' sacrifice — his death by crucifixion, which Christians believe brought about the redemption of mankind. Most crucifixes portray Jesus on a Latin cross, rather than any other shape, such as a Tau cross or a Coptic cross.

Western crucifixes usually have a three-dimensional corpus, but in Eastern Orthodoxy Jesus' body is normally painted on the cross, or in low relief. Strictly speaking, to be a crucifix, the cross must be three-dimensional, but this distinction is not always observed. An entire painting of the Crucifixion of Jesus including a landscape background and other figures is not a crucifix either.

Large crucifixes high across the central axis of a church are known by the Old English term rood. By the late Middle Ages, these were a near-universal feature of Western churches but are now very rare. Modern Roman Catholic churches often have a crucifix above the altar on the wall; for the celebration of Mass, the Roman Rite of the Catholic Church requires that "on or close to the altar there is to be a cross with a figure of Christ crucified".

The standard, four-pointed Latin crucifix consists of an upright post or stripes and a single crosspiece to which the sufferer's arms were nailed. There may also be a short projecting nameplate, showing the letters INRI.

Western crucifixes may show Christ dead or alive, the presence of the spear wound in his ribs traditionally indicating that he is dead. In either case, his face very often shows his suffering. The crown of thorns is also generally absent in Eastern crucifixes, since the emphasis is not on Christ's suffering, but on his triumph over sin and death.

Prayer in front of a crucifix, which is seen as a sacramental, is often part of devotion for Christians, especially those worshipping in a church, also privately. The person may sit, stand, or kneel in front of the crucifix, sometimes looking at it in contemplation, or merely in front of it with head bowed or eyes closed. During the Middle Ages small crucifixes, generally hung on a wall, became normal in the personal cells or living quarters first of monks, then all clergy, followed by the homes of the laity, spreading down from the top of society as these became cheap enough for the average person to afford. Most towns had a large crucifix erected as a monument or some other shrine at the crossroads of the town. By the 19th century displaying a crucifix somewhere in the general reception areas of a house became typical of Catholic homes. Richer Catholics could afford a room set aside for a chapel.

Roman Catholic, Eastern Orthodox, Oriental Orthodox, Anglican and Lutheran Christians generally use the crucifix in public religious services. They believe the use of the crucifix is in keeping with the statement by Saint Paul in Scripture, "we preach Christ crucified, a stumbling block to Jews and folly to Gentiles, but to those who are called, both Jews and Greeks, Christ the power of God and the wisdom of God".

In the West altar crosses and processional crosses began to be crucifixes in the 11th century, which became general around the 14th century, as they became cheaper. The Roman Rite requires that "either on the altar or near it, there is to be a cross, with the figure of Christ crucified upon it, a cross clearly visible to the assembled people. It is desirable that such a cross should remain near the altar even outside of liturgical celebrations, so as to call to mind for the faithful the saving Passion of the Lord." The requirement of the altar cross was also mentioned in pre-1970 editions of the Roman Missal, though not in the original 1570 Roman Missal of Pope Pius V. The Rite of Funerals says that the Gospel Book, the Bible, or a cross (which will generally be in crucifix form) may be placed on the coffin for a Requiem Mass, but a second standing cross is not to be placed near the coffin if the altar cross can be easily seen from the body of the church.

In modern times we find that in 2005, a mother accused her daughter's school in Derby, England, of discriminating against Christians after the teenager was suspended for refusing to take off a crucifix necklace.

A British prison ordered a multi-faith chapel to remove all crucifixes, presumably to avoid offending Muslims.

In 2008 in Spain, a local judge ordered crucifixes removed from public schools to settle a decades-old dispute over whether crucifixes should be displayed in public buildings in a non-confessional state.

A 2008 Quebec government-commissioned report recommended that the crucifix of the National Assembly be removed to achieve greater pluralism, but the Liberal government was supported in its refusal by a consensus of most legislators.

On 18 March 2011, the European Court of Human Rights ruled in the Lautsi v. Italy case, that the requirement in Italian law that crucifixes be displayed in classrooms of state schools does not violate the European Convention on Human Rights. Crucifixes are common in most other Italian official buildings, including courts of law.

On 24 March 2011, the Constitutional Court of Peru ruled that the presence of crucifixes in courts of law does not violate the secular nature of the state.

In 2019, I took a crucifix left to me by my dearly departed mother and placed it on my favourite black and grey bandana, which is usually part of my regular gym kit. I took some photographs.

Thereafter, one of the images was edited for the book cover that introduces this novel.

***

Shepherd

I found that the word shepherd is also deeply rooted in language, religion and culture.

A sheepherder is a person who tends, herds, feeds, or guards herds of sheep. Shepherd is derived from the Old English 'sceaphierde' or 'sheep hierde' 'herder'.

Shepherding is among the oldest occupations, beginning some 5,000 years ago in Asia Minor. Sheep were kept for their milk, meat and especially their wool. Over the next thousand years, sheep and shepherding spread throughout Eurasia. Henri Fleisch tentatively suggested the Shepherd Neolithic industry of Lebanon may date to one of the first cultures of nomadic shepherds in the Beqaa Valley of Lebanon.

To maintain a large flock, the sheep must be able to move from pasture to pasture. This required the development of an occupation separate from that of the farmer. The duty of shepherds was to keep their flock intact, protect it from predators and guide it to market areas in time for shearing. In ancient times, shepherds also commonly milked their sheep, and made cheese from this milk; few shepherds still do this today.

In many societies, shepherds were an important part of the economy. Unlike farmers, shepherds were often wage earners, being paid to watch the sheep of others. Shepherds also lived apart from society, being largely nomadic. It was mainly a job of solitary males without children, and new shepherds thus needed to be recruited externally. Shepherds were most often the younger sons of farming peasants who did not inherit any land. In other societies, each family would have a family member to shepherd its flock, often a child, youth or an elder who couldn't help much with harder work; these shepherds were fully integrated into society.

Dumuzid, later known as Tammuz, was an important rural deity in ancient Mesopotamian religion, who was revered as the patron god of shepherds. In his role as Dumuzid sipad ("Dumuzid the Shepherd"), he was believed to be the provider of milk, which was a rare, seasonal commodity in ancient Sumer due to the fact that it could not easily be stored without spoiling. Under this same title, Dumuzid was thought to have been the fifth antediluvian king of the Sumerian city-state of Bad-tibira.

In the Sumerian poem Inanna Prefers the Farmer, Dumuzid competes with the farmer Enkidu for the affection of the goddess Inanna and ultimately wins her favour.

Metaphorically, the term "shepherd" is used for God, especially in the Judeo-Christian tradition (e.g. Psalm 23, Ezekiel 34), and in Christianity especially for Jesus, who called himself the Good Shepherd. The Ancient Israelites were a pastoral people and there were many shepherds among them. It may also be worth noting that many biblical figures were shepherds, among them the patriarchs Abraham and Jacob, the twelve tribes, the prophet Moses, King David, and the Old Testament prophet Amos, who was a shepherd in the rugged area around Tekoa.

In the New Testament, angels announced the birth of Jesus to shepherd

The Good Shepherd is one of the thrusts of Biblical scripture. This illustration encompasses many ideas, including God's care for his people. The tendency of humans to put themselves into danger's way and their inability to guide and take care of themselves apart from the direct power and leading of God is also reinforced with the metaphor of sheep in need of a shepherd.

According to Muhammad, the Prophet of Islam, every messenger of God had the occupation of being a shepherd at one point in their lives, as he himself was as a young man. Narrated by Jabir bin Abdullah: We were with Allah's Apostle picking the fruits of the Arak trees, and Allah's Apostle (peace and blessings of Allah be to him) said, "Pick the black fruit, for it is the best." The companions asked, "Were you a shepherd?" He replied, "There was no prophet who was not a shepherd."

Sources: Wikipedia, and personal research across multiple websites into religious beliefs.

Paul Anthony
Reviews
~

'One of the best thriller and mystery writers in the United Kingdom today'....

Caleb Pirtle 111, International Bestselling Author of over 60 novels, journalist, travel writer, screenplay writer, and Founder and Editorial Director at Venture Galleries.

*

'Paul Anthony is one of the best Thriller Mystery Writers of our times!'...

Dennis Sheehan, International Bestselling Author of 'Purchased Power', former United States Marine Corps.

*

'When it comes to fiction and poetry you will want to check out this outstanding author. Paul has travelled the journey of publication and is now a proud writer who is well worth discovery.' ... Janet Beasley, Epic Fantasy Author, theatre producer and director - Scenic Nature Photographer, JLB Creatives. Also Founder/co-author at Journey to Publication

*

'Paul Anthony is a brilliant writer and an outstanding gentleman who goes out of his way to help and look out for others. In his writing, Paul does a wonderful job of portraying the era in which we live with its known and unknown fears. I highly recommend this intelligent and kind gentleman to all.' ...

Jeannie Walker, author of the True Crime Story 'Fighting the Devil', 2011 National Indie Excellence Awards (True Crime Finalist) and 2010 winner of the Silver Medal for Book of the Year True Crime Awards.

*

Printed in Great Britain
by Amazon